Bo〈

A Story of Keighton,

Yorkshire 1720 to 1727

Bonfires and Brandy

Joy Stonehouse

Grosvenor House
Publishing Limited

This book is published by
Grosvenor House Publishing Ltd
Link House
140 The Broadway, Tolworth, Surrey, KT6 7HT.
www.grosvenorhousepublishing.co.uk

A CIP record for this book
is available from the British Library

ISBN 978-1-80381-554-1
eBook ISBN 978-1-80381-555-8

Other titles in the series

Witch-bottles and Windlestraws
New Arrivals in Reighton
Whisper to the Bees

For Tom

Acknowledgements

I would like to thank the helpful and friendly staff at the Treasure House, Beverley, and the Hull History Centre; both sites make research a pleasure.

A huge thank you goes to members of Hornsea Writers. They have continued to offer support and encouragement as well as online critiques during lockdown. Without this group, the series would never have been published.

Special thanks must go to Lisa Blosfelds for her transcript of the Reighton parish records—an invaluable aid. She has also been most helpful in loaning local history books and allowing access to her collection of documentary evidence and maps.

Thanks must go also to Pat Sewell whose research into my Jordan family history provided the essential springboard for the novels. I appreciate her continuing encouragement.

Last, but by no means least, thanks to Pam Williams for the first reading and editing, and for painting the book cover (again) and for being the first port of call when the technology throws me a curveball.

Author's Note

The novels are inspired by the parish records and, although I have carried out extensive research into East Yorkshire in the early 18th century, I must stress that the stories in the series are works of fiction. The names of most of the characters are taken from the parish records, yet some are invented. Any omissions and deviations from these records are made for the sake of narrative interest. See the Appendix for a list of the Jordan family members.

The main characters, and those of higher social standing, speak in Standard English. Lesser characters and the older generation speak with a slight East Yorkshire accent.

Although Reighton is mentioned throughout as a village, the people of the time would have called it a town. I have opted to spell Bridlington as it is known today, though the town was formerly known as Burlington and was often referred to as Bollin'ton.

Contents

Part One

Young Love

Chapter 1

1720

It was springtime and young Francis Jordan was in love. Though he was almost thirteen years old, the object of his adoration, Milcah Gurwood, was twenty-one. The age difference did not matter to him except for one problem—his uncle Thomas. Here, sitting on a log in the garden beneath the apple tree, he could contemplate his chances in peace. After a day in the fields sowing beans, it was pleasant to be outside and alone while it was still light, much preferable to the cramped kitchen. If it wasn't his young brothers being noisy and fighting for space, it was the chickens and the dog.

He picked at a bit of loose bark, deep in thought. As far back as he could remember, his uncle Thomas had been Milcah's partner at every feast and celebration. He supposed this was natural since they were the same age, and yet he hated to see them dance together. He recalled only too well how Thomas had won the last bridal race, how he'd swaggered in front of her with the prize ribbon tied round his hat. He couldn't deny that his uncle was handsome and matched her perfectly for height; the pair could have been brother and sister. Both had the same dark hair and a way of smiling that would melt ice. And he knew that most of Reighton expected Thomas to choose her for a wife.

He stood up, stretched, and strolled round the garden. It had been so fortunate that Milcah had stayed behind in Reighton; she could so easily have gone with her parents and sisters to live in the vicarage at Rudston. It had worked out perfectly for Milcah to live here with her brother, and help his wife and growing family. Now he could visit her whenever he liked, could just turn up at the door to offer assistance. And that was something Uncle Thomas would never do. Francis smiled to himself. His uncle would never fetch water from the well or mind the children. No, and Francis didn't care what chores he was asked to do so long as he was near the lovely Milcah. She had such shiny hair and sparkling eyes, and was so gentle and graceful.

He took a last look at the buds on the tree, about to burst into leaf at any moment. They gave him hope. Right, he thought, my prospects might not look promising, but I'll never give up.

He walked into the house, his head held high for a change.

After the usual rush to the table, Francis and his family settled down to eat their supper. Halfway through the meal, his father put down his spoon and stared at Francis.

'You've been working hard lately, son. Would you like to go to Bridlington market with me?'

Francis gulped. His father usually ignored him, and never gave out praise. 'Yes, please.' His voice dropped a key unexpectedly as he added, 'I can buy a present for Milcah.'

His father smiled and shook his head. The boy, he thought, would be a man soon and had a lot to learn.

It was just before dawn, one Saturday in April, when father and son set out for Bridlington. As a child,

Francis had found the market a frightening place, but now he was nearly a man he was sure he'd be able to stomach the sights and smells. He sat behind his father on their best horse, sheltered from the worst of the wind and the blustery showers.

They arrived at eight o'clock when the major dealings were over and there was a little more space to move around the stalls. Having left the horse at the Nag's Head, they ordered trenchers of boiled beef with pots of ale. Francis was unused to the noise and the strangers pushing and shoving. He ignored his father's attempts at conversation, kept his head down and finished his food as fast as he could. Crowds of men made him uneasy and he was beginning to regret coming. He'd always got on better with women, like his aunt Elizabeth and the maids at his grandfather's Uphall farm. Now he was afraid he'd let his father down by being such poor company. It was purely the thought of choosing something nice for Milcah that made the day bearable.

William scrutinised his eldest son, an odd lad, one he couldn't fathom. Francis did a good day's work, had a way of handling the oxen, and all the workers at Uphall appreciated his application. Yet the boy had now reached that peculiar age of being neither man nor boy, and looked uncomfortable and ungainly in his growing body. His nose was too big for his face, his eyebrows bushy, his lips thick and his legs way too long. William sighed; he couldn't remember being that awkward himself.

'Come on, lad, if you've nothing to say and you've finished, let's be moving on.'

Francis was relieved to be outside in the fresh air, but it wasn't that fresh. In the marketplace, the smell of blood hung in the air, and he had to step through the slippery waste thrown down by the butchers.

The splinters of bone and raw flesh revived childhood memories of men fighting in the street and teeth being knocked out. All of a sudden, he felt queasy.

'Father—let's just go to the shops,' he begged. 'You see, I don't know what to get Milcah. Maybe I'll find something there.'

They threaded their way through the crowd and entered the nearest shop. While William bought sugar, Francis gazed at the yards of lace, the woollen stockings and the small gifts. He hadn't a clue what to choose and so they came out again.

'Oh, come on, lad, didn't you see *anything*?' When Francis shrugged, his father slapped him on the back. 'Right then, let's have another wander by the stalls.'

'I was thinking maybe I could get Milcah some lace edging. In the shop it was only two pence a yard.'

'Don't bother, I can get it cheaper from a man I know in Hunmanby.' He winked. 'It'd be better quality too— from Holland.'

Francis guessed the lace was smuggled. 'Well then,' he mumbled, 'maybe I could buy her stockings. There were some nice red ones.'

'Don't buy them from a shop. They'll be cheaper outside. Come on, we'll see up there at the knitting stall.' He marched off.

'I did see a nice wooden knitting sheath,' Francis offered as he tried to catch up. 'Perhaps Milcah would like one.'

His father turned to speak while he carried on walking. 'You ought to make her one yourself. I made one for your mother when we were courting.'

Francis shuffled up the street behind his father, tears of frustration pricking his eyes. Soon, they reached the trestle table run by the local knitting school. The children showed them a variety of red, blue and plain woollen stockings at a penny a pair. Francis wanted to get Milcah something special, not anything she could knit herself, but he was running out of ideas. Since his father was already tapping his foot and gazing at the sky, he bought two pairs.

As the two of them wandered back down to the Nag's Head, a quack stepped out, blocked their way and bade them inspect his array of medicines. Francis noticed there were pills to give a healthy complexion and, since Milcah was often pale, he plucked up courage and asked what was in them.

'Best iron,' was the reply. 'Taken by all ladies o' good breedin'. These put colour back i' their cheeks. Thoo can 'ave 'em fo' thruppence a box.'

When Francis saw that his father had already walked on and was chatting to a man draped in rabbit skins, he decided to buy a box. He hid it in his coat pocket knowing what his father would say, that the pills were probably just old iron filings crushed to powder, that they'd likely be mixed with unknown ingredients, and Sarah Ezard would have better things at home in Reighton. He caught up with his father. Neither of the presents were what he really wanted, and now he had no money left.

As he was about to ask if it was time to go home, there was a distant roar from the crowd. The noise came from further along the high street, towards the Priory. Everyone began to run in that direction, and Francis and his father had no choice but to go as well.

'It's a floggin',' was the general cry.

A pie man behind them yelled, "Is name's Edward Wilson. 'E was caught red-'anded wi' stolen tools.'

William pushed Francis forward so his son could get a better view.

The thief was stripped to the waist and roped to the back of a cart. The man's progress was so slow up the middle of the street, and the crowd cheered each time the whip cut into his back.

Francis saw the man had a piece of leather between his teeth; no doubt it stopped him from shouting out. At each sting of the lash, Francis flinched.

The men and women at each side cried for the whip to strike harder and faster. Their eyes glistened and their mouths drooled in excitement. Compelled to watch, Francis saw blood trickle down the man's back and onto his breeches. Then he lost sight of him as the cart was towed along to the pillory in the marketplace.

The jeering spectators soon turned to follow the cart, and swept Francis along in their wake. He saw the man untied, lifted semi-conscious and dragged towards the pillory. Edward Wilson was not a tall man; a stool had to be brought for him to stand on so that his head and hands could reach the holes. Twice, he nearly slipped off, and would have choked or broken his skull if someone hadn't held him in place.

It was the first time Francis had seen anyone in the pillory, and he soon realised it was a worse punishment than flogging; while one was disciplined and didn't last long, the felon was now left at the mercy of the crowd. At least in the stocks a man could defend himself with his arms, whereas here in the pillory, the wrists were clamped tight. Francis could see Wilson's fingers tremble as he waited for the onslaught. Being pelted with rotten eggs and cow dung, or even the odd dead rat, was one thing, but Francis saw that a few men had brought half bricks and cobblestones. The man would be lucky to get out alive.

Even William, who'd seen it all before, thought it was too much. He pulled Francis to the back of the mob where the boy puked by the roadside. William had hoped to have a few wagers at the cockfight behind the George Inn, yet it was obvious Francis was not up to it.

'Come on, lad, cheer up! Let's get you home. You'll soon be seeing your precious Milcah.'

As they journeyed back, the sun came out. Francis forgot about the man in the pillory for a moment as he admired the views. The winter wheat was green and healthy, the blackthorn in full blossom, and every step of the horse brought him nearer to Milcah.

When they reached the top field of Reighton, Francis saw his young brother William busy scaring birds from the crops, firing at them with a catapult. On getting closer, he noted there was already a row of dead or injured crows mounted on sticks. Just as he was about to shout at him, he saw Milcah racing towards the field, her gown held up in her hands.

She stopped in front of his brother and looked furious. Francis couldn't hear what she said, but she was waving her finger at William, and he was putting down his weapon and untying the crows. His father chuckled, amused at the scene as Francis slid off the horse and ran into the field. When he reached Milcah, he saw that she was upset.

'I am *so* sorry,' he cried, shaking his head in shame. 'I apologise for my brother's behaviour.' He then glared at William. He'd seen enough cruelty for one day.

She rested a hand gently on his arm. 'I'm sure your brother didn't mean any harm. No doubt he's been told to scare off the crows. It's not all his fault.'

With that, William sneaked off to join his father.

Francis was left alone beside Milcah. He thought she was so kind and thoughtful, like gentle rain on long-parched earth.

'I've brought you something from the market. Wait here. I'll get them.'

While he took the package from his father, she calmed down and smoothed her rumpled gown.

'I'm sorry Francis,' she said as he returned, 'I shouldn't let myself get so upset. I can't help it at times—especially when it's your brother.' She glanced beyond Francis at his father sitting placidly on the horse, not interfering. 'I think young William needs more discipline.'

'I'll see to my brother,' he promised. 'Don't worry.' He waved to his father to carry on home without him; he wanted to walk back with her alone.

They stopped when they reached the garden gate. He held out the woollen stockings in their brown paper parcel.

She opened it, hoping there might be a pretty cotton print inside. 'Oh, thank you—stockings.' She hid her disappointment well.

Then he drew the box of pills from his jacket. 'They're highly recommended,' he insisted as he pressed them into her hand.

Puzzled, she read the label. 'Iron pills?'

'Yes. Not that you're pale or anything,' he added quickly. 'Ladies of good breeding take them.'

'Oh... thank you very much.' Then, feeling sorry for him, she gave him a kiss on the cheek. He was a strange boy.

Francis almost skipped home. His day had been worth it after all.

Chapter 2

Throughout the spring, Francis paid court to Milcah. He gathered wild flowers on the cliffs and by the streams and always presented them to her on one knee. On Sundays, he took her and her young nephew George for walks to Speeton and back, carrying the boy on his shoulders while she carried presents of food for her sister Jane. Often, they were lucky enough to see her father as he still took the services there. Milcah's eyes would light up on seeing him; at such times, she was more beautiful than ever. When the hawthorn came out in May, the lane leading to Speeton became an archway of pink and white blossom, like a bridal bouquet.

'It's like being at a wedding,' he ventured, daring to dream of a future with Milcah.

She smiled but made no comment. As usual, she changed the subject and asked after his mother.

'She's well.' He didn't want to talk about his mother, now heavily pregnant and about to give birth at any time. The last thing he wanted was to be around when that happened.

On the day that Mary went into labour, Francis was out in the fields with his father. It was late in May, and Mary, left in the house with her three younger sons, had to manage as best she could. She wasn't worried. Seven times now she'd given birth, and each time was quicker and easier. As soon as the all too familiar pains grew more frequent, she sent young William to fetch Sarah Ezard. Remembering the midwife's arthritic hands, she sent John out as well to call for his aunt Elizabeth; the poor, backward boy, she hoped, should be able to achieve that at least. She enticed Richard to play under the kitchen table out of the way, and then paced the kitchen rubbing her back. She stopped to grip the table whenever her womb went into a spasm.

Richard, not yet three years old, crawled out and clutched the hem of his mother's skirt. He pulled himself up and let his hands stray to touch her stomach, so huge, hard and round. He'd seen it quiver sometimes and couldn't imagine the living thing inside. Whenever his mother gasped, he looked up with wide eyes.

'It's alright, Richard. Mother's alright. Aunt Lizzie will be here soon, and your brothers will take you out to play. You be a good boy.' Taken suddenly by another contraction, she lurched to grab the table again.

When young William returned with Sarah Ezard, the old woman told him to fill a pan with water and set it over the fire.

'I can't deliver bairn o' me own,' she warned Mary. 'Not anymore I can't.'

'I know, don't worry. Elizabeth's coming—I hope. I sent John to fetch her.'

'Poor lad,' Sarah said with a smile, ''e does 'is best wi' what brains 'e 'as.'

The back door opened and John almost fell through in his haste, followed by a concerned Elizabeth. He ran straight to his mother and wrapped his arms round her stomach.

'Steady, John, you're going to have a new brother or sister. It won't be long. Go into the garden with Will. He'll stay with you. You'll find something to do—won't you Will? And take your dog with you.'

Young William nodded. He certainly didn't want to be around when a baby was born. Seeing Richard holding on to his mother's skirt, he unlatched the boy's fingers and dragged him to the door.

'Come on, me and John will play with you.' As he opened the door he called to the dog. 'Come on, Stina—garden!'

As soon as the three women were alone, they moved to the parlour. There, Sarah gave her usual instructions for the birth. The curtains were drawn, candles lit and an old straw pallet placed on the bed. She took Elizabeth to one side.

'Listen, if owt goes wrong,' she whispered, 'it's thoo that'll 'ave to deal with it. Me fingers 'ave 'ad it—look.' She didn't need to hold up her claw-like hands; the whole village knew of Sarah's problem.

'Just tell me what to do,' Elizabeth replied. 'I'm sure Mary will be content with that.'

They listened for a while to the boys playing rowdily in the garden.

When Mary's pains strengthened and her waters broke, she decided to kneel on the bed in readiness.

'Leave tha shoes on,' Sarah prompted. 'It's lucky.'

There was a crash and a flurry of wings outside. Elizabeth fought the urge to look out of the window. The boys were obviously chasing the chickens and they were likely ruining the vegetable plot.

Mary didn't care. She focussed on the cramps now holding her womb in a vice. She faced the wooden bedhead and held on tight.

When she began to strain, Sarah signalled to Elizabeth to be ready.

Mary ground her teeth and pushed down hard. She squeezed her eyes shut and prayed it be over soon. It wasn't so easy after all. She'd had a baby almost every two years and she was tired. Experience was one thing, but she wasn't so young anymore, and looking after four boys had taken its toll. Resigned to her fate, she took a few deep breaths and then heard herself grunt like an animal as she gave a final push.

The tiny baby slid out into Elizabeth's waiting hands. She almost dropped it, not expecting it to come out so fast.

'Give it a good rub,' ordered Sarah. 'Make it cry.'

The moment Elizabeth cleared its mouth, the baby obliged and yelled. Relieved, she held it up for Sarah to inspect.

'Mary,' Sarah announced, 'thoo 'as another lad. Lisbeth—wash 'im an' wrap 'im i' yon sheet. In a while thoo can tie cord. Take me string, but wait till cord's stopped throbbin', then tie a good knot 'ere an' 'ere.'

While they waited, Mary turned cautiously onto her back, minding the navel cord that lay heavy between her legs. The baby was passed to her and she tried to fit a nipple into his mouth. A dark red, puckered face was all that was visible from the sheet; he looked healthy enough.

'Thank God,' Mary whispered. 'I don't think I can do this much more.'

Sarah glanced at Elizabeth. Both were thinking the same—women didn't have much say in that.

'Come on, cheer up,' Sarah said. 'Keep tryin' to feed 'im. It'll 'elp tha womb to clean out.'

Almost immediately, the cord grew longer, and Elizabeth gasped. 'Shall I pull it?'

'Nay, for God's sake! Stick yon sackcloth under Mary.'

The two helpers watched as the afterbirth flopped out and fresh blood clots followed. Sarah stood over the mess and examined it. She prodded and inspected it from all angles.

'Aye, I think it's all there. Now, Lisbeth, cord's stopped throbbin' so tie it where I said.' She then passed Elizabeth her sharpest knife. 'Cut it i' one go. I know it looks thick an' gristly, but yon knife'll cut through it like butter.'

Elizabeth's hand shook as she sliced through. Only a little blood appeared which she soon dabbed away.

'Now I'll show thee 'ow to make sure there's nowt left inside. Thoo'll 'ave to rub Mary's womb. I'd do that but...' She waved her useless fingers. 'Press down wi' both 'ands.'

Elizabeth did as she was told.

'Steady—not too 'ard,' advised Sarah. 'Be firm though. I can't explain... tha gets to know by feelin' around where to press most. That's right—move lower down.'

Mary felt the hot blood spurt between her legs. Soon there was just a trickle.

Sarah smiled with relief. 'Thoo can stop now, Lisbeth. Clear it all away. Thoo can burn it o' fire later—or bury it.'

Elizabeth folded the mess up inside the sacking and took it to the kitchen.

'Thoo's done well, lass,' Sarah crooned as she stroked Mary's damp hair away from her face. 'Thoo doesn't need me anymore, so I'll leave thee to rest. Lisbeth will wash thee an' swaddle tha bairn, an' I'll come back later.'

Mary thanked her and closed her eyes. All she need do now was let her body go limp and wait for her sister to wash her. Other women would arrive as soon as Sarah broke the news. They'd prepare the dinner and see to the boys, do all the cooking and housework. William would return from work with Francis, see the baby, and then he'd spend the next few weeks with his parents and family at Uphall. She smiled as she recalled how, years ago, she used to dread their separation. Now, she knew it was the best part of childbirth—to be left to recover in peace. She peered down at her new son, now asleep. Something about him reminded her of her brother Matthew. Maybe it was the high forehead. Perhaps he would prosper too.

Elizabeth returned to the parlour with warm water and began to wipe Mary's arms. It was quiet—even the boys had calmed down outside. The only sound was the distant bleating of lambs and the ewes' answering cries.

Mary closed her eyes again. The rite of being washed after giving birth was a time to cherish. After a while, as her legs were cleaned right down to her toes, she yawned and stretched.

'Do you think I should call him Matthew?' she murmured, half asleep.

'I thought you were going to call your next son Ben.'

'I was,' she sighed, 'yet the baby looks a bit like our brother, don't you think? It might be lucky to name him after one who's doing so well.'

'I suppose so.' Elizabeth still felt that the boy should be called Ben, but it wasn't her decision. 'Oh, alright,' she conceded, 'call him Matthew. He's worked hard. It's thanks to him that the Smiths are doing even better than the Jordans.' She rinsed out the cloth and gave Mary's legs a last wipe. 'You should see his cattle herd now and the amount of pasture land he uses.'

Mary opened her eyes wide. '*And* he knows folk in high places. He won't tell me, but I know he's had money from smuggling.'

'I bet you don't know what he's used his profits on—shares in that South Sea Company. He's done it with a group from Hunmanby, probably Sir Richard Osbaldeston himself.'

'Fine then, it *should* be a good omen to name the baby Matthew.'

Chapter 3

The birth of Matthew coincided with the annual spring fair at Bridlington. William thought it might be a good idea to take his three eldest boys. It would be their first experience of the Whitsun Fair, and would keep them away from all the women flocking to the house.

When Mary heard of the plan, her only concern was for John; the boy had little understanding and was small for his age. He might well have a face like a blessing, as the previous vicar used to say, yet he was a simple soul and easily hurt.

'Promise me you'll take good care of him,' she pleaded.

'Yes, yes, don't fret. Thomas and Samuel are going with me—we'll have a boy each.'

'Alright then,' she agreed, though she doubted that William's brothers would be of much use.

On the day of the fair, Mary summoned the boys to her bedside. It was a bright, sunny morning with a clear blue sky, perfect weather for a ride to Bridlington. She eyed them up and down as they gathered round the bed, scrubbed clean and in their best Sunday clothes.

Young William grabbed Stina by the collar. 'Can I take the dog?'

'No, and listen, boys, when you get there, mind the gypsies. If you're not careful, they'll cut your pockets and steal your money. Stay close to your father and uncles at all times—and keep away from the beer booths and the dancing. Now, don't look so glum. I do want you to have a good time—just don't forget what I've told you.' She smiled. 'And bring me back something nice.'

They promised to behave and took turns to kiss her goodbye. Young William also kissed the dog.

As they left the room, she held on to Francis for a moment. 'Keep an eye on John. See that he doesn't get upset. I can't trust your father or especially your uncle Thomas.'

As they made their way to Uphall, Francis glared at his brothers and wished they were not going with him. Young William hobbled along with such a lopsided gait it was embarrassing, and poor John shuffled alongside like a stray lamb. He hurried them up the hill as best he could. Even so, when they reached the stable, he found his uncles mounted and ready to go.

His father, annoyed by the wait, shook his head in exasperation and then hoisted up the youngest boys to sit behind their uncles. 'Come on, Francis, I'll give you a leg up. You're with me.'

He led the way out of the yard, and the group rode three abreast up the hill and out of Reighton. Once they were on the top road, he began to explain to his sons what they might expect.

'You know it's mostly a cattle fair? You must have seen your uncle Matthew's herd moving out of Reighton yesterday. Apart from the Smiths' cattle, there'll be lots of milk cows, some near calving, as well as heifers and bullocks. They're driven from all over and put to pasture near the Priory. Today, they'll be sold.'

Francis wasn't listening. It was very early in the morning and he was feeling at one with the fresh glory of the day. The hawthorn trees were still heavy with blossom, their branches weighed down almost to the ground, and the grass at the side of the road was lush and studded with dandelions. In a trance, he gazed at the profusion of colours—golden yellow standing brilliant against clusters of violet-blue bellflowers. Red campion, and what Milcah called soldiers' buttons, filled the hedgerows, the various pink and red flowers swaying in the breeze. He lifted his nose to catch the scent of wild thyme, and sighed as he imagined Milcah sitting there amid the grass and flowers.

His dream was broken as a group of men appeared suddenly behind them and yelled at them to make way.

As his father drew the horse to one side, the men raced past. 'They're eager,' he grumbled. 'Must be cattle dealers.'

'Aye,' Thomas agreed, 'you boys'll be seeing lots of them soon. As we get nearer town, there'll be big crowds and everyone will be heading to High Green.'

On the approach to Bridlington, young William and John hardly knew where to look. So many farmers and their families were arriving, and they were such a noisy lot.

'They're after a good time,' explained their uncle Samuel. 'You can't blame them. They'll want to meet up with people they haven't seen for a year.'

Thomas turned in his saddle and grinned. 'And tonight there'll be a pleasure fair on the green. There'll be even more folk then.'

'Yes,' his father snorted, 'and there'll be no grass left after all their stomping about.'

When they'd left their horses at the Nag's Head, they set off to walk to the green. On the way they passed a gang of lads leaning idly against a wall. Young William, sensitive about the way he walked, was sure the lads meant him when he overheard one snigger and remark to the others.

"E's got one leg shorter than t'other—or is 'e a mariner who's lost 'is ship? 'E wants to be down at quayside. 'E'd fit i' there right enough.'

Young William kept his head down. He told himself that he mustn't rise to the bait, must ignore them.

As they strolled on, John was puzzled and pulled on his father's sleeve. 'Why is Will upset?'

'I'm not upset,' his brother growled.

'Your face is red.'

'Shut up. You don't know anything.'

'Father, his face *is* red.'

'Leave him alone John. I'll explain later. Come on, let's get to the fair.'

They carried on in silence, John still frowning and sneaking glances at his brother. So far, John was not enjoying his first trip to Bridlington. Like Francis on his first visit, he was shocked. It wasn't the smell that bothered him; he was used to sweaty bodies, pissy straw and shit. What upset him was the noise. It was very quiet in Reighton, but here the men and women shouted and swore and laughed so loudly. And the animals were scary; cattle bellowed, pigs squealed as if being slaughtered, and the sheep bleated pitifully. Women jostled past him carrying live chickens upside down with their legs tied together and, as he went by the large pond at the bottom end of the green, there were dead rats floating in the scum.

His father hurried him past a stall displaying rows of freshly killed rabbits. They were hanging upside down with their noses dripping thick, dark gobbets of blood onto the grass. When he bumped into people, they all seemed to have something wrong with them, either a mouth full of broken, brown teeth or their faces scarred by pockmarks. A few even had an arm or a leg missing. Seeing ugliness and filth on every side, he began to cry.

2 1

Francis, although he'd suffered similarly as a child, showed no sympathy.

'Grow up. You're at a fair, not at home with Mother. What did you expect?' Yet Francis was not immune to the sights and noise. To distract himself, he thought of Milcah's smile and the way she smelled of lavender. He was daydreaming about how pure and clean she was when his uncles pointed out the sideshows. A placard advertised a female Samson.

They paid the small entry fee and squeezed into the tent for a peep. Francis turned up his nose; the place was hot and stuffy and stank of stale sweat and sawdust. His father pushed him and his brothers to the front where a rope prevented them getting any closer. There they saw a man standing beside what looked like a woman with a beard. Black hair sprouted from her armpits, and her bare arms bulged when she flexed them. The man prodded her various muscles with a cane and praised her extraordinary strength.

Francis hated her. She was the very opposite of Milcah. Why any woman would want to behave and dress so indecently, let alone grow a beard, was beyond him. He watched, disheartened, as the man fastened her long hair to an anvil and announced that she would lift it.

The crowd murmured in disbelief as the man counted to three. With a few grunts and then a great intake of breath, the woman's hair took the strain. The anvil rose into the air, a foot off the ground. The crowd applauded, impressed, and the anvil was lowered and her hair untied. The man then set up two chairs for her to lay across with her head and shoulders on one chair and her feet on the other. He asked for volunteers to come forward and sit on her stomach.

To Francis's shame, his father stepped under the rope to join two other volunteers. The first man sat very gingerly on the woman. The audience gasped as she took the weight.

The second man approached and decided to clamber over as if mounting a horse. The spectators laughed as he swung his legs back and forth.

'Gee up!' he shouted.

'Gee up!' echoed John.

'Shush,' Francis snapped. 'It's not right. And don't laugh. It's not funny.'

The boys held their breath as their father moved forward for his turn.

Francis crossed his fingers. 'Please,' he murmured through gritted teeth, 'sit on properly.'

His father stood by the woman, undecided where to add his weight. When he did sit down, the crowd cheered.

Even Francis was astounded. It was no mean feat to support three full-grown men. He was relieved when the show was over and his father rejoined them; now they could go back outside.

'Well, that was fun, wasn't it?' William prompted his sons.

'I liked it when she was a horse,' cried John, full of excitement.

Francis rolled his eyes.

'And,' added young William with a whistle, 'I thought she'd never be able to take *three* men!'

'I'll take you to other shows. There'll be lots to see.'

The tent with the mermaid was a disappointment. They could see it was just a young woman with a pretend tail attached, and Francis felt sorry for her having to lie in a trough of cold water all day. He had no idea what John was thinking; the boy gaped in silence, probably storing away things he couldn't understand. Having seen a live sheep with two heads, which was certainly real because he stroked both the heads, John had no reason to believe the mermaid was not real either.

The tent with the dwarf and the giant was interesting, though people shouted out bawdy questions. Francis could tell that the dwarf, at least, was getting angry. The giant, however, looked half asleep and seemed content to be gawped at for a half penny a time.

As the boys grew accustomed to the noise and bustle, they began to enjoy the day. There were jugglers on the green and dancing dogs wearing fancy hats. Music came from all sides, and brightly coloured flags waved from above the tents. They passed a whole hog roasting on a spit, the smell of burnt crackling making their mouths water. At this point, Thomas and Samuel slipped away to the ale booth, and William, seeing that the boys were hungry, bought small beer and pies.

They sat down on the grass, leaning against a tent, and sucked warm, greasy mutton through the hole in the top of the pastry. In no time, John had gravy dribbling down his front, ruining his best shirt.

Francis was disgusted. 'You're almost six! You should be able to feed yourself better by now.' He wondered if John would be like this all his life.

Once the piecrusts were eaten, William announced that there was one more thing they ought to see.

'Come on,' he said, brushing crumbs off his breeches, 'your uncles'll be there already. They'll want to place a bet.'

Francis pulled a face as he stood up. 'But Father, we won't have time to spend our money. We have to take something back for Mother.' And he wanted to buy a gift for Milcah.

'Oh, you'll have time for that. You can buy your trinkets and toys or whatever you want afterwards—and then we'll go home.' He grinned and rubbed his hands. 'We really don't want to miss this.'

Francis crossed his fingers again. He hoped whatever it was would be pleasant and wouldn't take long.

Chapter 4

William led his sons through the crowd, and then managed to wriggle them to the front where they could see a bull tethered. The butchers of the town were displaying their dogs and taking bets. The boys' uncles were also at the front; they were eyeing up the dogs, searching for scars of former fights and assessing which dogs looked most ferocious and primed for action.

Francis, trapped by the crowd, realised with horror that he was about to witness a bull baiting. The dogs had caught the scent of the bull and were slavering and pulling on their ropes.

His father pointed to them. 'See their jaws? That bottom one overlaps the top so it can get a good grip and not let go. They're bred specially.'

As he said this, the dogs shook their heads. Saliva and froth flew in every direction.

'And do you see their flat noses that stick up? That means they can still breathe if they have a chunk of bull in their mouths.'

Francis didn't want to know the details, but his father hadn't finished.

'And look at all those folds of skin on their faces. Those wrinkles let the blood drain away—it won't get in the dogs' eyes.'

Young William was impressed. He watched open-mouthed and gulped at the thought of what was to come.

Francis longed to escape. The spectators were rowdy and never stopped jostling for a better view. He thought of Milcah, tried to imagine himself in the garden with her, and presenting a better gift than last time.

Young William noticed the glazed stare in his brother's eyes and gave him a hefty shove. Francis was caught unawares and he fell forward towards the bull. He leapt back immediately.

'You fool!' he cried. 'What did you do that for?'

His brother had a smug grin on his face. 'You were dreaming again.'

John was silent, his face gentle and blank as he gazed at the curly-headed bull.

His father followed his eyes and remarked on the beast. 'Yes, John, it's a fine, young bull—just over two years old, I reckon. It'll make good eating. See its broad shoulders? It'll fight well, I'm sure. And those horns, look… I bet they could do some damage.'

'Will the bull come at *us*?' asked John.

'No, son, don't worry. You can see the rope round its horns—it's fixed to that ring in the ground over there. It can't come any nearer than this. The rope will hold it.' He didn't tell him that a frantic bull did sometimes snap the rope and charge the crowd; it was part of the excitement and entertainment. Though he'd never seen it happen himself, he trusted his brothers to help save the boys if anything went wrong.

John pressed back into his father's legs. Despite his fear, he liked the bull. It had a white blaze on its face and tawny curls between the horns. Its body was the colour of burnt gingerbread. He didn't like the look of the butchers. They held their dogs by the scruff of their necks or by their ears and, as the dogs growled to be set free, the men shouted and swore. He wondered why one of the men blew pepper up the bull's nose. The bull obviously hated it, and stamped its feet and shook its head, pulling against the rope.

Francis detested any kind of fighting, but there was no way out. The men had drawn lots as to which dog would go first and, at last, a dog was set loose. It was young and ran straight at the bull's head. The bull was quick to react and flipped the dog up with one horn. To the delight of the crowd, the dog flew howling high into the air while the butcher who owned him ran forward with a long pole. He wielded the pole so deftly that the dog slid down it and landed at his feet. After a quick inspection, the dog was found to be only slightly injured. It was deemed fit enough to be sent in later.

The next dog was older and had a torn ear. The butcher struggled to hold it back as it snarled and foamed at the mouth. Suddenly, it was released and set at the bull. This time the dog was sly. It crouched low, almost on its belly and inched forwards. The bull lowered its head in defence, ready to gore and toss its attacker. As the dog crept round in a circle, the bull kept track of its path. All at once, the dog sprang at the bull's head, intending to bite its nose, but the bull swivelled and the dog locked onto one ear instead. The bull roared in pain as the dog hung there, refusing to let go, blood spilling from the ear and flying into the crowd.

When young William's face was spattered, Francis couldn't tell whether his brother was pleased or horrified.

Uncle Thomas laughed. 'It's good for you, boys—it'll make men of you.'

The bull bucked and spun round, trying to rid itself of the dog yet without success. A minute later, another dog was sent in to distract the bull while the other was prised off. Half the ear came with it.

John was disturbed. There was a lot of blood about and the air smelled of rusty knives. As the men around him grew excited, they gave off a sharp smell; it was all very unsettling. He held onto his father's arm for comfort.

'You see,' his father explained, 'the idea is for the dog to pin the bull to the ground by the nose, and keep it still. The nose is rather tender.' He stood tall again and grinned at his brothers. 'Of course, there are other very tender places, though I wouldn't like to be the dog hanging onto those bits!'

As if William had tempted fate, the next dog did just that. It ran round the bull, shot under its hind legs and made a grab for the scrotum. The bull, however, twisted its head in time and managed to slide a horn under the dog's belly. The poor dog was tossed into the air. It landed close to the bull and was trampled. Three men ran forward with poles. They kept the bull off and dragged the mangled body to one side. The owner cursed and spat into the dust, angry at losing his bet. He then clubbed the dog on the head to put it out of its misery.

Both Francis and John were speechless. They had no time to recover for the crowd yelled for more action as the next dog was set on.

'That's a champion,' declared Thomas. 'We've seen it perform at Kilham. That's why my money's on it. Look—it's been stitched up a few times.'

Samuel turned to him. 'Do you remember that time they tied a cat to the bull's tail? *That* was at Kilham. We had fun *that* day.' Both uncles watched transfixed as the dog flattened itself to the ground and crawled forward, bull and dog eyeing each other closely.

'That dog,' boasted Thomas, 'can bite the bull's snout if any dog can. You'll see.'

For what seemed like ages, the dog manoeuvred around the bull, waiting for the moment to pounce. Then, without warning, it leapt up and grasped the bull's nose in its jaws. It held on tight as a vice, and hung on defiantly while the bull shook its head, stamped and kicked in an attempt to shake it off.

The spectators sensed the danger of the game. They shouted at the dog to keep hold, and cheered every futile move made by the bull.

Francis guessed a lot of money was riding on the outcome. All about him were contorted faces mad with excitement, yelling abuse at the bull and each other. A couple of butchers began to brawl, and the crowd cheered them on too. He knew his mother would never have wanted them there. He glanced at his father and saw only enjoyment in the flushed face and wide eyes. His brother John was so pale he might be sick any moment, while his brother William and his two uncles stood craning forward like young warriors out for the kill.

The bull had lost a deal of blood and, unable to rid itself of the dog, it began to tire. The disappointed spectators grew restless. One of the butchers sensed the mood of the crowd; he walked right up to the bull and threw salt at its torn ear.

The people had their fun a little longer. Enraged, the bull made a last attempt to shake off the dog, and yet the loose jowls were suffocating it and it soon tired again. Now, down on its knees, it was ready for slaughter. The dog still gripped the bull's nose, but the owner stepped forward and eased its jaws apart. He then held it up as the victor.

Thomas and Samuel grabbed each other and jumped up and down as the losing spectators wandered off, not interested to see the bull killed.

Francis and John did not want to see any more. They turned their backs ready to leave.

'We can't go yet,' said their father. 'Your uncle Thomas hasn't got his money. Anyway,' he added with a smile, 'it'll be good for you to see it to the finish.'

Francis took hold of John's hand. They could see the bull's head lolling wearily on its huge shoulders. It looked as if it was crying, for its face was wet below the eyes. When they saw a butcher walk towards it carrying a sledgehammer, they closed their eyes. This didn't stop them hearing the crack of the skull. They opened their eyes to see the bull being untied and hauled off through the dirt by two horses.

'Why?' Francis cried. 'Why can't bulls be killed like pigs? Kill them quick and have done with it?'

'You know why,' his father answered. 'You know perfectly well why bulls are baited before slaughter. Anyone will tell you the meat's better. It's the struggle of the fight—it makes the meat tender. You'd be glad to eat it. I can get you some if you like.'

'No, thank you. I'd rather starve.'

'Alright then. Next time we have beef I'll remind you.'

'I'll have his share,' piped up young William.

His father smiled and ruffled his hair. At least he could understand one of his sons.

As promised, there was time to walk round the stalls that sold local goods and trinkets. The men spent a while buying leather straps and belts, allowing the three boys freedom to choose whatever they wanted. Young William bought a small knife and tucked it proudly into his belt while John chose a tin trumpet. Francis spent his money on an embroidered handkerchief for Milcah. Between them, the boys bought a bag of bright red and green boiled sweets for their mother and, in their pleasure over their purchases, Francis and John forgot about the bull for a while.

On the journey back to Reighton, Francis looked forward to giving his gift to Milcah. The ride would have been pleasant but for disturbing thoughts about Uncle Thomas. Having seen the cruel pleasure on his uncle's face during the bull baiting, he was now more certain than ever that Thomas should never marry Milcah. How he might prevent such a match was as yet a mystery.

Chapter 5

Milcah felt sorry for Mary confined to the house and garden in June with her latest child. As her young nephew George could now walk for longer distances, she was able to take him down the hill to St Helen's Lane and so spend time there with Mary. The women could sit in the garden together and enjoy the warm weather. They could both sew and mend while minding the children. She knew that Mary's boy, Richard, was a restless child, yet having another toddler around focussed his attention and calmed him down. As for the new baby, Matthew was docile, took his milk without fuss and slept for hours at a time—by far the easiest of all Mary's children.

While the two women sat in the shade of the apple tree, they enjoyed long conversations. Mary wondered how Milcah had ever earned a reputation for being quiet, for the young woman had opinions on everything. It soon became apparent that Milcah did not get on too well with her sister-in-law. One afternoon, they sat knitting peacefully in the shade of the apple tree while the boys played at their feet with balls of wool.

'I love my brother,' Milcah confided, 'but I really can't see that Dorothy and I have anything in common—apart from my brother of course. All Dorothy wants to talk about is London fashions. And she never asks how George has been, she just wants to know who I've seen and who's doing what. She loves to gossip.'

'You'd better be careful then,' advised Mary. 'She's from Bridlington, and a woman like that can cause trouble. Watch what you say.'

'I don't tell her anything, but I can tell she hates me for it.'

'I'm sure she doesn't hate you. She'll just be disappointed.'

'She needs me—I look after George. That's the only reason she's polite.'

To change the subject, Mary asked after Milcah's brother.

'Oh, John—he's the same as ever. Every night he plays his fiddle. He's started buying sheets of music from that chapman who calls round. There are some lovely tunes—you know, for the children's rhymes. Maybe he could come here one night and play for you and the boys.'

'Only if you promise to come too, and sing for us.'

Milcah blushed. 'Oh, I don't know about that. I'll sing for the children, but only for them.' She was quiet for a moment and then sighed. 'You know I miss my sisters so much, and my parents, especially in the evenings. I know I see my father sometimes on a Sunday, but it's not the same. I loved it when we read together.'

Conversations often ended like this. Mary knew it had been Milcah's choice to stay in Reighton when the rest of her family moved to Rudston, yet she understood the girl's regret. She missed the vicar and his wife too; they'd been a comfort for so many years, and the Gurwood girls had brought life and colour to the village.

'Are your parents and sisters settled in their new home?' she asked.

'Oh, yes. It seems even Mother likes it. There's more room, and Cecilia even has her own bed.'

'You're not thinking of joining them?'

'No. I'm happy here.'

Mary could see that Milcah was putting on a brave face. She decided she must befriend her more, include the girl in tasks around the house and garden.

The fine summer weather meant that the hens were often giving two eggs a day. Mary and Milcah searched the garden with the two young boys and scrabbled about in the hedge bottom. Mary was keen to remind Richard about safe egg collecting. She called to him to come and feel one of the eggs.

'Is it warm at one end and cool at the other?' When he'd felt it against his cheek she asked, 'Has it just been laid then? Is it fresh?'

After gathering a basketful, she put any dubious eggs in a bucket of water. She stood Richard in front of it. 'What do we do? We throw away any that float.'

They also picked shepherd's purse to feed to the hens. 'That'll give darker yolks,' she explained.

One day, Mary noticed that the hens were bullying and pecking the smallest one, and it was losing its feathers. She sent Milcah to get pine tar from Sarah Ezard and then showed the boys how to smear it on the sore, bald patches.

'That'll teach those hens,' she said as she wiped her hands on the grass. 'When they try pecking her now, they'll get tar all over their beaks. They'll spend all day trying to get it off.'

Mary was so much happier having Milcah as a companion, a female presence in her all-male household. She often wondered if her own daughter, had she lived, would have grown to be such a close friend. Now, Mary woke up each morning in optimistic mood, knowing the day ahead would be shared with a sympathetic soul. She began to experiment with food again—something she hadn't done for years.

The children never knew what they'd eat next. Even their breakfasts were different as Mary added fruits in season or put raisins in their porridge. One day, she flavoured their omelettes with tansy leaves. The older boys didn't mind, but the younger two held their noses.

She laughed. 'That's why we use the leaves to keep flies off the meat.'

Milcah took an interest in Mary's herb garden and, over the summer, they made a variety of sauces together. William grumbled at first, yet grew to like the fennel sauce and the unnamed 'green' sauces his wife concocted. When he mentioned them to his father, he got a terse reply.

'Brown gravy an' white sauce,' he muttered, 'it's all we ever 'ad, an' more than some poor folks got.' William didn't mention Mary's food again. He should have known his father wouldn't approve of anything fancy.

Both women looked forward to their long days together. When the weather became hot, Mary got William to put a large tub outside and fill it with water.

'When Milcah arrives,' she explained, 'we're going to take all the bedding outside. We'll get rid of the winter bugs and give everything a good clean.'

They arrayed the various beds and mattresses about the garden until it resembled an auction sale. The boys toddled in and out of the rows while the women gathered the linen and put it in to soak. Mary made a flour paste to rub in wherever there were soiled patches. After much scrubbing, they held the sheets out between them and twisted them hard to get out most of the water.

By this time the boys were tired and so Mary wheeled two barrows into the garden; in one went the wet linen, in the other she put the boys.

'Wait, Milcah, while I get the baby. I'll strap him to my chest and then I can wheel one barrow and you can wheel the other to Uphall. William's told his mother to have a big pot of hot water ready.'

As they pushed the barrows up the hill, Mary knew she could not have done all the laundering on her own. Milcah was a godsend.

One morning, Mary chose to sweep the chimney. With Milcah's help, she moved every utensil and every bit of kitchen furniture into the garden. Then she improvised a pen outside for the children. As soon as the two boys were out of the way, and the baby was asleep in his crib in the parlour, she fetched the goose wing. With no warning to Milcah, she shoved it right up the chimney.

Milcah leapt back as more soot fell out than expected. Mary's bonnet, her face, her hands and her arms were black.

'Oh, Lord,' gasped Milcah and began to giggle. 'Oh, Mary, you should see yourself.'

'Don't laugh,' Mary spluttered and then began to giggle as well. 'If you don't stop, I'll chase you with my sooty hands.' With that, she lunged at Milcah who dodged out of the way and escaped into the garden. Mary ran after her and chased her round the children's pen. She stumbled and laughed while the two boys clapped their hands in excitement, and then she collapsed onto the square of grass, still giggling.

Milcah joined her, holding her aching sides. 'I think, Mary, you'd better find cleaner jobs for us. Come on,' she cried, and wiped the tears from her eyes with her new handkerchief.

Mary noticed the embroidery. 'That's pretty.'

'Your Francis brought it from the fair.'

Mary remembered she'd been brought nothing but boiled sweets. 'I hope he's not bothering you.'

'No, not really. He's kind and thoughtful.'

Mary was not so sure. She hoped the silly boy wouldn't make a fool of himself. 'Come on, there's the kitchen to put back together, and then we must wash ourselves. Dorothy won't want you bringing soot into her house. Tomorrow, let's go out and collect wild herbs.'

The next day was sunny. With her baby strapped once more to her chest, Mary showed Milcah where to gather butterbur leaves for wrapping the butter, and where young burdock stalks grew for the meat broth. The toddlers were content to pick daisies and roll on the grass.

'Come here boys—come and see this,' cried Milcah. 'This butterbur leaf is big enough for both you to hide under.'

They crept beneath it and nestled close together.

She knelt down, lifted up one end of the canopy and peeped in. 'Put your hands up and touch the hairs under the leaf. That's right, can you feel them?' She gazed upwards through the leaf. As the sun shone through, the red veins stood out against the green, making a beautiful pattern. 'Mary, come and see. It's heaven under here.'

Mary lay on her back beside her and ducked her head under the leaf. Like the boys, she was silent, in awe of the magical green world.

'So that's what thoo gets up to!'

Mary leapt up.

Sarah Ezard had spotted them and was waddling towards them with a large basket. 'Thoo spends over much time outside wi' them little lads, Mary. Thoo can't 'ave enough work to do.'

'Oh, we've plenty to do, but it's better to be out.'

'Aye, I understand. I've been out since dawn. It's poppies I'm after. The earlier I gather, the stronger the juice. It'll ease pain better.' She gazed into the distance towards Filey Brigg. Waves were splashing over the rocks at the far end.

'I miss Ben,' she said suddenly. 'I wander these 'ills an' meadows, but it's not same anymore. I'm oldest i' village now. I'll be next to go.'

Mary and Milcah avoided her eye. They didn't know what to say.

'I've taken all o' Ben's skeps,' Sarah added, 'an' like me, bees don't seem to thrive without 'im.'

'We all miss Ben,' Mary mumbled.

As Sarah left them and made her way home, Mary thought of her own grief for old Ben. It was her first summer without him, yet the fine weather brought back happy memories. Although there were tears in her eyes, she smiled as she recalled him talking with his pipe stuck in that gap between his teeth.

'If it's a wood 'un, it's a good 'un, he always said about tools. And he had so much to say about the weather. Robins sing 'igh, it's fine an' dry. Robins sing low, it's too wet to mow. That was a favourite of his. You know, Milcah, I've never worked out if it was true what he told me about migrating geese. He said they formed a number in the sky, and I think it was supposed to mean how many weeks of frost we'd get. I could have asked him so many things. It's too late now.'

'Come on, cheer up. Let's gather meadowsweet. I know where it grows best. It's this way.' Milcah led the way to the wet edges of the lower meadow.

As soon as they'd picked enough, they went home and spread the flowers over Mary's floors. As fast as they were strewn, the boys rolled about to crush them and release the scent; the aroma gave a fresh sweetness to the house.

Mary smiled and winked at Milcah. 'You do know what the plant means? It stands for courtship and matrimony.'

'Yes, of course I know.' She recited the old saying in a tired voice. 'The lovely scent of the flowers stands for courting, and the sharp smell of the leaves stands for marriage.' She sighed. 'I'm sure it's true for many.'

Mary teased her. 'William's brother Thomas is very handsome don't you think? You always choose to dance with him.' Then she had an idea. 'I know—why don't you ask him to drive you in the cart one day to Rudston? You'd have time on your own together *and* see your family at the same time.'

'Hmm.' Milcah was not sure. She shrugged. 'He is handsome, and I'd love to be related to you, but we're too young. He's just twenty-two. More to the point, he needs to have more money saved if he's to marry.'

'Oh, I don't know, maybe I should invite him to supper one night when you're here—and while there's still meadowsweet on the floor. Don't leave it too late. I wouldn't want you to end up like my sister—a long courtship and then be childless.'

Milcah nodded with a wry smile. 'I'll know when the time is right.'

Chapter 6

Mary had other concerns than Milcah's suitors: there was a ready supply of brandy in the area. William, she knew from experience, could be aggressive when drunk and, unfortunately, he wasn't sick and didn't collapse if he drank too much. Bart Huskisson the carpenter was the same, yet he was a large man, well built and had been violent in the past. Mary feared for his family.

When Bart hadn't come in for supper, his wife waited in fear. On previous occasions, she'd locked their daughters in the shed. Even then, Bart had once taken an axe and broken down the door. Now, on this quiet summer's evening, the three girls and their mother sat in the kitchen dreading his return. Probably, he was drinking at the forge. Maybe he'd been there for hours already. Easy targets, they listened out for the scrape of his boots outside and the lift of the latch.

All at once, the door opened with a crash, and Bart stumbled in.

He saw the familiar terror in his daughters' eyes—the craven look that always inflamed him. In two strides he reached his youngest daughter. He grabbed hold of Emma's hair and pulled her away from the table.

'Get over there, bitch. Let me see what supper's left i' pot.' With almost the same movement, he raised his other hand and slapped his daughter, Catherina, across the face.

She knew better than to cry out or resist, but her eyes filled with tears and a bright red weal appeared on her cheek. She scuttled quickly out of the way towards Emma. Only his wife and eldest daughter remained at the table. They stood up and rushed to get beyond his reach.

'What's thoo starin' at woman?' he bellowed, leering drunkenly at his wife. He turned from her and made a grab at his eldest daughter.

She was not going to give way. She stood tall and held him at arm's length. The two of them swayed in front of the fire, neither getting the upper hand, when the edge of Elizabeth's petticoat trailed too near the hearth. It caught fire at once.

Her mother, quick to see what had happened, bent down to beat out the flames with her hand. Bart couldn't see what she was doing and gave her a hefty kick. She reeled backwards clutching her ribs.

It was then that he noticed the smell of burning cloth. Thinking he was on fire, he released Elizabeth and leapt away.

Elizabeth screamed as the flames caught her leg.

Bart stared at her, uncomprehending.

'Lizzie!' screamed her mother. 'Sit down an' cover tha legs. Emma! Fetch yon blanket. Quick! Wrap 'er legs in it.'

Emma ran to get it and dived onto Elizabeth's petticoat. She forced the blanket over the flames and pressed down hard. The flames were extinguished and Elizabeth rolled onto her side, sobbing from the pain and shock. Her mother and sisters knelt down and tried to soothe her while Bart stood by in silence, swaying on his feet.

Emma removed the blanket. 'Tha petticoat's badly burnt,' she muttered. 'I think it could be mended.' Then she saw the burn on Elizabeth's leg. It looked nasty.

Their mother fetched a jar of chicken fat. 'Listen, Lizzie, I'll smooth this o' tha burns as gentle as I can. Maybe I can smear it on with a feather.' She did her best while Bart sat slumped in the corner. Under her instructions, the girls made a thick poultice of oatmeal and water.

'The fat'll stop poultice stickin',' their mother said as she applied the paste. 'Tomorrow I'll get summat better fro' Sarah Ezard. She'll 'ave plenty o' burn ointment an' thoo'll be better soon.'

'I 'eard that slime of a live snail were good fo' burns,' Emma offered.

Her mother pursed her lips. 'Thank you, Emma. Let's wait an' see, shall we?' With that, she ushered her daughters to bed.

They didn't even glance at their father as they went. It was as if he was invisible.

His wife glared at him and spat on the floor as she walked past.

Bart began to cry, as he'd done so many times before. Horrified at how he'd treated his family, he dropped to his knees and pleaded with his wife.

'I swear I love thee. Please forgive me. It's brandy what does it, not me.'

She wasn't listening. She'd heard it all before and yet, at the back of her mind, there was the niggling hope that maybe this time he would change. There was still the acrid smell of burning in her nostrils. She turned from him in disgust and carried on towards the bedchamber.

Left alone in the darkening kitchen, Bart wept again. He shook his head to try and clear it, even banged it against the wall. There was no escaping what he'd done. He wiped his wet face with both hands, sniffed back more tears and then put the cover over the fire and retired to bed.

When he climbed in next to his wife, he curled himself round her back and whispered how sorry he was. He carried on mumbling to himself as much as to her, saying how he'd make amends. Within a minute, the sound of his own voice had sent him to sleep.

His wife was wide awake. She couldn't block out his snores, and the room stank of his stale breath. She alternated between hope and despair. Having failed to keep her daughters safe yet again, she did not know how to improve their lives.

News of Bart's latest violence swept through the village. In the past, the vicar had intervened, and his wife had befriended Bart's family in an effort to ease their troubles. Now, in the absence of the Gurwoods, malicious gossip went the rounds. Milcah heard about it from her sister-in-law, Dorothy.

'That Bart Huskisson's done it this time. Almost killed his daughter... nearly burnt her to death. I heard he pushed her into the fire. He'd have pushed them all in if his wife hadn't stopped him.' She relished the details. 'I'm told poor Elizabeth has blisters on her legs the size of plums.'

Milcah hoped this was an exaggeration. She could never trust Dorothy to be accurate with her news.

Dorothy hadn't finished. 'Bart needs to be shamed in public, that's what. I'm going to go round and see people. We'll demand something be done about him.'

True to her word, Dorothy Gurwood knocked on every door and persuaded folk to join her in condemning Bart the wife-beater.

Milcah thought Dorothy was being unfair. Despite Bart's cruelty, he was repentant and should be forgiven. He should be allowed another chance. She went round the village speaking to people, calming them down and appealing to their better nature.

'Let he who is without sin cast the first stone,' she declared, and looked them straight in the eye. She reminded them that her father had always been tolerant of poor behaviour so long as people were truly sorry for their actions. It was as the Bible taught. She now realised it was true what they said about Dorothy—she did make the arrows for others to shoot.

Milcah visited the carpenter's shed and cottage. She talked with Bart and was convinced that he was humbled and would atone for his sins.

Within days, the angry mood of the village subsided. Bart promised to give up the drink and be kinder to his family and, for the time being, he was forgiven.

Young Francis Jordan was aware of the crucial role played by Milcah. He adored her already, but now she was a saint.

'Blessed are the peacemakers,' he murmured in his nightly prayers, 'for they shall be called the children of God.' Milcah was the salt of the earth and the light of his world. With this exalted notion, he looked forward to Midsummer Eve.

Chapter 7

Francis toured the village with his brothers to beg rubbish for the midsummer bonfire. Reluctantly, after young William's insistence, they took the dog along too. While Stina barked and ran ahead, they pushed their barrows in equally high spirits and reminded folk that it was unlucky not to give something. Already, their father had taken a cartload of whins as a base for the fire. When the boys turned up, they tossed on their collection of rags, withered May wreaths, odd bits of wood and old bones. They stood back to admire their contribution.

'That's good, lads,' praised their father, coming up behind them with another load of gorse. 'Stick this in between the other stuff, it'll help it burn. Mind your hands though—it's prickly. Then, when you've finished that, I want you to gather as many weeds as you can.'

They groaned. Weeding was no fun at all.

He ignored their glum faces. 'We want thistles and nettles and dock leaves—anything we don't want growing with the crops. Then go back to your mother and ask her for herbs from the garden—thyme and fennel, whatever she can spare. If she won't give you any, try Sarah Ezard. Then, when all that's on the bonfire, go down by the gill and gather mugwort and watercress.'

It sounded more like women's work. The boys frowned and glanced at each other, wondering how they could escape.

'It's an important fire,' their father insisted, 'so no horsing about. A good fire means a good harvest.'

They were not convinced, and trudged to the fields with a sack each to begin the weeding.

'Come on, Stina,' young William grunted. 'There's work now, not play.' The rest of the day would be boring.

It was late afternoon before the bonfire was ready and the boys could go home at last and get washed. They ambled into the kitchen that smelled of warmed, sweet milk and nutmeg.

Their mother was standing over the fire, stirring bread into a large pot.

'I'm not going to the bonfire,' she informed them. 'I'll stay at home with the baby and Stina. Your father can take this pot with you, and he'll make sure you all behave.'

Francis led his two brothers into the garden where he left them to have a wash from the tub. As he wanted to be especially clean and smart for Milcah, he went up the lane and fetched a fresh bucket of water for himself.

When they were ready, their father led the way to the top of the hill, carrying the pot of spiced milk. Francis had to carry Richard, and grumbled because the toddler wriggled.

'I'll be cross if he dribbles down my shirt.'

'Stop complaining.' His father had little patience. 'Look—most people are here already. Your grandfather's about to light the fire.'

Francis set Richard down, but held tight onto his hand. He saw his grandfather wave his arms for silence.

'I know it should be old Ben lightin' fire. I miss 'im as much as anyone, an' I miss our vicar an' all, but John Gurwood 'ere will 'elp light it. Now, let's say our bonfire prayer before we start.'

Everyone bowed their heads and uttered the words together. 'In honour of our Lord an' St John, to our good 'ealth an' prosperity. Amen.'

John Gurwood threw on the flaming torch. There was a loud cheer, and those who'd brought metal pans began to beat out a rhythm. John picked up his fiddle and began to play while mugs were filled with ale. Soon, everyone made their way to the trestle table loaded with barley bread, pies and cheeses.

'Don't make pigs of yourselves,' William warned his boys. 'Just because your mother isn't here, don't think you won't be noticed.'

Francis worried that his brothers would embarrass him. He wanted to be more grown up, accepted as an adult, and couldn't trust William or John to behave with any manners. It would be humiliating if Milcah saw them. There she was, standing with her brother and his wife, the flames lighting up her face and hair.

Obliged to stay with his father and brothers for the time being, Francis had little appetite. While others gorged themselves on the food, he kept an eye on Milcah, his heart beating fast at the thought of the dancing to come.

When everyone had eaten their fill, and the first roar of the fire had died down, married couples stood up. They moved hand in hand clockwise round the bonfire, singing as they went, and then courting couples joined in. Francis watched both Milcah and his uncle Thomas the whole time. So far, Thomas had not made a move.

Young William was aware of what was going on. 'It's not fair is it, Francis?' he teased. 'Uncle Tom is the same age as Milcah. I bet you hate that, and everyone expects him to marry her.'

Francis glowered back. He needed no reminders. His uncle would be waiting for the flames to die down further.

As Francis suspected, Thomas was the first to throw off his hat, roll up his sleeves and take a running jump over the fire. He landed unscathed on the other side, right next to Milcah—no doubt as planned. He gave her a sweeping bow, grinned cheekily and then stepped back for another run up to the fire. It was the cue for Francis's other uncles to join in. Later, when the fire sank even lower, courting couples held hands and leapt over.

Francis watched Milcah for any sign of a preference for Thomas, and held his breath when his uncle approached. He couldn't hear what they were saying, but Thomas was holding her hand and gesturing towards the fire. Francis's life was poised on the brink. With a thumping heart, he waited for his fate to be sealed. It seemed an age before she shook her head, declining the offer. He breathed out again and swallowed hard, not quite believing his luck. But then, suddenly, she'd changed her mind. She was lifting up her petticoat and was leaping over the fire with Thomas.

Sarah Ezard sidled up behind him. She laid a claw-like hand on his shoulder and whispered in his ear.

'I know it means they intend to start courtin'. Look though—I can tell fro' flames 'ow things'll work out.'

He didn't believe her, though he stared at the fire with interest.

'See them small flickers o' flame?' She pointed with a crooked finger. 'They died out before they got goin'. Nay, lad, I reckon there'll be no weddin' fo' that pair.'

His eyes widened in hope.

'Maybe she's fo' thee, Francis. Who knows?'

He turned his head away, mortified that Sarah Ezard should know of his feelings. Yet the seeds of hope were sown, and he could hardly contain his joy.

When the fire burnt lower still, it was the children's turn. Francis did not want to be seen jumping with his lopsided brother or John, the simpleton. He stood aside while they leapt over a few times. Even his aunt Lizzie was persuaded to have a go amid allusions to her husband's prowess, or lack of it, in bed. He thought it cruel since she was past childbearing age. It was lucky her husband wasn't there; Robert never attended what he termed ungodly rituals.

Francis looked on as his father grabbed young Richard and threw him over the fire to Uncle Samuel. Others began to toss over their youngsters and babies for luck. He noticed that Matthew Smith and his family stood apart, preferring to watch from a distance. Perhaps people were right when they said the Smiths aspired to be gentry.

When there was only a mound of red embers glowing against the darkening sky, Thomas was the first to strip to the waist and leap as high as he could to the other side.

Francis could see that his brother William was impressed. Sensing the danger, he put an arm out to prevent him getting up and trying it himself.

'Don't be daft, Will! You'll trip and make a fool of yourself. Besides, you can't really believe the higher you jump, the higher the crops'll grow.'

His brother scowled and batted away Francis's arm. Yet he didn't risk the jump. The brothers sat still as young men tried to outdo each other, cheered on each time by the crowd. When the men tired, Francis's grandfather put an old cartwheel onto the embers and, once it started to burn, he sent it rolling down the hill. It bumped along, sending sparks into the night, and kept burning even when it reached the bottom.

'That's a good omen,' he proclaimed. 'Next year's crops'll grow well.'

A few branches of gorse had been set aside. Now, these were passed to the younger men who lit them from the remains of the fire. They marched in single file to the fields, waving the blazing gorse above their heads in the hope once more of a good harvest. Thomas was one of them.

Francis and Milcah remained by the bonfire with the others to see the flickering procession grow smaller in the distance. Many people began to go home. Others chose to stay and keep awake on this most magical of nights. Though weary, and with eyes sore from the smoke, Francis did not want to leave; as Milcah's brother was still playing the fiddle, he hoped she'd stay a little longer.

When his father took the younger boys home, Francis loitered a while. Just as he was plucking up courage to sit next to Milcah, Dorothy Gurwood sauntered by and announced she'd had enough of the bonfire.

'It's getting cold, and it's time the children were put to bed.' She shouted out to any within earshot, 'You're all welcome at our house though. Follow us. There'll be food and drink—and fortune-telling.'

Francis gulped. The very thought of knowing his and Milcah's future set his heart thudding. Though wary of superstition, here was a chance he couldn't miss.

Like a stray dog hoping for a home, he followed a few steps behind.

Chapter 8

Francis dared not let Milcah out of his sight; Thomas was sure to end up at the house for the fortune-telling. As soon as they were inside, John Gurwood lit candles and began to serve drinks while Milcah and Dorothy saw to the children. The kitchen fire was stoked, pipes were lit and, by the time the two women reappeared, Thomas had arrived. He sat at the table opposite Francis.

'I'm told I can hear my fortune—well, I'm ready.' He grinned at the others and rubbed his hands together, eager for the fun to start.

Instead of sitting at the table, Milcah drew her brother aside. Francis could only just catch their conversation amid the chatter around him.

'I don't approve of all this,' she whispered. 'Father wouldn't like it.'

'No,' John agreed, 'but Dorothy's different. She hasn't been brought up in a vicarage like us, has she? It's not *her* fault she doesn't have the same respect for the Bible. I blame her mother—she was full of superstition.'

'So...?' Milcah pleaded. 'You won't stop it?'

He turned to see his wife walking in with the Bible. 'It's too late. We can't say anything in front of the others. It would shame her. Put up with it just this once.'

As Milcah went to sit at the table, both Francis and Thomas beckoned to her and made room on their benches. She ignored them and squeezed onto the edge furthest from the fire.

Dorothy set the heavy Bible on the table and found the first chapter of Ruth. Then she took a small key from her apron pocket and placed it ceremoniously on the page beside verses 16 and 17.

Francis's stomach flipped over. They were the exact verses that Milcah had read aloud last autumn, the words he'd loved to hear. *Intreat me not to leave thee, or to return from following after thee: for whither thou goest, I will go.*

Dorothy leant over the table, surveying her captive audience. She poked Milcah in the back.

'Say the name of the man you hope to marry.'

Milcah blushed. She lowered her head and mumbled, 'I can't, not in this company.' Then, angry at being the centre of unwanted attention, she raised her head and challenged Dorothy. 'I don't think we should be doing this. It's wrong.'

'Nonsense! Think the name in your head then. It'll work the same. Watch the key—if you are to marry him, it'll move and point to the verses.'

All eyes were on the key. Francis stared hard, afraid to blink. Whether Milcah had said a name to herself or not, nothing happened. The key did not move.

Thomas persuaded himself that it had moved a little. 'There,' he cried, 'did you see it? It twitched. I'm sure it moved that way a bit.'

'Nay,' the others answered. They suspected it was a trick of the candlelight in the draught. Each of the young men had a go with differing degrees of success, depending on whether or not they'd nudged the table with their knees.

When it came to Francis's turn, he refused to take part. Like Milcah, he knew it was wrong. He was relieved when the others grew tired and began to fidget and yawn.

Dorothy was disappointed to lose the attention of her audience. 'Perhaps I could bind the key with a length of cord and hang it up. That might work.'

Her husband raised his hand. 'That's enough, Dorothy. It's been a long day, let everyone go home.'

She had the last word though. As the men left the house, she stood in the doorway. 'If you want to know the future, I've got a well-scraped blade of a ram. I'd be happy to look through it for you.'

They nodded but made no arrangements. Tomorrow was Midsummer Day with better fun and games.

Francis said goodnight politely and followed the rest. He was disillusioned, shocked that Milcah had stayed to watch. His one consolation was that her future was still uncertain.

The next morning, despite a lack of sleep, the young of the village rose early. They adorned themselves with flowers and ribbons and paraded through the village. John Gurwood played his fiddle and led the way to the field below the church.

His wife was piqued by Milcah's lack of co-operation the previous evening, and still hadn't forgiven her for preventing Bart Huskisson's punishment. While others enjoyed the parade, she kept Milcah behind at the house to attend to the children.

As Milcah dressed George and fed the baby, she thought of the gossip that Dorothy had spread. The woman's rumours made everyone wary, and Bart Huskisson and his family had suffered exaggerated accusations. The Huskissons had not been at last night's bonfire, no doubt because of Dorothy's gossip. Milcah hoped the family would come for today's festivities, and then she had an idea. She took the children to the field, found Dorothy, and made an excuse to leave to collect flowers. Instead of going to the meadow, she made her way to the Huskissons' home.

Milcah was pleased to find Bart's daughters dressed in their prettiest clothes. He and his wife were also in their Sunday best for the day.

'I'm so glad you've decided to go out,' Milcah said with a beaming smile. As they left, she whispered to the girls, 'And don't worry about Dorothy Gurwood—the rest of us don't believe half of what she says.'

By the time Milcah had returned to the field with the Huskissons, the ash from the bonfire had been taken away and sprinkled onto the corners of the fields. She was sorry to miss this last blessing of the crops and said as much.

Dorothy overheard and sneered. 'You're getting soft— and you a country lass. It's the bone ash that's good for the crops. We can do without any long-winded blessing.'

Milcah ignored her and strode off with the Huskissons to see Matthew Smith laying out sacks for the sack race.

William and his son Francis also looked on. William nodded in Milcah's direction.

'That lass is too forgiving. Why is she standing next to Bart Huskisson? She's not the vicar—only a vicar's daughter. She should know better than to interfere.'

Francis didn't answer. He was too concerned about his uncle Thomas; his rival was strutting around like a cockerel. All the girls were eyeing him, giggling together and trying to catch his attention. At least Milcah was not one of them.

Young men from Speeton had walked over to take part and were now shouting mild abuse at the Reighton lads. Francis saw Thomas sidle up to Milcah and give her a wink.

'Watch me win this race,' he heard Thomas boast. 'Those lads yonder don't stand a chance. If I win, do I get a kiss?'

She blushed and shook her head. 'You'll just win a leg of mutton, same as always.'

A Speeton lad jeered, "E'd rather 'ave a leg o' tender young lamb!'

'Leave off!' Thomas warned. 'You'll watch me anyway, won't you, Milcah?'

'I'll watch all of you. I don't mind who wins.'

He shrugged and swaggered to the starting line.

Francis crossed his fingers, hoping Thomas would not win the race. Perhaps he'd fall flat on his face instead.

Matthew Smith waved the leg of mutton above his head. 'Winners—keepers!' he announced. 'Line up here if you intend to race. When I wave my hat, jump into a sack and race to yon gate.'

About a dozen young men joined Thomas, including his brothers, Samuel and Richard. When the hat was waved, they pounced on the sacks and climbed in. They rammed their feet into the corners, some choosing to jump while others tried to run. Samuel and Richard were jumpers. They were so intent on getting ahead that they crashed into each other and went flying. As they struggled to get up, everyone else overtook them with Thomas in the lead. He won with ease, and claimed his prize amidst cheering. Girls from both villages threw ribbons at him so that, when he strolled back to his brothers with a wide grin, he was festooned like a maypole.

Francis felt sick, but was surprised to see Thomas avoiding Milcah. Perhaps, now that his uncle was so popular, he was teaching her a lesson, making her wish she'd paid him more attention.

The next race was for the women. Matthew Smith's wife, Ellen, held up the prize—a white apron embroidered with red roses. The blacksmith's two daughters stepped forward, kicked off their shoes and hitched up their petticoats in readiness. Milcah overheard the Huskisson girls debating on whether or not to take part. Elizabeth said she wouldn't run because the burns on her leg had not healed yet.

Milcah stepped in front of them. 'I'll race if you will.'

'Let's do it,' cried Emma, excited at the prospect. 'Come on Cathy—'itch up tha gown.'

The three young women rushed forward to join the others at the start.

Francis was appalled. He never thought to see Milcah stoop so low. His angel had never raced before. She also kicked off her shoes and lifted up her petticoat like a common milkmaid. Maybe she was just like the other women after all. When the girls set off, he looked away, not caring to see the outcome. Something precious had slipped away from him, leaving him empty.

As soon as the race started, Milcah grew anxious. She was used to running barefoot with the children, but she had no idea how fast she should try to run. When she found herself in the lead, she realised her error; the field sloped much more steeply towards the finish at the far gate, and she was gaining speed. In a panic, and unable to slow down, she saw Thomas throw himself in her path. He flung his arms out to catch her—a moment before she collided with the gate. He held onto her briefly before letting go.

'You've won, Milcah! You've only gone and won!'

She was dazed and could scarcely believe it. The other girls congratulated her as they walked back up the hill where Ellen Smith handed over the apron.

'You're supposed to hold it up and wave it,' prompted Thomas. 'Come on—we'll wave it together.'

Francis turned his head when he heard the cheers. He saw the way Thomas held her in his arms and knew he'd never feel the same about her. The people around him were clapping and shouting. Everyone was happy while he was bereft. Milcah and Thomas seemed the perfect couple—two winners standing as one. Thomas was obviously thrilled as he waved the apron over their heads, and Milcah was flushed and smiling. Francis didn't know how he'd get through the rest of the day, or the days to come.

The last competition of the day was a race downhill to catch a wheel of hardened cheese. The same young men lined up as before. This time, Samuel and Richard kept well apart, not wanting a repeat of the sack race.

The cheese was bowled forward and, once it was halfway down the hill, the men set off in pursuit. Samuel and Richard, both with long legs, were deemed the most likely to reach the cheese first but, as the hill steepened, they lost control of their limbs and were overtaken by Thomas. He heard them yell and fall somewhere behind him, but kept his focus on the cheese still bouncing ahead. He caught it just in time before it hit the fence at the bottom. A couple of lads, not far behind, hoisted him onto their shoulders and carried him back up the hill in triumph. His brothers were left to carry the cheese.

Milcah ran forward and blew Thomas a kiss.

Francis slunk away in disgust at the sight.

'What's up wi' thoo, Francis?' asked his grandfather. 'Thoo looks as if tha'd seen tha backside an' 'adn't liked look of it.'

Francis forced a smile. He hated the races, the games and the banter. The day continued, but he was numb to any pleasure. Without his love for Milcah, his life stretched out before him like a grey, dirty sheet.

Chapter 9

For the rest of the summer, Francis avoided Milcah and, when this wasn't possible, he refused to look her in the eye. It annoyed him that she and his mother had become such good friends, and that Milcah was at their house almost every day.

Milcah couldn't understand the change that had come over Francis. She wondered if she'd offended him, or if he was ill. She missed his soft glances and devoted affection. Now, he wouldn't speak unless spoken to, and his eyes were furtive.

His mother had no idea what was wrong either. She put it down to his age.

His father paid little attention. 'He's a hobbledehoy, neither man nor boy. What do you expect?'

There were times when Francis's resolution weakened and yet, when he felt in danger of falling in love again, he always pulled back in time. He was determined not to suffer again, and whenever Milcah was near, he was cold and calculating.

He found unexpected comfort from John. His younger brother didn't understand the change in him and accepted him as he was. When John sat next to him at the table, he nestled up close. The warmth from his body, that gentle touch from another being, made Francis's days more bearable.

Dickon was a comfort too. Francis saw the old foreman at least twice a day as he started work at Uphall and returned at sunset. Dickon, limited in his work by arthritis, was left alone to do what simple jobs he could manage. Francis would always find him in some quiet corner and often sat with him. They'd oil harnesses together or tend a sick calf in silent companionship. Seeing Dickon's patience and uncomplaining acceptance of his lot gave Francis strength. He no longer hoped for love and happiness, but at least he could go on living from day to day, working from dawn to dusk, year in year out, like Dickon.

There was an abundant harvest that year, and the whole village worked hard to get everything in before the onslaught of the autumn mists. William was more than satisfied as his father had borrowed money to buy extra land. The two oxgangs in question were next to William's own strip, the idea being that, if William worked it and paid the interest on the loan, he'd inherit it one day. So far, the land had proved profitable, and William was not overly concerned about repayments. He was content for once as he strolled home from the barns filled with sheaves.

On entering the kitchen, he smiled as he watched Mary free their baby son's arms. He then frowned to see the rest of Matthew's body remain swaddled.

'I know,' she explained. 'I don't like our bairns held fast for so long either, but this way their bodies will grow straight. It's not my fault that young William has a bent spine.'

'No, it's no one's fault.' He sighed, wondering if the boy would ever be able to follow a plough.

Early autumn was Mary's favourite time of the year. She went brambling with Milcah and the younger children, and they spent hours making jellies and jams together. One day, they brought fresh, clean chaff down from

Uphall and stuffed it into the mattresses. They both looked forward to harvesting the garden produce.

Mary chose a day after dry weather to dig up her potatoes. The soil was warm and crumbly and, while the women forked them out, the boys dived in with their small hands to retrieve any the women had missed. John, scurrying on his hands and knees with Richard, thought it was like finding buried treasure. The boys helped put the potatoes carefully into sacks, and later they all stood back to enjoy the sight of a full storeroom.

Strings of onions hung down from hooks in the beams, and the shelves were stacked with jams and pickles, bottled fruits and cheeses. There was still plenty to do—pick apples to store in the loft, and salt down the meat—but the two women didn't mind because they'd be working together.

The hours spent outside, even with a bonnet on, had given Milcah a sunburnt face. Her sister-in-law was ashamed.

'Your sister's like a gypsy,' Dorothy complained to her husband.

He thought Milcah had never looked so well, but kept quiet. There was a bout of autumn flux going round the village and he didn't want to tempt fate. So far, the illness had just affected children and women recovering from childbirth. He never expected Milcah to catch it. She was strong and should be able to shrug off any infection.

Everyone was surprised when Milcah became housebound with the dreaded flux.

Sarah Ezard was shocked not to see Milcah in church; the young woman had seemed so healthy. She shook her head and clicked her tongue. ''Er looks don't pity 'er, but I'll send 'er an infusion to try.'

Milcah was made to drink as much raspberry leaf tea as she could force down as well as Sarah's concoction made from dried chamomile flowers. She lost her appetite and dared not venture far from her chamber pot. Often, all she expelled was discoloured water. It exploded from her into the pot, and the smell was rank.

Her sister-in-law showed no compassion. In disgust, Dorothy burnt mugwort leaves to fumigate the chamber, and told her husband she'd prefer it if Milcah was confined to the outhouse.

'If you're going to be that uncharitable,' he warned, 'I'll do the same to you if you ever get the shits. Do you want that?'

She kept her peace, yet made Milcah do her own washing and cleaning, and forbade her to touch the children.

No one was allowed to visit. Mary couldn't go anyway in case she caught the flux and passed it on to the baby. When Milcah's father heard of her illness, he wanted to visit, but she discouraged him as he might take the flux back with him to Rudston. Milcah lost so much weight that she could wrap her petticoats around twice.

After a few weeks, even Dorothy was sorry and, when Milcah was no better, she asked Sarah Ezard to bring a batch of her special pancakes.

'They're made fro' starch an' tallow,' Sarah told Dorothy as she plonked them on the table. 'They'll clog up 'er bowels nicely.'

When Milcah tried to swallow them, the claggy paste stuck to the roof of her mouth and made her retch. 'Please, Dorothy,' she begged, 'don't make me eat any more.'

Dorothy sniffed. 'Fine, if you don't want to get better...'

'Ask Sarah Ezard for something else to try. I can't go on like this.'

Later that day, Dorothy brought other remedies. 'Look, Milcah, I have a jar of chamomile flowers. They've been boiled in milk. Sarah says to put them in your chamber pot and sit over them.'

'I suppose that can't do any harm. What else have you got?'

'You won't like this so much. It's a clyster.'

Milcah stared in horror at the contraption on the table—what looked like a pig's bladder with a long tube attached.

'Don't expect *me* to administer it,' Dorothy added. 'You can do it yourself, or get your friend Mary. Sarah's given me this bottle of pearl barley and milk. She says if you won't eat, you'll have to be fed the other end... it's there if you want it.'

Milcah did not try the clyster. Instead, she drank pints of tea, and sometimes tried red wine with herbs. At last, after over a month of looseness, her bowels improved and her appetite returned. Unfortunately, she was left with piles. As she'd never had them before, she wasn't sure what they were like. She went to ask Mary.

'Ah, yes,' Mary said, 'my mother used to suffer from those. Like bunches of little grapes, hers were. Very sore. Sometimes, though, you could push them back in. Do you want me to have a look? I don't mind. I've seen enough bottoms in this house.'

They went into the parlour and closed the door, warning the children to stay on guard in the kitchen.

Milcah bent over a chair and lifted up her skirts.

Mary knelt down and peered up. Gently, she prised apart Milcah's cheeks and saw the purplish-red piles.

'What can you see?' Milcah asked, afraid to know. 'Is it bad?'

'No, I've seen worse. My mother had pile ointment from the apothecary at Hunmanby. I'll borrow it.

I think it has opium in it, but it's mostly lard. It'll soothe you while you get better.'

The shared intimacy over the piles brought Milcah and Mary even closer, so that Milcah often left her brother's house to spend the evening with Mary and the boys. In the autumn, the smuggling trade recommenced, and with William out most nights, Mary's sister Elizabeth would also visit. The three women could sit in peace by the fire to knit and chat.

One such evening, Mary made Francis and young William knit too. She handed them needles, and balls of freshly spun, unwashed wool.

'Get on with it. You know how to knit once I get you started.' She smiled at Milcah and winked. 'The wool will make your hands feel so soft and smooth.'

Young William laughed. 'Hey, Francis—Father won't want your hands like a woman's.' With a teasing grin he added, 'You won't be able to plough next year if your hands get any softer.'

Francis didn't care. He was having enough trouble trying to ignore the presence of Milcah. He kept sneaking a glance at her to test his resolve, like prodding a raw wound. Did he still hanker after her? Was he still moved by her voice? Did he still love her after all? He was glad she was well, although he'd enjoyed a few weeks of peace while she'd been ill. Now he was confused again.

Thomas Jordan had never reckoned on Francis as a possible rival, thinking there could be no competition between a man and a boy. One night, when it was just the women and boys at home, he turned up unexpected at Mary's house. He disturbed them with his manly presence, bringing in the cold autumn air and the smell of tobacco. He sat on the settle beside Milcah and made

Francis pull off his boots, a degrading task befitting a servant. Then he gave Milcah a present.

'Something for your knitting needle,' he said, his eyes twinkling.

Mary, sitting on Milcah's other side, gave her a nudge. She remembered when William had courted her. He had given her a knitting sheath with a heart carved in the middle. She was eager to see Milcah's reaction.

Francis, sitting opposite by the fire, held his breath. In Milcah's hands, was a thin yet beautiful sheath carved from what looked like pear wood, with a hole bored in the top for the needle. Her initials were carved on the front. It was obvious how pleased she was. She blushed as she thanked him.

Thomas rubbed his large hands up and down his thighs as if trying to warm them. No one knew what to do next. Francis sulked and ground his teeth. After what seemed like ages, Mary broke the silence.

'Let's have a drink to celebrate. We won't have beer or tea. Let's try Geneva. William brought a bottle home last week. I'm sure he won't mind.'

None of them had tasted gin before, so Mary only gave them a little to try. 'Here, boys—you can have a watered-down sample.'

The boys held back until the others had tried it. Milcah took a tiny sip and pulled a face. She didn't like it one bit. Thomas swallowed his in one go, then coughed, his face turning bright red.

'I don't know why it's so popular,' he spluttered. 'It smells better than it tastes.'

Young William showed off by taking a big swig. He tried not to screw up his face, but his eyes watered and, like Thomas, he began to cough.

Francis didn't even try it.

'Alright, I'd better make some tea then,' Mary decided. 'Tonight should be special.'

As they sipped from their saucers, she smiled. 'Now I know what it's like to be gentry—having friends and family round drinking tea.' She winked at Thomas. 'William won't drink it, you know. Be careful, Tom, he thinks that tea weakens a man, makes him foppish.'

Thomas grinned and rubbed his thighs again slowly while eyeing Milcah sideways. 'I don't think you need have any fear of that.'

Young William groaned and kicked Francis's foot. He hated to see his uncle acting like a lovesick bunch clot.

Francis glared back. He was disturbed. Thomas had so quickly and easily destroyed the calm. He hoped his uncle would leave as soon as he'd drunk his tea. One thing was certain now—despite all his efforts, he still wanted Milcah.

Chapter 10

1720-21

Francis couldn't bear the thought of his uncle Thomas with Milcah. After a sleepless night, full of jealous imaginings, he made a new resolve. He would love Milcah again and show her he was a better suitor than Thomas. Once he'd made that decision, he threw himself into the evening activities with relish. He was the first to pick up his knitting and choose a place by the fire, and when his mother served food and drink, he leapt up to help. If Milcah happened to hum a tune while she knitted, he was in heaven, and as Thomas did not visit very often, restricting his courting to Sundays, Francis saw his way clear.

His mother and Milcah were relieved at the change in him, but his brother, William, was embarrassed. He couldn't believe how pathetic Francis was in female company.

'If Francis had been a dog,' he told his mother, 'he'd have rolled over for his belly to be tickled. He even chews spearmint leaves, and the looks he gives Milcah…' He shook his head. 'Stina gazes into nothing like that when I stroke the back of her ear.' He had to admit, though, that he benefitted from his brother's improved mood; Francis sometimes let William have his second helping of supper.

Francis's brothers, John and three-year-old Richard, also appreciated the change. Francis let Richard sit on his knee and he played kindly with him, never getting cross. One night the boys played Puss in the Corner; they moved the beds to one side in the parlour to make a space, and each boy went to a different corner. Milcah stood in the middle. Whenever the boys rushed to swap places, she tried to reach an empty corner before them. The game soon became hectic, and John got over-excited. He never fully grasped the simple rules and collided with the others, often hurting them. Young William was so frustrated he thumped John in the back.

Francis flew to the rescue. 'Leave him,' he shouted. 'He's got past himself. He can't help it.' He sat John on his knee and cuddled him, but John was so worked-up he was sick all down his front. 'Don't worry, Mother,' Francis said with great command. 'I'll wash him down in the kitchen.'

Young William was amazed. 'Saint Francis,' he mumbled under his breath. 'No wonder John was sick.'

On a dark winter's evening, not long before Christmas, Milcah came to the house with her brother John. He brought his fiddle and some music he'd bought recently. While he played the tunes, Milcah taught the boys the rhymes. Seeing the children love it so much, he began to visit more often, leaving his wife alone with their children. He was most impressed that John, with his simple mind, was soon able to hum the tunes for 'Ride a Cock Horse' and 'London Bridge'. When her brother couldn't come, Milcah sang while she knitted.

Francis couldn't believe his luck for she'd never sung on her own before.

Milcah and her brother also encouraged the boys with their Bible reading. When they chose the more uplifting psalms, it took Francis back to the time when his sister sang in bed at night—bits of the Bible mixed up with her own fancies. He was charmed once more by the words and the rhythms and, with Milcah in mind, he read the Song of Solomon on his own many times.

His mother understood his need to be alone to read in peace, and made sure the others were occupied elsewhere so as not to bother him. Glad that Francis was taking more interest in the Bible, she didn't pay heed to his choice of content.

'As the lily among thorns, so is my love among the daughters,' Francis read aloud. To him at least, Milcah had always been the most beautiful of the Gurwood girls. He loved the repetitions of *Rise up my love, my fair one, and come away*, and imagined saying such words to her. *For, lo, the winter is past, the rain is over and gone. The flowers appear on the earth; the time of the singing of birds is come.* If only her brother had a tune to go with the words. 'Arise my love, my fair one, and come away,' he read, wishing he could sing it close to her ear.

He closed the Bible and sighed; he could never sing to her. Apart from anything else, his voice would let him down. He could trust himself to speak the words though, and decided to learn parts of the Song of Solomon by heart. That way he could tell her how he felt.

One evening, Francis waited until his mother was putting his brothers to bed. He was alone with Milcah in the kitchen. Standing behind her, he whispered.

'Many waters cannot quench love, neither can the floods drown it.'

Somewhat surprised, Milcah ignored him and stood up to poke the fire. Then she crashed around among the pans as if looking for something. She busied herself until Mary returned.

A few nights later, Francis was bolder. Alone once more with Milcah, he put his hand on her arm. When she turned to face him, he gazed intently and spoke the words he'd learnt.

'Set me as a seal upon thine heart, as a seal upon thine arm: for love is strong as death.'

'I know those words,' she replied with accustomed calm. 'They're from the Song of Solomon. My father liked to read it.'

Francis had hoped for more recognition, but she drew away from him again and busied herself with the fire. Despite her aloof behaviour, the winter seemed more like spring.

The winter did not suit the rest of the village, for the new year began with heavy rain. Sarah Ezard had forecast this, as had the apothecary in Hunmanby who had a jar of leeches; he'd reported how restless they'd been—a sure sign of wind and wet weather. The previous autumn had been too mild, Sarah complained—another bad sign. November had been oppressively warm and humid. It was unnatural the way the bees had kept working, and vegetation had grown when it should have died back. Now, in January, the lower meadows had flooded and the fields could not be ploughed.

At Uphall, Francis Jordan called for his sons and Dickon, their old foreman. They sat around the kitchen table to debate how best they might manage.

'I've been thinkin',' he began, 'I'd like to plough up more of our old pasture ground o' Land Moor.'

Dickon screwed his nose up at the idea, always averse to change, yet William and his brothers listened with interest.

Francis continued. 'Nobody wants to start ploughin' top field yet, but there's nowt to stop us gettin' started on our own ground over o' north side.' He turned to Dickon. 'Remember, we ploughed up old pasture once before. We 'ad a ploughin' match about ten year ago to get us started. Thoo must remember.'

William thought of a problem. 'And like last time, the Smiths' land is right next to ours. We should let Matthew know—it's only fair since he's the chief freeholder.'

Dickon frowned. 'That land 'as been pasture fo' years now.' He scratched the bristles on his chin. 'It'll take some ploughin'.'

Francis wasn't in the mood for Dickon's gloom. 'Listen, yon pasture's been gettin' poor for a long while. It needs more than manure. Ridges an' furrows are still there from me gran'father's time—thoo can see 'em plain enough. We'll plough an' then plant peas. They'll do soil a lot o' good. Aye, an' then later on we can sow rye grass an' clover.'

His sons began to see the sense in this; they glanced at each other, nodding their heads.

'Aye,' Francis concluded, 'i' years to come we'll end up wi' really good pasture again.'

Dickon, though reluctant, prepared the ploughs and supervised their haul on sledges to the northern field. The Jordans went ploughing while others remained idle. They regretted the decision when their boots were weighed down with clods of mud and the oxen tired. Every hundred yards both man and beast had to rest, which meant the work took twice as long.

After a day's ploughing, young Francis was too exhausted in the evening to enjoy the songs and readings. As soon as he'd had supper, the warmth of the room and a full belly made his eyes close. He fell asleep despite his best efforts to keep awake for Milcah.

His father was worn out too, working on his own land as well as doing his share of the ploughing for Uphall. He maintained a presence with the smugglers, but kept his role as a riding officer ambiguous, closing his eyes to most of the free trading while reaping its rewards. However hard he worked though, and whatever he did, he'd never make the same amount of money as Matthew Smith. Rumour had it that the Smiths had sold their shares in the South Sea Company last summer, just before it collapsed. The Smiths, it seemed, had the luck of the devil.

Following the wet weather, there was a renewed outbreak of the flux. One morning Milcah woke up with a familiar rumbling in her bowels. She didn't feel well at all and dreaded to face the illness again. As she stood and leant her forehead against the cold window-frame, she began to shiver. Suddenly, her bowels cramped and she rushed for the chamber pot, hitching up her nightdress as she went.

Dorothy found her still there half an hour later, squatting with her head in her hands, her elbows propped on her bare knees.

Milcah didn't dare get up. Despite being empty, her bowels kept straining, ever straining until merely the thinnest slime was ejected. Still her bowels convulsed and it was wearing her out. It was obvious that she hadn't recovered properly from her autumn bout of the illness.

Chapter 11

1721

As soon as Milcah could leave the chamber pot, Dorothy helped her back into bed. Milcah couldn't stop shivering, so Dorothy added an extra blanket and then brought her a large mug of hot, weak tea.

'It's important,' she warned, 'to keep drinking. Even if you can't stomach any food, you must drink.' She didn't look forward to tending the children all by herself again. 'Listen, I've had enough of Sarah Ezard's remedies. They didn't work. I'll get John to ride to Hunmanby and get something from the apothecary. Don't worry about the cost. We just want you to get well.'

Later that day, John returned with a cordial and laudanum. 'The apothecary advised bleeding,' he said as he put the bottles on the table.

Milcah raised herself up in bed. 'Not that, please,' she begged. 'It'll make me feel worse... but thanks for the laudanum.' She sank back down again. 'It'll ease the cramps... then maybe I can sleep.'

Milcah watched Dorothy make up a dose of cordial. She drank it obediently, but not without pulling a face. It was a revolting mixture of bitter herbs and strong spices.

By chance, no one else in contact with Milcah caught the illness, yet despite the apothecary's cordial, she suffered throughout January. Violent, griping pains doubled her up and, after painful evacuations, she dreaded checking the contents of the chamber pot. She was horrified at the sight of the mucus and blood. It was as if her body wanted to get rid of everything in it. She lost weight again and didn't want to see herself in the mirror. The last time she'd looked, she'd hardly recognised the gaunt face staring back.

In early February, when she developed a slight fever, she asked Dorothy to send away any visitors. 'I don't want them to see me like this.'

'What about your sister, Jane? She's in Speeton—she could walk over. Or your father?'

Milcah shook her head. 'No, Jane has young children, and there's another on the way, and I don't want to worry father on his busy Sunday. Send him word that I'll have someone drive me to Rudston when I'm better.' She knew Mary would have loved to visit, but Mary had children too.

The two 'suitors', Thomas and Francis, were out all day working, and Dorothy persuaded them not to visit the girl in the evenings. She told them that Milcah would be deep in sleep by suppertime, exhausted by another painful and worrying day.

'Come on Sundays, if you really must,' she advised them. 'That's your best opportunity.'

Mary tried to discourage Francis. 'Leave the poor girl alone. Let her recover in peace.'

He couldn't stay away though, and neither could Thomas. They contrived to visit at different times despite the warnings.

Thomas always took a small present, but was ill at ease in the sick room. He was never one for sitting around and making polite conversation; it was a relief when it was time to go. He didn't like to think of the future. If Milcah recovered, that would be good. If she didn't... well... there were other women.

When Francis visited, he noticed the small gifts from Thomas arrayed on the table by the bed. They were things bought from shops: a bar of soap, a pack of cards and a set of wooden buttons. Francis decided to make a present; the effort involved would prove his love for her. He remembered old Ben carving a dove for his sister. With this in mind, he thought he could do the same.

As soon as he returned home, he searched around for a suitable bit of wood.

'What are you rummaging for?' his father asked. When Francis explained, he agreed to help. He found a piece of apple wood at Uphall, pruned the year before. 'Here you are. Although it's a hard wood, it's strong and it'll take fine detail. She'll love the colours of the grain.'

That evening, Francis sharpened his knife and sat by the fire with the lump of wood in his lap. He took off the bark and then pondered what to carve. He could try and make a dove as Ben had done. It would be most appropriate since, in the Song of Solomon, doves and doves' eyes were mentioned more than once.

After two hours of hacking away at the wood and cutting his fingers, he gave up the idea of carving a dove. What he had left was a shapeless thing.

'Don't give up,' coaxed his mother. 'Get to bed now and have another go tomorrow.'

The next night, Francis sat staring at the wood. He thought to make it into an animal, maybe a sheep, but knew he couldn't do the legs.

Eventually, his mother put down her knitting. 'Here, pass it to me. Perhaps I can think of something.' She closed her eyes as she turned it over in her hands.

'You might laugh,' she said at last, 'but why not make it into an apple?'

He grinned and took it back. 'That's perfect. I'll do it.' After a while, and after cutting his hand twice, he gave up once more. With tears in his eyes, he threw it down.

'It's no good. The wood's too hard. It's impossible.' He stood up and began pacing round the kitchen. 'What am I going to do? What can I give Milcah on Sunday?'

'If you're so intent on carving, your father brought driftwood back last week. I was going to burn it. You might be able to make something instead. It's over there. It should be dry by now.'

He found the piece she mentioned and cut into it with his knife. Compared to the apple wood, it was like slicing butter. It was a long, thin piece though, and it wouldn't make a dove. It didn't have much colour either.

'Mother!' he complained, and let it fall to the floor. 'I can't make anything.'

'Look, Francis, you could make it into a nice shape. Smooth it and decorate it with holly. Maybe you could add red berries or rose hips. I'll give you a bit of red ribbon, and she can hang it over her bed.'

Francis's face lit up. 'Yes! And it will bring her luck.' Straightaway, he began to shave the wood and didn't stop until it resembled a small, shapely yoke.

When Sunday came, he cut down a branch of holly that still had a few berries, and his mother helped him fix it on with ribbon. They finished by tying a fancy bow.

He set off with his gift and, when admitted to see Milcah, he blushed and hid the ornament behind his back.

'I made it myself,' he said as he presented it to her. 'I wanted to carve a dove but... Anyway, this will bring you luck.'

She managed a faint smile and whispered, 'It's very pretty. Hang it here on the bedhead so I can see it.'

He didn't get the chance to stay any longer as Thomas turned up. Undaunted for a change, he strode home inches taller and with a huge smile on his face.

As the weeks went by, Francis grew more uncomfortable on his visits. He could see that Milcah had lost a lot of weight since Christmas. Her arms were like pale sticks laid on the bedclothes. Her dark eyes were enormous in a white, pinched face and her hair, once so black and shiny, was now dry and brittle.

He stared at her, searching for signs of the old Milcah, but only her eyes showed any animation, and the predominant look was one of fear. It upset him that he couldn't be more prepared. The truth was, despite the lavender strewn on the floor, the smell of sickness in the room put him off. Milcah's brother and wife had grown accustomed to it, yet it made Francis want to retch. More often than not, he wished he hadn't gone to visit.

The Song of Solomon taunted him: 'the smell of thy garments is like the smell of Lebanon.' That was so untrue of Milcah now. Her cheeks were no longer 'as a bed of spices, as sweet flowers.' Her lips were definitely not 'like lilies dropping sweet smelling myrrh.' His love for her was not strong enough; it had failed.

When he lay in bed at night, the words of Solomon droned in his head, keeping him awake. He thought with shame of his wooden gift hanging from her bedhead. The holly leaves had turned pale and crisp, the berries were dry and wizened, and the wood was as bleached of colour as Milcah's face. His gift now looked a miserable thing, an apt reflection of the love dried up in his heart.

As for Milcah, she was past caring. She had longed for spring to come and her health to return, hoping to visit her mother in Rudston on Mothering Sunday if not before. Thomas had promised to take her. Now, any such hopes seemed unrealistic. News came of her sister Jane giving birth to her first daughter. It was hard to believe that life was carrying on without her.

One morning, Dorothy took Milcah her morning infusion of raspberry leaves. The young woman was peaceful, in a deep sleep, but when Dorothy touched her cheek, it was stone cold. She stepped back in horror. She hadn't expected death, not in one so young. Milcah should have recovered; she should have seen her family again. Oh, Lord, Dorothy thought, her family had no idea she was this ill. Francis's bit of wood and ribbon was dangling above the bed. With tears in her eyes, she tore it down and flung it into the corner.

Chapter 12

Dorothy Gurwood braced herself to break the news about Milcah. She walked into the kitchen twisting her hands, and avoided her husband's eye. He might be tempted to blame her, and yet she had done her best this second time around.

'I couldn't have done any more,' she pleaded after she'd told him.

He stared down at his bowl of porridge and pushed it away. 'I can't eat that.' He got up and went into the chamber to see Milcah. When he came back, he put his head in his hands and wept. 'God knows how I'm going to tell my parents and sisters.'

After a while, he wiped away his tears and stood up. 'I'd better get this done. I'll ride straightaway to Rudston.' He reached for his coat and hat, then turned as he lifted the door latch. 'You'd better go across to Uphall and let them know. Word will soon get round.'

Dorothy had to see to the children on her own. After their breakfast she had no option but to take them with her to Uphall. By the time she arrived, William and his son Francis had already left to work on the fencing. Relieved not to see them, she asked Dorothy Jordan to pass on the sad news. Next, she called on Sarah Ezard; although the old woman's hands were clumsy and almost useless at times, she could still help wash and lay out the body.

After riding to Speeton and breaking the news to his sister Jane, John Gurwood headed to the rest of his family in Rudston. He avoided the roads with their water-filled ruts, and took the route along the ridge of the Argam Dike. He saw no one to speak to. A southwesterly breeze blew across the fields, and the weather was unnaturally warm for February. From the high ground he could see open country for miles. In other circumstances, it would have been a pleasant ride. He rehearsed what to say to his mother and father, but the more time he had to think about it, the more upset he became.

William and Francis had hardly got started on the fencing when they saw one of the farm lads running up to them. At the sight of the lad's face, Francis's hands began to shake. He dropped the mallet when he heard the news. Apart from that, he showed no reaction at all. William put an arm round his shoulder.

Francis shrugged him off. 'I'm alright,' he growled. 'Let's get on with the fence.' He picked up the mallet and began to knock in a post.

'Steady, lad,' his father warned, 'you'll wear yourself out going at it like that.'

Francis ignored the advice and struck the post again as hard as he could.

At noon, the two went home for dinner to find that Mary had heard about Milcah and had told the boys already.

John, as expected, did not fully understand; he carried on playing with Richard as if nothing was wrong.

As soon as William and Francis had taken off their boots, Mary took her husband aside. 'How has Francis taken it?' she whispered.

'Who knows? He doesn't say anything to me.'

'I can't fathom young William. He smirked when I told him.'

'Maybe he's nervous and doesn't know how to react. It's hard for a lad.'

She sighed. She'd never understand boys and men. 'I've made Francis's favourite meal for dinner. That's something I can do.'

William lifted his nose to the aroma of mutton, apple and onions. 'That smells good,' he said as he took off his jacket. He nudged Francis. 'I bet your mother's got the pickled cabbage out as well.'

Francis couldn't care less. He sat at the table, and when the food was shared out, he pushed it around his plate.

His mother watched and didn't say anything for a while. There was the usual clatter of spoons as everyone else ate their dinner. Eventually, she dared to speak.

'I do understand, Francis.'

'No, Mother, you don't. You really don't.' He banged down his spoon and rose to leave the table. 'I'm going back to work, Father. I'll see you at Uphall. There are more posts to fetch.'

The family ate in silence while he grabbed his boots and jacket. When he'd closed the door behind him, they glanced at one another. No one spoke.

George Gurwood arrived early for the funeral. He came alone and went straight to the house to view his daughter. As soon as John opened the door, father and son embraced. They clung to each other, reluctant to part and face the day ahead. At last, George stepped back.

'You can imagine we've had a hard time these last few days. It would be February! Your mother and sisters can't get here. The roads are in a terrible state. I've struggled even on horseback. It just wasn't possible to bring them by carriage.'

'I know. I understand.' John ushered his father into the parlour where Milcah lay in the open coffin. 'As you can see, I managed to get one made especially for her. I thought you'd want that. I hope you don't mind.' When his father didn't answer, he added, 'It's a pity Jane couldn't come. It's only two weeks since she gave birth.'

George peered into the newly made coffin. All he could see was Milcah's face, the rest covered by the white shroud. He was shocked to see her cheekbones standing out and her nose sharp like a knife. He staggered and clutched the coffin for support. Milcah had been so beautiful in both body and spirit. He reached for his son's arm and pinched it hard.

'Why weren't we told how ill she was?' he snapped. 'How are we supposed to deal with this?' He began to cry. 'Was it your wife, John, who stopped us coming? I could have been here for Milcah.'

'No, it isn't Dorothy's fault. She did her best. No one thought Milcah would...' He bit his lip as he saw the disbelief in his father's face. 'Blame me. I should have been more firm. It's just that Milcah didn't want to bother you. She knows how busy you are. Dorothy will say the same when she comes back. She's just taken the children to Uphall so she can attend the service.'

George crossed over to the window and looked out on the dismal day. He couldn't believe he was back in Reighton, not for Milcah's wedding but for her funeral. They sat, desolate and silent by the coffin, waiting for Dorothy. When she didn't return, George decided to go to the church and see the new vicar.

'I want to take the service,' he explained as he left. 'It's only proper. John Sumpton barely knew Milcah.'

George left the house and slouched through the mist that hung over the churchyard. The low sun couldn't break through, and the thatched roofs along the street dripped as if weeping in sympathy. Everything was damp. Already the bells were tolling six times for the death of a maid, and mourners were making their way up the hill.

John Sumpton was waiting in the porch. He was not at all surprised to see that the previous vicar, the father of the deceased, wanted a private word. He was relieved to hear he need not conduct the service.

'I would have liked to give a short sermon as well,' George explained, 'but I don't think I can manage it.'

The vicar rested a hand on George's shoulder. 'You do what you can,' he said kindly. 'I'll be there if you need me.'

George Gurwood returned to the house to lead the procession. He walked behind the coffin draped in its white pall.

It was a short walk to the church, and villagers were already huddled by the gate waiting to follow. John's wife was one of them; she linked arms with her husband as he passed.

'Where have you been?' he hissed. 'My father wanted to speak to you.'

'I've been helping decorate the church.'

He wondered if it was an excuse because she dared not face his father.

They entered a cold but brightly lit haven of green foliage. Ivy and laurel hung from the end of each pew and shone in the light of the best beeswax candles. The place smelled of rosemary sprigs, left here and there for people to take to the graveside.

As the congregation sat down, George Gurwood mounted the pulpit. Instantly, his eyes welled with tears; he knew he could not utter the words he intended to say. Instead, he opened the Bible at Psalm 91 and sought comfort from his faith.

'He who dwells in the shelter of the Most High will rest in the shadow of the Almighty. I will say of the

Lord, He is my refuge and my fortress, my God, in whom I trust.' He then turned to the first letter to the Corinthians.

'As in Adam all die, even so in Christ shall all be made alive... We shall not sleep, but we shall all be changed, in a moment, in the twinkling of an eye, at the last trumpet, and the dead shall be raised incorruptible, and we shall be changed.'

He closed the Bible and cast his eyes over the congregation. Here were people he'd known most of his life. Both young and old were stricken with grief; Milcah had affected so many. He knew by heart his next reading from Ecclesiastes. Despite his distrust of Dorothy, it was his Christian duty to show forgiveness. After all, she had tended his daughter through her illness.

'The race is not to the swift, nor the battle to the strong... but time and chance happeneth to them all.' He held his arms out. 'The ways of God are indeed strange. To God pertain the issues of life and death. Let Him do what seemeth good in His own eyes. Thy will be done. Amen.' He struggled through other verses and then signalled to John Sumpton that he couldn't carry on.

The rest of the service was conducted outside. Milcah's two suitors, Francis and Thomas, followed the coffin to the open grave where it was lowered into the dark, wet earth. With stern and solemn faces, they doffed their hats and bowed their heads. Tonight was Valentine's Eve, and they had no sweetheart. There would be no gifts for Milcah.

George Gurwood stared fixedly at the grey sky as he awaited the inevitable words.

'Earth to earth, ashes to ashes, dust to dust,' John Sumpton intoned. 'In sure and certain hope of the Resurrection to eternal life, through our Lord Jesus

Christ. Blessed are the dead which die in the Lord. Amen.'

Mary, standing beside Francis, began to tremble. The companionship of Milcah had made every task a pleasure. How bleak would her life be now. Hot tears blinded her as she realised anew the enormity of the loss.

Francis gazed unseeing into the grave. He'd let Milcah down. His love was not even strong enough to face illness. He recalled what he'd said to her—'many waters cannot quench love, neither can the floods drown it.' He'd seen an abandoned premature rat once in his garden—it was hairless, cold and pale in the wet grass. His love was like that, withered like something born before its time. Tears came as he acknowledged his weakness.

His brother John peered up into his face, not fully understanding, as usual. He smiled and squeezed his hand. Then he began to sing softly out of tune.

Ride a cock horse to Banbury cross
To see a fine lady upon a white horse
With bells on her fingers and rings on her toes
She shall have music wherever she goes.

Part Two

Idle Hands

Chapter 13

Dorothy Gurwood chuntered as she trudged to the well to fetch water. While Milcah had been ill, John had another woman to do the carrying, and he'd helped with the children himself. Now, she had so many jobs to do, and her two boys were always under her feet. She cursed as her youngest fell over for the fifth time and banged his head. It was hopeless, and with spring on the way, her husband would be busy organising work on the glebe lands with Robert Storey; she'd have no choice but to do everything at home herself.

When she reached the well, she joined the queue. Women were chatting as they waited. Bart Huskisson's wife was there, a bright red weal on her cheek. The woman next to Dorothy murmured as she gave her a nudge.

''E's at it again.'

The others ignored the comment, yet Dorothy Gurwood recalled only too well how, last summer, Bart had got drunk and burnt his daughter's leg. She never believed it was an accident, and neither was this ugly mark on Ann's cheek. The woman wouldn't lock her daughters in the shed for nothing. She leant forwards and tugged Ann's arm.

'You can't tell me that's an accident,' she said, pointing to the red mark 'Your Bart's been drinking again, hasn't he?'

The chattering stopped. The women stared at Ann, wondering what she'd say.

Ann Huskisson lowered her head in shame. 'We thought 'e'd stopped,' she mumbled. 'We thought Milcah 'ad 'elped to change 'im.'

The women glanced at each other and whispered among themselves as Ann left with her pails of water.

Dorothy sensed the mood. It was time something was done. 'We needn't wait for the vicar to condemn Bart's behaviour,' she ventured. 'Right is on our side, and we can deal with him ourselves.'

'Aye, maybe we could,' they agreed.

'So, when you go home, tell your menfolk.'

Without a resident vicar or the presence of Milcah, the villagers were easily swayed. No one could say who first mentioned riding the stang. John Gurwood had his own ideas.

'I bet it was Dorothy Jordan and her sons at Uphall. They'd soon get all the farm hands roused up.'

Others thought it was more likely to be John's wife. She was the one who spread gossip, and she still nursed a grudge about Milcah and the Huskissons. Whoever it was, the idea of riding the stang soon circulated the village. Young men, who'd heard of the tradition from their elders, were the most keen to take part. It sounded like good sport.

The Huskisson family received no warning. Late one afternoon in early April, William Jordan and his brothers removed the thick, heavy pole from their ox cart and sent word round that tonight was the night.

Dorothy Gurwood, in expectation, had already made a straw man—an effigy of Bart. She handed it over to the young men who carried it to Uphall.

Young Francis Jordan knew of the event and was reluctant to attend. Milcah would never have let this happen.

'Oh, come on, you should join us,' his father coaxed. 'It'll seem very odd if you don't.'

'But Milcah would have helped Bart,' Francis argued. 'She'd never have made a mockery of him.'

'I know. She was always most forgiving, poor lass. But, come on Francis, your brothers want to go, and you can mind them. Don't argue with me.'

When the time came, Francis sulked as he put on his coat and went out. His brother William left the dog at home for a change and took the jam pan and a wooden spoon. John, not wanting to be left out, carried his little tin trumpet bought at Bridlington Fair. Francis was determined to remain an onlooker and stay in the background; he took nothing to add to the noise.

Their father was waiting for them at Uphall. Francis suspected that the men had been drinking ale for they were slouching against the stable wall with grinning faces, waiting for it to get dark. A crowd of children appeared, afraid to miss anything. Standing well back, he and the children watched the men get his uncle Thomas ready.

The men strapped the effigy of Bart Huskisson to Thomas's back. Then four men stood each side of the long pole. They raised it a little and waited for Thomas to sit astride. Once he was in position and had gained his balance, they hoisted it onto their shoulders and set off towards Bart's house.

The men walked while the children skipped on either side, making as much noise as they could; they banged kettles and pans with sticks or blew whistles, trumpets and horns.

'It's a hell of a din,' young William shrieked. 'I can't wait to tell Mother.'

Francis noted the sky darkening. Now, their faces looked like demons in the glow from the lanterns. Milcah would have hated it.

When they reached Bart's house, someone rang a bell. The noise stopped immediately. John, who couldn't control his excitement, found his father's hand clamped over his mouth. The only sound was the shuffling of boots in the dirt. On a signal from Dickon, Thomas shouted out the traditional verse.

'Ere we come with a ran tan tan
It's neither fo' me nor thee
That I ride this stang.
If any o' thoo 'usbands tha good wives do bang
Let 'em come to us an' we'll ride 'em the stang.

Only the older generation could remember the rest of the words. They yelled to make up for the lack of voices.

'E beat 'er, 'e banged 'er, 'e banged 'er indeed.
'E banged 'er before she ever stood need.
'E banged 'er wi' neither stick, stone nor stover
But 'e up with a saddle flap an'
knocked 'er back'ards over.

Dickon and his master finished the verses by shouting alternate lines.

Now if this good man doesn't mend 'is manners,
Skin of 'is 'ide shall go to the tanners,
An' if tanner doesn't tan it well,
'E shall ride upon a gate spell,

An' if spell should 'appen to crack,
'E shall ride o' devil's back,
An' if devil should 'appen to run,
We'll shoot 'im with a wild goose gun,

An' if gun should 'appen to be misfired,
I'll bid thoo goodnight, for I'm almost tired.

The two men then shouted together, 'God save the King!' It was the signal for everyone to beat on their pans again and make even more noise.

After a minute, Thomas waved his arm. 'That's enough for tonight.'

They made their way back to Uphall in good spirits, and dispersed for the evening.

Francis went to bed but couldn't sleep. He was thinking about the Huskissons. He couldn't be sure that the wife and daughters would gain any benefit. Bart might even blame them and grow more violent.

The same thing happened the next night, the only difference being that Bart Huskisson was expecting it. He didn't dare leave the house; he and his family lurked miserably in the kitchen as far from the street and the hubbub as they could get. His wife and daughters sat by the fire spinning and knitting, trying to pretend that nothing was happening though they blushed with shame.

The third night was almost a repeat of the others. The unruly crowd paraded the village, making the usual racket. After the last verse though, the clamours died down, and everyone followed Thomas to the prepared bonfire at Uphall. Tankards of ale were passed round, and the straw effigy, now much the worse for wear, was lifted from Thomas's back.

Francis kept his brothers at a distance. He didn't know what was going to happen next. He watched as his father and Dickon used their lanterns to set the fire alight. The dry gorse caught instantly, and everyone stepped back as the flames roared. His brothers' eyes glittered with excitement as their uncle Thomas slipped a noose round the neck of the straw man. Then his father held the pole aloft and hung 'Bart' from it.

Francis was sickened by the sight. The men and lads stood in a circle around the fire and hurled abuse at the effigy as it swung in the smoky night air.

After a few minutes, William lowered the straw man. At this, the men booed, but when Thomas tossed it into the fire, they cheered like mad men.

'That's the end of that then,' Thomas yelled above the crackle of the burning gorse. 'Bart had better watch his temper in future and stop beating his womenfolk... or *he'll* be on the fire next.'

Subdued cheers followed that announcement, and as the fire died down, tankards were refilled. Francis took the opportunity to drag his brothers away and take them home to bed. He knew his father would linger a while, would drink more than he should and, like the others, would be smug and satisfied with the evening's work.

At home, in his kitchen, Bart Huskisson knew what would be going on at Uphall. He could not look his family in the eye. Restless on the stool in the corner of the kitchen, he kept his head down. He resented what the villagers had done, and wondered how much his wife was to blame. He also knew he was at fault. From time to time he muttered that he was sorry.

'I'll stop drinkin',' he offered.

His wife and daughters ignored him. They had no faith in his promises. He'd been sorry and had vowed to make amends before. It was unlikely he'd change now.

Chapter 14

Mary and Francis missed Milcah's presence throughout the spring. They accomplished one menial task after another in order to tire their bodies and distract their thoughts. Francis wandered about with a lost look. There was nothing to replace the joy of being in love. As his body developed and he became a man, he scrutinised the village girls; not one attracted him. Though he'd never been violent or aggressive, he began to have daily arguments with his brother William. Often, their rows led to a fight with fists, or they lashed out with their feet. If they happened to be wearing their boots, they both suffered terrible bruises.

Outnumbered in an all-male household, Mary despaired. One day she was missing Milcah so much she could hardly bear it.

'You two lads are driving me mad,' she shouted, clutching her head. 'For pity's sake get out of the house or leave each other alone. I swear you'll drive me to an early grave.'

The other boys cowered in a corner. John put his hands over his ears.

'You just wait till your father comes home,' Mary yelled. 'He'll sort you out.'

But their father was rarely at home these days.

One afternoon in May, Mary sat knitting with Elizabeth in the garden. John was in charge of his younger brothers, making them daisy chains while the women relaxed in the warm sunshine. The peace and quiet encouraged Mary to confide in her sister.

'If William isn't busy in the fields or at Uphall, he's up to something with the smugglers. He's never around when I need him, and I can't control the boys.'

Elizabeth cocked her head on one side. 'He's not the only one getting too involved. Did you know Matthew's bought land in Flamborough?'

'Flamborough? Are you sure?'

'I think I'm right. More to the point is that he bought it from that Richard Woolfe. You know, he's that merchant from Bridlington, the one sent to prison for shipping malt—illegally.'

Mary dropped a stitch. 'Ah, so you think Matthew's mixing with the wrong people?'

'*I* think it's to do with the smuggling. I've heard there are two caves they use to land the cargo. It would be perfect to own land nearby. One cave's called Rudston Church Garth. You don't suppose our old vicar has some connection?'

'I shouldn't think so, but who knows? William tells me nothing. All I know is that the so-called free traders just used to work in winter. Now it's all year round. William was worn out the other day, scouring ditches and then patrolling the cliffs.'

Elizabeth stopped knitting and frowned. 'Maybe I'm misjudging Matthew. Maybe he bought the land to celebrate having another son.' She took up her needles again. 'We've two Matthew Smiths in the family now!'

They knitted quietly for a while, both pondering their brother's rising fortune. Mary thought her sister might have misunderstood about Flamborough; she'd overheard William speak of the Jordans' piece in the

'Flamborough Lands' in Reighton, part of the estate that used to belong to the Constable family from Flamborough. Maybe Matthew had bought more of that same old estate. She glanced a few times at her sister, debating whether it was worth discussion, and decided against it; their men didn't include them in the complex matters of land sales. Instead of talking about property exchanges, she was desperate to have a more intimate conversation. She didn't want any more children, and hoped to discuss ways to avoid conceiving. However, since Elizabeth had spent years trying to have children, Mary dared not broach that subject either.

They continued to knit in silence, occasionally calling to the boys to be careful and stay in one place. As the garden grew cold in the encroaching shade, Elizabeth put down her knitting and sighed.

'I ought to be going home. I don't want to go, but Robert needs me—he has a lot to think about just now. It's being a churchwarden...'

Mary grinned. 'He does take his role so seriously, doesn't he?'

'It's only right and proper he takes such care, but it's not just that. No, what is worrying is that there's to be an official inspection of the church.' She then added in a pompous voice, 'A visitation by the archdeacon no less.'

'Ah... I can see your problem. And I thought *I* had worries.'

The church visitation was not expected until June 24th. Although there was time to make repairs, funds were low and so was willing labour. Everyone was busy in the fields, and with the vicar living in Filey, it was left to the two churchwardens to prepare for the archdeacon's visit.

Robert had Elizabeth polish the pews and clean the windows within reach. He took the men from their jobs on the glebe land and made them scythe the grass and clear the brambles in the churchyard. Then, with the other churchwarden's help, he repaired part of the fence. When they'd finished their task, they surveyed the church and yard yet one more time. Richard Maltby agreed it was a daunting sight. Both sides of the porch had become built up over time with the gravediggers' soil and other rubbish. The mounds should be removed, yet time was running out and work in the fields was not going to wait.

'It'll have to do,' Robert decided. 'We've done our best.'

On the appointed day, Robert and Elizabeth Storey were up early. As soon as she was dressed, she went out to gather fresh flowers. She returned and went to the church with pink campion and violet bellflowers; they'd add some much-needed colour.

Sarah Ezard was standing in the porch with a basket full of dropwort, mint and gorse. 'This'll mask any damp smells i' there,' she said as she passed over the basket. 'Tell Robert I wish 'im luck.'

Robert arrived at the church soon afterwards to check everything was in order. He marched in and then stopped, amazed to see the pots of flowers.

'Thank you, Elizabeth, you've done well,' he said, humbled by her thoughtfulness. 'Go home now to your other jobs. God will be pleased with your efforts.' He was not so sure about the archdeacon.

As Elizabeth left, Richard Maltby strolled up the path. He entered the church to find Robert praying on his knees before the altar. After allowing a respectful time for him to finish, he coughed to get his attention.

'I see vicar's not arrived from Filey yet.'

'No,' Robert answered as he stood up. 'Let's hope he won't be long. It's going to be a hot day so he'd best be here early.'

Although there was little that could be done at this late stage, they went outside for a final walk round. In spite of the sunny morning and the clear blue sky, both men were gloomy and tight-lipped.

'Even if we'd levelled the ground here by the porch,' Robert argued, 'we couldn't have repaired *that*.' He pointed to the nearby buttress.

As the two churchwardens stared at the damaged stonework, the vicar, John Sumpton, arrived at last. He tied up his horse and walked stiffly towards them. Overdressed for such a warm day, he looked flustered, hot and uncomfortable.

'Come into the porch,' Robert invited. 'It's cooler there.'

The vicar was only too glad to be out of the sun. 'I can see that fence hasn't been mended very well,' he remarked as he entered the church. He paced slowly through the nave, ignoring the flowers and noticing faults everywhere. Suddenly he stopped and turned to face Robert.

'Your former vicar, whatshisname Gurwood, has not left his church in very good repair.'

'It's not all George's fault,' Robert retaliated. 'A place like Reighton can't afford the repairs, and labour's hard to get at times. That's right, isn't it Richard?'

Richard Maltby nodded.

'Well,' concluded the vicar, 'the archdeacon and his registrar will arrive sometime this afternoon between one and six o'clock. The sooner this is over, the better.'

Robert didn't fancy sitting and waiting in church all day. He made a suggestion. 'Why don't we wait at my house? I can get one of the lads from Uphall to run and let us know when they arrive.'

The vicar agreed and, with a heavy heart, went back outside and into the bright sunlight.

The archdeacon and his man rode into Reighton at two o'clock, having already visited other churches in the morning. They dismounted at the churchyard gate and walked up the path to meet the vicar.

John Sumpton was surprised and awed to see the archdeacon in a full wig. No wonder the man looked hot; it was bad enough to wear a long, black cassock in the middle of summer. He stepped out from the cool of the porch to greet him.

The smaller of the two churchmen, also dressed in black, began the introductions. 'My name's Thomas Jubb. I'm the registrar, and this is the venerable archdeacon of the East Riding, Mr Heneage Dering.'

'Good day to you, Mr Archdeacon,' the vicar answered with feigned confidence. He gave a nervous bow, and was about to shake the archdeacon's hand, but the man did not remove his glove. Embarrassed by this overt sign of their different social status, the vicar could only bow again. Ill at ease, he didn't want to keep the archdeacon standing for too long outside; the less seen of the exterior structure the better. He introduced his churchwardens and welcomed the visitors to Reighton.

'It's rather hot today,' he concluded. 'Do come inside where it's cool and more restful on the eyes.' He stepped aside to allow them to enter the church, but the archdeacon stood his ground.

He gazed down at the raised mounds on each side of the porch, and waved an arm. 'All this will have to go,' he said in a voice used to giving orders. 'The ground here must be made level.'

The registrar made a note in a small book.

The archdeacon inspected the south buttress. 'And put this down for repair.'

John Sumpton gulped. They hadn't even entered the church. He managed to coax them into the porch with Robert Storey and Richard Maltby bringing up the rear.

The churchwardens glanced at each other. The visitation was not going well.

When the heavy oak door was opened, the archdeacon raised his nose in the air. He ignored the flowers, sniffed to check for damp, and then scuffed his boots deliberately against the cobblestone floor.

'This won't do. The floor must be even. And make sure it's plain. There's no need to have fancy tiles or stones laid.' He stroked a hand along the first pew. 'The same goes for these—no carving or ornamentation. Pews must be plain and simple.'

It was worse when he reached the chancel and saw the floor.

'This is no good at all, not—at—all! The whole of this chancel needs to be re-laid.'

'With small cobblestones again?' the vicar ventured.

'No, certainly not. I suggest you use flags or plain tiles or bricks. Have you written that down, Mr Jubb?' He didn't wait for a reply. 'Now, let's see what we have in the vestry, shall we?'

Robert Storey set out the Bible, the surplice and communion ware while the registrar stood poised, pencil in hand.

The archdeacon stifled a yawn. It had been a long day and he'd already been to Flamborough and Speeton. He still had Burton Fleming and Grindale on his list, and had more visits arranged for Monday. Relieved that tomorrow was a Sunday, a day of comparative rest, he stuck to his task.

'Are you ready, Mr Jubb? The surplice must be made good and also the flagon, and a new linen cloth must be bought for the communion table.' On his way back up the aisle, he waved both arms around. 'These walls...

they're a disgrace. They need a good whitewash. Mr Jubb, write out the usual certificate for next Michaelmas. The advowson, Edward Hutchinson, Esquire, and Sumpton, the vicar here, must see that it's all done by then.'

Mr Jubb settled down at the tiny table in the vestry. He opened his leather bag, and taking out a piece of parchment, a quill and inkpot, began to write.

'We'll leave you for a while, Mr Jubb. Perhaps our good friend Mr Sumpton can provide us with sustenance at the vicarage.

The vicar apologised. 'I'm afraid, your worship, that I don't live here yet. The vicarage is empty.' He gave Robert Storey a meaningful stare.

'Oh, please let me entertain you at my house,' Robert obliged. 'It would be an honour.' With that, he bowed and showed them the way.

When the archdeacon found there was nothing stronger to drink than mead or small beer, he made the visit brief. Within the hour they'd returned to the church.

Mr Jubb had the document ready for signing. Robert, though an avid reader, could only leave his mark. As John Sumpton wrote his name, he hoped that when the archdeacon made his visitation to Filey church next Wednesday, there'd be a better outcome. He said farewell at last, and the churchwardens closed the door. They left the church with drooping shoulders and the same worried frown. God alone knew how the work could be done by Michaelmas.

That night, William climbed into bed with Mary hoping she was in a good mood. As soon as he began to nuzzle into her neck, she pushed him away.

'Did you hear about the visitation?' she asked him, keen all of a sudden to talk.

'Oh that… yes. Richard Maltby came down to the meadow. It's bad news—there's a lot to do. Still… let's think about that tomorrow.' He leant towards her and began to nibble her ear.

She took a deep breath. 'William—stop! We have to talk. I don't want any more children.'

He opened his mouth to speak, but she put her hand over it.

'Listen, I've given birth eight times and we have five sons. Surely that's enough for anyone. Let's be thankful and have an end to it.'

He couldn't believe it. 'Does that mean I can't share the bed anymore?'

'No, you fool, there are other ways. I've been to see Sarah Ezard.'

He groaned, dreading what Sarah might have prescribed.

She leant towards him on one elbow, eager to instruct. 'There's an enema you can take. It's to ease your lust. It's made of hempseed and bruised cowcumbers. And there's a drink we can buy made from water lilies and purslane.'

He sat up immediately. He wasn't an old man and didn't want to lose his lust as she called it. 'I'm not using an enema. Is there no other way?'

'The trouble is, I've finished feeding Matthew now, so something has got to change.'

'What if I wear armour?' He'd never used a sheath, though he'd heard you could buy them made from sheep's gut.

She thought about it, wondering whether she could trust such a thing.

'On second thoughts,' he murmured and sank back down in bed, 'I think they're too expensive. And the apothecary might think one of us has the clap.'

'Oh, Lord! I don't want that.'

They both lay on their backs to reflect.

Suddenly, Mary came to a decision. 'This is what we'll do—we'll carry on as normal, except you'll have to pull out in time.'

He thought about this. For a year now, Mary had been steadier in her moods, even obliging in bed, especially when she'd had Milcah for company. She'd been content, even happy. He'd enjoyed Mary whenever he wanted. If that was to continue, he'd have to compromise.

'You're right,' he agreed with reluctance. 'Something has to change. I can see it's for the best. I'll try.' He rolled over to face her. It was still quite light, one of the longest days of the year. 'You do know all my instincts will be against it? I'll want to push right in, not pull out. You'll have to help. It's up to you to remind me.'

'I'll help you,' she whispered and turned towards him. Though it was a sultry night, they snuggled up together. Aroused by his kisses, she surrendered to the lovemaking.

Chapter 15

Dickon set to work on the church repairs. Robert Storey gave a hand, and noticed how slow Dickon had become. The old foreman found it difficult to wield the large brush when he whitewashed the walls, and he kept missing bits.

Sarah Ezard offered to help him though she was just as stiff in the joints. 'Them young uns i' village should 'elp more,' she complained. 'They're neither use nor ornament.'

As Robert started on the floor of the nave, he heard Dickon and Sarah chuntering in the background. He couldn't deny that the young Jordans at Uphall were fit and healthy, and yet they always found other jobs when asked to help at the church.

William's son, Francis, though just fourteen, did offer to assist, and welcomed the extra labour. Ever since Milcah's death he'd held himself in low regard; if not actually wicked and sinful, he knew he was poor in spirit. To repair and renew the church was his atonement. As a result, he spent more time with Robert Storey and found consolation in his uncle's strict approach to life. The shunning of any kind of pleasure suited Francis's mood perfectly.

His parents were wary of their son's growing friendship with Robert as the boy was at an impressionable age. They voiced their concern in bed.

'That Robert Storey's filling his head with all sorts,' William whispered in case Francis overheard.

'I know,' Mary agreed. 'The poor lad should be left to find his own way. It's a shame he's taken Milcah's death so hard.'

'Well, I want him to enjoy his youth while he can. If he gets like Robert, who knows where it'll end.'

With that alarming thought, they turned over to sleep.

Francis was in awe of Robert Storey; his uncle had read so many devotional books, each one promoting the ascetic life. Whenever they worked together in the church, he listened avidly and lapped up advice on how to conduct a pure life. He was relieved to hear it was good to have a low regard of yourself, to be quiet and submissive, to be humble and let yourself be an instrument to honour God. His imperfections and weaknesses were to be accepted gladly, for they were a means to nourish humility and resist pride.

One morning, when Francis arrived at the church, Robert bid him kneel first in front of the altar, and said a prayer for them both.

'O eternal God, give us thy grace, that we may be a prudent spender of our time, so we may best resist temptation, and glorify thy name. Take from us all slothfulness and fill up the spaces in our time with works of charity, so that when the devil assaults us he may not find us idle. Amen.'

They said the Lord's Prayer together before picking up their tools.

Late one summer's afternoon, while they levelled the ground by the church porch, Francis took the opportunity to ask Robert why he fasted so much.

'By starving the body, you feed the soul,' Robert replied as he stamped down heavily on the loose earth.

'And if I'm tempted to eat, then I suppress the desire. I read or busy myself in the fields. That way there's no room for temptation.'

When Francis went home, he told his mother that he didn't want to eat as much meat.

'Robert says you have to be moderate with your food if you want to save your soul.'

She rolled her eyes and grumbled. 'Robert says, Robert says... it's a good job we're not all like him. Get on with your supper.'

'Can I say grace?' he asked. Not content with that, he added an extra prayer. 'Let thy holy angels be ever present with us. Keep us from the malice and violence of the spirits of darkness, and from the ways of sinful shame. Amen.'

Mary pursed her lips. Francis was putting a dampener on their evening meal, and without Milcah around anymore, there was little enough pleasure in her daily life. She watched him as he began to eat. He chewed each mouthful slowly and deliberately, often gazing upwards as if to heaven. His brothers attacked their food as usual, like pigs in a trough, eager to get second helpings.

Francis put down his spoon and reprimanded them in a calm, authoritative voice. 'You should eat solely for your health's sake, not for greedy pleasure.'

Young William stared, his cheeks bulging with potato and bacon.

John's mouth fell open and his food dropped out.

Mary banged her spoon down on the table. 'Francis, that's enough! Let your brothers enjoy their supper. They're only young.'

'Mother,' he replied, 'they need to know that such pleasures will ruin them. Their souls will become loose and soft—they'll wander.'

John listened intently, his eyes wide; he feared that one of his arms or legs might drop off.

'We must prefer the soul to the body,' Francis continued, 'reason before appetite, and prefer the pleasures of eternity before the pleasures of our short lives.'

'That may be so,' his father interrupted at last, having finished eating, 'but I think you're spending far too much time with Robert Storey.'

'Listen, Francis,' said his mother. She rested a hand gently on his arm. 'You don't know Robert like we do.' She wondered how much she could tell him. 'I know your aunt Elizabeth would have something to say. It's all very well putting God before everything else, but people have to live.'

She stood up and began clearing away the empty bowls. 'I think charity should begin at home. Perhaps Robert should think more about Elizabeth than his soul for a change.'

Francis did not reply. He didn't know what she was getting at. 'Can I say an evening prayer, now that we've finished?'

'Don't you ever stop?' groaned his father. Seeing the earnest look in his son's eyes, he relented. 'Alright, but after tonight, let's have supper in peace. Keep your thoughts to yourself. We'll look out for our own souls, thank you.'

Francis put his hands together and closed his eyes. 'O Lord, our souls are troubled as we remember our sins. Our flesh is frail and sinful, exposed to every temptation, and without thy grace, we are unable to resist. We give ourselves up wholly to thy service. Amen.'

'Amen!' they echoed loudly, glad that it was over.

When Mary and William lay on their backs in bed together that night, they pulled the sheet up to cover their mouths. Then they whispered. Mary argued that a middle-aged man who refused to have normal relations with his wife, for whatever reason, was not the person to be influencing their son.

'I want Francis to carry on repairing the church though,' William countered. 'We'll just have to try and stop him getting too involved with Robert.'

'If only George Gurwood was here, he'd have made the lad see sense.'

'Someone needs to knock it into him.' William yawned. 'At least Francis is spending his spare time being useful, not like my brothers at Uphall.'

'Mmm,' Mary agreed.

'I know they're full of themselves,' he said as he turned over, preparing to sleep. 'They find Reighton boring, but they'll settle down in time.' He closed his eyes. Thomas, Samuel and Richard were a worry to his parents; thankfully, they were not his problem.

Since the Gurwood girls had left the village, there were just the blacksmith's two daughters of a suitable age for the Jordan brothers to court. Bart Huskisson's daughters didn't count, as no one wanted Bart as a father-in-law; besides, only Emma was close in age.

Each Sunday after dinner, the Jordan brothers left Uphall and strolled around the village with nothing to do but look for mischief. The three of them made half-hearted attempts to court the blacksmith's daughters, and the girls, flattered by the attention, proved amenable. The boys took turns with them and afterwards recounted how far they'd got. Thomas boasted of fingering Anna up her petticoat.

'What was it like?' the younger two asked, their eyes wide in anticipation.

'It was like...' He stopped, unable to find a comparison. 'You'll find out.'

They suspected he didn't know because he hadn't done it. Nevertheless, they encouraged each other and became obsessed with women's bodies. Knowing how Francis was aping Robert Storey, they teased him whenever they could.

'A proper little saint, aren't you?' Richard taunted him one morning while out in the yard. 'I bet you'd have liked to tup Milcah if you'd had the chance.'

Without warning, Francis dived at him, knocked him to the ground and began to beat him with his fists. A crowd of young labourers gathered round to watch as Thomas and Samuel hurried to haul Francis off. Still shaking with rage, Francis stared down at Richard in the dirt. Suddenly, he was ashamed of himself. It was unforgivable to lose his temper. He'd fallen far short of his ideals. Since his uncles and his brother William goaded him often, it was something he'd have to endure. He despaired of ever being calm like Robert Storey.

'Sorry, Richard.' He offered his hand and pulled Richard to his feet.

Richard dusted down his jacket and breeches. 'I'm fine,' he smirked. Francis's punches had been wild and ineffective.

That night, when he thought everyone was asleep, Francis whispered a heartfelt prayer.

'O God, I am not worthy to be called thy servant. I am the vilest of sinners and the worst of men. I am proud and intemperate. Lord, pardon and wash away my sins. Blot them out of thy remembrance. Be pitiful and gracious to thy servant. Amen.'

His parents heard and were sorry. They knew how often he was provoked. William also knew that his three brothers at Uphall were not helping matters. More to the point, they were becoming the talk of the village.

By harvest time, not only were the three Jordan lads 'courting' the blacksmith's daughters, they were also flirting with the youngest Huskisson girl. Folk thought this a cruel thing to do as none of the lads had any serious intentions.

Emma Huskisson couldn't believe her luck; three eligible young men, each attractive in their own way, desired her company.

On Sundays, the young Jordans went first to the blacksmith's where the wife brewed her own beer. There they could sit with the family and drink as much as they liked before walking out with the girls. When they escorted them back, they had another beer before moving on to the Huskissons.

Emma was used to men smelling of drink, and as long as the Jordan brothers were polite and gentle, she didn't fear them. She was so glad of their attention that she let them do as they pleased.

The brothers thought the empty vicarage would be the perfect place to take the girl. They broke in through the back door and, apart from finding the place cold, damp and unfurnished, it seemed a safe hiding place. They carried in armfuls of straw to make it more comfortable.

The next Sunday, once they were settled in the vicarage parlour, Thomas began first as usual. He was the eldest and, he believed, the most handsome. As he lay on the straw beside Emma, his soft, lingering kisses aroused her, and while she allowed him to feel her breasts, the other two looked on.

Then Samuel had his turn. Thomas shook his head in dismay as his brother groped in a clumsy fashion. Samuel had a lot to learn.

Richard, the youngest, watched with a mixture of awe and horror; he declined to have a go.

Each week, with Samuel's encouragement, Thomas enticed Emma to remove more of her clothing. As a fair exchange, he offered to take down his breeches. His 'courting' was progressing and, as the nights drew in, he took a lantern.

It wasn't long before a light was noticed in the empty vicarage. Robert Storey, as a churchwarden, was notified, and he went straightaway to the vicarage with his key. He let himself in at the front door, and closed it quietly. Seeing light coming from beneath the parlour door, he pushed it open.

Thomas Jordan, with his breeches down, was standing astride a woman laid on the floor. He couldn't run away, or deny what was going on.

Robert stood open-mouthed. Then he noticed Samuel and Richard sitting in the shadows. When the woman got up and straightened her clothes, Robert could see it was Emma Huskisson. He found his voice and held a hand out towards her.

'Come with me. Come, I'll take you home.'

'Don't tell me father,' she begged. 'Please don't tell 'im. 'E'll kill me.'

Robert thought that might well be true. 'I'll not tell him. Come on, you must pray for guidance. God will help you.'

He glared at the young men and was so angry he could barely speak. 'You three!' he spluttered. He waved his arms in despair and bit his lip. 'This must *never* happen again!'

He paused to gain control, and then at last spoke calmly and with great sadness.

'I haven't the heart to inform your poor parents. They don't deserve it, Francis and Dorothy. They're innocent, God-fearing folk.' He turned his back on them and escorted Emma home.

On the way back from Emma's house, Robert puzzled over the girl's apparent willingness. He put it down to a kind of witchcraft. Emma's normal powers of reasoning must have been suppressed somehow and her will enslaved. As for the young men, he put it down to idleness. Lust crept in when the soul was unemployed and the body at ease. If only the Jordan boys had spent their time repairing the church; their bodily labour and occupation would have proved so useful in driving away the devil. With that in mind, he decided the boys should finish the whitewashing. It would be their penance and, in the light of what he'd seen, they wouldn't dare refuse.

Robert told no one of the goings-on in the vicarage and, though the Jordan brothers did whitewash the walls, the rest of the church was not repaired on schedule. In early October, a few days after Michaelmas, Edward Hutchinson, Esquire, inspected the church with the vicar to find that the new floor of the chancel remained half-finished. John Sumpton signed to say it would be completed within the month.

Old Dorothy Jordan was ashamed that her sons had done so little to help at the church. She complained of them to her husband, but he disagreed.

'Our lads toil 'ard enough i' fields,' he argued. 'They do enough. They deserve their few hours o' rest.'

Dorothy snorted. 'If only they did rest o' Sundays. They're a worry to me.'

The next day she felt vindicated; she heard that her sons planned to go to the Bridlington fair and take their whole year's earnings. God alone knew what they'd find to do.

Chapter 16

Earlier in the year, at Shrovetide, the Jordan brothers had been to the cockfights at the George in Bridlington. There they'd acquired a taste for gambling, along with a lust for blood and violence. When they heard a three-day event had been advertised at the October Fair, they couldn't wait to go. Thomas persuaded his brothers to attend the last day when there'd be an elimination contest; only the best cockerels would be left and the stakes would be highest.

After leaving their horses behind the high street, Thomas swaggered into the George's crowded yard, followed by his brothers. Bets were being taken on eight cockerels, the eight left out of the original sixty-four. They paid the entrance fee and lost no time in inspecting the birds in their pens. Bred for aggression, strength and stamina, they were impressive despite their clipped wings, tails and neck feathers. Thomas noticed blood on some of their necks. He barged his way forward to get a closer view.

'Is that a good sign, I wonder? What do *you* think, Richard?'

'It *could* mean they're tough.'

'Or maybe they just weren't quick enough to avoid being hurt,' Samuel countered. It was a quandary, but it was all part of the gamble.

After scrutinising each bird and paying heed as to which ones were the favourites, they placed a bet.

Neither a rank outsider nor the favourite, what appealed to them about one bird was its colour—a deep russet red; the odds were favourable too. It was the same size as the others and had an old scar on its comb from a former fight.

Thomas rubbed his hands in anticipation. 'If it loses early on, we'll still have money to bet on the others.'

As they waited for the first fight, they bought mugs of ale, and took hasty gulps while being elbowed and jostled. The noise and the crush of bodies added to the excitement. It was so different from working in the quiet open spaces of the Reighton fields. Money was still changing hands, and Thomas's heart thumped faster as the time approached. The sharp odour of poultry dung mingled with tobacco smoke and the tantalising smell of rum punch. He inhaled deeply; there was nowhere he'd rather be.

The pit master entered the yard to a huge round of applause. Then, as the first two birds were announced, everyone rushed to the cockpit to get a place at the front. The Jordans had to be content with a view between shoulders and hats. Their chosen bird was not yet involved.

'It's fine,' said Thomas, licking his lips and unable to keep still. 'We can enjoy the fight for its own sake.'

Spectators yelled banter from every direction and raised their hats to cheer on the birds. The fight was about to start.

While Samuel craned his neck to see into the pit, Richard gazed around and noted the number of rich men and gentry in attendance, wearing their best attire and fashionable wigs. He admired their brocade coats in plum, orange and green, much more pleasing than the browns and greys he was used to. One day, he hoped to buy such things. Maybe, if they won today, it would be sooner rather than later.

The master stood in the middle of the pit. 'May I remind you gentlemen,' he shouted amid a few jeers, 'there are to be no weapons used, no brawling and no complaints against my decisions. If need be, I will fine any person in breach of these rules, or expel them from the pit.'

He moved to one side, and the two owners entered with their birds carried in sacks. As soon as the cockerels were pulled out, hoods were put over their heads while more money changed hands. Once the betting closed, razor-sharp spurs were attached to the legs. The hoods were then removed. The birds were held up a foot apart and thrust at each other. Once they displayed signs of aggression, they were thrown into the air. Their owners sprang away to avoid being hurt and joined the master and spectators behind the wooden wall.

Although it was the middle of autumn, the birds still had plenty of fight in them and attacked each other immediately. One soon bullied the other and remained dominant. The weaker bird tried to escape, yet there was nowhere to go; it flapped in a panic round and round the edge of the ring. It was just delaying the inevitable. Amid boos from the crowd, the fight ended, though the process of dying took time.

Richard wanted to turn away, yet found his eyes drawn to the scene. When the bird had its lung pierced, the winning cock crowed and leapt on top of it, holding it down and pecking its head until it died. The spectators around him showed no pity, and Richard's brothers joined in and jeered with the rest.

'Well,' Thomas explained, 'you have to admit—that fight was a poor one.'

There were three more matches before noon, and Thomas managed to place bets on each one. They lost money on two in a row, but trusted it would be third time lucky when they saw their original chosen bird brought out at last for its match.

They watched wide-eyed as the red cockerel was held out in the pit still wearing its hood. Final bets were placed, and their bird was the favourite. The rival was black. Thomas and his brothers held their breath as the hoods were removed. When the two birds were lifted up, they struggled like falcons to be let go. After a count of three, they were released.

Instead of attacking straightaway, they fluttered to the ground and stood cautiously eyeing each other. The crowd urged them on, but they strutted round each other, clucking more like chickens than cocks.

Thomas shouted into Richard's ear. 'I think they're waiting to see who's going to make the first move.'

The standoff lasted a few minutes before the black leapt suddenly into the air. The red also flew up and the two birds met in a flurry of feathers. They repeated the leap over and over again, each trying to get on top of the other and peck its head.

'Their beaks will have been sharpened,' Thomas shouted again. 'That way, they'll peck the hell out of each other.'

The birds succeeded in damaging each other's necks and, as spots of blood appeared, both birds took a brief rest. They shimmied carefully round each other, seeking signs of weakness. Again, the crowd urged them on, jeering and swearing.

Thomas and Samuel held their breath as the birds circled each other like trained boxers, feigning moves and dodging away. The last of the brothers' money was on this one cock. It had to win. With rapid nods of the head, their bird dived in and out, avoiding most hits while occasionally striking the other.

Thomas nudged Samuel. 'Our bird's faster, don't you think? It has more fight in it.' He cheered it on at the top of his voice, but both birds looked exhausted.

After a few minutes, and without warning, their bird flew high over the other. It landed plumb on the back of the black cock. Forced to the ground, the black lay flattened with its wings outspread. It tried to get up and defend itself as the red cock pecked out its eyes. Blinded, the bird gave in.

Samuel cheered. 'We've won!'

'No,' warned Thomas, 'it's not over yet—not until the bird's dead.'

Victory was ensured a minute later as the red cock pecked the other to death. It stood over the bloodied head, puffed out its few feathers and crowed loudly. Thomas echoed the cry. Their year's savings had increased, and the red cock had at least one more match to come.

Richard's mouth filled with saliva. He thought he might be sick as he saw the mangled body of the black cockerel dragged through the bloodied sawdust.

'Come on,' said Thomas. 'Move yourself, it's time for dinner.'

After a rushed meal in the smoky, overcrowded inn, everyone moved back to the cockpit for the last matches. The four birds that had won so far were paraded round with their hoods on. Those who'd drunk too much with their dinners were now gambling with no heed for tomorrow. Stakes were high as a white cock and a brown one faced each other, evenly matched. As usual, the birds strutted and clucked, edging ever closer until one braved the first move. Then they flew at each other time and time again, so quickly that no one could gauge the damage inflicted. Feathers flew and, when the birds went too near the top of the wall, men pushed them back in with clubs. The birds were strong and fought for almost half an hour. No one could predict the outcome.

First, the white cock seemed to be gaining an advantage, only for the black to have a surge of energy and retaliate. The crowd, sensing a great battle, cheered and whistled. When the black one's belly was slashed, the crowd groaned in disappointment, but the fight was not over. Bleeding yet still defiant, the black fought back and somehow managed to pierce the chest of the other with its spur. The white cock fell sideways to the ground, blood oozing through its feathers. It fluttered for a moment and then its wings drooped.

Everyone held their breath, not knowing if it was dead or not. They kept an eye on the other bird. The black one seemed to have a fatal injury too. It staggered about and then fell over, belly uppermost, with its legs stuck out in a helpless fashion. The audience gasped. It was a pitiful sight. The question, now in everyone's mind, was which bird would die first.

The owners jumped into the pit. The pit master joined them to inspect the almost lifeless bodies. He poked each one with his boot, and then had the owners lift them up. He declared the white cock dead. The black one outlived it by less than a minute, so was declared the victor. The men with the winning bets cheered.

Thomas and his brothers, along with other neutrals and those who'd lost bets, were saddened by the outcome. They'd admired the courage of the birds and hadn't seen such a close contest for a long time. With the death of both birds, there was just one match left to decide the champion.

'Cross your fingers,' urged Thomas. 'Our cock is in the final.'

After a short break for refreshments and the chance to place more bets, the red cock was brought from its pen to face a dark brown bird, its feathers streaked with black. Both the birds' plumage shone with health and they looked ready for the fight. Thomas's mouth was dry. All depended on the next half hour—if the fight lasted that long. He linked arms with his brothers, saying nothing, and gazed with wide eyes into the pit.

The birds were kitted with their spurs, hoods were removed, and they were held close to each other, beady eyes locked onto their target. The owners waved them about to the cheers of the crowd and poked them at each other.

Suddenly, the birds were loose in the air. They flapped and fought together on the way to the ground. Once on their feet, they leapt at each other, nodding and pecking, their sharp beaks cutting each other's heads repeatedly.

After a few minutes they drew away as if resting, their necks still outstretched in an aggressive pose. The crowd jeered, and the birds shot into the air again, flailing their wings and pecking, each trying to get above the other to bring it down. It looked as if it might be another great contest, but as they were falling to the ground, they lashed out with their spurs. Their crops were slit open. Both landed awkwardly, tried to get up, squawked feebly and then lay still. The crowd was silent. It was most unusual for both birds to be dead outright, though it looked that way. The pit master jumped in to confirm it.

Thomas stared at his brothers aghast. He swallowed with difficulty before finding his voice. 'Oh Lord, our total savings are on the throw of a dice.'

The pit master explained the rules. There would be only one throw of the dice, and he would do it himself. 'Winner takes all,' he said.

He took the two owners aside, and they flipped a coin to decide who had the low or high numbers. It was announced that the red cock would have the numbers, four to six. The three men stood in the middle of the pit for the crucial throw of the dice.

For Thomas, the suspense was so great that he felt sick. He crossed his fingers and looked down at his boots, not daring to see the outcome. His brothers watched for him, praying for a high number.

'Here we go then,' shouted the pit master. He flicked the dice up into the air. To the Jordans, it took forever to land.

'Two!' the pit master bellowed.

Chapter 17

The Jordan brothers rode home from Bridlington in silence. Penniless, they didn't know how they'd explain the loss of their earnings, and each dreaded what their father would say or do. It was growing dark when they reached Reighton, and managing to avoid Dickon, they sneaked their horses into the stable. Though it was too late for supper, they knew their parents would still be in the kitchen.

Thomas walked in first. His brothers followed one step behind, twisting their hats in their hands. The two dogs were lying by the hearth and rose to greet them. Samuel and Richard grabbed the opportunity to kneel down and stroke them—anything but face their father.

Their mother was covering the fire for the night. She stopped and turned to them. The look on their faces said it all.

Their father, sitting at the table, also guessed the worst.

'So—thoo's come 'ome at last!' he taunted. ''Ow bad is it then? Thoo'd best tell us.'

'Our money's gone,' Thomas admitted. 'It was the cockfights.'

His father leapt up from the table and raised his arm to strike, but Thomas dodged out of the way. His father's arm fell to his side as he sank back down on the bench, red in the face. His mother glared at him. Thomas had nothing to say. He knew he was to blame.

The three brothers waited. The only sounds came from the old clock and the dogs re-settling themselves by the fire.

Eventually their father spoke. 'Summat must be done,' he said, gazing vacantly into the hearth. 'I don't know what.' He turned to his sons. 'I'll give me decision i' mornin'. I need to sleep on it.' With that, he rose slowly from the table and left the room.

Their mother followed him. Her glance in their direction was as cold and penetrating as ice.

In bed that night, Francis and Dorothy Jordan lay wide-awake, their bodies tense. Francis wanted to send all three sons away—exile them for a while.

Dorothy hated the idea. She'd grown so close to her youngest. 'Not Richard, surely?' she pleaded. 'It's Thomas who's led 'im astray. Just punish 'im.'

'Listen,' Francis was about to argue. What he planned to say would upset his wife. The truth always hurt. He took a deep breath. 'I think it'll do Richard good. 'E's eighteen now. It's 'igh time 'e stopped clingin' to thy apron strings. It's not natural. Thoo's gotten far too fond o' that lad.'

She felt her face redden. Richard did spend more time with her than any of her other sons. Ever since he was little, he'd liked to help her with chores and he'd chat away while they worked together. He was as good as a woman friend. She didn't know how to reply. Anything she might say in his defence could make thing worse.

'So, you agree?' Francis demanded, knowing he was in the right.

She turned away from him. 'I'm not 'appy about it,' she grumbled into the pillow.

He stared into the dark. An unhappy wife made for an unpleasant life. Yet he was master of the house and his word should be law. He rolled over to sleep, though his eyes remained open. He had to make a decision.

At breakfast, the three brothers were reluctant to go down and join the farmhands. Each hung back in the bedchamber, hoping he wouldn't have to go first.

'We can't be late,' argued Richard. 'Let's get it over with. Go on, Thomas, you're the eldest.' You're also the most to blame, he wanted to add.

'Alright,' agreed Thomas. 'What's the worst father can do? We're his sons, he won't chastise us in front of the hired lads.'

When they entered the kitchen, the table conversations stopped. As if on command, the lads bent low over their food and avoided any eye contact. The brothers sat down, and in ominous silence, they were served their porridge. Their father ignored them as he finished his breakfast. Thomas managed a sidelong glance at his brothers. There was no doubt they were in serious trouble.

Suddenly, as one, the farmhands rose from the benches and made for the door. Thomas, Richard and Samuel made moves to join them.

'Not you!' their father growled.

They sat down again.

Richard looked to his mother for help, but she lowered her eyes.

'A sleepless night I've 'ad,' their father began, 'an' thoo's not worth it. Thoo's all lazy an' spends over much time o' daft games an' women. This damn fool gamblin' o' cockfights is last straw. I've made up me mind, an' it's no good lookin' at tha mother. Come next month, when we take on new lads at 'Unmanby, thoo'll leave Up'all.'

They gasped in disbelief.

Francis was determined not to be swayed by their open mouths and sorry faces. 'Aye, I see thoo's shocked, but I mean it. Thoo'll move on to another farm, at least for a year—nay, make it two. If *I* can't knock sense into thee, some other poor yeoman might, God 'elp 'im.'

'But, father,' Thomas insisted, 'how will you manage? How will you get our work done?'

'I'll find a way.'

Thomas was desperate. 'It's me that sees to the plough lads. It's me that works longest out in the fields.' He glanced at his mother standing behind his father, still holding the porridge pot. She gave him a wild look and shook her head. He ignored her warning and carried on. 'Listen, father, listen to me, I can do the work of two.' He spoke so fast he began to stammer. 'I'm s-s-strong. I'm never ill. And, and William can't be relied on.'

Samuel was keen to agree. 'No, he can't. With that customs work he does, he's never here when we need him.'

His father held up a hand. 'Enough, you two, enough!' It was true that Thomas was invaluable. 'Give me time to think.' He put his head in his hands. It was a dilemma. His sons needed to be taught a lesson, Thomas most of all, and yet Thomas was the most useful. His wife had kept her peace, yet he knew that she'd prefer to keep Richard at home. He weighed the practicalities against his wife's displeasure.

'This is what I've decided,' he pronounced at last. 'Thomas, thoo can stay, but Sam an' Richard must go.'

His wife slammed the porridge pot onto the table.

Samuel and Richard were speechless. They turned to their mother, but she held up her arms in despair. She was as shocked as they were. Thomas was most to blame and, instead of being punished, he was getting away with it.

'It isn't fair,' mumbled Samuel.

His father banged down his fist. 'Me word is final! Who's i' charge 'ere?' He pointed a finger at Thomas, 'An' thoo must change tha ways! Now get out, get on wi' tha work.' With that, he strode out of the kitchen.

Thomas followed close behind.

Richard wiped a tear from his cheek. He didn't want to leave his mother, or Uphall. Chewing his lip, he asked Samuel, 'What do *you* think?'

'It doesn't matter what I think. We do as we're told.' He stood up. 'Come on, there's work to do. They'll be threshing corn.'

As Richard got up, his mother put an arm around his shoulder. 'I'm so sorry... thoo knows tha father...'

Over the coming days, Samuel resigned himself to a November move, yet Richard could see only misery ahead. One afternoon, as they led the oxen home from ploughing, he confided in his brother.

'Apart from leaving home,' he complained, kicking a stone away, 'I'll have no money to buy clothes at the hirings, and if I want anything, I'll have to borrow from next year's earnings. It'll be ages till I can get sorted and save up again.' He scuffed his boot against another stone. His hopes dwindled of ever being in fashion.

Samuel offered little sympathy. 'I shouldn't fret, if that's all you're afraid of. *I'm* going to save up hard. I'll leave Reighton for now... maybe find a wife. That's *my* plan. There are too many sons in this family. If we don't show them we can work hard, we'll never get a decent share of land. That's what *you* should be worrying about, not fancy clothes.'

When the time came for them to leave for the November hirings, Richard's mother wrapped both her arms around him and held him for a while. Upset to lose her favourite, she kissed his downy cheek and whispered, 'Don't go too far away. Remember, you'll always be welcome here, no matter what.'

Richard's throat ached with unshed tears. He nodded and kissed her in return before leaving the kitchen.

Samuel was waiting in the yard with his father and the lads. He saw his mother appear in the doorway with Richard, and he gave a nod in her direction. It was a meagre farewell, but he'd not be missed like Richard. No doubt she'd wave until they were out of sight.

Thomas was nowhere to be seen.

Chapter 18

During the day of the hirings, Thomas found work to do well away from Uphall and his mother. In the late afternoon, he waited at the blacksmith's for news of his brothers. He heard that Samuel had a new home close by in Hunmanby, while Richard was far away in Carnaby, near Bridlington.

Partly as a punishment, and partly to instil better habits, Thomas was made to work with Dickon. From now on, he had to put up with Dickon's perpetual advice and slow explanations. After just two days, he was losing patience.

'Aye,' Dickon sighed, laying down his tools for the tenth time in the day, 'secret o' doin' a job well is to concentrate on ev'ry bit... go steady like... never rush.'

There's little chance of that, thought Thomas.

'Thoo'll 'ave less accidents an' do a better job,' Dickon went on. 'It doesn't matter what thoo's doin'— repairin' a fence or 'angin' a gate. If tha takes tha time, thoo'll enjoy tha work more. Thoo'll see.'

Thomas was not convinced. His life, without the companionship of his brothers, was tedious enough without having to listen to Dickon all day. Courting the blacksmith's girls was no fun without his brothers, and even he hadn't the gall to repeat his trysts with Emma Huskisson. He shuddered as he recalled Robert Storey catching him with his breeches down. A long and boring winter lay ahead, unless he could find distractions.

Winter was a difficult time for Mary's family. The boys were confined indoors far too often for her peace of mind. Though Francis was content to knit on bad days, young William hated to sit still. He moped around with Stina, the dog equally miserable at being cooped up. She hated to see them both looking so forlorn and tried to involve the boy in jobs around the house. He never took to the tasks though, believing them to be women's work. If it wasn't for John, she'd have despaired. With his limited understanding, he followed her around the house like a lost lamb, watching how she did things. She spoke to him like talking to herself, or like talking to a dog, for company.

Now that she'd weaned Matthew, Mary wanted to get back into making her own yarn for their knitting. Spinning was a task she'd neglected, and maybe John could help. With this in mind, she had her husband fetch a fleece from Uphall.

'It's not been washed,' William confessed as he dumped it on the kitchen table. When Mary blinked in horror, he added, 'Mother's got most of the muck out and untangled it. And it's been skirted. Look—there's nothing from the belly and back end. You've got the best wool, just the back and shoulders.'

Somewhat pacified, Mary unfolded the fleece and buried her hands deep in the warm, oily wool.

John, close behind as usual, copied her. When he pulled out his hands, he found his fingers stuck together.

'Don't worry,' she said, 'it's the grease in the wool that makes the rain fall off. It'll make your hands soft too.'

John thought about this. 'The shepherd says he never gets wet,' he announced with a smile.

'That's because he's always rubbing up against the sheep. His clothes are ingrained.'

William saw that he was now surplus in the kitchen. He called to his older sons to take them out to work.

'And yes, Will, you can bring Stina. She needs to have a run.'

As soon as they'd gone, Mary put Matthew under the table and penned him in. Then, happy that she could work without interruption, she went to a wooden box and took out her pair of carders.

'See here,' she explained to John, 'I've kept them clean and dry. They're a bit like your shuttlecock bats, but without the long handle. One's for my right hand and one's for my left. I'll pull a bit of wool off and show you how I get it ready for spinning.'

He watched her take wool from the bottom of the fleece.

'It's softer down here,' she told him, and he nodded. 'I'll knit you something to keep you snugly and warm.'

He nodded again and smiled.

She placed a bat in his hand, and immediately, he touched the wire hooks. 'Careful, they're sharp!' she warned. 'And don't bend any of them. Watch—I'll show you what to do.' She put the tuft of wool onto the left-hand bat and sat down with it in her lap. 'On second thoughts,' she added, 'I'd better put an old cloth on my knee. It'll save my clothes from getting snagged on the teeth, and that wool's bound to have dirt in it still. I don't want to spoil my apron.'

Once settled again, she began to draw the right-hand carder over the left. 'I do it gently. Look, it's like stroking a cat.'

He listened to the scrape and swish as she worked, and gazed in wonder at the fine particles of dust as they fell through the air. Once all the wool had transferred to the other carder, she turned it back the other way onto the left, and eased the sheet of wool off the hooks.

'I'll do it again and again until the wool is even. See, John, the bats are slipping easily against each other now. It's almost done.'

'It's like when you comb my hair in a morning.'

'That's right. And you've no idea how hard it was for me to comb your sister's hair.' She sighed as she remembered the ordeal. Quickly, to avoid other thoughts, she examined the wool on the right-hand bat. It was clean and even, with no tangles. After pushing it onto the left one, she rolled it from the edges with her fingertips.

'See how I stretch it out now.' She held it up to the window. 'Can you see my fingers through it?' He nodded. 'That's how it should be—soft and light and airy.' She rolled it into a tube shape and set it aside. 'We'll need lots and lots of these. It'll keep us busy this morning. I think you'll make a fine carder and, one day perhaps, I'll teach you how to spin.'

No matter how long Mary worked at the task, John was content to watch. Both were happy in the quiet house. All too soon, William and the boys would come clomping home for dinner.

The foul weather of January and February made the winter drag on. Bad habits had started, like young William taking the dog to bed with him. There was little enough room as it was, and Stina twitched her legs as she dreamed. When his mother complained and warned him of fleas, he insisted that Stina stay to keep him warm. Thinking of young Mary's love for the dog, she hadn't the heart to say no, but it was such a relief when Shrovetide came at last. Though the weather was still cold and unsettled, the dog could be outside more, and there were rituals to break up their routine.

On the Sunday night before Shrove Tuesday, Mary lifted the cured bacon off its hook in the kitchen and carved three thick slices. With John helping, she chopped the bacon into small chunks and put them in a dish. When she put the lid on, she whispered in his ear.

'Tomorrow we're having a special breakfast.'

The next morning, she rose before everyone else, as usual, and revived the fire. She took out the bread and cut it into cubes to add to the bacon. Then she set the mixture over the fire in a pan to fry.

The boys woke up to the smell of fried bacon, and smiled as they remembered it was Collop Monday. Then, as fast as they could, they left their beds, put on their extra clothing, and hurried to their places round the kitchen table.

As William entered carrying the year-old Matthew, Mary wondered, not for the first time, how she'd ever produced such a family of boys. Apart from Francis, who murmured a prayer, the boys tucked into their food as fast as she could dish it out. Their spoons banged against the bowls as they scooped up the collops. No one thought to thank her, not even John. The only response was from young William.

'Pity we hadn't any eggs left to go with it,' he complained with his mouth full. 'It was better last year.'

Francis rolled his eyes in despair while his mother sighed as she tidied away. She felt as empty as the bowls.

Chapter 19

Thomas heard of young William's boredom and decided to further his education by teaching him about dog and duck wagers. He knew that William spent a lot of time with his dog Stina; the boy might enjoy training her and there was money to be won if she proved capable.

Young William was captivated by the idea. From the moment Thomas mentioned it, he found time each day to work with Stina. At first he used the village pond, except everyone complained that the ducks were unsettled and the water was muddy for the animals to drink. In desperation, he took her down to the sea and threw in a piece of wood for her to retrieve. To make it more authentic, he covered the wood in a brown cloth to which he'd sewn duck feathers. Stina was reluctant, so he rewarded her with a titbit each time she entered the waves. As she responded well, he threw the wood further and further out until she had to swim a good length to retrieve it. A pond, William reckoned, would be simple after training in the sea. A month later, he told his uncle that Stina was ready.

It was a Saturday in summer when Thomas took young William on his horse and set off along the road to Bempton and then on to Flamborough. The dog sniffed the roadsides and ran ahead.

William was unusually quiet. 'By the time we get there,' he frowned, 'she'll be too tired to chase the ducks.'

'No, no,' Thomas replied with a grin. 'She'll be fine, you'll see. She'll soon settle down and walk.' He was enjoying the ride. Though it was early morning, the sun was bright and a stiff southeasterly breeze felt fresh on his face. The pink hawthorn was still out, and wild flowers bloomed like bridal bouquets. He laughed at himself. What was he doing thinking of weddings when there was a dog and duck chase in prospect?

By the time they reached Flamborough, the sky had clouded over, and Thomas's spirits fell with the change in the weather. He began to have doubts about taking a day off work. He had hoped that, with the market on at Bridlington, men would return home to Flamborough with money in their pockets. They'd be tempted to place a bet on Stina.

To while away the time, they went into the Dog and Duck Inn. It was William's first time in such a place. He put Stina on a rope and tried to be nonchalant, hoping no one would remark on his limp. It was generally the first thing that strangers spotted. He shuffled towards a corner seat to be out of view, and Thomas brought him a beaker of milk. His uncle seemed in better spirits and settled down to a tankard of ale and a hunk of bread and cheese. As William picked at the cheese and took furtive glances round the room, Thomas scrutinised the other customers.

'Well, William, I don't think they're the sort to wager bets—not with outsiders anyway. Finish your milk. I'll get us another drink. You can have beer this time.'

An hour later, a noisy group entered the inn. Thomas waited until the men had ordered their drinks, and then told William to stay in the corner with Stina while he had a chat. Minutes later, he came back with a twinkle in his eye to say it was on.

William's stomach fell; he wondered why he'd ever thought he could do this. After all, he was just a boy and with only a smallish mongrel bitch for a dog.

Thomas saw his downcast face, and punched his arm. 'Come on, cheer up! You said you were ready.'

William nodded and swallowed hard.

'Right then, drink up, lad, and we'll head outside. There'll be no bets taken till we get to the mere. The landlord has a duck—he'll strap its wings. Come on.'

William tipped his mug and pretended to drink the last drops. Then, as if savouring the taste, he wiped his mouth on his shirtsleeve and stood up to go. The beer was stronger than the diluted stuff he had at home. Feeling lightheaded, he stumbled towards the door. He focussed on the sneck, and tried to keep in a straight line, but he knew he was walking like a drunken sailor. His limp was a curse. There was no mistaking the sound of sniggers behind him.

The customers drank up and followed Thomas and William to the large pond at the north end of the lane. The landlord had already gone before them with the duck. When a few locals saw the men troop by, they followed to watch; they also took their dogs along.

The landlord announced that if the dog from Reighton could catch the duck inside ten minutes, then he'd buy a round of drinks.

In a sudden panic, William tugged on Thomas's arm. 'What if Stina can't do it?'

'Then I'll have to pay for the round.'

William gulped.

'Don't worry.' Thomas clapped him on the back. 'Other dogs will have a go, and I can win money on the bets.'

William couldn't follow his uncle's reasoning or feel his optimism. He knelt down and put an arm round Stina.

'Please,' he whispered into her ear, 'watch the duck and do your best—do it for me.' He kissed her head quickly, stood up and announced she was ready. He still held her tight on the rope.

The landlord put the duck in the water, and it began to swim out towards the middle. He held up his sandglass for all to see, and then turned it upside down. 'Let the dog go then!' he shouted.

Stina was set free. She stood gazing at William, not realising what was required. The spectators laughed and made snide comments.

Thomas's heart sank; he didn't want to look a fool. 'William,' he growled, 'do something for God's sake!'

William shook Stina and pointed at the duck. 'Fetch!' But she stood still. He glanced at Thomas. 'I'm going to have to throw a stick.'

'No, don't do that! There's trouble if you throw at the duck.'

'Well, I'll pretend to throw then.' He made a frantic effort, throwing his arms out towards the duck while urging Stina to fetch. Instead of getting the message, she sat down with her ears pricked and her large soft eyes on her master.

The landlord felt sorry for William. It was obviously the boy's first time. To the annoyance of the crowd, he declared the match void. The dog, he explained, could have another go later.

Thomas's face was dark. He kicked the clump of grass by his feet. 'I thought you said you'd trained her!'

'I did, but it was in the sea—and not with a real duck.'

Thomas clicked his tongue in disgust and shook his head.

William's eyes filled with tears as two men stepped forward with a dog and said they'd have a go. He knelt down again by Stina and fondled her ears, telling her to watch and learn.

Thomas put money on the duck winning. This turned out to be a shrewd move as the duck was full of energy and dived the moment the dog came anywhere near. The dog soon became confused and began to tire. When the ten minutes were up, Thomas heard whispers that the next to go was a veteran duck courser. Relishing the risk, he put money on the duck again.

As soon as the dog was released, it leapt into the pond with a great splash. The crowd cheered it on as it swam steadily onwards. Suddenly, the duck dived. It stayed underwater for an age and then popped up right on the other side many yards away. Meanwhile, the dog swam round in circles searching. Once the duck was sighted, the dog set off again. For ten minutes the swimming and diving continued. It was then announced that the duck had won. The landlord winked as Thomas collected his winnings. He suggested Thomas might have one last bet.

'Does thoo 'ave nerve to put all tha money on yon dog there?' He pointed at Stina.

William's mouth went dry. Surely, his uncle would not put him in this position.

'Aye,' replied Thomas. 'Why not?'

William glared at him and shook his head. Was his uncle completely mad? He looked on helplessly as new bets were taken. The duck was the favourite, and yet Thomas put his winnings on Stina. He couldn't believe his uncle would be so stupid.

Thomas, though, had been keeping an eye on Stina. He noticed how she watched the duck, how she pulled on the rope each time it dived and resurfaced. He guessed she was as ready as she'd ever be.

When Stina was let off the rope, William flung his arm in the duck's direction and told her to fetch. She shot into the water and swam strongly towards the duck. To no one's surprise, the duck dived and escaped. This chasing and diving went on for quite a while. William eyed the sand trickling through the glass. There wasn't much time left, and he could tell that Thomas was concerned. Stina was getting nowhere. Frustrated at not catching the duck, she was now yelping as she swam around.

As the time was almost up, William yelled more encouragement, and to his amazement, Stina responded. The duck was tiring after already being chased by two dogs, and Stina seemed to sense this. The duck had swum and dived now for nearly three quarters of an hour with little chance to rest. The next time it dived, Stina predicted where it would reappear. She grabbed it in her mouth and swam back to William as the last grains of sand fell through the glass.

The men standing round the pond were silent, tight-lipped. All except Thomas had lost their bet. William knelt down, and with trembling fingers, took the duck unharmed from Stina's jaws. He handed it to the landlord who, alone, congratulated him.

The crowd dispersed, leaving Thomas to count his winnings. It came to five shillings. William's eyes were still wide in shock. The money amounted to a whole crown.

'There,' said Thomas, flipping him a coin. 'You've earned that. Best not tell your parents how you got it.'

William stared at the money in his hand—a whole shilling to spend how he wanted. A grin spread across his face.

Thomas guessed the boy's thoughts. 'Just don't you dare go waging any bets on that dog without me.'

Chapter 20

Young William wanted to boast to his father about Stina and the duck, but thought better of it. He hid his winnings behind a loose stone in the cowshed wall, and waited impatiently to show off to his brothers. As soon as his parents were preoccupied, he lured Francis and John to the cowshed. He fished out his shilling.

'There!' he said.

They stared at the coin in his open palm.

'I won this with Stina. She caught a duck in the Flamborough pond, and Uncle Tom had a bet on her.' He saw the look in Francis's eye and added quickly, 'Don't you dare tell! Father will belt me.' He turned to John. 'He's so cross these days, even *you* keep out of his way.'

Francis folded his arms and leant against the wall with a smug smile. '*I* know why Father's cross and loses his temper. I've heard them talking in bed at night. While you two are snoring, *I've* been listening, so you'd better hide that shilling again quick.'

Deflated, William slid the coin back behind the stone. He faced his brother. 'Well, are you going to tell us about Father, or not?'

'Alright, but it's nothing to do with us. It's about the smuggling and the Stutville family in Hunmanby. Old Charles Stutville died, and his son's taken over. Father's worried about the change.'

'Why would that worry him?'

'I guess he doesn't know who's running things anymore, whether it's the Stutvilles or the Osbaldestons.'

John was none the wiser. He stared with wide, vacant eyes, and began to fidget.

Francis was beginning to feel exasperated. 'Listen you two, surely you understand what Father does. He's a customs officer *and* he helps the smugglers.'

'Wait,' interrupted William, 'he's got nothing to do with the landings on the beach. He just watches and gets a share if he keeps his mouth shut... doesn't he?'

'He gets paid by the customs in Scarborough, so he still has to send in reports. Perhaps he's afraid someone might betray him. It can't be easy pretending to be a loyal officer.'

John shrugged. It didn't make any sense to him. He took hold of Francis's hand and moved closer for comfort.

William had to concede that his older brother knew more. 'You keep your ears open then, and tell us if you hear anything else.'

Two nights later, in bed, Mary and William discussed the smuggling problem.

'They all used to know their place,' William grumbled in a low voice. 'The landers *and* the carriers—they had a good idea who was backing the operation. Now they complain and skulk around. There's no trust anymore.'

Mary yawned. 'Don't worry,' she whispered. 'It's been fine all this time. Nothing will change.'

William raised his voice a little and spoke more urgently. 'You don't know! The stakes are higher now. The government's passed new laws. They only apply to the south, near London, but they could just as soon apply up here as well. Listen, if a boat's found with more than four oars and within two leagues of the coast, it'll be forfeited. And, on top of that, the owner will have to pay a £40 fine.'

She yawned again. 'It won't affect *you*. Go to sleep.'

'Mary, listen—anyone buying *or* receiving clandestine goods might have to pay a £20 fine… or end up in prison for three months.'

'Oh, Lord!'

'Yes, and it's worse for the Dutch crews and those men on the Filey cobles. Now, if they're found with foreign goods within twenty miles of the coast, and if they happen to be armed or have blackened faces, they'll be treated as runners. And if they're found guilty, they can be transported for seven years to one of those plantations in North America.' He paused for a while and sighed. 'It doesn't bode well.'

'But you work for the customs. You'll be safe. I remember you told me when you first became a riding officer, you said if the runners resisted you or hindered you in your work, then they'd be punished.'

'Look, I don't actually seize their goods, do I? So they're not going to resist me. You don't seem to understand… I have an agreement with them. I "seize" just enough to keep the customs masters appeased. I tread a fine line.'

Francis was wide awake. He'd been straining his ears to listen, but didn't hear the end of the conversation; it was lost as his father buried his face in the pillow. In the morning, he reflected on what he'd heard. He didn't like what his father did but, so far, there'd been no trouble.

There was one thing neither Francis nor his father had taken into account—a local official who would not take bribes. Henry William Lumley, Officer of Excise, was one such man, recently appointed and conscientious. So diligent had he been that the 'more lenient' customs officers at Scarborough had packed him off to Hunmanby to be out of the way. The young man, still in his mid-twenties, was proud to represent His Majesty's Excise. His role was a noble one, bringing his king and country the vital revenue needed to discharge the national debt. He also enjoyed his job.

Only one day after renting a room opposite Hunmanby church, Lumley set out to peruse the records that the farmers were obliged to keep. He hoped he was not too late, for it was already sheep-shearing time. He knew that somewhere nearby, fleeces were taken down to the shore. They'd be hidden there until they could be loaded onto boats bound for the Netherlands in return for brandy and God alone knew what else. The illicit free trade had been going on for years. It was time it stopped. Rigorously, he noted the number of sheep owned, the number of fleeces sold and where the fleeces went. He wrote everything in his book.

Over the next few days, Lumley pored over his pages of figures. He double-checked them and found discrepancies. Staring out of his tiny window at the yews in the churchyard, he wondered why no one had reported anything before. He knew there was a riding officer living close by in Reighton. Rubbing his newly shaved chin, he decided to pay that man a visit.

Early next morning, he trotted along St Helen's Lane and asked for the house of William Jordan. Like other members of the excise, he felt far superior to the customs men, and especially to a mere riding officer. He was more efficient, and far more effective. He was also free from corruption.

When William's wife opened the door and let him in, he refused the offer of a drink. He stood almost to attention in the kitchen, his eyes flickering as he grew accustomed to the dark, smoky room.

William and the boys, seated at the table, stopped eating. They stared, spoons in hand, at the strange man in the neat white wig and with a sword at his side.

At the sight of the family sitting there with bowls of an unidentified broth, Lumley blushed suddenly and apologised to Mary for interrupting their meal. Blinking his eyes, he remembered what he'd rehearsed. He straightened his back even further, cleared his throat and faced the master of the house.

'My name is Henry William Lumley, Officer of Excise. As you are the riding officer for these parts,' he warned, 'you're expected to be a valuable link between the customs and the excise. It is your duty to report regularly and not hold back information.' He swallowed. 'I trust you have not been negligent.'

William tried to appear affronted.

The young officer cleared his throat once more. 'I'm going to be in this area for quite some time. There are going to be changes. I'll see you again soon.' With that, he marched out of the house, his sword and silver spurs clinking as he went.

William looked at Mary. He shrugged and managed a weak smile that belied his thudding heart. This man, Lumley, presented an unexpected problem. William had no idea what he might have to do to placate him.

Lumley did not waste time. He collaborated with fellow officers based in Bridlington, Beverley and Driffield. Together, they soon figured out where the fleeces were being shipped out. Hunmanby was one key area—a perfect place to graze sheep while situated near a coastline with many ravines and a flat, sandy beach. Also, as

Lumley discovered, there was a huge rabbit warren on the north moor with its own lodge, owned by Sir Richard Osbaldeston. Since Osbaldeston was also a Justice of the Peace, Lumley thought it inadvisable to search any of his properties, and yet the warren would be an ideal place to store fleeces and much more besides. Instead, he decided to make another visit to Reighton.

One warm evening, William was walking home after a long day scything hay in the meadow. He was sweaty and tired, in need of a wash and a rest. As he turned to go up St Helen's Lane, he saw the young excise officer riding along ahead, no doubt going to his house. He hailed him, hoping to avoid a long conversation indoors in front of Mary. The less she knew now, the better.

Lumley stopped and twisted in his saddle. He waited for William, but did not dismount, preferring to give his orders from an elevated position. He aimed to put William at an immediate disadvantage, standing at the roadside in his working clothes.

'Good evening.' Then he cleared his throat. 'I have work for you. You are to come with me and search these properties in Hunmanby tomorrow. I'll need you as a witness.' He handed down a piece of paper.

William glanced at the list and his heart sank. There were so many people to forewarn.

Lumley didn't wait for a reply. 'I'm going to be in Speeton early in the morning to check a few things there, and then I'll call on you. Be ready, and we'll ride together.'

As soon as the excise man was out of sight, William went to Uphall for a horse and then rode out to Hunmanby. First, he went to the tanners' yard, one of the hiding places for brandy, and found the two owners, Palmer and Watson, sitting outside smoking. They looked as if they were enjoying a last pipe before going home for supper; both grimaced as soon as they saw him approach. William knew he was never welcome.

'What's up now?' Palmer asked and spat into the road.

'I'll be here tomorrow with the new excise man. You'd better make sure we don't find anything.'

'Damn it all! We were just about to close up an' go.' Aggrieved at having to start shifting the tubs to an even better hiding place, they were horrified when William suggested they leave a tub of brandy in a nearby ditch.

'I'll have to find something,' he explained, 'otherwise I'll be under suspicion.'

'But it's still double-proof!'

William shrugged. 'You have time to tip some out and water down what's left.'

Palmer grumbled to himself, and then spat again as he thought about it. 'If we 'ave to lose a tub...let's leave it where it'll be 'ard to retrieve, like in a clump o' gorse.' He chuckled to himself.

'Aye,' agreed Watson, 'let's put it where it's thickest over by top road.' He raised his eyes to William, still on his horse. 'Tha knows where I mean?'

William nodded in agreement, bid them goodnight and proceeded to the other names on the list.

The next morning, William was tense as he waited outside his house for the excise officer. He gazed at the sky. It would be another hot day once the sun burnt off the early mist. He cursed the day he'd ever become involved in the customs. He should be spending his time in the hay meadow, not on a fool's errand prancing around Hunmanby. Before long, he heard a horse's hooves and the now familiar jangle of a sword. There he was again—the young, clean and bright Henry Lumley.

'Ready then?' Lumley shouted from a distance.

'Yes, sir, let's go.' William mounted his horse and murmured under his breath, 'The sooner it's done, the better.'

They rode in silence side by side until they reached the main road, and then Lumley turned to William and smiled.

'I'm looking forward to this search,' he confided. 'You see I need more practice in calculating the dimensions of casks. You've no idea how various they are, but I have tables to assist my calculations. I'll show you them later, if you like.'

William scratched the back of his neck and frowned. He did not want a lesson in arithmetic.

Lumley carried on talking. 'I need to find the diameter at the bung, the length of the cask, and the head of it, and then do my multiplications and divisions. I have a sliding rule. I'll show you that too. It's a beauty, made of ivory. I can calculate the mean diameter of any cask. I can gauge *any* vessel by finding the diameter every ten inches from the bottom upwards.'

Oh, Lord, thought William. *Would this man never shut up?*

'And then I can test the gravity of the liquor. That's interesting, and I have my own areometer. My father purchased it in London. With that, I can measure how dense *any* liquid is. You see, it depends how far the quicksilver sinks. If it doesn't sink far, then the liquid is heavy. I'll show you today if we find any brandy. I can show you anyway.'

William stifled a yawn. It was going to be a long day.

Lumley hadn't finished. 'You know, I have a table of specific gravities. You name a liquid, and I bet it's in that table. Go on, name one.'

'Milk.'

'That's no problem. Name another.'

William tried to think of something else that had nothing to do with ale or spirits. 'Seawater... no, better still, urine.'

'Aha—both are in my table. And there's pump water, vinegar and olive oil as well as claret, brandy, ale and beer. Nothing can fool me!'

Chapter 21

The excise officer was determined. He began at the tanners' yard and made it clear to William that he intended to work through the list until he reached the end, even if it took all day.

William sighed. He did not want to be seen fraternising with the man. With hunched shoulders, he followed doggedly into the sheds.

The two tanners and their workers ignored them and carried on working. They were at ease, though quite aware that their yard was the perfect place to conceal brandy or French perfume; the stench of stagnant water and rotting flesh overpowered any pleasant aromas.

Despite Lumley's zeal, nothing was found, and he had the same negative results wherever he went. William feigned enthusiasm and, late in the afternoon, after unsettling every tradesman in town, he saw that the excise officer was looking despondent at last. Although he wanted to go home, he made sure that his face reflected similar disappointment.

Lumley turned to William. 'We've been on the wrong tack here,' he said, wiping the sweat from his brow with his neckerchief. 'Show me where the runners carry their goods from the beach.'

William was not going to give away that information. He pointed in the wrong direction. 'Over yon, sir. It's a devious route, not the one you'd expect.'

'Let's explore then!' Lumley was full of enthusiasm again.

William led him on a roundabout route through the town and out the other side where it grew hilly and thick with gorse.

'They come up through there, sir,' he explained and peered around for the hidden tub. On noticing it pushed deep into a thicket, he called out. 'I think I've seen something, sir—over here!'

The excise officer dismounted, drew his sword and began to slash at the gorse. Once he'd cleared an entrance, he sheathed his sword and ventured in.

'Come on, man, help me pull it out. I can see it's a tub of some sort. Let's hope it's not just a broken one thrown away.'

William slid from his horse, happy to oblige. His work was almost done. Together, they rolled out the tub and set it upright.

Lumley laid one hand on it and declared pompously, 'I seize this tub for the proper use of His Majesty, and William Jordan is my witness.' In a normal voice, he added, 'I'll write the details out later, and you can sign it.' Then he wiped his brow and grinned. His blue eyes sparkled in the sunshine. 'I reckon that's half an anker. It's heavy enough to be full— maybe four gallons in there. It's too heavy to carry though.' He rubbed his chin as he pondered how to take it back to his lodgings. Suddenly, he began to undo his belt.

'Jordan, I have an idea. We can lift it onto your horse. I'll use my sword belt to strap it down, and you can walk alongside—make sure it doesn't slip off.'

William had no option. It was humiliating to be seen walking when the officer was on horseback, but it was better than lugging or rolling the tub.

It was past five o'clock when they reached Lumley's place. William heaved the tub onto his shoulder and carried it up the narrow stairs to the chamber. He dumped it on the floor and turned to leave.

'Oh, don't go yet.' Lumley waved his arm and invited William in. 'I haven't shown you my areometer. It's here.' He opened a beautiful, monogrammed wooden box, and took out a small glass tube, about four inches long. He held it out to William.

'Can you see that quicksilver in there? See the stem all divided up into degrees? This is what I'll use to test the contents of the tub. It could be well overproof— quite lethal if you drank too much.'

William trusted that the tanners had succeeded in watering it down to at least normal proportions. It wouldn't do to let Lumley know there was a highly lucrative trade going on. He tipped his head to one side as if interested while taking a step nearer the door. He even had the sneck in his hand when Lumley thrust a length of wood at him.

'This is my gauging rod,' he said with pride. 'I'll wager you think it's only a foot long, but watch.' He flicked it out, watching it unfold into four lengths joined by brass hinges. 'With this I can measure the diagonal of a cask. Then, once I know the height and the radius at the top and the middle, I can calculate the volume.'

'I'm sorry, sir, I really must go. I'm needed in Reighton. We're busy haymaking.' He opened the door and stepped out.

'Some other day then,' Lumley called out as William descended the stairs. 'You haven't seen my slide rule yet. Thank you for your efforts today. We'll meet again soon, no doubt.'

William kept smiling to himself all the way home. That excise man was made for jokes. He couldn't wait to tell others that he was asked to see the man's rod, and that Lumley boasted it was more than a foot long.

William's sense of humour was short-lived as Lumley's presence in Hunmanby set everyone on edge. Rumour spread that young Charles Stutville was asserting himself, putting more money and men into the free trade enterprise than ever his father did. The old rivalry between the Osbaldestons and Stutvilles was resuming. As a result, people grew suspicious of each other. They were afraid of betrayal, and when the officer continued to question and search, fights broke out.

William regretted once more any involvement with the customs. A fine brother-in-law Matthew Smith had turned out to be, getting him hired as a riding officer in the first place. Right, thought William, he ought to know how bad things are. When he heard that Matthew was inspecting his cattle herd on his land closest to the sea, he set off in that direction.

'Now then, Matt,' he shouted as he approached, 'your beasts are looking well.'

Matthew smiled. 'Yes, and so they should. We've always said the pasture's best by the sea. I expect to get a good price at the next market. But you haven't come to talk about my cattle, have you?'

'No.' William lowered his eyes to the lush grass beneath his feet, and trod it around with his boot. Then he peered at Matthew and squinted against the sun. 'I've come about the trouble in Hunmanby.'

'Yes… I did hear about the excise officer. The devil's offspring, they call him.'

'Oh, he's not so bad really, but he has thrown the cat among the pigeons. There's been trouble between Osbaldeston and Stutville tenants. Did you know one of the butchers was reported for a breach of the peace?

And the Buck brothers attacked George Humpton. He was only walking home. It was brutal. Now both brothers have been reported too.'

'You'll be alright though,' Matthew winked. 'You're a customs officer. If *you're* molested you can ask for treble costs.'

'And what consolation is that? I can't work in the fields with a broken arm or leg. It's getting serious. And everyone's watchful, anyone might be an informer. Listen, Matt, if they inform, they get £40. That's my whole year's pay as a riding officer. They know that even if they're caught with any goods themselves, they'll be let off. No one's safe—least of all me.'

Matthew put a hand on his shoulder and stared directly into his eyes. 'You carry on as normal. I have a feeling things will get a lot better before long.'

William gritted his teeth and set off for home. He was convinced that Matthew knew more than he admitted. His brother-in-law always seemed to have more money these days, and it couldn't just come from cattle sales. If it was true that he had land in Flamborough, then it was probably for landing and concealing goods. And it was certainly possible for the Osbaldestons' influence to stretch that far. He stopped in his tracks, spun round and headed straight back to the field.

Matthew was on his way back to the village. William stood in his path with arms folded.

'It's time you told me a few truths. How much do you know about the Hunmanby runners?'

Matthew smiled, but not with his eyes. 'Very well then, I do have the ear of Osbaldeston. Listen, William, it's best you don't know details, though I will tell you this—there's a plan afoot to get rid of Lumley. You stay away from Hunmanby this week—especially at night.'

William agreed, though he thought it was tough on Lumley, a young officer too keen for his own good. Yet he had a family to support and he must not get involved. Besides, the officer had a pistol *and* a sword. Surely, the man could defend himself.

Chapter 22

One week later, the young excise man was heading out at night to patrol the cliffs. He hoped to find the riding officer there doing his duty. Although late in the evening, the sky was still light over Filey as he trotted eastwards. The cool night air held the aroma of freshly cut meadows, and he sat comfortably in the saddle, enjoying the gentle motion of his horse. As he rode by one of the fields, he whistled a tune softly to himself.

Osbaldeston's men lay out of sight in the ditch, fully prepared. They wore shepherd's smocks as disguise and they'd blackened their faces. They also carried clubs. With them was Andrew Briggs, a hefty man who'd do anything for money. He also happened to have a trained bulldog. On a word of command, it would attack a horse, a useful trick on many occasions.

Lumley had little warning. Out of the corner of his eye, he glimpsed a dark shape fly from the ditch. With a terrifying snarl, the thing leapt at his horse's nose. At once, the horse stumbled to its knees, and Lumley was catapulted over its head. He landed heavily as the men rose silently from the ditch like phantoms. They gathered in a threatening circle around him and raised their clubs.

Lumley panicked and hurried to his feet. Far outnumbered, there was no point drawing his sword; with their black faces and smocks, he couldn't identify a single man. Remembering his role as His Majesty's

Officer, he stood tall, straightened his hat and dusted himself down. Despite his assumed air of superiority, he eyed their weapons and wondered if it was his last day.

'What do you think you're—?'

His demand of an explanation was cut short. Grabbed from behind, a rag was stuffed in his mouth and someone tied his hands together. Silent and efficient, someone else tied up his ankles. Still possessing his sword and pistol, he was pushed over into the ditch. He landed awkwardly on his side, the sword wedged under his ribs. Not one word was spoken by his assailants. As he manoeuvred his body to look upwards, he saw they were walking off with his horse. They were leaving him there. He closed his eyes and gave a muffled curse. It was going to be a most uncomfortable night, and he didn't know when, or even if, he'd be found.

The next morning, one of the Osbaldeston men 'discovered' him. Lumley was stiff and cold from his ordeal, but as soon as the rag was removed from his mouth, he began asking questions.

'Do you know anyone around here who has a bulldog? He's a large man.'

The man shrugged and pulled a face. 'Can't say as I do, sir.' After pretending to ponder for a while he added, 'Per'aps there's a chap like that i' Flamborough. They're a wild bunch there.'

'Did you see any men roaming around here last night—dressed in smocks?'

'Why, it's mostly shepherds wear smocks. I did see them two tanners though, Palmer an' Watson. I don't know what they were up to... I wouldn't trust 'em... they're Stutville tenants.'

Having sown the seeds of doubt, the man waved goodbye. The Osbaldestons would be pleased with him.

He could report that the officer looked shaken by his experience, didn't know who had assaulted him, and would now be after the tanners and their Stutville cronies.

Lumley spent the rest of the day in his chamber. Ashamed to admit the incident to his superiors or even to his riding officer, he had no one to turn to. After changing his clothes and asking the landlady to clean his boots, coat and breeches, he picked up his book of calculations. He needed a distraction, but his eyes were blurred with tears and the tiny figures danced in their columns. He was too tired and too humiliated by his night in the ditch to concentrate. He dropped the book onto the table. Then, wiping a tear from his cheek, he wandered over to lie on the bed. He stared at the beams above him and vowed to show more courage and do better tomorrow.

The next morning, Lumley's landlady reported that his horse had turned up. This was an excellent piece of news. Somewhat refreshed and with renewed hope, he set out to question the people of Hunmanby. He soon realised that folk were either afraid of the man with the bulldog, or were his friend. No one gave information as to the man's whereabouts, yet Lumley was determined to get to the truth. He haunted the tanners' yard for days and made the men's lives a misery.

Palmer and Watson were furious. The Osbaldestons were doing as they pleased, safe in the knowledge that the excise man was concentrating on others, particularly Stutville tenants. Something had to be done to redress the balance. The two tanners came up with a plan.

Two nights later, a piece of meat was lobbed over the hedge and into the garden of Andrew Briggs. The dog, on a long chain, awoke with the thud of meat on the grass. It wolfed it down and then settled to sleep again, licking its lips.

Early next morning, Briggs found his dog motionless beside a heap of vomit. He knelt down and cradled its head, but when it flopped heavily to one side, he knew the worst; his dog was dead. He leant over and hugged it closer, scarcely believing what had happened. His lips brushed against its soft ears. It was then that he noticed an unmistakeable smell of garlic—the telltale sign of arsenic. Someone had poisoned his dog. He leapt up and saw the half-chewed meat amid the mess of sick. His first thought was the butcher. Yet it couldn't be him because he was an Osbaldeston man, and he was one of the men with him in the ditch. Yet he might know something. He crouched down again and stroked the dog gently with his huge hands. Then he jumped up. It was time for action.

He strode up the street and banged on the butcher's door.

'Whatever's the matter?' a voice shouted from an upstairs window. 'I'm not open yet.'

'Did thoo sell any meat yesterday to any o' Stutville's lot?'

'As a matter o' fact I did. John Palmer, yon tanner, bought a piece o' beef. Why?'

'Then it's 'im, damn 'is eyes. 'E's gone an' poisoned me dog.'

'Thoo'd best fetch constable then, an' don't waste any time. I'm right sorry, Andrew. It were a good dog.'

Andrew Briggs did not seek the constable straight away. Instead, he stomped up to the Hall to speak with the Osbaldestons.

It was Sir Richard's son, George, who dealt with him. He hadn't even had his breakfast, but he realised it must be serious and so took Briggs for a stroll in the grounds. When he'd heard the news, he commiserated politely.

'I'm very sorry, Briggs. Your dog was a fine specimen, so well trained and not to be replaced easily.'

'Butcher thinks it were them tanners. John Palmer bought meat yesterday.'

George Osbaldeston stopped walking and thought for a moment. 'Yes, it could be them. They're Stutville men. They'd be brazen enough to do such a thing. Or ...' He began walking again. 'Maybe it was Lumley, the excise officer.'

Briggs spun round. His eyes glittered. 'Aye, maybe thoo's right, sir. Aye, that could be it. That viper, Lumley, would want revenge, wouldn't he?' Briggs began to believe that the young excise man really had deliberately poisoned his dog.

'Leave it with me,' concluded George Osbaldeston. 'You can trust my father to see justice is done.'

Before noon, the constable had been informed. Henry W. Lumley and the two tanners were charged with the crime of poisoning the dog. They were ordered to appear at the next quarter sessions in Beverley.

Matthew relayed the news to William. 'And best of all,' he added with a grin, 'Lumley's hardly left his lodgings since.'

William felt sorry for the young man. Annoying he might be, but the officer would never do anything unlawful and certainly nothing so underhand.

Weeks later, Matthew told William the outcome of the Beverley sessions. On leaving church one Sunday, he walked alongside William and the family. Pleased with the turn of events, he clapped William on the back.

'Those tanners, Palmer and Watson, have been fined.'

'And what about Lumley?'

'Oh, he was let off. His father has influence.'

William nodded. He couldn't help feeling relieved.

'It's not gone well for Lumley though,' Matthew continued. 'Apparently, the experience was too much for him. I suppose it was finding himself on the wrong side of the law. He hasn't given up being a revenue man, but he's asked for a transfer. He's already left Hunmanby. Cheer up, William, the Osbaldestons have killed two birds with one stone. The authorities are going to see the Stutville gang as the local lawbreakers, and Lumley won't be bothering us anymore. Pity about the dog though.'

William, to his surprise, missed the young excise officer. He couldn't share Matthew's optimism and now, more than ever, he regretted his dual role. Brutal assaults were something new, and poisoning a dog meant that the men would stop at nothing. The thought of receiving treble costs, if molested, was little recompense if he was crippled and unable to work.

Chapter 23

William puzzled over the troubles in Hunmanby, though things had quietened down since the departure of Lumley. Perhaps the rest of the summer would prove uneventful. He chose a beautiful balmy evening to ride out on his horse, more to escape the house than to show a presence as a customs officer. Heading south for a change, he paused near Speeton church, somewhere he'd long suspected as a place to store contraband. Lumley had found nothing on his searches. This was a relief since George Gurwood continued to give the occasional service there and probably took advantage of the free trade like everyone else. No, William thought, I'm not going to upset my old friend and, without getting in too deep, I'll continue to take bribes for keeping my mouth shut. He slowed his horse. There was the nagging suspicion that, behind his back, the free traders were laughing. No doubt goods were stored all over the place, and his brother-in-law, Matthew, would never divulge them even if he knew.

As the horse came to a standstill, he sighed and fondled its ears. 'What do you think, Duke? It's a strange business. I don't like being kept in the dark.'

He turned his horse around and gazed out across the sea. Cobles from Filey were setting out on the tide, aiming for the Brigg and beyond, the tops of their tan sails caught by the setting sun.

'Come on, Duke,' he said as he flicked the reins. 'We're wasting our time here. Let's head home.'

Once he'd reached the high open fields above Reighton, he slowed the horse in order to survey the barley. Lush and green, it swayed and separated like fur in the sea breeze. Life had been so much better, he thought, when the Gurwoods were here. The vicar's daughters had kept the lads in check; Milcah, especially, had been such a good influence on his sons.

The horse fidgeted beneath him, impatient to move on.

'Alright then, Duke, we'd best go home.'

He made his way down the hill into the village, thinking about his family. 'It's not that I'm openly disobeyed,' he confided to the horse, 'it's just that I don't understand them. There's Francis still harping on about the good of his soul, and young William's hellbent on having fun no matter the cost. And as for poor John, well...'

The boy, he mused, offered peaceful company and affection, rather like a favourite dog, but William did not expect any meeting of minds. At least John could follow simple instructions and might just about earn his keep. As he turned into the Uphall yard, he felt sorry for him. The boy was often bullied, and it wasn't fair.

Young William had teased and tormented John for years and the older he grew, the more pranks he devised. He got one of his ideas from watching the mole catcher. The old man arrived one morning with his clay traps and stayed at Uphall while he carried out his work. Young William took Stina and followed the old man down to the pasture where the grass was littered with the telltale mounds of fresh soil. There, he studied the man as he inspected the field; he admired the man's moleskin waistcoat and was fascinated by the traps. Eventually, he enquired how they worked.

'Clear off!' was the reply.

At least that's what William thought the man said; he couldn't say for sure as the mole catcher had his mouth full of little wooden pegs, which he was fitting into holes in the traps. The man waved his arms about, shooing William away, but William wandered only as far as the ditch, and hung around there with his dog. After a while, he edged closer to the man and saw how he kept prodding a rod into the ground near the molehills.

When the man found a tunnel, he dug out the soil carefully and then inserted the trap, setting it to spring with bendy willow sticks. When he noticed William's shadow creeping up on him, he shouted and waved his arms again.

William stood his ground and watched as fine soil was taken off the molehill and sprinkled onto the top of the trap. The mole catcher then got up off his knees and readied to leave.

'When are you going to check the traps?' William asked.

The man ignored him so he walked on behind. 'I said when are you going to check the traps?'

The man stopped and flicked his hand as if a fly was annoying him. 'Is thoo that interested?'

William nodded with a cheeky grin.

The man rubbed his bristles on the side of his face. 'I reckon I'll be back before sunset. That'll gi' mowdywarps a few hours, an' then I'll see.'

'Alright, I'll come back then.' William gave a broad smile and waved goodbye as he set off to run home. Stina bounded after him as usual, barking with excitement.

People in the village knew from experience that the sound of Stina's barks meant trouble; young William was up to no good.

As the sun began to go down, William returned to the pasture with Stina. The mole catcher was already there with his bucket and his club. William ran over to him and counted the dead moles already collected. He ran a finger over the dark, velvety bodies, impressed by their claws, the perfect tools for shovelling soil and perfect for ruining a good pasture.

'Are you going to skin them?' he asked.

'Aye.'

William grew talkative. 'I once saw a tree at Bridlington. It was full of moles. They were all strung up and swinging like hanged men.'

'Since when did thoo see an 'anged man?'

William shrugged, not wanting to admit he'd never seen one. He was not discouraged, though, and had an idea.

'Are you going to hang *these* moles up in a tree?'

'Nay.'

'Why not?'

The man ignored him and moved on to the next trap. He'd marked the places with sticks and there were many still to check. He let out a long breath and paused in his work. He preferred to be left alone, but realising there was no escaping the lad, he spoke more kindly.

'I don't need to 'ang up moles to show off me work, not like some. Ev'ryone knows me round 'ere an' I get enough jobs. I'll be catchin' 'undreds on 'em, thoo'll see.'

'What *will* you do with them?'

'Just skin 'em, what else?' He knelt down by the next trap and saw that it had gone off. He prised it out of the soil and waved it at William, revealing a large dead mole caught round its middle, almost snapped in two. He took it out and threw it for the dog. Stina leapt on it and tossed it into the air before pouncing again and shaking it. Afraid that she'd wreck the traps, he ordered William to keep a tight hold of her.

'Can I keep this mole?' William asked as he wrested it from her mouth.

'Aye, no point me 'avin' a skin wi' teeth 'oles in it.'

'When are you going to skin them?'

'Doesn't thoo ever stop spoutin'?' The man blew out his cheeks. 'I'll likely skin 'em tonight.'

'When tonight?'

'Why, what does thoo want to know for?'

'I was wondering if I could have them, just for a while. I could bring them back to you at Uphall.'

'Thoo's a strange lad.' He scratched his chin and stared at William.

'I promise I'll bring them all back—no teeth marks in them, nothing spoilt. I promise. I'd swear on the Bible if I had one.'

The man wavered in his decision and then had an idea.

'Only if thoo 'elps me skin 'em afterwards.'

William grinned and shook the man's calloused hand, filthy with caked soil. 'Good. I'll wait until your bucket's full and then I'll be off... and bring them back later.'

William saw that the man was keeping a careful count of the dead moles and, as the sun disappeared behind the hill, he was handed a full bucket. When he got home, instead of going indoors, he crept round to the back garden. He took a ball of twine from the outhouse and used his knife to cut it into lengths. Then, with Stina sitting bolt upright and attending every move, he tied a piece of twine round each mole, and then hung them from the apple tree. There they swung in the dwindling evening breeze.

His plan had worked well so far. Satisfied, he went to the kitchen where his mother was busy preparing supper. As he'd hoped, his father and Francis were not home yet; only his mother and younger brothers were there.

'John,' he whispered urgently. 'I've something to show you. Have you been a good boy lately, or have you been very bad?'

The boy thought for a moment. He couldn't remember being bad. He'd never harmed anyone or anything on purpose.

'Don't know,' John replied, upset at not knowing the answer to his brother's difficult question.

'Well,' answered William, 'I think I know the answer. You've been very wicked. Want to know how I know?'

The boy nodded, his eyes beginning to water.

'Did I ever tell you that, for every bad deed, one of God's creatures has to die? And they'll come back to haunt you. Think of that.' He waited until the information had sunk in. 'Listen, John, I noticed the apple tree looked weird as I walked past... it looked as if some very odd things were hanging there, and they certainly weren't apples.'

John stared with enormous eyes at his brother. He bowed his head, thinking it must be his fault.

'Want to see?' William asked cheerily. 'You'll be safe with me. We'll go out and see together. Here, hold my hand.'

They went into the garden, John still with his head down to avoid seeing the tree. William led him right beneath it and told him to look up. It was now dusk and the branches of the tree were black against the darkening sky. Strange objects dangled down. John shuddered and closed his eyes.

'Here, I'll lift you up. If you don't open your eyes, at least you can feel one.'

'No.' John flinched and pulled away, but William lifted him up and guided his hand onto a mole.

Although it was soft, John also felt a sharp claw. He wasn't sure whether it was one of God's creatures or one of the devil's. He yelped in fear and pulled back his hand.

William set him down before he squirmed free. 'Just look,' he coaxed, 'see all those creatures hanging there?'

John gazed at the tree in horror as the breeze stirred the moles. They twisted and turned silently on their strings. He screamed and ran straight into the house towards his mother.

She was about to lift the simmering pot from the fire. He rammed into her and gobbets of hot broth slopped onto his face. He screamed again.

'Oh Lord!' she cried and set the pot down. In a panic, she shoved her hand into the nearby tub of hog's grease and scooped up plenty to daub on his scalded cheek.

'There, now. Oh, dear, that will have to do for now. I'll make up a poultice later—once it feels easier. There now, don't sob so.'

He tried to talk, but he was choking so much she couldn't catch what he said. She had no idea what else was bothering him.

Out in the garden, William heard the racket and guessed he might be in trouble. As fast as he could, he untied the moles and put them back in the bucket. Then, before he left to go to Uphall, he shouted quickly through the doorway.

'I'm going to help skin moles. I'll have supper at grandfather's.'

That evening, the truth came out. John had spoken such a lot of gibberish about God punishing him for his wicked ways that his parents made him sit down and relate everything that had happened. While not surprised to find young William behind it, they were alarmed at the lengths he'd taken to frighten his brother.

When the boy returned after supper, his father yanked him aside and pushed him up against the kitchen wall.

'You will be punished for this,' he growled through his teeth. 'Tomorrow I'll give you a rake, and you will go to the pasture and rake every single molehill flat.'

'What—on my own?' Usually, they used an ox for the job, pulling a moulding sledge.

'Yes, and you're not taking Stina with you. Dickon will check your work later and, if it isn't done to his satisfaction, he'll find you some ditch-digging to do.'

Next morning, young William sulked. The rake was too heavy for him and gave him blisters. He thought of last evening's lesson in skinning moles and wondered if it had been worth it. The answer was no, it had been a disappointment. The mole catcher made it look simple; it took him merely a couple of minutes to skin each mole. Although he'd shown him how to do it, William had struggled. No matter how hard he tried, he was all thumbs. Worse still, he'd been left to nail the skins to a board and rub salt into them—a task that was women's work.

As he returned the rake, Dickon asked him if he'd learnt his lesson. William's face reddened as he glowered back. He didn't reply. On his way home, he kicked at any loose stones in the road and grumbled under his breath, 'I wish Uncle Thomas was my father. He wouldn't have punished me; he'd have laughed at my mole trick.'

Chapter 24

Mary worried about John. The burn on his cheek healed, but his mind remained scarred. He wandered aimlessly about the house and garden, never straying far from her and, when he helped her pull thistles and dirt from the new fleeces, he had such a haunted expression. She tried to allay his fears.

'Put that comb down, John, and listen to me. You're the most kind and tender-hearted boy I've ever seen. Don't go thinking you're evil because you're not. Come on, let's have another hug.'

He wrapped his arms around her and pressed his face into her apron. Her warm body and her smell of baking soothed him, yet he continued to believe he was bad at heart. At supper, he hung his head in shame and peered at the rest of the family from the corner of his eye.

Mary was at a loss how to cheer him up. The least she could was to keep him at home each day and away from his older brother.

'I have an idea,' she said to him one sunny July morning. The others had left the house and she was alone with her three youngest sons. 'Matthew can walk further now, so why don't we take him and Richard for a walk? We can go up on the moor. We can take a sack and pull the bits of wool caught on the gorse. Then, when we get home, you can comb it and card it.'

John nodded and gave her a smile not seen for days.

Mary let Matthew toddle by himself halfway down the lane before he fell headlong. Then she carried him on her hip. John walked barefoot beside Richard, holding his hand tightly and feeling protective.

'Look, John.' Mary pointed to the blue sky. 'The swallows are flying high. It's going to be a fine day.'

He shielded his eyes from the sun and squinted upwards. He hoped no harm would come to the birds because of his wickedness. Crossing his fingers, he also prayed to God.

When they reached the moor, Mary led them to the gorse. Still balancing Matthew on her hip, she showed them the clumps of fluffy wool caught on the thorns. John ran ahead and began to pluck off the wool, handing it to Richard who then passed it to his mother. They worked together for almost an hour. As it was such a hot day, Mary soon gave up carrying Matthew. She set him down on the grass and wiped her brow.

'You stay here, there's a good boy. You're too heavy for me.'

The gorse was in full flower, and the heady scent rose with the heat from the ground. Mary regretted not bringing a drink. She wiped her brow again. Through the shimmering haze, she kept her eyes on John and Richard in the distance.

'Come on, you two,' she shouted at last. 'I think we have enough wool now to keep you busy.'

'Where are the sheep?' John asked as he handed her his last bit of wool. The moor was bare except for the numerous sheep tods dotted about the grass.

'They'll have been moved onto the fallow, and the lambs will be taken from their mothers.' Since John was taking more interest in sheep and wool, she added,

'Perhaps Greasy Jack'll let you help him. You like the shepherd's company, don't you?'

The blissful smile on John's face brought tears to her eyes. It took so little to please him. 'Now, there's something for you to look forward to.' She brushed his wavy hair from his eyes. 'Come on now, we're hot, and Matthew feels very damp. We'll go home and have a cool drink of water straight from the well.'

As they ambled back, John was his old self again. He smiled at everyone and everything. The sky, the trees, the ducks on the pond, they all received his blessing.

Mary watched him and shook her head. If only her eldest two were as easy to manage.

Neither parent had much control over young William. Throughout summer, he behaved as if carrying out a vendetta against anything that breathed. He got a thrill out of tormenting animals, and seemed to hurt creatures purely because he had the power. So long as his victims were classed as vermin, his father didn't mind; he appreciated him doing a necessary job.

Young William trained Stina to catch mice, but she was never quick enough and, besides, the cats at Uphall did the job well enough. Then he tried to catch the small birds that were becoming a nuisance in the growing crops. He pestered Dickon to help him make a snare.

Dickon sawed a piece of wood for a flat board, and they tied loops onto it that Dickon had made patiently out of horsehair. William then took the board into the pea field, sprinkled a few barley grains over it and walked away to wait. The idea, Dickon had said, was that the birds, in their greed, would get their necks caught in one of the many loops. It was disappointing though. After waiting an hour, William caught nothing except two sparrows. Bored, he left the snare to do its work and ran off with Stina to look for something else to do. He forgot all about checking the trap.

Two days later, John and Richard were at work, scaring birds from the pea field. John found his brother's snare. The sight of the small, dead birds with their necks twisted in the loops made him sick.

That night, when he couldn't eat his supper, his mother took him into the garden and questioned him gently. As soon as she understood, she marched back indoors.

Young William was about to put his spoon in his mouth when she clipped him round the ear. Taken by surprise, he dropped the food back into the dish. He rubbed his ear and scowled.

'What was that for?'

'Just think yourself lucky your father isn't here. And you'd better get rid of that snare if you're not going to use it properly.'

He glowered at his brothers, still rubbing his sore ear and, when his mother's back was turned, he stuck out his tongue.

The next day, young William sought out his uncle Thomas and explained the trouble over the snare.

'Cheer up, lad, and don't worry. I'll show you how to set up a different kind of snare—a pulling one. Come with me after supper, and you can help me.'

That evening, William went out with his uncle to collect a few strong and bendy twigs. Thomas showed him how to attach a noose to one end of a twig. Then, wandering around the Jordan lands, they chose various sites where Thomas stuck a twig into the ground. He then bent it over before pegging down the other end.

'If a bird pushes the peg,' he explained, 'the twig will spring up, like this.'

Intrigued, William saw how the noose would catch the bird, probably round its neck.

'You must make sure,' Thomas warned, 'that you check each snare every day.'

All went well until one of the Uphall cats was almost captured in error. William was then told to think of another way to keep the bird population down. He moped around the village with Stina, getting in everyone's way. Eventually, his father made him a sling—a simple enough device using a bit of leftover leather and a thong made from animal gut.

'Here you are,' he said. 'See how you get on with this.' As the boy waved it about, his father added, 'I haven't time to practise with you, but I bet your uncle Thomas'll help you. He's never yet refused a chance for some sport.'

After supper, young William ran all the way to Uphall with Stina barking alongside. He found his uncle in the yard scraping the muck off his boots.

When Thomas saw the sling, he smiled to himself. 'You're going to need the right kind of stones, William, before you try that out. Go down to the beach at Speeton. You'll find plenty there that'll do. You want them smooth and round—about the size of a pigeon's egg. When you've filled a bag, come and find me again. Then I'll show you what a sling can do.'

Late the next day, young William went to Uphall with a bag of stones. The men were just returning from the fields, so he waited in the yard for Uncle Thomas. On seeing him, he held up the bag and grinned.

Thomas didn't hurry. Hot and tired, he sauntered into the yard and dunked his head in the trough of cool water. Refreshed, he shook the water from his head and turned to William still standing by and waiting.

'I'm warning you—that sling is not a toy. It's a weapon. Come on, then. Pass me it, and a stone, and I'll show you.'

He led William onto Reighton Hill, a good distance from any stock. 'You'd best keep a tight hold of Stina. We don't want her being hit. See, William, once you've put a stone in the pouch, you put your middle finger through this loop on the end, and pinch the knot on the other end between your thumb and finger. Only pinch it lightly, mind, as this is the end you let go. Now watch— you stand sideways to whatever you're aiming at. I'll aim at that gorse bush. You spread your feet apart, lean onto your back foot, like this, and let the sling hang behind you, ready. Then, look at your target, and... whip it fast over your head.'

The stone flew out and hit the bush with force. William licked his lips. 'Can I have a go now?'

'Keep your eye on the target as you do it, and don't forget to let go of the knotted end as you turn and throw. The timing will come with practice. Here you go then.'

William tried to sling the stone as instructed, but it flew straight into the ground barely a yard away.

'Never mind, you'll soon master it. Maybe it'll help if you point your finger at the target once you've let go.'

William tried again, and again.

Thomas put an arm around his shoulder. 'It's practice you need. It'll take time to get your eye in and hit the target. Be patient—and don't forget it's a powerful weapon. Over a range of about thirty yards, it's deadly. It can crush a bird's or a rabbit's skull, so be very careful where you aim. Perhaps it would be better if you didn't take your dog along. Make sure you practise well away from your house—and mind there's nobody within range.'

William didn't improve much that day, yet after daily practice he began to hit his targets with increasing accuracy and strength. He often ran down to Speeton beach, threw bits of wood into the sea and then aimed at them. Once satisfied with his skill, he collected a large bag of stones and began to do the proper job of keeping the bird population down. He spent hours roaming the fields and moor, picking out his targets, often returning home with a string of dead birds.

One evening, he came home late for supper and plonked two pigeons on the table. Both parents were pleased. His mother was glad of the extra food, and his father was proud of his son's prowess with the sling.

John gazed at the birds and began to stroke the soft, grey feathers. Suddenly, his brother, Francis, gave him a shove.

'Don't be daft, John, they're not pets. They've been killed to eat.' Unimpressed by William's skill, Francis glared at the pigeons laid on the table.

'And what's the matter with *you*?' his father demanded. 'You've a face like a long sermon. Can't you be happy for your brother?'

Francis didn't reply.

'Perhaps if you spent more time practising useful skills instead of sneaking off all the time to be with Robert Storey...' He would have said more, but Francis had jumped up from the table and was heading to the door.

'That lad,' he shouted as the door slammed. 'He needs to sort himself out. He should face up to his *real* lot in life.' He turned to his wife. 'He's never going to be a churchman, is he? He has to work the land like the rest of us. The sooner he accepts that the better. I've had enough of his harping on about the good of our souls. He's fifteen now. Tomorrow he's going to do a proper man's work—or else!'

Chapter 25

For the rest of the summer, William kept an eye on his eldest son and made sure the youth did more than his share of the work. He noted with disappointment that Francis always set himself apart. The lad refused to drink ale, and never joined in when the farmhands were having fun and teasing the girls. It was obvious that most of the workers avoided him, especially as he was in the habit of saying an unexpected prayer. One day, William was amazed to find his son being bold or stupid enough to chastise the older lads; he wasn't surprised when they shoved Francis into the dung heap.

At the end of August, and with the harvest well underway, William was still puzzling over his son. Now, at least, Francis looked the part. His face and arms were chestnut brown, and his body was growing hard with muscle. William was gratified to see the palms of his son's hands calloused like his own, his fingernails short and full of dirt and his knuckles scarred from numerous scrapes.

When Francis glanced down on his body, he hardly recognised himself. The hours spent with Robert Storey made him view the lean, fit body with distrust. Now, at fifteen years old, he was facing greater temptation. Whenever his body became aroused, as it often did at any time and for no reason whatever, he gritted his teeth and muttered a prayer, one taught him by Robert.

'Teach me Lord to walk always in thy presence. Let the employment of my whole life be to serve thee, to advance thy glory and to root out all the accursed habits of sin.' He spat out the last words with venom.

When he explained his problem to Robert, he was given short meditations to use during the night.

'Francis,' Robert advised, 'you must think of Jacob wrestling with the angel, and then commune with your own heart and be still. Then, once you are calm, you must pray for pardon and the grace of chastity.' Robert also recommended fasting and, if Francis felt he was losing the battle, then the total abstinence from food for a whole day.

After one such fast, Francis collapsed out in the field and had to be sent home. At supper, his father gazed at his son and frowned.

'I just don't understand you, Francis. You look fit and strong enough, but I do wonder at times.'

'I am strong enough,' Francis assured him. 'I didn't eat today.' Under his breath, he added, 'Or much yesterday.'

His mother put a hand over her mouth, upset that she hadn't noticed. 'Oh, Francis, you have to eat!'

His father was less forgiving. 'For God's sake, lad, what's up with you?'

'Robert says, if I eat less, I can combat temptation and sin.'

William was speechless. He'd hoped his son was getting over that nonsense, had thought the hard, physical work of the summer and harvest would change him. Obviously not. As he settled down to his plate of pigeon pie with onions, he still pondered the mystery of his eldest son.

The next evening, William came home with news of a Jacobite plot that had been discovered. Over supper, he told the family how thousands of soldiers from Spain and France had intended to land.

'Don't worry. The plot's failed, thank God. The chief suspects have been arrested, and they've already been tried and sent into exile. One of them has been hanged, drawn and quartered.'

Young William's eyes glittered. 'How do they do that?'

Francis rolled his eyes.

'I reckon,' said their father, 'the man was hanged until he was almost dead, and then taken down and his John Goodfellow cut off. Then his bowels and heart ripped out. And then beheaded and his body cut into four pieces.'

The boy's eyes widened with horror and delight. 'That's the most grisly thing I've ever heard!' he exclaimed with a smile.

Francis lost his temper and cuffed the side of his brother's head.

'You disgust me!' he hissed. 'You have the devil in you!'

Everyone stared as if Francis had lost his mind.

He coughed in embarrassment. 'Well, I mean... look at poor John here. *He* doesn't need to know such things. Or Richard either—he's old enough to understand.'

No one spoke. They were still shocked by his outburst.

'Even mother shouldn't have to hear such things,' he mumbled as an afterthought.

His mother opened her mouth, about to say that it didn't affect her that much, yet he had more to say.

He turned to his brother and wagged a finger at him. 'I'm sorry, Will, but you need to think more about the poor man's soul... and his suffering. You think only of yourself and the fun you can have.'

In an instant, young William rose from the table, launched himself at Francis and punched him in the face. Mary hauled John out of the way, as the two boys fell in a heap on the floor. When the boys wrestled their way across the kitchen, she made a grab for Matthew, lifting him out of his little chair so he wasn't trampled.

'Oh, stop them, William,' she begged, holding Matthew on her knee. 'They'll break something—or each other. Oh, Lord!' she exclaimed as the meal bin tipped over.

'Leave them be. It'll do them good. I want to see who comes out on top. Francis should be a man for once and give Will a good beating.'

Five years older, and much taller and stronger, Francis should have won easily, but he relaxed suddenly, went limp and stopped fighting.

Even young William could not find it in him to continue punching. The fight was over. 'You've had enough then, have you?' he gloated, sitting astride his brother. Then he climbed off and swaggered back to the table with a smug grin.

Francis got up slowly and brushed the dust off his shirt and breeches. He was almost in tears.

'You made me forget myself, miserable sinner that I am,' he growled. In despair, he stared at his family, his arms hanging loose by his sides. 'Who shall deliver me from this body of sin?'

John held out his hand. 'Don't cry, Francis.'

'I'm not crying. I'm fine, John. Let me be.' Then, to the rest he announced, 'I'm going out. I need to get away, be on my own for a while.'

Young William shrugged his shoulders. 'Go where you like,' he taunted as the door closed. Then he shouted after him, 'I don't care where—so long as you're out of the house.'

'Well, well,' his father said as he passed his son another slice of pie. 'Fancy you getting the better of him.'

Francis strode up the hill and knocked loudly on Robert Storey's door.

His aunt Elizabeth was surprised to see him so late. It would be getting dark soon. Perhaps he'd come for evening prayers. Alarmed by the wild look in his eyes, she let him in without asking questions, and followed him into the kitchen.

He found Robert sitting hunched on the window seat, intent on a book in the fading light. Francis sat beside him, his body trembling and his throat sharp with unshed tears. Robert ignored him and carried on reading. There was a stillness in the house; the only sound came from Elizabeth's spinning wheel. As Francis began to feel at peace once more, he explained the kind of temptations he was facing at home.

'And I'm afraid I lost my temper with William... and worse still... I had a fight with him... I'm so ashamed.'

Robert was quiet for a while. He'd listened with great patience. 'I think, Francis, we should kneel together and pray. I'll lead. Elizabeth, you come and join us.'

Obediently, she stopped spinning and knelt beside her husband.

'Please, O Lord,' he began, 'look down with mercy upon us. Grant Francis the strength to withstand all sin, for he is sorely tried and in great need of your grace. Amen.'

William and Mary retired for the night still wondering about their eldest. Francis had returned and gone to bed without a word. They lay on their backs, staring into the dark.

'I just don't know what to do for the best,' William confessed in a whisper so that Francis could not hear. 'I wish George Gurwood was still here. He'd have given me some advice. And now I can't even see him at Speeton because our new vicar's going to be taking the services. Did you know he's been appointed the curate there?'

'No. Has he heard rumours about tea stored at the church?'

'He knows nothing about that. I hope not anyway, but that's another worry. Right now, we have Francis to deal with.'

'I don't think Francis is going to change, do you?'

'No. Perhaps we'll have to think of sending him away.'

'What, to another farm?'

'Why not? My father's done it with Samuel and Richard. It might do us all good.'

Mary didn't believe he'd really do this. She turned away from him, onto her side, to go to sleep.

Tomorrow, thought William, I'll tell Francis at breakfast time—before Mary has time to argue.

Chapter 26

Next morning, as soon as the porridge had been dished out, William put down his spoon and cleared his throat.

'I've been thinking, Francis... I'm sure it's all for the best if you live somewhere else.'

Francis caught the smirk on young William's face. How he wanted to swipe him. Instead, he stared at the bowl before him while his eyes brimmed with tears. He didn't dare look up to see his mother's face. She'd gripped the table, and he could see her white knuckles from the corner of his eye. Neither could he face John. Any sympathy and he'd lose control and cry.

'So, Francis, what do you think?'

For a moment, Francis thought he might be sent to live with his aunt Elizabeth. That wouldn't be a bad idea. He nodded, unwilling to risk his voice. He began to eat his porridge though it was hard to swallow.

'Listen, Francis,' his mother said quietly, 'you won't have to leave straightaway.'

'Oh but he will—almost. He can leave at the November hirings in Hunmanby. Don't worry, I'll find him a good place.'

It was worse than Mary thought. She was furious that William had sprung this on her over breakfast. The blood rushed to her face as she rose from the table to say her piece. The moment she opened her mouth to speak though, she realised deep down, that it would be a good idea to get Francis away from Robert Storey, and the sooner the better. Resuming her seat, she bit her lip.

Francis turned slightly towards her and raised his eyes.

She saw the betrayed look on his face. Standing up again, she walked round the table. Resting a hand on his shoulder she murmured, 'I'm sorry, Francis. Your father really does think it's for the best. And perhaps it is. It might not be as bad as you think, and you can always come home to see us.'

He didn't respond, and the family finished the porridge in silence.

Francis had never thought to leave Reighton. Once the initial shock had worn off, he was surprised not to be too despondent. He knew he'd be free of the Uphall lads, free of his annoying brother as well as a father who didn't understand him. As for his mother, he would miss her; at least she'd tried to be kind though she'd so little time to spare. He'd miss John too. Most of all he'd miss Robert Storey. His uncle's prayers and meditations had helped him through many difficult times.

On the eve of the November hirings, Francis visited Robert one last time. His aunt smiled kindly as she opened the door, yet thought it best to leave the two men alone in the parlour.

'As soon as Robert's finished with you, come into the kitchen. I've made fresh oatcakes, and there's my new bramble jelly.'

When Francis walked in, Robert leapt up, overjoyed to see him.

'I'm *so* glad to have one more opportunity to speak with you. I want to make sure you have the correct attitude towards women. Come, sit here with me.'

Francis obeyed and they sat together in the candlelight. There was no fire in the parlour and the air was icy.

Robert didn't waste any time. 'You do realise there are evil consequences for the enjoyment of carnal pleasures?'

Francis nodded and squirmed on his chair.

'You see,' Robert continued and gazed in the direction of the kitchen, 'the very nature of that kind of pleasure is vain. It's empty and unsatisfying. You may expect great things from it, especially from being with a woman, but it's only great in expectation. Believe me, it leaves a sting and a thorn behind.'

He paused for a while, again glancing at the kitchen door. He rubbed his nose, almost blue with cold, between his finger and thumb, and sniffed. 'You see, it's a real war and we must fight against *all* temptations. You must pray and fast and work very hard. Oh, and avoid festive occasions. It's the only way to fortify your spirit and be a good Christian.' Again, he paused.

Francis, always the avid listener, had nothing to say. It wasn't long before Robert resumed, this time quoting from one of his books.

'Chastity is that grace which forbids and restrains. It keeps the body and soul pure. Listen, Francis, the choice is either abstinence or continence. Let me explain... abstinence is for virgins and widows; continence is for married people. Now, I happen to believe that chaste marriages are honourable and pleasing to God.'

He put his hand on Francis's shoulder, looked him in the eye and whispered, 'Virginity, though, is the life of angels... it's the enamel of the soul.' Speaking up again, he explained. 'You see, virginity, when it's chosen and voluntary, is better than married life because it frees you from cares. You have more time to spend in spiritual employment and converse with God. *I* believe there is a special reward from God for those who have not defiled themselves with women.'

Francis couldn't help wondering, not for the first time, whether Robert should ever have wed Aunt Elizabeth. Perhaps both could have led happier lives. He shivered and made a decision there and then never to marry, hoping he wouldn't weaken.

'Help me, Robert... to keep pure. I falter... often.'

'Listen, lad, the trick is not to let impure thoughts and feelings get a hold. As soon as they start, you must suppress them.' Robert stood up and began pacing around the room, his voice growing louder. 'It's like a fire—you must extinguish it, or it flares up again.'

Francis noted how his uncle, when stirred, always chewed his lips. Robert was now staring into space. He often did this when reciting memorable passages from his books.

'Francis, you must develop a loathing for swinish lusts and the parings of the apples of temptation. The taste of sinful pleasures,' he spat out, 'must be as unsavoury as the drunkard's vomit.' Without warning, he slumped back down on his chair.

Francis gulped. He faced a long battle ahead. Realising that Robert had finished, he got up to say goodbye.

'You've been like a father to me. Thank you. I promise I'll do my utmost to live my life in all godliness.'

'Goodbye then, Francis. May God be with you. I won't join you in the kitchen. You spend some time alone now with your aunt, and I'll finish my reading.'

In the kitchen, Elizabeth had set the table ready. She pulled a chair out for him, telling him to help himself. 'Eat them while they're still warm.'

The oatcakes were more crumbly than the ones his mother baked, and the bramble jelly tasted both sweet and sharp. Francis knew he shouldn't eat so much, but it was obvious that his aunt was happy to feed him. He relaxed and helped himself to a few more. With his mouth full, he gave her a wistful smile and mumbled, 'I'll have plenty of time to abstain tomorrow.'

Francis's parents woke their son while it was still dark, hoping to avoid any difficult farewells over the breakfast table. His mother raked the two potatoes from the ashes of the fire.

'Here,' she said, 'it'll be cold walking to Hunmanby. Stick these in your pockets.' Then she bent down to blow on the embers and add more kindling. 'I'll soon have the milk heated up and then I'll pour it onto the oatmeal. Your porridge won't be long.'

Francis sensed her discomfort as she jabbered away. It was most unlike her; usually, she was quiet at breakfast.

'I'm thinking it's cold and damp outside today,' she added. 'You must both wrap up warm.' She only stopped talking when the milk was hot enough.

Francis and his father didn't know what to say. They ate their porridge in silence.

When it was time to leave, his father went out of the door first, carrying his son's new wooden box of clothes. He left Francis and his mother to say their goodbyes.

Francis hovered in the doorway unsure how to behave. His mother had never been one to hug or kiss him, always too occupied with the younger children. Even as a child, he couldn't remember ever sitting on her knee. It had always been their servant Kate or Aunt Elizabeth who cared for him. It came as a shock when she held him close. Now taller than his mother, he could see over the top of her cap as she rubbed her hands up and down his back.

'There now,' she said as she pushed him away. 'You'll be fine. You work hard wherever you end up, and I expect we'll see you at Christmas.' With that, she turned her back on him, wiped her eyes on her apron and saw to the fire.

He closed the door gently behind him.

Father and son did not speak as they walked to Hunmanby carrying the box between them. It was a dreary day, the sky low with threatening, dark clouds. As they crossed the high ground overlooking Filey Bay, a light drizzle and haze obscured any view of the cliffs. The sun could not break through the blanket of grey, and they could not differentiate between the sea and the sky.

By the time they reached the town, their coats were quite wet. Francis appreciated his father's forethought to be at the hirings before the Uphall lads arrived. At least he could see what was for sale without their snide comments and jokes. The marketplace was already filling with all sorts of people intent on selling clothes, tools and trinkets to the lads with a year's pay in their pockets.

'You wait here,' his father ordered as they stood outside the White Swan. 'Don't wander off. I'm going in here to ask around—see which farms will be hiring men.'

Francis leant against the wall and peered in misery through the mist that dampened the newly erected stalls. Groups of young men were now appearing from every direction and were sauntering about waiting for others to arrive. Well-dressed yeomen passed by and even more lads, including those from Uphall. His grandfather was among them, in his best coat, no doubt aiming to impress potential new farm hands. Francis edged round to the sidewall of the inn to be less conspicuous, but it was too late. The Uphall lads had spotted him.

'Look over yon,' one of them shouted. 'If it i'n't our Francis!'

'Ey up, Francis—'ow about workin' with us? No? Thoo's right—we wouldn't want it either.' They nudged each other and sniggered.

''E's too soft,' remarked another in a voice that carried across the square. ''E's allus prancin' about an' prayin'.' They laughed as one of them went down on his knees in prayer.

Francis coloured up. To hide his anger and embarrassment, he turned the corner and shot inside the inn. Men were standing over the fire to let their clothes steam dry, oblivious to the smoke seeping from the chimney. His father was in there somewhere, hidden amid the suffocating fog of tobacco fumes. He couldn't find him, so worked his way through the crush of people to search the other room. Suddenly, a heavy hand landed on his shoulder. He spun round to find his father standing beside a large man with a ruddy face.

'This might be your new master, Francis. This yeoman's from Rudston, and he might take you on. If he does, he'll speak to George Gurwood, and then you'll be able to visit our old vicar.'

Francis muttered a thank you, and the three of them left the inn.

The yeoman stepped out first into the cold, fresh air, planted his feet wide apart and took a deep breath.

'That's better,' he declared. 'Inside yon it's as crowded as candles in a tallow-chandler's basket. I can't abide bein' cramped.' He looked Francis up and down, assessing the lad's build and his muscles. 'Tha father tells me thoo's ready to learn at another spot. 'E tells me thoo can 'andle oxen an' can mow an' stack corn. Is that right?'

Francis nodded.

'Tha father also tells me thoo can start straight away. Thoo doesn't want a week's 'oliday first. Is that right?'

Francis cast a glance at his father before nodding again.

'So, thoo doesn't want to spend time drinkin' an' larkin' wi' lads an' lasses then?'

Francis shook his head.

'Glad to 'ear it. Thoo's a sober lad. Thoo'll set a good example.'

William changed the subject. 'He just needs to buy a few things and then he'll join you.'

The farmer thrust money into Francis's hand. 'There's your godspenny—that's our bond. Thoo's one o' *my* lads now.'

Francis watched the man stride away. He noted his left shoulder was higher than his right, evidence of years at the plough. His new master also swayed as he walked, as if he was mowing a meadow.

'If I were you,' his father whispered in his ear, 'I'd spend your money on stuff you'll need to mend your own clothes. You won't have your mother to do it.'

The enormity of the change hit Francis. He hadn't thought of such things. He'd learnt to knit but had never done any sewing. Taking his father's advice, he bought needles and strong linen thread. The money did not run to a pair of scissors so he bought a new comb instead and a block of soap. He put the purchases into his box and then sought his father to say goodbye.

He found him eyeing up the lads for hire, some chewing a bit of straw, others with a clump of wool in their hats to be hired as shepherds, or with a whip round their necks to be taken on as horsemen. Other lads, already hired and free for the week, were capering about in gaudy neckties; they'd be set on getting drunk and molesting the girls. Francis couldn't wait to get away.

'I'm ready, Father,' he said, pulling at his father's sleeve. But he wasn't ready. He was wondering what kind of a place would be his home for at least a year, and whether he'd have to share a bed.

'Come on then, son, and give up staring like a scared rabbit. There's your master over there. Off you go. Work hard and don't disgrace the family. See you at Christmas.' He watched his son pick up his box and join the farmer. 'Good luck.' Out of earshot, he added, 'You'll need it.'

William grew more hopeful as he strolled back to Reighton for the sun had finally broken through the mist. Yes, Francis would work hard, and maybe George Gurwood could curb his son's religious zeal. His old vicar had always put people before cold commandments.

At home, young William was also full of hope. With Francis gone from the house, he was now the eldest and could sit nearer the head of the table. Better still, he need no longer share the truckle bed with John; he could sleep in Francis's bed. He would miss goading his brother, but he wouldn't miss the prayers or being told off all the time for gobbling his food. Now he could look forward to suppertime more than ever. He could tuck into his food with relish, and burp and eat as noisily as he wanted. No one was going to stop him.

Chapter 27

1722-3

In the middle of December, the villagers celebrated a new arrival. Their previous vicar's son had a daughter and named her after his mother. Mary was one of the first to visit, not minding the long, uphill trudge through the slush. She was glad that John Gurwood had christened the girl Susanna; it kept alive memories of the Gurwoods when they lived in Reighton.

When she set off for home, she glanced at the vicarage, still empty, its windows shuttered. Snow lay heavy on the thatch, not melted by the low winter sun or by any fires from within. Whenever Mary passed by, she had a pang of nostalgia for the days when it was full of young girls and the vicar was part of everyone's life.

Treading carefully back down the hill, she realised how much she also missed her eldest son. No doubt Robert Storey was missing Francis as well, yet she had to admit that life was easier for her family without the constant call to lead better lives. As she approached the lane to her house, she thought of poor John who missed his brother the most. Never mind, she thought, it will soon be Christmas, and Francis will come home.

Francis did not return as planned. Snow fell for days, and gales blew it into deep drifts. No one travelled anywhere. The family didn't even spend Christmas at Uphall. Huddled close to their own kitchen fire, Mary tried to make the best of it. She prepared the frumenty and the special seasonal cakes as usual, but their Christmas was a quiet affair.

Even young William was subdued, seemingly lost without Francis to tease. He was bored by having to stay indoors and tormented John instead. There was no older brother to stop him and, with his mother too busy to notice half of what went on behind her back, he bullied John at his leisure. While no one was looking, he put salt in John's beaker of milk.

'This is a medicine for you,' he explained. 'If you gulp it down in one go it'll make you grow taller.'

John grinned, gullible and trusting as ever. He took a huge mouthful. Then he gagged and brought it back up, along with his breakfast.

Their mother gritted her teeth. Harassed enough, she had to boil water and scrub the table clean. When she saw the smirk on young William's face, she sent him out to fetch another bucketful.

He found that being sent on extra errands was a drawback of being the oldest. As he left the house, he stuck his tongue out at John, vowing to make his brother pay for it.

When the weather eased in January, making it possible to venture further from home, young William went out with the dog. They leapt together through the dwindling piles of snow in the lane, and made their way onto the hill to the nearest gorse. He had a small tin in his pocket. Although he scratched his hands, and his fingers grew numb with cold, he removed the sharp spikes and put them in the tin. He smiled to himself. Hiding gorse thorns in John's bed was a good idea; they'd prick him no end and he'd never sleep. He had a better idea, though, when he saw rose hips on his way back.

He returned home at last and went straight into the milkhouse. No one was about. The rest of the family were in the kitchen. He emptied his pockets onto the table and, using his knife, split open each rose hip and scraped out the hairy seeds. Stina sat watching him with ears pricked.

'There's nothing for you,' he said. 'You can't have these, they'd make you scratch. I've made itching powder.'

The only problem was how to get the seeds into John's bed without making himself itchy as well. He couldn't put them in his pockets. Reluctantly, he went outside and tipped the collected gorse thorns into the bottom of the hedge. Then, with his knife, he scooped the seeds and the tiny white hairs into the tin and wiped the table clean with his coat sleeve.

That night, when the children retired to bed, he hid the tin under his pillow. He waited until his mother had tucked them all in and said goodnight and gone back to the kitchen. Then, tin in hand, he tiptoed in the dark to the truckle bed.

John was now sharing the bed with Richard, one at each end, head to toe. William knelt by John's head.

'You don't like being sick, do you?' he whispered. 'I have something that will stop it.'

John couldn't see his brother's face. He was afraid and lay still, holding his breath.

'It's an all-over medicine,' William explained. 'You don't have to drink it. I have it in this tin here. It works best if you sleep with it inside your clothes.'

John didn't move. Even though he still had most of his clothes on since it was winter, he didn't want to get out of bed.

'Come on, John, get up,' William urged as he pulled down the blankets. 'I can't give it you otherwise.'

John crawled out.

Richard wondered what was going on, but it was dark. He didn't see William tip the tin down the inside of John's collar and then down the front of his breeches.

'There, I think that's the lot,' William said, satisfied the tin was empty. 'Now, John, get back into bed... and sleep well.' He stifled a giggle as he groped his way back to his own bed.

In the morning, John's neck was red raw from scratching. His more tender parts were in a worse state. When he used the chamber pot, his urine stung so much he cried.

His mother couldn't understand what ailed him. It couldn't be the chaff in the mattress, and it couldn't be lice either because Richard was not affected. Besides, John had not been anywhere to catch anything. In desperation, she ripped off all his clothes and hung them outside.

'I'll give them a good airing and a beating. This cold breeze should kill anything off.' In her hurry, she never noticed the rose hip seeds.

John stood as near to the fire as he could while his mother washed him from head to toe. He shivered so much his teeth chattered, yet not once did he mention his brother's visit in the night.

Richard, not knowing what went on, was silent on the subject. As for young William, he'd made himself scarce.

Mary had her suspicions and kept a closer watch over her sons, particularly William who had sneaky ways of teasing and annoying his brothers. She caught him nudging John with his elbow at suppertime so that food was spilled. If only he'd been older, she'd suggest *he* be sent away.

As soon as the worst of the weather was over, Mary thought about sending John to work with the shepherd. Instead, she opted to have him help Dickon. The man had arthritis and could use a pair of young, supple hands. He could train the boy to see to the horses, and John would be safe from his cruel brother.

When John heard of the plan, he couldn't wait to spend time with the old man. The next day, he leapt out of bed at dawn, grabbed his coat, rammed his feet into his boots and ran to the Uphall stable. There he met Dickon leading one of the horses to the drinking trough.

Dickon hailed him. 'Now then, young un. Come an' talk to Duke 'ere. Allus be gentle, never shout.'

John found that easy. He never had a lot to say and what he did say was simple, repetitive and invariably quiet.

After listening to the boy's murmurings for a while, Dickon ruffled John's wavy hair. 'Thoo's born for it. Now 'elp me clear out stable. Thoo can shovel all muck onto yon midden while I fetch fresh straw.'

Once the stable was clean, Dickon told him they'd prepare the 'oats an' chop' to feed the horses.

'Now, John, come an' 'elp me crush these oats an' we'll mix 'em wi' hay. Then thoo can 'ave first go wi' sieve to get rid of any dust. Then I'll tip it into their mangers.'

When they'd finished, they went into the Uphall kitchen for breakfast. They joined the large table where the lads were already stuffing their faces with cold meat. It was the same routine every day, yet John grew to love it and was never bored. Before long, the three horses recognised John's approach from a long way off. He'd never learnt to whistle, so he sang the nursery rhymes as he came up the hill. The horses would hear him, turn their heads and whinny softly.

During the lighter spring evenings, John often returned to Uphall after supper. That way, he avoided young William's snide remarks about him stinking of horse manure. One evening, Dickon showed John how to look after the leather traces and harnesses. He passed him a bar of soap, a brush and a bucket of water.

'Sit o' this stool an' take 'old o' this leather strap. See all that muck an' dandruff? Thoo must clean it off. Then we'll leave it to dry, an' tomorrow I'll show thee 'ow to oil it.'

Dickon stood and watched for a while to make sure John was doing a good job.

'That's right—thoo's framin' well. I'm just goin' to put these broken shinbones i' this pot. I'll simmer 'em to get marrow out, an' I reckon stuff's as good as any lard or linseed oil.'

Dickon remembered teaching John's sister how to oil harnesses. Lost in memories of young Mary, he leant against the stable door and gazed across the yard as the setting sun cast long shadows. It seemed like yesterday that he was here with the girl, but it must have been after his wife had died. He was muddling the years. There'd been so many changes. Too many farmhands had come and gone. Too many folk had either left Reighton or died, and the new vicar didn't even live here. He peered down at his hands, no longer useful for the finer tasks, and wondered how many more years he could work.

John sensed something was wrong. He came up behind Dickon and tugged on his jacket.

For a moment, Dickon didn't recognise the boy.

Suddenly, John wrapped his arms around Dickon's waist and held him as tight as he could.

Slowly, Dickon remembered where he was and what he was doing. He pulled free of John, shook his head to clear it, and tipped the bones into the pot.

'Finished cleanin' yon leather strap eh?'

John smiled and nodded.

'Right... well seein' as I 'ave a pot ready to boil, we could make a balm for 'orses' feet. Come wi' me to Sarah Ezard's. She'll 'ave what we need.'

It was a treat for John to visit Sarah's cottage. They found her busy in the kitchen, fumbling with her crooked, swollen hands to fill bags with herbs and hang them up to dry. She stopped on seeing John and made a fuss of him.

He hugged her and pressed his face into her apron. She smelled of mint and ginger, lavender and liquorice. He stepped back and wrinkled his nose, trying not to sneeze, and then stood to attention by her side.

Dickon told her what they needed—tallow fat and beeswax. While Sarah measured it out, he explained they were going to make a balm. He asked if he and John could dig up a few comfrey roots from the garden.

'Aye, go on an 'elp thassens.' As they went outside, she shouted from the back door. 'Thoo knows 'ow to make a good balm then?'

'Why, aye,' grumbled Dickon. 'Though I may be old, I'm not daft.'

Once they'd dug up the roots, they wandered back to the kitchen. Dickon began to explain to John how they'd make the horse ointment.

'We'll warm up Sarah's tallow fat over a good fire, then bruise these roots an' add 'em to pot. Then we'll strain it an' add beeswax. We'll warm it up again an' pour it into a jar. After it's cooled an' set, then we can use it.'

Sarah smiled. 'It'll smell bonny when you've done.'

'As bonny as you,' John replied with a serious face. She pressed him tight against her ample bosom and, once more, he breathed in her unusual but distinctive aromas.

That night, when John climbed into bed, Richard turned up his nose at the odd smell coming from his brother's direction.

'Pooh! What's that?'

'It's stuff to cure horses' feet. Dickon showed me how to make it. Tomorrow he's going to show me how to oil the horses' straps.'

The next day, John found Dickon on a stool in a corner of the yard sheltering a candle.

'I'm keepin' this marrow jelly an' linseed oil warm,' he explained. 'The stuff'll rub into yon straps better. Grab another stool an' join me.'

John fetched a stool and saw how Dickon worked the oil into the leather.

'Now, lad, thoo 'ave a turn.'

John was so slow that Dickon worked with him, giving encouragement when he struggled.

'That's right, John. Soak cloth an' make sure ev'ry bit o' leather is oiled. Bend straps like this. Watch me. Bend 'em back an' forth to let oil soak into ev'ry bit.'

Though it seemed to take ages, John liked the feel of the soft, warm leather and the smell of the oil.

'Another day I'll show thee 'ow to buff 'em up with a piece o' cuttlebone an' a soft cloth. Thoo can rub 'em till they're black an' shiny.'

Dickon's eyes pricked with pleasure to see John smile. He'd not had such an eager apprentice for years, or one so easy to please.

It wasn't long before John had to learn how to deal with a lame horse. Dickon had him wash the hoof with a stiff brush and a bucket of water, and was amazed how the horse stayed so calm.

'Well, John, seein' as thoo's done such a good job, thoo can rub this pine tar on its foot, to stop it goin' bad.'

John's hands grew sticky as he smeared on the pine tar. When the smell made him sneeze, he rubbed his itchy nose against his sleeve and grinned.

Dickon smiled. 'I know...it even smells as if it'll do good. Allus remember—no foot, no 'orse.'

When John went home, he repeated what he'd learnt to his mother. He put his hand on her arm to stop her chopping up the bacon, making her listen as he told her that horses needed a clean stable that was dry and airy.

'But,' he added, 'they mustn't have draughts. And, if they get a cut leg, you can make a hot plaster of something... I think Dickon said to use turpentine and... something else.'

She smiled. 'You're becoming a proper stable lad. I bet Dickon's pleased with you. Perhaps you can help him when the Uphall sow farrows.' She kissed his head and smiled again as she caught the scent of pine in his hair.

It was just days now before Mothering Sunday, and she expected Francis to be home for the day. While she did look forward to seeing him, she feared that his visit might disrupt the recent harmony in the house.

Chapter 28

As Mothering Sunday approached, Mary grew excited at the thought of Francis being at home. She started spring-cleaning in an agitated fashion, and shunted Matthew from corner to corner of the kitchen as she moved things and swept behind. Unused to the sudden upheaval, the other boys kept out of her way as she shifted and crashed about the chests, pots and pans. At last, she calmed down and told her sons to sit at the table.

'There now,' she announced, 'you've been good so you can watch me make a special pudding for Sunday.' Seeing her youngest two grin and bounce up and down, she added, 'As long as you don't put your grubby fingers in it! Sit on your hands, that's best.'

Obediently, they slipped their hands under their bottoms, and then with wide eyes they saw their mother add the dried fruit, spices and almonds to a bowl of pudding mixture.

'Isn't that good!' Mary said as the boys inhaled the rich aromas. She spooned the pudding into a cloth and tied it up to be boiled. 'It smells just like Christmas. When it's cooked, I'll wrap it in pastry. Then you can come with me to Uphall and your grandmother will bake it for us.'

On the eve of the big day, Mary brought out the pan of wheatears that she'd left to soak. She put them in a bag and then called to her boys.

'Come on, it's like Yuletide. I'm making frumenty. You go first, William, you're the eldest. Bash the bag and knock the husks off.'

'No,' he grumbled and stepped away. 'It's for children.'

'Oh, well, I suppose you're a man now you're nearly eleven. I'll remember that when there's heavy work to do.'

He stood behind his brothers and scowled as they took turns to thump the bag on the floor. 'Richard's too rough,' he complained. 'He'll break the bag.'

'He's fine,' encouraged Mary. 'All he has to do is copy John.' She remembered how her daughter had been the same—far too eager and clumsy. Richard had been born the same year young Mary had died, born in October when geese were flying south—a sure sign of a restless child, or so his grandmother had foretold. Mary watched with a rueful smile as he gave the bag another wallop.

'Go steady, there's a good lad.'

When she tipped the bag into a bowl of water, young William stood to one side while the others picked out the floating husks.

Just then, their father walked into the kitchen. 'You're doing a good job, boys. Mother will be able to make frumenty tomorrow. Are you looking forward to seeing Francis again?'

Three boys nodded and smiled; young William stared at the floor.

Francis, in his best clothes, set off at dawn to walk from Rudston to Reighton. He carried a gift tucked inside his coat for his mother—a small, spiced fruitcake made by the Gurwood girls. It was early March and, though the day had started sunny, there was a light frost on the grass and a cold wind blew in off the sea. He gazed across the wide expanse of open fields and pasture, pleased with the way his life was turning out. In Rudston, he was accepted. No one taunted him, and he was always made welcome at the vicarage. Smiling to himself, he hummed a ploughboy's tune and kept time with his stride.

As he descended into St Helen's Lane, the sky darkened and a sudden shower of hail sent him scurrying to the house. His confidence plummeted with the change in temperature so that, by the time he fumbled with the door latch, he was the same anxious boy who'd left last November.

Mary heard the door open, and rushed into the passage. 'Oh, Francis, I'm *so* happy you've come.'

He bent over to kiss her politely on the cheek and then followed her into the kitchen. Everyone was seated at the table.

'About time,' cried his father. 'Come in, lad, get sat down. Mother's been waiting to make the frumenty.'

'And there's a special pudding pie for us later,' she added.

'That sounds good,' Francis replied. As he removed his coat, he took out the gift, wrapped carefully in paper. 'Mother, here's something for you. It's from the Gurwood girls, and made by them. It comes with their love.'

The boys craned their necks to see.

'That's so thoughtful of them,' she said as she unwrapped the cake. 'You must thank them for me.' She wiped away a tear. 'Now, I must get on and boil that milk.'

Francis sat beside John who had the widest of grins and was so overjoyed that he couldn't stop wriggling.

Young William scowled and helped himself to a slice of cold ham. 'Francis,' he asked with his mouth full, 'who do you have to share a bed with in Rudston?'

'No one. We don't have beds as such. We sleep on mattresses on the floor. There are six of us.'

Young William smirked. 'That must be hard for you!'

'No, it suits me. I've got used to it. A soft bed leads to temptation.'

'Don't start,' warned his father.

'But it's true.'

'Now don't spoil the day,' Mary intervened. 'Here's the frumenty ready, nice and hot and sweet. Sniff it— you can smell the nutmeg.' She began to pour it into their beakers. 'This will warm us up and keep us cheerful. Francis, you can tell us all about Rudston.'

'Aye,' echoed his father, 'it's strange you haven't been home once since you left. It's not far to walk. There must be someone keeping you there... someone special... a lass perhaps?'

Young William choked on a bit of ham.

'No.' Francis was quick to reply though the colour was rising to his cheeks. 'It's just that every Sunday the Gurwoods ask me to dinner.'

'Ah... more than one lass then—six, in fact. No wonder you don't come home.'

Remembering Francis's obsession with Milcah, young William was desperate to tease him. He opened his mouth and then had second thoughts. His older brother had put on more muscle and had grown at least another inch. If there was a fight, Francis might give him a beating.

His mother guessed what he was thinking. 'John,' she asked to change the subject, 'why don't you tell Francis about the work you do with Dickon?'

Mary was relieved when the breakfast conversation meandered peacefully to a close without further provocation or argument. Yet there was still the church service to get through, and she knew that William did not want their son to meet up with Robert Storey.

On their way to church, Francis strolled ahead with John. His parents swung the two-year-old Matthew between them. Young William slouched behind with Richard.

As the family neared the church, William halted. He leant towards Mary and hissed into her ear. 'Listen, on no account must Francis and Robert get together. I'm not having it. We must see to it.'

She agreed yet wondered how it could be done without causing offence. 'We'd best sit Francis between us. That might help.'

When they entered the church, they saw that Robert Storey was already there in his pew with Elizabeth, their heads bowed in prayer. William stood by while Mary nudged John into the pew first with instructions to keep Richard quiet. She seated Matthew next to her as usual and hoped to entertain him with various things from her pocket.

'Francis,' she coaxed, 'you come and sit beside me for a change. It *is* Mothering Sunday.'

On hearing the commotion, Robert spun round. He noticed Francis and nodded in welcome.

William spotted that hopeful look on Robert's face. He frowned as he sat down and wedged young William into the small space left at the end of the pew.

As the service progressed along the traditional lines, Mary relaxed. Matthew was content with a ball of wool, and the only time she had any qualms was when the vicar read the customary reading for that

Sunday—Jesus feeding the five thousand. She glanced at Francis. Would the mention of food make him think of greed and self-indulgence?

When the service was over, young William was propelled from the pew by his father and hurried towards the door. To avoid Robert, Mary bustled Francis after them. The other boys trailed behind. As soon as they were outside, they headed for the gate.

'Wait!' Robert Storey hailed them from the church porch.

'Keep walking,' William urged. 'Pretend we haven't heard.'

'We can't,' whispered Mary. 'Everyone's looking.'

'No, we can't,' agreed Francis. 'I'm going back.'

Mary and the rest of the family also turned back though William's face was set hard. Elizabeth was standing at Robert's side. Mary could tell by her sister's red cheeks that she was embarrassed by the awkward situation.

Robert was undaunted. He ignored William's stony expression and shook the youth's hand. 'It's wonderful to see you again, Francis. You must spend some time with us.'

William gripped Francis's arm. 'You're not to go,' he growled.

Other folk, making their way out of the church, sensed a family row brewing and stopped to hear.

Mary blushed with shame. How rude must people think William.

Suddenly, Francis held up his hand. 'Robert, I'm sorry. I have so little time in Reighton and I must get back before dark. Today of all days I should honour my mother.'

Mary was amazed at his tact. To use one of the Ten Commandments as his excuse was a brilliant ploy.

Elizabeth smiled and whispered something in Robert's ear.

He cleared his throat. 'Very well said, Francis. Honour thy father and thy mother: that thy days may be long upon the land which the Lord thy God giveth thee.'

'Believe me,' added Francis, 'you and Aunt Elizabeth are always in my prayers. May God be with you.'

Mary took the chance to link arms with Francis and lead her family out of the churchyard.

William was subdued as he walked back home. Though he carried Matthew on his shoulders and pretended to be a horse, he was deep in thought about his eldest son; Francis never ceased to amaze him.

When they sat down for their pudding pie, Mary handed Francis the largest slice. She was proud of the way he'd conducted himself outside the church and remembered what Jesus had said: 'Blessed are the peacemakers.'

He returned her warm smile and accepted his slice in the spirit given. He was not about to lecture them on the rewards of fasting.

Young William glowered throughout the meal and hoped he'd seen the last of Francis for the year.

When it was time to leave, John was sad and hung onto Francis's coat.

'Don't go.'

'I have to, John. You look after your young brothers for me. And mother tells me you might be helping Dickon with the piglets when they come. You'll like that.'

John nodded with tears in his eyes. He loosened his grip on the coat when his mother kissed Francis farewell. He had no idea when he'd see him again.

The next day, when John went to Uphall, he almost crashed into his uncle Richard who was striding out of the yard, head down and oblivious of anyone in his path. John heard him grumbling to himself as he barged past.

'Sorry, John… didn't see you. Are you alright?'

John nodded.

'Listen, when you grow up, be careful. Make sure you let your parents know when you're courting.'

John's face was vacant.

Richard gave a half smile, removed his hat and plonked it on John's head. 'There, you look like a man already.'

'I'm only eight.'

'Yes, I know, but you will be a man one day. Well, I'm going back to Carnaby now. If you go in the kitchen, beware—your grandmother is in a foul mood. I should never have come home for Mothering Sunday. I've just stirred up trouble.' He took back his hat and ruffled John's hair as he left.

John stood for a moment in the middle of the yard, puzzled by his uncle. Suddenly, his grandfather shot out of the house, followed closely by his grandmother. They were yelling at each other. He had no idea what had upset them, though he heard Richard's name mentioned. When they turned back to the house, he remembered why he'd come. He wanted to see if the piglets had been born.

The sow in question wasn't with the others; she'd been moved into the sty. He found Dickon leaning over the half-open stable door keeping an eye on her.

'John, thoo's too small to see properly. Stand o' this stump o' wood.'

He joined Dickon and leant over the door. 'Grandma's upset,' he mumbled.

'Oh, aye, that she is. It's Richard that's set cat among pigeons. Says 'e wants to marry a lass an' live

206

i' Bridlin'ton. Tha gran'mother's allus been fond o' Richard—she won't want 'im livin' that far away.'

John wasn't listening; he was more intent on the sow. He thought her behind looked very peculiar.

'I think a piglet's coming out,' he gasped.

'Nay, lad, not yet, but she's about ready. When thoo sees 'er backside swollen an' red like that, it won't be long.' Dickon brought fresh straw for the sow and poured food in through a chute. 'I reckon she'll farrow in a few days. I'll let you know when.'

Three days later, the sow began to gather mouthfuls of straw and used her feet and snout to make a nest in one corner. Soon, there wasn't a scrap of straw left anywhere else—it was all in one pile. She began to pace around in circles and, when she refused the food offered, Dickon told John it was another sign that her time was near.

'We must be very quiet,' Dickon whispered. 'She mustn't be disturbed. Don't make any noise or she might go mad an' kill 'er piglets. Thoo can stay an' watch as long as thoo doesn't frighten 'er.'

John rested his chin on the stable door and waited. Before long, the sow ceased her pacing and flopped down on her side in the straw. She stretched out her back legs and panted. All at once, she pulled her back legs up to her stomach and strained. A piglet popped out headfirst. It looked so easy. Every fifteen minutes or so, another piglet came out and, after each birth, the sow swished her tail. Soon there were four white piglets suckling at the nipples. Then nothing happened.

'Is that it?' asked John. 'Only four?'

'Nay, lad. Let's go an' 'ave summat to eat an' come back later. She just needs a rest. I reckon there'll be more. She's lyin' very still.'

When they returned, they found another piglet had been born, and she was pushing out number six. It didn't seem to bother her which way they came out, head or tail first.

'It's like shellin' peas,' Dickon whispered as another two followed at ten-minute intervals. The straw was wet through with blood and fluids and bits of placenta as the ninth piglet slid out. The sow then got up and waddled away to urinate before going back to the nest of straw. There she suckled the piglets while she ate the placenta.

'That's that then,' announced Dickon. 'Nine piglets i'n't bad. I know she's finished, but we mustn't disturb 'er. We don't want 'er to eat 'em.'

John was horrified at the thought. He held his breath, bewitched, as he stared at the piglets. They suckled happily, each to their own nipple. Only the last piglet, much smaller than the rest, was not suckling; it hadn't even moved.

'What's up with that one?' John whispered anxiously.

'I reckon it's runt o' litter. It'll not live long. Best leave it to die i' peace.'

John could not take his eyes from it. He remembered his brother often called him by that name—runt. He couldn't just watch it die.

'Let me have the runt. I'll look after it.'

'Thoo doesn't know what thoo's lettin' thassen in for.'

'Please,' John begged. 'Please! I'll do extra work... I'll do anything.'

When Dickon saw a tear slip down John's cheek, he hadn't the heart to deny him.

'Stay 'ere then while I fetch it.' Making no noise, he opened the door and trod softly into the sty. He scooped up the runt and passed it, cold and shivering, to John outside.

'Rub its chest—it'll 'elp it breathe.'

'It feels so cold.'

'Never mind, stick it down tha breeches. That'll soon warm it up.'

'What?'

'Thoo 'eard me. Stick it down there where it's warmest.'

Without further question, John slipped the almost lifeless piglet down his breeches, leaving its head poking out. He listened carefully to Dickon's instructions on rearing it; they came with a warning.

'And don't get too attached to it. If it does live, it'll 'ave to join rest of 'em one day. Aye—an' be treated same.'

John left the yard, proud as any new father, cradling the piglet against his bare stomach. Against Dickon's advice, he'd already given it a name. The sow was called Queenie, so the piglet was to be Prince.

Dickon watched John walk slowly down the hill. He was already regretting what he'd done. He shouldn't have let his heart rule his head. The runt could hardly be kept as a pet in the house, and God knows what William and Mary would say.

Chapter 29

Both John's parents objected to the piglet. Mary passed a weary hand across her forehead. She hadn't wanted any more children, and certainly didn't look forward to more broken nights feeding a runt.

'Oh John, I have enough to do without seeing to a weakling pig.'

'*I'll* see to it. *I'll* feed it,' he promised.

That didn't satisfy his father. 'What are you going to do with it if it lives?' he demanded. 'We're not having a pig rooting round the house. It's not like having a pet dog.'

Young William added his reservations. 'Yes, and what about Stina? Why should she have to share the house with a pig?' He knelt down by the dog and whispered into her ear. 'We've already got one runt in the family. We don't want another, do we?'

The two younger boys were curious. On seeing the piglet's head poking out of John's breeches, Richard wanted to hold it, and when he heard it was called Prince he begged their father to keep it.

'Alright,' he agreed and, while the boys fussed around John, he turned to Mary. 'You'll see—the pig won't survive the week. It'll be a good lesson to the boys. They'll soon learn.'

John fed the piglet with milk from a cow that had just calved, and kept it in bed with him to keep warm. This wasn't such a good idea. In the morning, the mattress was smelly and wet.

Mary held her nose as she put the mattress out to dry. 'Now see here, John, we can't have this. It stinks to high heaven. From now on, if you want it in bed with you, you'll have to tie a wad of cloth round its bottom and rinse it out every morning.'

That night, Prince's lower body was wrapped up like a baby and, like a newborn, it couldn't drink much at a time. John found he had to feed it three or four times during the night. In the daytime, he laid it in a basket packed with wool by the fireside and then, to keep the pig out of draughts, he put the basket on a stool.

After just a few days, even his parents had taken more interest in the piglet and now hoped it would thrive. Only young William remained cynical.

'It'll never grow up,' he sneered. 'And, if it does, we'll make sausages.'

John paid no heed. His face was transformed whenever he nursed the pig, and his parents were proud of the way he'd persevered.

Once Prince had survived that first week, Dickon called in to give more instructions. It was already growing well yet still had to be kept warm.

'Just feed it three or four times a day now. An' if thoo feeds it late at night, then that should last it till mornin'. Thoo needs more sleep. Thoo looks worn out.'

The piglet could also be given a little water to drink, and John should try to wean it off the bottle by putting milk in a bowl.

The second week was trying in a different way. The piglet did not take readily to drinking from a bowl, and kept spilling the milk. By the third week though, it would eat food mashed up with milk and water. It also ran about the kitchen squealing and chasing after the dog. It gave no one any peace.

'That pig is gettin' spoilt,' Dickon pronounced when he next visited. 'Let it outside more, John. Let it root i' garden.'

'No!' Mary shrieked. 'I can't have that. Listen, John, I'll put up with this chaos in the kitchen so long as you promise to return the pig to Uphall before May Day.'

'Aye,' agreed Dickon. 'That's probably fo' best, an' don't forget—yon piglet 'as to be castrated before it gets any bigger.' He didn't add that it was to prevent its meat tasting musky.

'It won't 'urt 'im much... 'ardly at all,' Dickon explained. 'It's done i' blink of an eye. Listen, I've got me knife 'ere. Why not get on with it now?'

Young William grinned. Keen to watch, he followed John and Dickon into the garden.

Dickon said he didn't need any help, and sat down on the chopping log with the piglet tucked under one arm. He took out his knife.

'Don't look at me like that, John. It'll be fine.'

He laid the piglet across his knee and made two quick cuts. John flinched as it squealed, but Dickon had already pulled the testes out through the sac and cut the cords before the piglet or John knew anything else. He tossed the bits onto the grass and asked John to fetch honey from the kitchen. When John returned, Dickon smeared a gob of it over the wounds.

Young William was disappointed by the speed of the process. He lowered his gaze, poked the tiny wet bits with his boot and called Stina over to eat them. As he watched her lap them up, he saw John trying not to retch. He approached Dickon with a sly smile.

'When are you going to put a ring in its nose?'

'Not yet. We'll wait till it's at Up'all.'

John, as William suspected, hated the thought of a metal ring being forced through Prince's snout.

He grabbed Dickon's arm and implored him not to do it.

'Sorry, lad, but we 'ave to, otherwise it'll root up our pasture an' our crops.'

John ran into the house in tears, and got little sympathy from his parents. They were too busy discussing the latest rumours in the village. Apparently, the new vicar, since he'd become curate at Speeton, might be coming to live in Reighton after all. John didn't understand why his father looked so alarmed; it was something to do with having to move things quickly out of Speeton church.

At Uphall, Francis Jordan was anxious. He was a churchwarden for the year, and the vicarage had been empty for two years. More to the point, it had been neglected and was in need of repair. As soon as William arrived in the yard, he pulled him to one side.

'Listen, if that new vicar moves 'ere, we're i' trouble. It's not just vicarage that worries me, it's that tea stored i' Speeton church. Thoo knows all about it, so I don't care 'ow busy we are—that tea must be shifted. An' thoo, with all thy connivin', must see to it.'

William scratched his head. As a lenient and obliging customs officer, he did not want to be too involved. 'I'll see what I can do,' he replied with little confidence.

Instead of heading to the top open fields, he went in search of Matthew Smith. He guessed he'd find him in the pasture by the cliffs. Sure enough, Matthew was there supervising fence repairs. William hailed him as he strode across the new spring grass.

'This pasture's in good condition,' he said as he approached, 'and I hear you've plenty of calves this year.'

'It's true. This year should be the best yet. But, come on, what's your problem?'

William looked out to sea, avoiding Matthew's steady, suspicious gaze. Cobles were scudding over the waves in the bay, the stiff breeze filling their tan sails; to him, they appeared carefree.

He sighed. 'It's about the tea hidden at Speeton. The vicar might be living here soon. He'll get to know of it, or he might even find it. Who knows how he'll react?'

Matthew winked, unconcerned. It was as if he'd already made plans. 'The moon's in its last quarter. The tea will be moved just before midnight in two days' time. Make sure you're there on watch.'

Two nights later, William was standing on the hill overlooking Speeton church. He could see nothing below. There was no moon, and the darkness enveloped him like a cloak. The only sound came from the lapping of the tide. After a while, he picked out the jangle of harnesses. Below him were shapes, blacker than the night, moving towards the church. He preferred not to know who they were or where they went afterwards. Having heard of a riding officer from Flamborough, a Thomas Whitehead, who was rumoured to be conscientious, he glanced around in each direction. There were no ominous flickers from warning lights so he presumed all was well.

He loitered awhile until the anonymous figures below disappeared into the village. It should have been a relief when it was over, and yet he shivered at the thought of what he'd do if things went wrong. He was in such an unfair and precarious position. 'Damn Matthew and the free traders,' he cursed under his breath. He thought of Lumley and the young man's troubles. Maybe, he decided, his own life would be easier if he resigned his post.

By the time he'd walked back to Reighton, he'd changed his mind. It was better, he argued, to know what went on and, besides, there were benefits... like the brandy and the annual pay. He decided to work for the customs a little while longer... maybe another year or so.

On the morning of the piglet's return to its natural family, John spent ages feeding it. He scratched its ears and rubbed its back until young William warned him he'd rub holes in it. John wondered how this might be possible, but stopped rubbing just in case. When he started kissing it, his brother lost patience and stomped out of the house with Stina.

John felt his mother's arm around his shoulder.

'Don't let him upset you,' she said as she gave him a squeeze. 'I'll come with you when you take Prince to Uphall, and Richard and Matthew will want to come too... won't you boys? They both love this pig of yours.'

When the time came, the piglet struggled so much in John's arms that they had to put it on a rope and walk it up the hill. They met Dickon waiting for them in the Uphall yard. He took the piglet from John, led it to the sty, untied it and pushed it in. As they watched to see how the other pigs would react, Dickon reassured John that it was for the best.

'A pig needs to be a pig. It's no use it bein' treated like kith an' kin.'

John nodded and fought back his tears. His pig cowered by the wall and looked lost.

'Don't forget, John, thoo an' tha brothers can always come an' see Prince anytime. It'll remember thee, so don't worry.'

Mary sighed. She knew the pig would be fattened up like the other hogs to be slaughtered later in the year. Also, Prince would have to be ringed soon.

Young William found out when the ringing would be done. He'd seen the blacksmith curving the nails in readiness, and he was determined to be present when Dickon performed the deed.

When his mother heard of it, she found John some work to do at home so that he wouldn't fret. With luck, he wouldn't even know about it until it was over.

On the appointed day, young William set off at a run for Uphall with his dog Stina leaping and barking alongside. He was looking forward to the event and the chance to tease John later with all the gory details. When he found his uncle Thomas with Dickon, he was told to stand out of the way if he wanted to watch. Stina sat at his feet, alert as ever, her ears pricked.

Thomas restrained the first hog. He held the jaw secure with a pair of tongs while Dickon greased the awl. Then, in an instant, Dickon pressed the spike through the middle of the snout.

The pig let out such a loud, high-pitched screech that young William put his hands over his ears. It must have hurt a lot because the pig snorted and gasped for air as if in shock. It was almost human in the way it reacted. Even the dog was affected. She lay flat with her head between her paws and began to whimper.

Young William bent down to stroke her head. 'There, there, it's alright.' But it wasn't alright. The pig recovered a little and began to breathe easier, yet a nail had still to be pushed through. William tensed as Dickon placed a curved nail into the hog pliers. The nail was held in place over the snout and then it was clamped shut to make a ring. The pig squealed as if being slaughtered.

Each time Thomas grabbed another hog, young William prepared himself for the ordeal. He clenched his fists and tried to look as if he didn't care, but the ensuing squeals were always terrible. He'd never have guessed the rings would cause so much pain. Stina couldn't bear it either. She was quivering against his leg.

'I'm sorry, Dickon,' he lied. 'I've just remembered mother wants me at home.' With that lame excuse, he rushed from the yard and never did see Prince ringed.

He calmed down once he reached St Helen's Lane. He stopped, knelt down and wrapped his arms around the dog. Hugging her tightly, he kissed her soft, black head.

'I'll never hurt *you*, Stina. No one will ever hurt *you*, I promise.'

Chapter 30

The rumours continued about the new vicar leaving Filey and coming to Reighton, yet nothing was confirmed. No one, not even Robert Storey or the churchwardens, liked to question him directly and, so far, John Sumpton had given no indication of a move. Keen to know why the rumours had started in the first place, William called on the blacksmith.

Phineas Wrench was busy repairing hinges. The shed was stifling, though the doors were wide open and, even with his sleeves rolled up and his shirt loose, the blacksmith looked most uncomfortable in the heat.

William didn't waste time with polite greetings. He asked him straight out about the vicar's intentions.

Phineas stopped hammering and frowned. 'I only said what I'd 'eard. It's not *my* fault if it comes to nowt.'

'Usually, you hear right.'

Phineas put down his hammer and rolled up his sleeves further as if for a fight. 'Look, I can't always be right. God knows what's i' vicar's mind—I certainly don't.' He began hammering again. Above the noise he shouted, 'Why don't you ask Mary? It's wives often know what's afoot.' He stopped work again and tapped his nose with his finger. 'They know plenty, but they don't always let on.'

William took the advice and asked Mary.

'I can't help you,' she confessed, 'though I bet there's someone who *will* know—Stinky Skate. He'll be round here tomorrow with his fish. He's bound to know what's going on in Filey.'

The next day, Mary saw the pedlar limping along the lane, getting too old now to be tramping round the countryside. She called him over and did her best to ignore the smell as he approached, grateful that it wasn't high summer for then he stank of crabs. The basket weighed heavy on his back, and he winced in pain as he swung it to the ground. Feeling sorry, and eager to ask questions, she invited him in for a drink.

Glad of the rest, he slumped at the table.

Only the youngest boy was at home and wrinkled his nose at the fishy stink that had suddenly pervaded the kitchen.

'Matthew, go and play in the parlour, there's a good lad.'

As soon as he'd gone, she poured the pedlar a beer and began to wheedle out information.

'So—I expect you're still doing a good trade?'

'Mustn't grumble.'

'I expect you see our vicar sometimes in Filey, do you?'

'Only o' Sundays, i' church.'

'I mean, do you ever meet his family... like when you sell fish?'

'Nay, but I see their kitchen lass. Always of a Friday she's sent out to get a codlin' or a few dabs.'

'Does she mention her master and mistress? Are they happy in Filey? Or do they perhaps think of moving here?'

'Ah, well, there's been some goin's on. Between thoo an' me, it's vicar's wife who's master. She can't abide to leave.'

'I've never been to Filey. Is it a large vicarage they have there?'

'Oh, aye. Not just bigger than 'ere i' Reighton—there's a garden wi' trees an' all sorts. An' there's a great big brick wall round it. It's very grand.'

'No wonder she doesn't want to leave then.'

'She likes to think she's o' good terms wi' Richard Osbaldeston. 'E lets 'em live there. Nay, they'll not be movin', not while John Sumpton's still curate there.'

Satisfied with her information, Mary let the pedlar finish his drink in peace. She gave him a slice of curd cheesecake, and looked forward to telling William the news.

The villagers most involved in the smuggling took the news about the vicar as a good omen. They also thought it boded well when, towards the end of April, Matthew Smith's wife gave birth to twins. He'd fetched a midwife from Filey, a Mrs Foster, who despite her experience was not as friendly or as comforting as Sarah Ezard had been.

Both baby girls were small and weak. As they were deemed unlikely to thrive, Ellen wanted them baptised there and then, yet the vicar was in Filey.

The midwife, after another close inspection of the twins, assured Ellen that they'd survive the week at least.

The babies were christened the next day and, in deference to the Smiths, the vicar offered to carry out a brief service in church. Although it was a Wednesday, many attended. William and Mary took their family dressed as if for a Sunday. The boys fidgeted, miserable at having to be in their best clothes and in church on such a sunny day.

'We won't be here long,' Mary whispered.

John had heard that the twins were very small. 'Are the babies like runts?' he asked loudly.

Young William began to giggle.

'Shush, you two,' Mary snapped. She was ashamed, yet he was merely saying what everyone thought. Perhaps her brother's good fortune was running out.

Robert Storey, standing near the font with his wife, believed that the tiny babies were God's judgement on a family getting above itself. He didn't voice this opinion to Elizabeth, being Matthew's sister, but Matthew was too proud for his own good. Her brother had been lucky so far with five children already, and he'd made money on his South Sea Company shares, or maybe from the smuggling. Yet, mixing with the local gentry and buying more land was like tempting a downfall.

As everyone left the church, William glanced at the tiny twins, Mary and Martha, cradled in Matthew's arms. Apart from the one great loss of young Mary, he could count his blessings. Each of his sons was healthy. Even John could do a good day's work if given simple instructions. His wife had escaped major accidents and ill health, and even his own troubles as a customs officer had not ended too badly. So far, so good.

When the twins survived the rest of the spring, William and everyone else felt the babies were out of danger. The summer weather would see them thrive, and then they'd be strong enough to face the winter. It was good news, yet in early summer William heard an unsettling report, not about Matthew's offspring, but about an assault on an excise officer in Driffield. This time the blacksmith had all the facts.

'Thoo'd better watch out, William,' he taunted. 'That excise officer was afraid for 'is life. Men were armed wi' great clubs an' found out where 'e lived. They warned 'im they'd knock 'im on 'is 'ead an' kill 'im if 'e didn't stop seizin' their goods.'

'It wasn't that young Lumley, was it?'

'Nay, someone called George Parkin. Never 'eard of 'im before.'

Though glad it wasn't Lumley, and relieved that Driffield was far away inland, William was alarmed enough to do fewer patrols on the cliffs and concentrate his energies on Uphall and farming. He knew that double-strength brandy was still being brought in and diluted at Hunmanby to drinkable proportions, and he suspected the apothecary there was selling on French perfume. Good luck to them, he thought. The weather was fine and dry, and he wasn't going to spoil a good summer by worrying over things he wouldn't or couldn't prevent.

William threw himself wholeheartedly into the haymaking that year, surprised to gain so much pleasure from physical exhaustion. One evening, satisfied with another long day's strenuous work, he strolled home very late from Uphall. He took deep breaths of the cool night air, and inhaled the aroma of new-mown hay. Cattle were lowing occasionally from the pasture, and it was so still he could hear frogs croaking in the distance.

Suddenly, an owl flew past. It tore him from his trance and, for some reason, he thought of his lost daughter. He wondered what young Mary might have looked like now had she lived—probably very bonny and full of fun. He stared at the darkening sky, remembering how he'd shown her the constellations. Somehow, he'd never found the time to teach his sons. Maybe it didn't matter. The boys would learn enough working at Uphall. He continued his walk home, content with life for a change. If he still had his daughter, then he'd have counted himself truly blessed.

The fine, dry weather led Francis Jordan to consider making a better pigsty. Initial discussions began in the yard with Dickon and William.

'It 'as to be warm an' free fro' draughts,' Dickon reminded them.

'Aye, we know all that,' Francis replied, annoyed at such an obvious statement. 'It's whether or not to build floor below level o' yard. If it's below,' he argued, 'it'll be warmer i' winter an' cooler i' summer.'

'Aye,' grumbled Dickon, 'but what about floodin'?'

William smiled. He enjoyed listening to the pair.

'Why, that's no problem,' Francis answered back. 'All we need do is build a big step i' doorway.'

'I think,' interrupted William, 'the floor will have to be ground level anyway—it's too hard to dig out.'

His father conceded that point, and the next debate was over whether to use cobbles and chalk, or clay and gravel for the walls. William was content to listen; it was preferable to thinking about the latest smuggling runs.

When he went home for supper, he asked John if he'd like to help build the new sty. John was delighted, thinking that Prince would live in it. William didn't remind him that Prince would never live long enough to need permanent housing.

Young William knew very well, though, and made cruel jokes about black puddings, all lost on John.

'Right,' interrupted his father, '*you* can help build the sty too. *You'll* be doing most of the carrying.'

The next day, William borrowed five donkeys from the brewers at Hunmanby and led them down to the beach with his two sons. Dickon and Thomas were already there with the Uphall mule and had begun to collect large cobbles. The boys held the donkeys still while the stones were heaved into panniers. It amused William to see Dickon fussing, making sure the loads were balanced. He was as daft about animals as old Ben had been.

When the baskets were full, John was allowed to lead the first donkey and make his way slowly back up the track to the top of the cliff.

'We'll have a drink at Uphall,' his father announced. 'We'll have a bite to eat and then we'll sort the stones.'

The refreshment was brief. They gulped down their beakers of small beer, stuffed cheese into their mouths, and soon went back to the yard to face the pile of cobblestones.

Young William complained straightaway. 'It's too hot for me, and I can't lift them anyway. Can't I do something else?'

'Thoo an' John can work wi' Thomas if tha likes,' said his grandfather. 'Thoo can see 'im make lime mortar. Go on. If thoo watches carefully enough, thoo'll be able to make it thassens one day.'

The boys stood by while their uncle Thomas measured out lumps of quicklime and made a ring of damp sand around the pile. Young William thought his uncle was being too fussy, like his mother with one of her recipes. He grew more interested when his uncle added water to the quicklime and it began to bubble.

'Careful, lad,' Thomas warned, 'it's hot. Don't touch it. Keep out of the way while I mix in this sand.' He stirred it round and added more water. 'There, that's done. Now, you lads can fill yon buckets with it and take it to the new sty. Keep it coming as we work. Don't be slack.'

Young William yawned. It was such dull work. He reckoned it was a job for a simpleton.

'Hey, John,' he teased, 'I bet you can't carry two buckets at a time.'

'I think I can.' John picked up his brother's bucket as well as his own and struggled to the sty. The buckets banged against his legs, and twice he slipped.

His grandfather saw what was going on. 'Never mind, John, thoo's doin' a good job.' He gave young William a stony glare and added in a louder voice, 'Better than some!' He turned back to John and told him he could have a rest. 'Thoo can see us build instead. Thy brother can do all carryin'.'

John saw the way the men chose the stones that would best fit together, and watched in awe as Thomas pushed mortar into the gaps.

The hot, sunny weather was ideal for the lime to dry so that the bases of the walls were finished by sunset. Francis stood back to admire the work.

'We'll 'ave chalkstones delivered i' mornin' an' then we can finish off them walls. Then we'll get Bart Huskisson to put up roof timbers, an' then we'll get a thatcher in. Clay floor'll 'ave to wait.'

William blew out his cheeks. 'That's a relief. I don't fancy digging a pit in this heat.'

'It's not just that,' said Dickon as he mopped his face with a grubby neckerchief, 'we'd not get a spade through. Ground's far too 'ard an' dry. We'll 'ave to wait till it rains.'

The rain never came. The month of June was so dry and hot that a major fire broke out in Bridlington. William told his family about it over supper. 'They say it was the timber frames of the houses. They caught fire and there were no fire carts to put it out. I think as many as fifty bays were lost.'

Young William spluttered through a mouthful of mutton stew. 'I wish I'd been there to see it.'

His father clouted him across the head. 'Don't be so heartless. A fire can happen anywhere. Think yourself lucky. We don't have fire carts either.'

William could never understand how he could have raised such different sons. If only John had more brains...

'I hear your brother John's been out gathering elderflowers to make a cordial with your mother, while *you've* been out killing birds we can't even eat.'

'So?' Young William grumbled. 'And now the whole house stinks of elderflowers. Even my shirt smells like a girl.' He received another clout.

When the rain did come in July, it came in buckets. The fields grew sodden, and a poor harvest was predicted. The rain, however, allowed the Jordans to make the clay floor for the new pigsty. William and Thomas dug a pit until they reached clay, and then took off their boots and trod around in it.

'Come on, John,' William shouted. 'Get yourself in here and trample it with us. We want it smooth, then we can use it.'

Young William jumped in the pit as well. Finally, there was a fun job to do. At first, he enjoyed the feel of the clay between his toes, but he soon tired. The heavy clay stuck to his feet so that he could hardly lift them.

'Father,' he whined, 'my legs are aching...'

'Oh no, you're not getting out,' said his father, 'not until the clay's ready. Stop sulking. It'll do you good.'

Eventually, the boys were hauled out of the pit, and the clay was spaded up onto a muck cart. The boys followed the cart wearily to the Uphall yard where the clay was mixed with gravel and lime. Dickon appeared with a bucket of bull's blood to make it congeal, and the men spread it over the floor of the new sty.

Dickon beckoned to them. 'Come on, lads, get i' there wi' tha father an' uncle. Stamp it down flat.'

Though tired, the boys joined in and began to paddle down the clay. When Thomas saw them flagging, he sang a bawdy song. The singing took everyone's minds off the coming harvest, and the numerous verses and choruses kept them going until the job was done.

August and September brought no reprieve from the rain. It stayed wet, and the harvest was one of the poorest for years. As Mary feared, the pigs, including Prince, would be needed for food more than ever.

Chapter 31

1723-24

In November, the newly hired hands arrived at Uphall with their master. William happened to be in the kitchen with his mother, and was most surprised to find his two exiled brothers among them. They were unusually subdued.

His father shot a glance towards the fire where his mother had just taken the pot off the hook. 'Dorothy... look who I found... tha long lost sons. Thoo'll be pleased to 'ave 'em back, eh?'

Richard and Samuel stepped forwards as their mother rushed forward to greet them.

She was overjoyed to have Richard home again, her youngest and favourite. 'Oh, tha father didn't let on who 'e was bringin' back. Thoo's both so tall I can scarcely reach up to kiss thee.'

Samuel blushed, and the reason soon became clear. 'There's someone I need to introduce,' he murmured. 'I've persuaded Father to hire this lass here.'

His mother turned to see the girl, assessing her in an instant; she was typical of many a country lass, broad in the hips and with full, rosy cheeks. She also had dark blonde hair curling from the sides of her bonnet.

'This is Elizabeth Clarkson,' Samuel explained. 'As you know, I've worked for her family on their

Hunmanby land these past three years. Well, we've been courting for over a year now.'

'Not another one! Thoo's as bad as Richard. What is it wi' thoo lads? Why court so young?'

He took hold of her hand. 'Listen, Mother, please don't start—she'll suit Uphall. She's a good worker, and she's used to tending a large family.'

His father looked sheepish and avoided his mother's eyes. He couldn't divulge what he'd learnt from Richard on the way home, that their youngest had obtained a licence to wed in Bridlington, and that the marriage was likely to take place at Christmas. Worse still, Richard might work there for a ship's chandler. He tried to placate his wife.

'Our Samuel's been savin' up to get wed. At least 'e 'asn't squandered 'is wages, 'asn't spent 'em o' cockfights an' gamblin.' He didn't know what else to say and wandered towards the door with an excuse about seeing Dickon. His wife could deal with the new servants.

She narrowed her eyes but said nothing more for now. She beckoned everyone to sit at the table, and then went back to the fire to finish preparing the dinner.

Samuel could sense his mother's mood by the way she threw salt into the stew. He didn't want the new servants to witness her bad temper so early in their stay.

'Mother, *I'll* show the new workers around the yard, and show them where they'll sleep… save you a job.' He led the newcomers back outside, leaving William and Richard alone with their mother.

William could hardly believe that Samuel had the nerve to bring his sweetheart to live at Uphall. 'I wonder what Thomas will say when he finds out. Richard, did you know about it?'

Richard nodded. He looked at his mother, her back turned to him. He thought to tell her about his own wedding while William was there; his mother might make less of a fuss. He stood up and moved towards the fire.

'Mother, you remember I was courting too?'

She spun round, her lips tight.

'I'm getting married... this year—probably late December.'

Her face darkened. 'Does tha father know?'

When he nodded, she threw down her spoon and stormed out of the house.

He and William exchanged glances. 'Poor Father,' they said in unison.

William hoped for more information from Richard, but found his brother awkward and difficult to engage in conversation. Usually young men were eager to talk about their future wives. Samuel was besotted with *his* woman. Maybe Richard would say more once his mother had grown accustomed to the idea. It was natural that she'd been shocked. After all, he'd always been her favourite, and she'd want to keep him at home.

When William could discover no more than the girl's name being Hannah, he shrugged and left the kitchen. Outside, he bumped into his father loitering by the barn door and surveying the damp, gloomy yard.

'You've seen Mother then?' William asked.

'Aye. She's now gone off to see to chickens, God 'elp 'em. Can't say I blame 'er fo' takin' news so badly. She won't want Richard to live so far away.'

'I can't fathom him or Samuel.'

'Nay, neither can I,' his father confided. 'Richard won't look at me straight.'

'No. He was the same with me. I suppose we'll get to know one day why he's not telling us more.'

His father frowned. He took his pipe from his pocket and prodded it at William. 'Let's 'ope we're not last to find out. Summat's up wi' that lad.'

William strode home with his news. 'You'll never guess who turned up today at Uphall,' he shouted as he walked down the passage to the kitchen. 'Samuel and Richard are back. And Samuel's courting. His girl is going to live with him there.'

'I bet your mother won't like that,' Mary said as she put the bowls onto the table.

'There's worse—Richard's getting married—and in Bridlington of all places.'

'Richard? Never!'

'It's true. It's odd though—he won't talk about it.'

'You know he's always been different,' she added as she fetched the spoons.

'Has he? You've never said that before. What's different about him?'

'Oh, it's just something...' She paused with the spoons in her hand. 'He's not like the rest of you. For a start, he gets on so well with your mother. He's more... how shall I put it? He's gentle in his ways.'

William bridled. 'What are you implying?'

'Nothing.' She began to set out the spoons. 'Forget it. Any minute now, the boys will be in from the garden. It's women's gossip, that's all.'

'Women—ha!'

No more was said.

John visited Prince every day. The pig knew its name and always trotted up for a tidbit. John did not think for a moment that his pig would be killed. Yet it was winter now, Prince had fattened up nicely, and pig-killing time was fast approaching.

Early in the morning on the appointed day, his mother offered to walk to Uphall with him. The lane was white and sparkling with frost as they set out with half a warm potato for the pig. John held her hand, explaining that he didn't want her to slip.

As they began to walk up the hill, he peered into her face. She couldn't bear to see the hurt.

'Oh, John, please be brave. You must have known we couldn't keep him as a pet.'

He didn't answer. He stopped walking and stood in front of her to bar the way. 'It's not fair,' he cried through his tears. 'Prince is not like other pigs. He's *my* pig.'

She put her hands together as if in prayer. 'Please, John, I'm begging you. Don't make this harder. Listen—don't spoil Prince's last morning. You can talk to him and feed him, and then he'll think today is just like any other day.'

John wiped his face with his coat sleeve and sniffed. 'But I love him.'

'I know.' She stood up and took his hand again. 'Come on, John. Prince will be waiting for that potato. Best get it to him before it goes cold.'

When they reached the sty, the pig was already at the half-open door expecting food. As soon as John entered, Prince barged into his legs, almost knocking him over. He held out the lukewarm potato and, while he watched the pig eat, he scratched him behind the ears. Tears scalded his cold cheeks as he realised this really was the last time. Too upset to speak, he kissed Prince's head. Then he turned away, ran from the sty and didn't stop.

Mary shut the door after him. 'Sorry, Prince,' she whispered and wiped her eyes. As she walked home, she vowed never to have a runt in the house again.

That winter, John refused to eat anything connected with pork. Luckily, young William went out at dusk seeking woodcocks. He knew the male bird would fly over its territory at this time, and sometimes he managed to hit one in mid-air. More often, he had Stina search for the birds as they were well camouflaged against the earth and bracken. Despite his hands growing numb with cold, the birds were worth the effort; they were plump and made a decent roast dinner. Both parents sang his praises for, thanks to him, the family now had a little variety in their meals.

Christmas was a poor celebration at Uphall, and not just because of the food shortage. Richard was to be married on St Stephen's Day and, partly due to the state of the roads, his mother forbade anyone to attend. She spent Christmas Eve plucking chickens, ripping out feathers with a manic force, occasionally spitting out bits of fluff. Her husband avoided her, so did the maids, the hired lads and the rest of the family. It was the most miserable Christmas they'd ever spent.

In the new year, Dorothy Jordan continued to fret over the food supply. Also, she was increasingly unhappy at having Elizabeth Clarkson under the same roof as Samuel.

'Mark my words,' she grumbled to her husband. 'They'll be up to no good. They'll be at each other as sure as bees make 'oney.' She made every attempt to ensure the couple were not left alone, but the winter was cold and the nights were long.

By spring, there was an extra twinkle in Elizabeth's eye, and Samuel gazed at her like a moonstruck calf. His mother's fears were justified in late April when she overheard Samuel singing Elizabeth's praises.

'Oh, Thomas,' he said with a sigh, 'she's lovely. When I hold her close she's so soft, and as sweet as fresh hawthorn buds.'

She doubted this very much and butted in. 'Aye, she may look an' feel sweet... beware though—she might be more like a nettle. If thoo's over gentle with 'er, thoo'll get stung.'

Samuel blushed. The advice, asked for or not, was too late; yesterday, Elizabeth had told him she was with child. He'd keep that quiet for now.

That spring, Matthew Smith celebrated his twins' first birthday. Against all odds, and thanks to Sarah Ezard's tonics, the tiny girls had survived the winter. Equally important, even though basic foods were running low, their mother was still able to provide them with enough of her own milk. Despite all the care given, the twins remained small for their age, and few villagers expected to see the girls outlive their childhood. Many were convinced they'd only lasted this long because Ellen had not cut their hair.

When Mary was queuing for water at the well, she heard the women discussing the twins' chances. Young Emma Huskisson thought the danger lay in the damp mists that crept up and over the cliffs.

'Nay,' countered the blacksmith's wife, 'it's teethin' that's main risk.'

'Aye,' the older women murmured. They knew one had to take extra care at teething time.

Martha Wrench wanted to make sure that the younger women understood the full implications. 'Tha knows tha must preserve every single tooth. If Ellen doesn't, then she must destroy 'em utterly on a fire wi' salt.' Martha was enjoying their rapt attention. 'If she lets just *one* tooth get lost,' she warned, pointing a finger, 'then bairn won't live long.'

As everyone eked out their dwindling food supplies, different birds arrived in the area. The dotterels always stopped off to feed on the fields at the top of the village, and young William was ready. They were so easy to catch that he could dispense with his sling. He could simply walk right up to one and grab it. At times, he had so many birds that he went round the village selling them.

Instead of praising him, his mother was furious. 'How could you! How dare you ask for money!'

'But I only charged a penny a pair.'

'And what have you done with the money?'

He shrugged, unwilling to reveal his hiding place in the cowshed wall.

'I think you should give back the pennies and say you're sorry.'

'Uncle Thomas was proud of me.'

'Never mind about Uncle Thomas. Do as I say.'

Reluctantly, he obeyed. Later that day he was seen slouching through the village returning the pennies and mumbling his apologies.

Samuel bided his time. Each week he put off telling his mother about Elizabeth. As he was plucking up courage in early June, a severe thunderstorm hit Reighton, and hailstones wrecked the crops; he couldn't face giving his mother more bad news. He put it off until later in the month, thinking if he left it any longer, it would be too late; everyone would notice.

He took the opportunity one morning to speak to his mother while she was out feeding the hens.

'Mother, I'd like to be married next month.'

'No one gets wed i' middle o' summer,' she protested as she threw out the scraps. 'Unless...' She spun round to face him.

'Yes,' he nodded with a grimace, 'we need to be married soon.'

She bit her lips and then sucked in her breath before speaking through clenched teeth. 'Let God be me witness, I did me best but thoo young uns will not be stopped. 'As thoo nowt to say?'

'We're not sorry. We want to be wed.'

'Well, don't go thinkin' thoo can stay an' live 'ere afterwards. This 'ouse won't abide two mistresses.'

He'd expected that reaction. 'We've already thought about it. Lizzie says we can go back to live in Bartindale. Her father will be glad to have me work on his land again, and there's a cottage empty.'

'So—it's all settled then?' She began to march back to the house.

'If you like,' he said, rushing after her, 'we'll move there straight after the wedding feast. You *will* be giving us a feast?'

She'd already slammed the door on him.

Chapter 32

Dorothy Jordan complained for days about the coming wedding. She didn't even stop at bedtime, and her husband was losing patience.

'Just remember,' he said as he lay down beside her, 'last Jordan weddin' i' Reighton were some year ago. It's time we 'ad another.'

'Aye,' she replied, 'an' it was i' depths o' winter as all weddin's should be. If it interferes with 'aymakin', there'll be trouble.'

'Nay, it won't interfere, woman. Why, we won't mow yon old meadows till last week i' July. It's time we celebrated summat. Everyone's spirits need liftin'.'

'Tha knows I can't be supplying same amount o' food as other years.' As she rolled away from him she added, 'But I don't want to appear begrudgin'.'

'That's more like it, there's a good lass.' He turned over as well, a wry smile on his face.

On the day before the wedding, Dorothy Jordan made her final preparations. She worked with an ill grace at having to complete all her tasks in one day, tomorrow being a Sunday and a day of rest. She blamed the vicar; he wouldn't ride out midweek to conduct the service. She sent her two maids out to milk the cows, and told them to pick wild raspberries on their way back. When they returned, she had them mash the fruit in a large bowl. Once satisfied with the pulp, they sieved it, and she added sugar. Then she poured in the foaming fresh milk.

'Get tha fingers out,' she warned them. 'No tastin' yet.'

She lifted a jug of ale and poured it gently into the bowl, mindful it didn't froth over the rim.

'Now, I'll just add a sprig o' rosemary an' thoo can take this syllabub to milk'ouse to keep fo' tomorrow. I'll wash out yon posset pots ready. All thoo needs do i' mornin' is whisk it up.'

The girls pulled long faces. The bride wouldn't be helping, and the whisking would be hard work.

'Oh an' don't forget to cover it tight. There's that many flies around.'

'We won't,' they replied in unison.

They carried away the bowl but, before they covered it, they took a spoon and tasted the froth. The syllabub was so good they dipped the spoon in deeper and drank as much as they dared. Wiping the foam from their lips, they walked innocently back to the kitchen.

In the afternoon, Richard arrived from Bridlington, minus his wife. He was keen to run in the traditional garter race although, as a married man, he would not aim to win. It was another hot day without a cloud in the sky. Thomas and Richard gathered at the church with the Uphall lads and the youths of Reighton. They were to race from the church gate to Speeton mill and back. Richard assumed that his brother would win; Thomas had always been a good sprinter and would be keen to win the right to remove the bride's garter.

Francis Jordan, in a large straw hat, lined them up in a haphazard fashion across the main street. He warned them that folk would be watching at various points along the way to prevent cheating. Then he waved his hat and they set off.

Most of the lads sprinted up the steep street and then along the lane towards Speeton. They soon flagged, but Thomas and Richard, who'd paced themselves better, began to catch up. The two brothers ran side by side until they reached the mill. By then they were in the lead, and the rest of the way was downhill. Thomas, the better runner, could easily have won the race yet allowed Richard to forge ahead.

On the approach to Reighton, Richard couldn't slow down on the hill. His long legs took him further into the lead. As he skittered round the corner by Uphall, his arms waved like a windmill.

The villagers, lining the street on both sides, saw he was out of control and couldn't stop. Dickon and William were the first to rush forwards and grab him as he was about to fly past the church gate.

'Whoa, Richard!' they yelled, and were pulled along by his momentum until their feet acted as brakes.

Close behind, Thomas ran into them. 'Well done,' he panted, 'well done, brother.' He slapped him on the back and gave a wicked grin. Tomorrow, Richard would have to remove the bride's garter. He couldn't wait to see how his brother would perform.

The next morning, Richard hung about the kitchen, half helping and half in the way. His mother was still venting her displeasure about the wedding. He had little choice but to listen patiently to her complaints.

'Thoo young uns these days don't do owt like i' my day. Why, when tha father wooed me, we only saw each other once a month. Aye, things were done prop'ly then. 'Ere, pass me yon knife.'

As she cut a curd cheesecake into slices, she paused and waved the knife at him. 'An' tha father even wrote a letter to me father askin' permission to start seein' me with a view to marriage. Aye, it were diff'rent then.'

A knock on the door interrupted her. Richard opened it to find the bride's family waiting outside. The Clarksons had arrived in plenty of time to have a late breakfast at Uphall.

While Richard left to find his father, Dorothy bade them sit at the table and help themselves. Her first impressions were favourable. The mother and daughters wore identical straw hats—not homemade ones either but made of the finest straw, and the brims were lined with blue silk. They wore pretty linen prints over hooped petticoats, and they wore gloves. The father and sons were equally well dressed. They were also well mannered; they didn't grab for food as her sons might have done. Perhaps Samuel had made a good choice of bride after all.

At that moment, the bride entered the kitchen. Elizabeth was dressed in green and wore a garland of rosemary. She was the epitome of womanhood and rude health and yet Dorothy thought the choice of green rather bold, even shameless in the circumstances. Elizabeth certainly needed no luck with fertility. Dorothy assumed the Clarksons had guessed the reason for the July wedding, yet they were smiling, overjoyed to see their daughter again. She cleared her throat.

'Thoo looks lovely, Elizabeth. Come an' sit wi' tha fam'ly. Richard'll be back soon... to take tha garter.'

Elizabeth had no sooner sat down than Richard entered with his father and Thomas. She leapt up, curtsied and then raised her gown to reveal the fancy garter above her left knee.

Thomas whistled.

Richard gulped. 'But I thought it was to be removed after the service, after the dinner even.'

'Not today, it's Sunday,' his mother explained. 'Less o' that kind o' thing i' public, the better.'

'Go on, lad,' encouraged his father. 'Get down o' tha knees an' untie it. It won't bite.'

Richard blushed and knelt down. He'd never been so embarrassed. His fingers were carrots as he fumbled to undo the slender band.

Thomas stood by with his hands on his hips. 'Good God, Richard! I'd have had it off by now.'

'There,' mumbled Richard, 'it's done.' Still blushing, he held up the pretty red and white band for all to see.

Elizabeth clapped her hands and grinned. 'An' guess what—I found a spider i' me gown this mornin'.'

'Oh, that's very lucky,' her parents cried.

Dorothy thought that, with marrying in summer, the bride would need any luck she could get. Disguising her thoughts, she smiled and introduced her husband and sons properly to the Clarksons. The formalities over, she bade them start on the breakfast—thick collops of cold bacon and the cheesecake.

The bridegroom, Samuel, was kept out of the way. Dickon had him in the barn sorting the trestles and benches to be set out in the yard. He also had him sprinkling the ground with water to keep the dust down. It was going to be another hot, sultry day.

'Best get thassen ready,' Dickon said once everything was prepared. 'Wash i' yon trough to save goin' i' kitchen. Tha brothers'll be comin' fo' thee soon to walk to church.'

The last thing Samuel wanted was to have words with his mother in the kitchen. He persuaded Dickon to go in and fetch his clean shirt. As soon as he was ready, he waited at the end of the yard for his brothers.

Thomas joined him first, also in a clean white shirt. 'Richard's nearly ready at last. You won't believe what he's wearing. He must spend all his wages on clothes.'

Samuel had often wondered why Richard loved to dress up so much. Most men were much more comfortable in their working gear, and yet his brother seemed more at ease in his best clothes.

'Maybe it's living in Bridlington makes the difference,' he decided.

At that moment, Richard appeared. He almost strutted towards them and, after planting his feet in front of them, he twirled round.

'What do you think?'

Samuel didn't know where to start. Richard looked as if *he* should be the groom. His white linen shirt had voluminous sleeves and he wore a blue waistcoat to match his breeches.

Richard opened his waistcoat further. 'How do you like my shirt?'

Samuel was speechless. The shirt was so ornate that it projected from Richard's chest.

'And look at his stockings,' Thomas prompted.

Pure white, like the shirt, the stockings had fine, scroll-like patterns. Richard pointed to the way they were fastened with a tiny buckle.

'Good Lord, Richard! You ought to be in London, not Reighton.'

Richard beamed with pleasure. 'On to the church then. Let's go.'

When William arrived with his family at the church gate, Mary was the first to notice Richard standing by the porch in the full sunlight. He was a vision in blue and white as he waved his hat at her.

'You see Richard there? See what I mean?'

William had never seen his brother so smart or so confident. 'Wonders will never cease,' he mumbled. 'And you boys, don't gawp. Keep your mouths shut. Just smile and walk past.'

As he led his family down the aisle to their box pew, there was much whispering and turning of heads. He caught the words 'sickle and scythe'. He could guess what people were saying: 'wed 'twixt sickle an' scythe, bride an' groom will never thrive.'

The congregation was restless, and the vicar looked uncomfortable. He'd had a miserable ride from Filey with the sun full in his face. His wig was awry and, though he wiped his face from time to time, his forehead remained shiny. Before he began the usual Sunday service, he explained it would be curtailed in order to conduct the marriage ceremony.

Mary whispered to William, 'And I bet the wedding will be brief too. He doesn't know Samuel, and probably suspects the reason for choosing July.'

Throughout the marriage vows, William noticed that Mary, interested as she was in the bride, couldn't take her eyes off Richard. He tried to remember what his youngest brother had been like as a boy. He'd never really had the chance to know him because he'd left Uphall to be married when Richard was just two years old. Suddenly, Mary was nudging him again. The service was over.

Due to the food shortages, John and his brothers threw petals rather than grain over the couple's heads as they left church. When their grandfather raised his gun and fired, John held his hands over his ears, and then scrambled with the other children to snatch the feathers as they floated down.

As soon as people had congratulated the couple, Francis and Dorothy ushered the guests to the Uphall yard. They shooed the chickens from their path and pointed out where everyone was to sit, making sure that the hired labourers and the unrelated villagers were seated far away from the main table.

As everyone took their places on the benches, the kitchen maids rushed out with plates of food, and carried across the jugs of ale that had been kept cool in the shade.

Mary was not surprised to see very little bread set out; flour had been short this year. There were no pastries at all. There was no bride-cake and no gingerbread either. To compensate, great chargers had been loaded with slices of ham and beef. There were also plenty of cheeses.

'Keep your hands on your knees,' she instructed her boys. 'The vicar will say grace and then you must wait for the toasts.' She saw one of the maids standing to attention by the milkhouse; she'd bring out the syllabub as soon as grace was said.

When Dorothy Jordan whispered into the vicar's ear, he stood up and clapped his hands to get attention. When that didn't work, she banged a pewter mug on the table.

'Grace!' she shouted. There was an immediate hush.

'O Lord,' began the vicar, 'bless our food today that we may eat and drink, not to ourselves alone, but to your glory. Help us to be yours in body and spirit, in all our work and all our refreshments—through Jesus Christ, Amen.'

A loud amen echoed around the tables as the maid carried across the tray with its four posset pots. The pots were full of syllabub, frothy from the whisking. They were also cool from being stored in the milkhouse. Everyone watched as the bride and groom were handed a pot to share; their parents also shared a pot while the vicar had one to himself. When ale had been poured out for the other guests, Francis Jordan stood up.

'We're 'ot an' thirsty, so I won't make a big speech.' He acknowledged the cheers of relief and raised his posset pot. 'I just want to wish long life an' 'appiness to Samuel an' Elizabeth.'

'Aye, long life an' 'appiness,' the guests repeated. Mugs were raised and drained, and then the food was passed round.

It was the first wedding dinner that the boys had attended, and John still had his hands on his knees.

'What's the matter, John?' asked his mother. 'You don't have to eat the ham—there's beef too.'

'I'm waiting for the toast.'

Young William choked on a piece of cheese.

'That'll teach you to laugh at your brother.' She turned to John. 'There won't be that kind of toast—there's not enough bread to go round. Here, have a bit of cheese.'

While John ate, he kept his eyes on Samuel and Elizabeth drinking their syllabub. They sucked from the spout first, taking turns. Then they drank from the top. Even when they'd licked their lips, they still had foamy pink moustaches. He wished he could have tried some instead of his watered-down ale.

'Normally,' explained Mary, 'we'd have dinner in the barn. That's what we do in the winter.'

Young William frowned and asked with his mouthful, 'So why are we stuck out here?'

'Ah, well... maybe your grandmother thought it would be nicer to be outdoors like this.'

'She doesn't look very happy about it.'

'Oh, that's your grandmother for you. Perhaps she's hot. See—the vicar's had enough of the heat. He's saying goodbye already. He'll want to get back to Filey.'

As the vicar left, there was a general murmur of discontent from the furthest table. Sarah Ezard summed it up. She leant across the table towards Dickon.

'That John Sumpton doesn't care about us—only 'imself. 'E's killed two birds wi' one stone 'avin' this weddin' on a Sunday. We can't 'ave our entertainments on a Sabbath, but 'e'll still get 'is weddin' fee.'

'Aye,' Dickon announced to the whole table, ''e's that mean 'e'd skin a fart.'

John, ignoring the sudden burst of laughter, was gazing at his uncle Richard who was walking round the tables helping to pass food and pour more ale. 'He's pretty,' he observed.

Young William almost choked again. 'Don't be daft. You don't say that about men.'

'No, you don't,' Mary agreed. 'Though you *can* say he's very handsome, like Samuel there with his new wife.'

Her eyes lingered on the main table. Among the bride's family was another daughter, a girl on the verge of becoming a woman. Her own daughter would have been fifteen this year. Like young Mary, the Clarkson girl had chestnut hair. Curls escaped from beneath her hat in just the same way. She even twitched her nose from side to side when her brothers teased her. Mary saw that William's eyes were also drawn to the girl. She tried to get his attention but he was lost in thought. She left it a while before trying again. When she pulled on his arm, he turned on her, a wild look in his eyes.

'Can't a man have any peace? What's the matter with you?' He rose from the table. 'Come on, we've had enough of this eating and drinking, we'll go home.'

There was to be no dancing or singing because it was a Sunday, and many had already begun to leave.

The boys turned to their mother, hoping to stay longer, but she shook her head.

'Come on, boys,' she said quietly, 'we'll say thank you to your grandmother and wave goodbye to Samuel.'

William did not join his family in saying farewell. He avoided the main table and strode from the yard with his head down, scattering the chickens.

Mary was afraid. She dreaded to think what had so unsettled him. 'When we get home,' she warned her children, 'you'd better keep out of your father's way.'

Chapter 33

After the wedding, William had realised how tired he was. Perhaps he'd overdone it this year. After all, he wasn't a young man anymore. The trouble was that his labour was not going to be rewarded by a decent harvest. More often of late, he'd wondered why he bothered. Every year was a struggle. Mary had never questioned his poor temper at the wedding, and his unspoken thoughts about young Mary had added to his misery.

To crown William's growing despair, he heard that Matthew Smith had sold his 'Flamborough Lands' on the Moor to Reighton Manor. That land had once belonged to the Jordans. William now regretted that sale, for now it would make a fine profit. Perhaps Matthew would use the money as capital in a smuggling venture; it was certain he'd never tell William. It galled him to think that he and Matthew used to piss up the same tree. That had been in a former life, before the increase in smuggling, when Matthew had been simply another yeoman.

More troubling was that, with the free trade being so lucrative these days, violent attacks were becoming more frequent, or so he kept hearing from the blacksmith.

Phineas Wrench always seemed to know what went on. One evening, he hailed William as he caught sight of him passing the forge on his way home.

''As thoo 'eard latest?'

'What is it now?' William was impatient to get home for his supper.

'Trouble at Bridlin'ton. Thy fellow customs officers tried to board a boat, an' got assaulted.'

'They're not *my* fellow officers. I have nothing to do with them. You know I'm attached to Scarborough.'

'Well, funny thing is—sailors' boat were called *William an' Mary*. 'Ow's that for an omen?'

'So, what happened?' William asked wearily.

'Don't know details, but a bunch o' sailors are now i' York Castle.'

William turned to leave.

'Nay, don't go yet—there's more, an' closer to 'ome. Does thoo remember Andrew Briggs?'

'Of course. It was his dog got poisoned.'

'Well, I 'eard 'e'd been attacked. Aye, i' Flamborough an' by Flamborough men.'

William sucked in his breath and shook his head. He wondered if it had anything to do with Matthew and his smuggling friends. He preferred not to know. 'I've heard enough, thank you very much. Goodnight.'

As William left the forge, Phineas shouted after him. 'Sleep well then... if thoo can!'

Robert Storey heard of William's low spirits. He observed his brother-in-law closely and decided to intervene. One evening, as the sun was setting, he knocked on William's door.

Mary let him in, guessing his intentions and knowing that William was in the kitchen with no escape. She sent the boys to bed, and joined the men at the table.

William prepared himself for a lecture, one probably about misfortune being the school of virtue. He thought to get in first and explain his state of mind, reckoning a quote from the Bible wouldn't go amiss.

'The work that is wrought under the sun is grievous unto me for all is vanity and vexation of spirit.'

'Ah yes,' replied Robert, 'though the ox, when he is weary, treads the surest. And let me remind you, William, the greatest evils are those within us, therefore take sanctuary in religion. Cast out an anchor for your soul, to keep it from shipwreck. Reach out to God. He is the fountain of all good, but you must reach out with your own hands. Come on, let God be your friend and save you.'

William rubbed his hands up and down his face. He took a deep breath, about to vent his frustration. Just in time, he glanced at Mary. She gave the slightest shake of her head.

He breathed out with one big sigh. 'Alright, I will try,' he agreed, more to appease Mary and get rid of Robert than for any better motive. He stood up to show that the visit was over.

'Very well,' said Robert, rising to his feet. 'I'll see myself out.'

Mary leapt up to usher Robert from the kitchen before William could change his mind.

As soon as William heard the door close, he sighed again, this time with relief. He'd got off lightly. As he looked at Mary though, he knew he couldn't talk to her about his feelings, nor the one thing they never mentioned.

As expected, the harvest that year was poor yet again. Despite the meagre yields, Robert Storey insisted that the correct tithes be stored in the vicarage barn. He took pride in supervising the church lands for the absent vicar, and even defended the man.

'I know he insists on living in Filey,' he argued, 'but we must render unto Caesar that which is Caesar's.'

The villagers complied, though with an ill grace.

In October, most of the cattle were killed or sold, and the vicar gave little comfort to his post-harvest congregation. William listened miserably to the nasal voice of John Sumpton as he read the familiar words from Isaiah.

'He shall feed his flock like a shepherd: he shall gather the lambs with his arm, and carry them in his bosom, and shall gently lead those that are with young.'

The words brought no reassurance to William. He felt that God had ignored them.

The vicar lifted his head and then intoned, 'Who hath measured the waters in the hollow of his hand, and meted out heaven with the span, and comprehended the dust of the earth in a measure, and weighed the mountains in scales, and the hills in a balance?'

William wondered, if God is so powerful, why can't He send some decent weather? It didn't seem a lot to ask when they were putting in all the hard work.

As if to make matters worse, the very next day, William hurt his back. He'd always prided himself on the strength of his body. Now he felt betrayed. He didn't know how it happened. One day he was fit and in full charge of himself, and then he'd just bent down to pick up his boots... and now he could hardly move.

The boys stared at him with wide eyes for they'd hardly ever seen their father ill. They watched him crawl to bed and lie flat on his back.

Their mother didn't bother to undress him but covered him up to keep warm. She pulled out the chamber pot so that it was handy.

'I'll let you rest. I'll see if you need anything later. Come on boys, we have chores to do. And don't look so sad, John, your father will be fine tomorrow.'

For what seemed like hours, William gazed at the tiny window, watching the light change as clouds drifted overhead. He listened to women chattering as they passed the house on their way to the well. Sometimes they lowered their voices as they went by, maybe having a gossip at his expense. He closed his eyes to concentrate on the sheep bleating on the moor. Perhaps John would help the shepherd grease and mark them. It would soon be time to send out the ram.

He must have dozed off for he suddenly realised the room was quite dark. As far as he knew, no one had visited or been to see why he was not at work. He was alone and hungry with a sickening ache across the middle of his back, and there was a long evening ahead.

The gloom suited his mood. He allowed himself to dwell on that Clarkson girl, the one he'd seen at Samuel's wedding. In a dreamlike state, he imagined young Mary as a bride; how proud he'd have been walking her to the church. She might have married into the Smith family and shared their new wealth. As his thoughts became ever more fanciful and muddled, he fell asleep once more.

At different times during the day, Mary had checked on him to see if he needed anything, yet each time she'd found him fast asleep. She let him be, and it was evening before she went in with a candle and a plate of food.

'Oh, good, you're awake at last. I've brought you supper. Look, here's cheese and ham. I've cut it up so it's easier for you, and there's a mug of beer—I'll leave it here where you can reach it. Thomas is in the kitchen. He heard about your back so he's come to see you. He'll help you eat and drink.'

William was glad it was Thomas and not Robert Storey. He needed good cheer as well as distraction, and who better than Thomas. His brother did not disappoint.

After asking about William's back, and drinking half his beer, Thomas was full of the latest news about the notorious London burglar, Jack Sheppard. The blacksmith had been informing the village for some time of the burglar's arrests and subsequent escapes; the methods of breaking out of jail were so ingenious that he'd become a legend. Most people now wanted the man to escape.

'Somehow,' said Thomas excitedly as he sat on the bed, 'Jack's always managed to get tools smuggled into his cell. You might remember how he escaped in spring with his woman, Bess. He did it twice—even broke through the cell wall. They found saws and all sorts of stuff on his bed afterwards.'

William sighed. 'He's an amazing man, that Jack Sheppard.'

'Well, seeing as he was free again, he burgled a draper's shop on the Strand, and this is the sad bit—one of his fellow criminals betrayed him. Can you believe it! So, he was arrested again and put in Newgate prison. They were going to execute him, but yes, you've guessed it, he escaped again. This time he cut through a bar in his cell. He walked straight out with a cloak hiding his face. Ten days later, they re-arrested him, this time in possession of two silver watches. Of course he was sent back to Newgate. And William, you'll not believe it… this time he was chained to the floor of what they obviously thought was a secure room.'

William raised his eyebrows in anticipation.

'Yes, you know what I'm going to say. He had a small file hidden in a Bible and, not only that, two more files, a chisel and a hammer were concealed in the bottom of a chair. Apparently, he undid his chain and handcuffs with a crooked nail between his teeth. Then he broke through six locked doors and climbed from the prison tower onto the roof of the next building.'

William rolled his eyes in disbelief.

'But that's not the end by any means. Ten days later, they arrested him again, this time in a Drury Lane gin shop. And he was dressed like a lord, wearing a wig and in a fine black suit. He even had a diamond ring on his finger.'

'I suppose he went back to Newgate?'

'Yes, back he went, now quite the hero. I heard at the trial there were so many crowded into the courtroom that people got hurt in the crush. A constable even had his leg broken.'

'But you're going to tell me he escaped again.'

'No, sadly, I'm not.' Thomas stood up and moved towards the window. He peered out, deep in thought. It was now pitch black outside. He turned back to William.

'You know Jack Sheppard was only twenty-two years old when he was taken to be hanged at Tyburn... just a year older than Richard.' He pulled a newssheet from his pocket. 'Listen, I'll read it to you.' He smoothed it out and began.

'At the place of execution he behaved very gravely, spoke very little and, after some small time allowed for devotion, he was turned off the scaffold, dying with much difficulty, and with uncommon pity from all the spectators.'

'Fancy him being so young. A rogue certainly, but what a character. I've never heard anything like it.'

Thomas folded the newssheet back into his pocket. 'Well, I can't stay here all night. You get yourself better.' He pushed William's supper nearer to him and stood up ready to go. 'Have you sent Mary to Sarah Ezard yet? She'll have something for your back.'

'No, I'm hoping I'll be better after a night's sleep. I'll see how I am in the morning.' He used his elbow to try a more comfortable position. He grimaced in pain and gave up.

Thomas watched him grit his teeth as he lowered himself down gingerly. 'You don't look too good. You'd best get help sooner rather than later.'

'Maybe. Thanks for coming, Tom. If I'm still laid up tomorrow, then I'll get help.'

Chapter 34

When William was no better the next day, Mary brought Sarah Ezard. Both women blamed overwork and the damp autumnal weather. Under Sarah's supervision, Mary made a hot poultice using crushed linseed and brown paper, and as soon as William was comfortable, Sarah fed him her posset of ale and comfrey roots.

'That'll ease tha pain.'

He sighed. The instant relief from the poultice was bliss. 'I feel a bit better already.' His muscles relaxed and, after drinking the posset, he began to fret about the jobs that he'd missed.

'I should be helping to finish the ploughing, and there's the muck to spread, and then there's all the gear and the carts to store away for winter.'

Sarah clicked her tongue and shook her head. 'Now, go steady. It's a good rest, think on, that'll 'elp most. Mary'll change that poultice later, an' thoo can 'ave a sleep.' She left the house, confident that William would soon be out of bed.

Two days later, William could walk about the house. He shuffled along stiffly, but by the end of the week, he was able to recommence light work.

Sarah Ezard's ointments and medicines were in great demand as autumn turned into winter. Despite her arthritic hands, she worked long hours at her table, chopping and grating roots and grinding various seeds into powder.

One morning, just before Christmas, she was busy in her kitchen warming up a pot of turpentine. Instead of concentrating on the job, she began to think about William. His bad back might be a symptom of whatever else ailed him. She'd noticed him at the wedding feast, gazing at that sister of the bride. The reason was obvious; the girl reminded everyone of young Mary.

As the fumes from the turpentine filled the kitchen and dulled her senses, she became lost in a reverie about William and his daughter. She stopped stirring the pot, and realised too late that the liquid had overheated. She tried to lift it off the fire, but the handle was so hot it burnt her fingers. She dropped it, and immediately the turpentine burst into flames. Burning liquid splashed over her and across the floor. When her gown caught fire, she fell backwards, hitting her head on the edge of the table. Semi-conscious on the floor, she stared in horror at the flames. How had it happened? Why hadn't she used the sand bucket?

She struggled to get up and put out the fire, but the reeds on the floor were now catching. She could only watch as her bunches of dried herbs hanging from the rafters began to smoke and then burst into flames. She flapped at her smoking clothes yet merely succeeded in burning her hands and arms. In a panic, she threw herself onto the floor and rolled over, frantically trying to smother the flames. She caught hold of her cloak on the back of a chair, wrenched it off in desperation and wrapped it over her head.

By now the whole kitchen was ablaze. The dried herbs acted as tinder and set fire to the roof timbers. Black smoke began to seep through the thatch and was seen at last by the neighbours. Bart Huskisson was the first to arrive. He charged in to look for Sarah and found her lying close to the door, barely alive.

He carried her outside and laid her on the wet grass and mud, her clothes still smoking.

Phineas came running to help. He rushed indoors, but it was too late to save anything. All the herbs had gone up in smoke; all the jars and bottles had cracked in the heat. The medicines were lost.

By now, half the village was standing around shouting for water. Francis Jordan arranged a chain of buckets from Uphall, and the men began to douse the smouldering thatch.

Martha Wrench knelt by Sarah's head and gently removed the cloak from her face—the only part not burnt. Sarah was still conscious. Between gasps of pain, she whispered something about poultices of oatmeal and groundsel, but Martha could tell at a glance that Sarah's injuries were way past the help of poultices. Cloth had adhered to her arms, and the exposed skin on her legs looked like melted candle wax. The smell was disturbing, like roast pork. Suddenly, Sarah began to shiver violently.

'Oh, God! Fetch laudanum!' Martha yelled to anyone listening. 'Someone must 'ave it. Someone—rush to 'Unmanby an' get it. Quick!'

Bart Huskisson brought a wide plank of wood, and they managed to lift Sarah onto it and carry her into his house. There the women eased off the still-smoking garments, ignoring Sarah's cries as they cut away the cloth where it had stuck to the skin. They were aghast to see the burnt flesh on her arms, raw like fresh meat.

When they covered her with a clean sheet, she cried out again. The slightest of touches gave her such pain, and all they could give her was water sweetened with honey.

Within the hour, Thomas Jordan had brought laudanum; Sarah could find relief at last.

Dickon visited her and was shocked at the extent of the burns. He reported his worst fears to Uphall.

'If she's as long out of 'eaven as tomorrow morn I'll be surprised.'

This news shot round the village, and so did the worrying fact that all Sarah's salves and potions were gone. Poor Sarah couldn't even treat herself.

She suffered for two days, relieved to some extent by strong doses of laudanum. Everyone in the village called to see her, each with their own reasons to be grateful for her existence and equally helpless and afraid for the future. Sarah survived one more day before lockjaw set in. She died in a drug-induced coma.

Mary and her sister Elizabeth went into Sarah's cottage to see if anything could be salvaged. It reeked of charred wood and had the unpleasant lingering smells of overcooked pork, burnt lavender and turpentine. It was hard to believe that such a cottage, once so welcoming and packed with herbs and medicines, could be destroyed so quickly. The smoke, if not the fire, had ruined everything of value. The two women stepped over the debris and walked into the garden at the back. They stood gazing at the herbs and beehives.

Mary sighed. 'We need to tell the bees.'

'I'll do it later, and Robert will say a prayer.'

They turned to leave. There was Sarah's body to prepare for burial.

Mary chewed her lip as she took a last glance at the blackened cottage. 'It's going to be hard to wash her, what with her skin being so damaged.'

Elizabeth rebuked her. 'Sarah always did it, no matter who it was or whatever state the body was in. We must do the same—attend her with the greatest respect.'

Mary began to cry. 'She delivered my children.'

Elizabeth put an arm round her sister and walked her home.

Later that day they returned and, with great tenderness, they helped the Huskisson women to clean Sarah and lay her gently in a woollen shroud. They prayed, placed candles beside her and left her looking as peaceful as in sleep.

The next day, Mary felt the need to keep busy, and so made special biscakes for after the funeral. She asked John to help her, knowing he liked to get his hands sticky. There was plenty of cold porridge kept back from breakfast to mix with the dough, and she had jars of chopped apple preserved in honey. To get young William and Richard out of the way, she sent them to fetch more water.

She added the sticky pieces of apple to the dough and the porridge, and mixed them together well.

'Now, John,' she said with a smile, 'here comes your favourite part. Start getting handfuls and make them into little balls. Let Matthew sit next to you so he can learn.'

John grinned and rolled his sleeves up.

'Wait—are your hands clean?'

He waved his slightly grubby hands in the air.

'Alright, they'll do.'

John's fingers were soon clagged together with the mixture, yet he carried on making the balls and passing them to his mother who rolled them in dried oats. When he wiped his sticky hands down his shirt, she didn't get cross.

She even let Matthew help to sprinkle sugar over the cakes before they were baked.

'After the funeral, you two can eat some, but John, don't try any ale—it'll be too spicy and you'll burn your throat.'

On the night before Sarah's funeral there'd been a fall of snow. In the morning, the trees had a light dusting of white, and there was a heavy frost on the ground. As the day progressed, the snow began to thaw and, without a breath of wind, drops of water hung from the trees and hedges.

Dickon and the Jordan men helped carry the coffin into the church. They rested it on the low trestle at the front where the vicar stood waiting.

John Sumpton had known Sarah Ezard for a few years now and understood her importance. Once everyone was seated, he chose to read from a psalm.

'Ye that fear the Lord, praise him… For he hath not despised nor abhorred the affliction or the afflicted; neither hath he hid his face from him; but when he cried unto him, he heard.'

Mary knew that Sarah had never turned her face away, had always been there for them as a confidante and healer even when suffering herself. Yet who would deliver the children? She felt John quivering, so put an arm round his shoulder to comfort them both.

He was shivering with cold and trying not to cry. He could not believe that Sarah's dark, warm cottage was gone, or that he'd never be able to bury his face into her apron and smell her lavender and liquorice again.

Dickon, sitting with the hired lads, wondered stoically if he'd be next.

'We brought nothing into this world,' he heard the vicar say. 'And it is certain we can carry nothing out.'

Yet, Dickon thought, that's not true. Sarah Ezard left behind the love of a whole village; it wouldn't die with her passing. People would remember her good deeds, but would they remember him?

When everyone shuffled outside into the cold December air, people were torn between wanting to pay their last respects and needing to be indoors by a warm fire, preferably with even warmer ale. The sky had already turned a sickly, dim yellow by the time Sarah was lifted from the coffin and lowered into her grave.

John thought she looked strange, all bagged up in the sheet with just her face poking out. It wasn't the Sarah Ezard he knew. To confuse him more, the vicar seemed happy that she was dead.

'We give thee hearty thanks,' John Sumpton cried, raising his arms to the sky, 'for that it hath pleased thee to deliver this our sister out of the miseries of this sinful world.'

Robert Storey said 'Amen' to that.

John grew more alarmed as he listened to the vicar.

'We who are still alive, and are left, will be caught up together with those in the clouds—to meet the Lord in the air.'

John had visions of being caught alive in one of his brother's snares and then thrown into the sky. He peered up at his mother who was crying silently. She held his hand and forced a smile. He gazed around and saw other women weeping. So the vicar was wrong. It *was* a very sad thing to die. Even the men wiped their eyes.

Mary gripped John's hand harder and tried to stem her tears. Without Sarah, who would be their healer now?

Chapter 35

1725

The winter following Sarah Ezard's death proved to be very mild and dry as if she was helping folk from beyond the grave. This was just as well since no one in the village had stepped forward to replace her. William had wondered if his mother might take her place, though to a lesser extent. She'd kept her family's recipes and always had her own ointments and tonics. He waited until she seemed in a reasonable mood before he dared broach the subject.

She shook her head immediately. 'I'm not 'avin' folk wanderin' in 'ere any time they like wi' their broken bones an' what not. Any good wife 'as 'er own medicines passed down from 'er fam'ly. Aye, an' keeps a stock o' what they need. I look after me own—an' our lads an' lasses who work 'ere. I'm doin' nowt else.' When William raised his eyebrows, she added, 'An' don't expect me to 'elp deliver bairns neither. I've 'ad enough wi' me own.'

William was saddened although not surprised. The villagers would be left to their own devices.

The showers came in mid-April, as was natural, yet the rain did not stop. The first casualty of the wet spring was one of the twin daughters born to Matthew Smith.

What had appeared as simply a normal cold had turned into whooping cough, and the little girl, who was almost two years old, had violent coughing fits. Matthew would never have gone to Sarah Ezard anyway, preferring to pay an apothecary or a physician, but this didn't stop people debating the correct cure. Most agreed that drinking thyme tea and rubbing goose fat on the chest would see the girl right. The older generation had different ideas as they walked back from church through the light drizzle.

'Boil a mouse an' make mouse tea,' said the blacksmith's wife.

'Nay, that won't 'elp,' argued Dorothy Jordan. 'Thoo needs to skin a field mouse an' bind its warm skin, furry side down, against bairn's throat. Do it fo' nine days. Aye, an' make a mouse pie to eat.'

Dickon preferred spiders. 'Fo' kink-cough thoo 'as to find a dark spider i' bairn's 'ouse, an' 'ang it over bairn's 'ead. Then say three times, "Spider, as thoo wastes away, 'oopin' cough no longer stay." Then 'ang spider in a bag over fireside. When it's dried up, cough'll be gone.'

Dorothy Jordan smiled. 'Now then, if it's a spider cure tha wants, thoo 'as to put as many spiders in a small muslin bag as is bairn's age. Put bag i' bairn's mouth a while, then 'ang it above 'er bed all night.'

Matthew Smith and his wife overheard these 'cures' and, when a pedlar stopped by the next day and suggested catching a frog and putting it in a jug of water for their daughter to cough into, they felt it was time for more serious action.

Matthew rode to the apothecary in Hunmanby and returned with a tar concoction. He was told to heat it up for his daughter to inhale, and it would loosen the mucus in her chest. The coughing fits persisted though and, when his daughter began to choke and be sick with the effort, he decided to fetch a physician; the man could come and bleed her. His wife hated the idea but he persuaded her it was for the best; it would clear out the girl's infected blood.

When people saw the physician arrive, they stopped what they were doing and gawped. Unlike the local barber-surgeon, he was well dressed, had fine black boots and spurs and even wore a substantial wig. Martha Wrench was standing outside the forge, and it had just started to rain again. She chuntered to her husband as she went back inside.

'No wonder Smiths prefer *'is* treatments. It'll cost 'em though, tryin' to keep up wi' gentry.'

'Good luck to 'em,' replied Phineas as he brought down his hammer with a loud clang.

Matthew Smith led the physician into the parlour where his daughter, Mary, lay feverish in bed. Ellen was wiping the girl's brow while her other children stood by with anxious faces. She sent them into the kitchen with instructions to the eldest two to help the maid prepare dinner.

The physician opened his bag. He made Mary grip a pole in one hand, and waited for the vein in her arm to dilate. Then, very carefully, he made a quick cut and drew out ten ounces of blood.

She didn't cry but had a choking fit afterwards. When she could scarcely catch her breath, her lips turned blue and she fainted.

'Don't worry,' said the man as he packed up his bag. 'Your daughter should feel better in a day or so, or I can take more blood.'

Matthew paid him and trusted he'd done the right thing.

Less than two weeks before the twins' birthday, Mary's condition worsened. When she coughed, her phlegm was bloodstained and she struggled to breathe. Her parents were still so confident of her recovery that her death came as a great shock.

Ellen could not believe it; she'd always been in the best of health herself and her other children had never given her a moment's worry.

Matthew was stunned. Since he'd wed Ellen, he'd had one success after another. Now he felt vulnerable. His hand shook as he pulled the sheet over his daughter's face. No amount of money or good connections had prevented this untimely death.

At the funeral, his wife was sullen, still blaming Matthew's insistence on a physician. It wasn't bleeding the girl needed; she should have had something to clear her lungs. Mary had suffered needlessly.

Less than two weeks later, the family did its best to celebrate the other twin's birthday. It was an anxious time as Martha had always been the weaker of the two. The parents endeavoured to keep her free from draughts and damp air, but they could not keep her away from her siblings; five other children in the house would always pose a threat from one ailment or another.

To add to the Smiths' worries, the wet weather throughout May and early June brought an outbreak of foot rot in the cattle. While Matthew kept his stock on his own pastures, everywhere was sodden, and there was every chance his cattle would suffer too. The spongy ground softened the skin in their feet, and even a tiny cut was enough for infection to set in.

Each day Dickon ambled down to the common pasture with John to look out for limping cows.

'It's usually just one foot that's affected,' he explained. 'We'll 'ave to treat 'em wi' pine tar ointment.'

'Like when the horse was lame?'

'Good lad, aye, thoo's remembered.' He ruffled John's hair. 'Now, if cows are goin' to get better, they need to be kept o' dry ground for a few days. We'll 'ave to walk 'em to Up'all an' tend 'em there. That's a lot of extra work what wi' feedin' an' cleanin' out.'

John smiled and took Dickon's hand. 'I don't mind. The cows must get better. I'll bring Richard to help.'

The next day, Dickon, John and Richard led a couple of cows from the pasture to Uphall. What the boys hadn't bargained for was the rank smell of the rotting feet and the pus in the wounds. They held their noses while Dickon did the cleaning. After helping fetch straw for a while, they ran home to tell their mother. They shot through the door and along the passage to the kitchen.

'Mother, cows' feet stink like a poke o' devils,' they cried in unison.

'It's this blashy weather,' pronounced Richard with a serious frown. 'The cows get all blathered up. Dickon says that's why they're getting lame.'

'You two are beginning to sound like Dickon. I think maybe you're spending too much time with him. I hope you're not getting in his way.'

'No,' said John with a smile. 'He needs us.'

Many of Dickon's methods were based on superstition, but John and Richard couldn't tell one cure from another and learnt them all regardless. One day he took them to cut a piece of turf from the foot of the large apple tree at Uphall. He brought the turf into the fold yard and had the lame cows walk over it. Then he got Richard to climb the tree and hang the turf from the highest bough.

'It 'as to be largest tree an' 'ighest branch,' Dickon shouted up as Richard climbed. 'When turf dies off, foot rot'll go.'

Soon they were facing another problem. Many of the cows had loose bowels; their coats looked rough and they were losing weight. Dickon blamed the wet pasture ground and the large numbers of parasites the cows ate with the grass.

John was keen to report the latest to his mother. 'The cows are getting the squits now. Dickon says it's the plothery field to blame. We're trying another remedy tomorrow.'

The next day, John and Richard watched as Dickon carried out a box of old broken clay pipes. He crushed them up and used the powder to make a gruel for the cows. Then he put onions in various places around the cowshed. Still not satisfied, he hung up the lower jaw of a pig.

He apologised when he saw John's face. 'I'm sorry, lad, but cheer up, it's not Prince. Listen, we can't be over careful. I think I'll put a rowan branch above byre to keep evil away. There's maybe a witch out at Argam, or one even closer, that's causin' all this trouble.'

The vicar heard from Robert Storey about the strange 'preventions' and tried to instil in his congregation a more God-fearing approach. Dickon, however, was not taking any chances. Without Sarah Ezard's wormwood and vinegar mixture to dab on the cows' noses and mouths, he'd have to do his best with other means. He'd always believed in the efficacy of rowelling the cattle regularly to maintain their condition.

'Come on, lads, I'll show thee 'ow it's done.'

The two boys accompanied him and flinched when he made two small holes in the cow's dewlap. Then Dickon took a length of tarred cord from his pocket and poked it through the holes, leaving the ends free. From another pocket, he drew out a hagstone and tied the cord ends through it.

John could see the stone was weighty as it pulled on the cords. 'Doesn't it hurt?' he asked.

'Nay, lad. That stone'll keep witches away, an' cords'll draw any badness out. We 'ave to keep pullin' cords back an' forth. Thoo'll 'ave to 'elp—it needs doin' three times a day. We 'ave to keep wound festerin' to make sure all the pus comes out.'

'Won't they get smelly?' asked Richard.

'Aye, that they will. The smellier the better. Once we see good matter oozin' out, then I'll take out them cords.'

When they wrinkled their noses, he added, 'I tell thee what thoo can do—find me a four-leafed clover. We'll 'ang it above byre fo' luck. An' if all this won't work, I reckon we'll 'ave to light a need-fire.'

The boys frowned, puzzled by this new word.

'Aye, thoo's not lived long enough to see one. Sometimes, we 'ave a bonfire i' mid-summer to protect our livestock. An' if that won't work...' He bent down to whisper to them. 'I might steal a sheep from up o' moor an' bury it alive as a sacrifice.'

John gasped and shook his head, tears already in his eyes.

'I'm sorry, lad, I was forgettin' thoo's fond o' them sheep. Listen, I promise I'll never do that. Cheer up.'

As rumours of a need-fire spread through the village, Robert Storey made a point of talking to people to dissuade them from taking part; he hoped to convince everyone that it was a pagan idea. As Christians, they should shun heathen superstitions.

William Jordan, as a churchwarden for the year, was obliged to side with Robert Storey. He knew that most people couldn't care less about the arguments for or against, but for the need-fire to be beneficial, any other fires in the village had to be doused and only re-lit from the bonfire. Although it was summer and fires weren't needed for warmth, everyone used them for cooking; it would be an inconvenience to extinguish them.

Commonsense prevailed in the end, much to Dickon's disappointment. Robert Storey felt he'd triumphed for once, but his pleasure was short-lived. In mid-June, when the weather had not improved, Matthew Smith's other twin daughter fell ill.

When William heard about Martha's symptoms, painful memories resurfaced of his own daughter's last illness. It sounded like throat distemper. While Matthew's other children had sore throats, they soon recovered. Martha, though, had difficulty breathing, and she developed a fever.

Against Ellen's wishes once more, the physician came and took blood from the girl. Ellen refused to be party to such a treatment and left the room crying. From the kitchen she heard her daughter sobbing and asking for her. Suddenly, unable to bear it, she rushed back into the parlour and knelt by the bed. She held Martha's hot, damp hand to her cheek and kissed it.

Matthew stood to one side as the physician packed away his implements and prepared to leave. Ellen had begged him for days not to allow any bloodletting, and now, as he escorted the man out of the house, he was full of regret. He should have paid more heed to his wife and not forged ahead regardless.

Martha struggled to breathe for hours afterwards. She passed away in the night with both parents at her side.

When Matthew broke down in tears, Ellen ignored him. Full of self-blame, he held out a hand to her, but she turned away. He remembered how low he'd felt after the death of his first wife. He'd blamed God, and then his life had changed when he courted and married

Ellen. How wonderful his life had become. Now, with the death of both his youngest daughters, he feared once more that God had deserted him.

'Don't abandon me too, Ellen...'

At the girl's funeral, John Sumpton chose to read from Ecclesiastes Chapter Two. Matthew Smith was a successful man, now facing misfortune and, while the congregation did not wish ill on the Smith family, the vicar's reading was deemed appropriate.

'I made me great works; I built me houses; I planted me vineyards; I made me gardens and orchards, and I planted trees in them of all kinds of fruit... I had great possessions of great and small cattle... I gathered me also silver and gold... So I was great, and increased more than all that were before me... I withheld not my heart from any joy; for my heart rejoiced in all my labour... Then I looked on all the works that my hands had wrought, and on the labour that I had laboured to do: and, behold, all was vanity and vexation of spirit, and there was no profit under the sun.'

William sympathised. His own life, since the death of his only daughter, had been a struggle against despair. He thought back to the way he'd mistreated his wife and children, how he'd taken to drink as an escape from his misery. It was years before he could respect himself again. In a similar situation, Matthew might be humbled by his experience, or he might strive for greater prosperity. It rankled William to think that Matthew would most likely choose the latter, and even view success as recompense for his ill fortune.

Chapter 36

The rain continued throughout June and early July; it was the coldest summer in living memory. When haymaking was postponed, Richard even left his wife for a while to come back to Reighton and help the family; he knew that a poor harvest would mean the third in succession, bringing the real possibility of famine. Those involved with the smuggling also had a hard time; their pack animals sank in the mire, and mud splashed as high as the girths.

Dickon despaired when he arrived at the Uphall stable soon after dawn to find the mule chilled and sweating. He sought out William and led him straight to the stable.

'Just look at 'er,' he complained. 'I feed 'er an' brush 'er an' then she's misused be'ind me back.'

William scratched his head, knowing she'd been used to carry contraband. He pretended innocence. 'Perhaps it's that witch from near Argam that's been riding her all night.'

Dickon knew the truth and spat on the ground. 'Oh, aye, if thoo says so, that'll be it.' He began to rub down the mule, grumbling under his breath.

William took the opportunity to leave. On his way to the house, he noticed his youngest brother leaving the barn. Richard's face was flushed and he was smoothing down his breeches. Aye, aye, he thought, I bet Richard has found some lass in there. But it wasn't a girl that came out—it was one of the hired lads, Bullock Rob.

The sight gave William a jolt; he felt almost a physical punch in his stomach. He didn't know why it was such a shock since he'd seen how Richard was dressed last summer at Samuel's wedding, and Mary had hinted as much. All the same, he was shaken and unsure what to do. If he was the only one to know, then he could keep it to himself. He wouldn't tell a soul. It was best that no one knew, especially Robert Storey. If *he* found out, then who knows where it would end?

As Richard ambled past, William looked deliberately in the opposite direction. He told himself that he had far more pressing worries with the bad weather; Richard's business was his own. While he went about his work though, he kept thinking about it. At least he ought to let Richard know he'd been seen. He waited all day until he and Richard were alone.

Richard blushed when he realised he'd been found out. He avoided William's eyes and stared at the mud drying on their boots.

'I can't help it,' he mumbled. 'It's the way I am. I've tried to like lasses. I thought, if I married, I might cope better.' He raised his head. 'You know I even groped Emma Huskisson.' When William shook his head in disbelief, Richard dropped his head and murmured, 'I only did it to prove I could.'

William sighed and gazed at the distant cliffs. His brother would embarrass the family; worse still, he left himself open to blackmail.

'Listen,' he said, exasperated by Richard's revelations, 'if you carry on, you're going to have to be more careful. If *I* could catch you, as sure as eggs are eggs, someone else will, and they won't keep it to themselves. I know I shouldn't judge—I've been twice to court in

Beverley—but it *is* against the law.' When Richard looked so despondent, William reassured him. 'At least you can trust *me* to keep quiet.'

'Thank you, William.'

Richard did nothing to tempt fate in the village. Instead, he rode back to Bridlington. There were plenty of men there, and his work for the ships' chandler gave him plenty of opportunities.

Richard, at twenty-two years old, was no longer a gawky, clumsy youth. He'd grown tall and attractive. Women cast longing glances as he sauntered by, admiring his full thighs and his long legs in riding boots. Unlike his brother Thomas, who relied on swagger and a mischievous grin to get attention, Richard was languid in his manner and had an innate reserve. Whenever he had work on the quayside, he knew there'd be mariners willing to have a bit of fun up an alleyway. His good looks ensured that he never had to pay for it.

Richard became a well-known figure at the quayside inns. He never drank much, and kept his eyes open for the telltale signs of a likely encounter. It wasn't difficult; even those not normally drawn to another man would find themselves gazing at him. He never went home but that he'd enjoyed someone, and it was a different man each time. What he didn't know was that one of the mariners who arrived regularly from Hull had spied him in action with a fellow crewmember.

The mariner, Michael Watson, was disturbed as well as disgusted. Unnerved by his thudding heart, he convinced himself that it was the result of his passionate hatred of such unnatural acts. Yet he couldn't get Richard out of his mind and so, whenever his ship sailed to Bridlington, he made sure to frequent the same inn and alleyway.

At Uphall, Dorothy Jordan waited in vain for news of Richard's wife being with child. He'd breed such handsome sons. If only Thomas would settle down too, get married and work as hard as Samuel and Richard.

Thomas usually avoided extra jobs, yet on the day when Jack the shepherd announced that he was moving the ewes away from the lambs, he was one of the first to offer help. As he strode to the moor, he stopped at William's house to see if John wanted to join him. The family was just finishing breakfast.

As soon as John heard he could spend time with the shepherd, he leapt from the table and upset the milk jug. Amid groans from his brothers, he threw himself at his uncle and wrapped his arms round his waist.

'Alright, John, go steady.'

John turned his head to ask his parents. 'Can I? Can I go?' He was still clinging to Thomas.

His father nodded, but his mother shook her head. She frowned at having to be the one to speak sense.

'Look, John, it's not pleasant to see the lambs split from their mothers. You've been upset before by all the bleating.'

John knew she was right. He let go of Thomas, and his eyes filled with tears.

Thomas rested a hand on John's head. 'Never mind, cheer up. I'll come another day and we can help Jack do something else.'

'Yes,' echoed his mother, 'why don't you help the shepherd when he sees to the ewes. He'll be glad of your way with animals when they need a bit of milking.'

John wiped his eyes. 'Can I start helping tomorrow?'

His father rolled his eyes. He never thought to have a son so keen on sheep and shepherding.

The next day, John was the first out of the house. He ran barefoot up the lane, the ground wet from the night rain. He sped up the hill, past the church, past Uphall and then on to the top fallow field. Out of breath, he stopped at last and bent double with his hands on his knees. His lungs hurt and he had a sharp pain in his side. After a short while, he straightened up to see the morning sun shining in a bright blue sky. There wasn't a single cloud anywhere. He knew what Dickon would say, 'If it's early an' sun's too glary, rain'll come soon before afternoon.' Today, that was hard to believe.

He gazed across the field that had grown oats last year. Now all the village ewes were penned there and grazing on the weeds and oat husks. They bleated for their lambs in vain for their offspring were out of earshot, still eating the grass on the northern moor. He stood outside the pen and watched the shepherd wander around the flock, inspecting each sheep's udder.

'Jack,' he called, 'can I help?'

The shepherd turned and shielded his eyes from the sun. When he saw who it was, he smiled. 'Aye, come on in.' He lifted a hurdle to one side, just enough for John to slide through.

'What are you doing, Jack?'

Never one to waste words, Jack pointed out one of the ewes and beckoned to John to follow him. He knelt to take a closer look at its udder.

John knelt down too. He could see that the teats were swollen and the ewe seemed uncomfortable. He saw Jack squeeze out a little milk. Then he followed him to another ewe.

Jack stood by the sheep's head and prepared to hold her steady. 'Go on, John—your turn.'

John got on his knees and began to milk the ewe.

'Squeeze 'arder. Lambs suck a lot stronger than that.'

John was soon able to work by himself. Together, he and Jack went through the whole flock, making them comfortable for the day. The task was repeated for two more days until the shepherd was satisfied that the udders were neither sore nor infected and there was no more milk; every ewe was dry.

As John and the shepherd walked back down the hill, it began to rain. Jack put his hand in his pocket and took out the knee bone of a sheep that he kept there.

'I don't like damp weather,' he grumbled. 'This cramp-bone'll 'elp.'

'How?'

'Why, I put it under me pillow of a night—it stops me leg crampin' up.'

John took hold of Jack's other hand. It was enormous, as broad as a bucket yet soft from touching the fleeces. He held on tight until they reached St Helen's Lane and it was time to say goodbye.

'Can I help you again?'

'Aye.'

'Soon?'

'Wait till autumn, when it's greasin' time. Run off 'ome now—thoo's gettin' wet.'

John let go of Jack's hand. He sprinted down the lane and then turned to wave. He was already looking forward to autumn.

On a glorious day in July, Richard set off once again for Bridlington Quay to put in a few hours for the chandler. There was a clear blue sky with no hint of rain and he was in high spirits. As he neared the quayside and left his horse, the familiar sounds and smells excited him. Shouts in unknown languages assailed him from all sides, and even many of the English accents sounded foreign. The tide was in and there was a hectic loading and unloading of boats. Coopers hammered barrels together, and Richard had to leap out of their way as they rolled them along the quay. It was so different from the peace and quiet of Carnaby and Reighton, but he relished it and his heart beat faster at the prospect of an inn full of sailors.

He decided to do a bit of chandlery work and then sit in his favourite inn to wait until the tide went out. Then the harbour would quieten down a little and the men would take time off to eat and drink.

As he strolled along, he took a deep breath and inhaled the smells of the town. The cold summer meant that the malt houses were still operating and a yeasty aroma hung over the streets. Less pleasant were the whiff of fish and the stench of the raw hides stacked in piles. He walked up Ship Hill, past the shops selling coffee and spices. Finally, he manoeuvred past the timber stored on King Street and entered one of the yards behind. As soon as he opened the door of the Newcastle Arms, he was engulfed in the fog of tobacco and the welcoming scent of rum. He ordered a quart of ale and settled down lazily in a corner to watch and wait.

He loved Bridlington so much. Apart from the abundance of busy people and the pace of life, he approved of the fine houses. Brick dwellings were going up all the time for rich merchants and master mariners; Bridlington was going up in the world. Mostly though, he knew the area around the quay. There the fishermen's cottages were crammed close together with numerous narrow alleyways. These places were convenient for his purposes, and he knew which ones were least frequented.

He had time on his hands. There was no hurry, although a few mariners were already sitting at different tables keeping themselves to themselves. One group of men sat well away; he assumed from their blackened clothes that they'd sailed with coal from Sunderland or Newcastle. He suspected another group of men were from the Low Countries. He took out his pipe and lit up. Through the smoke, he noticed one of the men staring at him. He crossed his legs slowly and made eye contact.

Chapter 37

Richard drank the last of his ale. Instead of putting out his pipe, he continued to smoke and watch the man through the fumes. Though he hadn't seen him before, he assumed from his clothes that he was a mariner, and quite a handsome one too. The cleft in his chin was particularly attractive.

After half an hour, the man stood up. He glanced at Richard with a slight nod of his head and then made his way outside.

Richard waited a minute then put out his pipe and followed. As he guessed, the mariner was loitering by the yard exit. Richard winked as he passed and, sure enough, the man followed a few paces behind. Richard led the way down towards the harbour, in and out of passages before reaching a particular blind alley behind a coal store. He leant his back against the wall, bending one leg lazily behind. Though he couldn't guess the man's preferences, he was game for anything.

The mariner licked his lips.

To reassure and excite, Richard put an arm out casually and stroked the man's cheek. The effect was instant. With one blow to his face, Richard was on his knees, blood pouring from his nose. He tried to get up, felt dizzy, and staggered forwards. When he was kicked hard in the groin, he crumpled to the ground in agony.

'That'll teach thee... filthy bugger.'

Richard fought for breath and hoped he'd be left alone.

The mariner cleared his throat and spat on Richard before giving him a last kick in the stomach. As he turned to walk away, he warned, 'Tha'd better not come 'ere again or tha'll get same.'

Alone in the alley, Richard waited until the pain eased. Wincing, and taking his time, he rose to his feet. He brushed the muck off his best breeches and used his kerchief to staunch the nosebleed. As he limped back, he passed a trough of water. He rinsed out his kerchief and used it to try to dab the blood off his shirt. This only made things worse. By the time he returned to the harbour to get his horse, he was a mess. He dared not go home and face his wife, so he collected his horse and set off on a long, sore and miserable ride to Reighton.

It was early evening when he arrived above the village. He thought to avoid Uphall and go to William's house for clean clothes. It meant a circuitous ride, but he reached the house unseen and sneaked in.

Mary and the boys gazed in surprise.

'What on earth happened to you?' she asked.

'Oh, nothing much. When will William be home?'

'He's working late tonight, what with the weather being so good.'

'Can you lend me some of his clothes? And wash these? I can't go to Uphall. I don't want my mother to know about it.'

'Oh, yes, Richard, I do understand, but I can't believe you've been in a fight. It's not like you.' When he didn't offer any explanation and looked so sorry for himself, she added quickly, 'Don't worry. Go into the parlour and get undressed. I'll find you something to wear.'

When she brought his soiled and bloodstained clothes back into the kitchen, she warned her boys.

'Don't you go thinking this is what men get up to. It isn't. Fighting won't get you anywhere.' She sent young William out for a bucket of water. 'You especially,' she said as he went, 'don't you dare think this is amusing or exciting in *any* way.'

He tried to look unconcerned, yet he was fascinated.

As soon as William saw his brother, he knew he'd been in a fight and, later, when he heard the facts in confidence, he wasn't surprised. It would have happened sooner or later.

'You know, Richard, it could have been a lot worse. I suggest you stop going to Bridlington Quay for a while. Listen, why don't you give up your work in Bridlington and go back to farming?'

'Maybe, maybe, but that man misled me, and that's not fair. I'm going back. I'll find him and...'

'And what?'

'I don't know, but I need to get my own back.'

'Revenge is not always the best thing.' William thought for a moment and then went against his better judgement.

'Alright, seeing as you're my brother, I'll go with you one day to Bridlington, to that inn, and we'll sort him out. Don't go there on your own though. Wait for me.' He doubted they'd see the man again.

When the harvest was delayed by the wet summer, William found time to ride into Bridlington in early August. The day was not promising, the wind coming from the north-west and the sky overcast. He called on Richard at the chandler's and, after leaving his horse, they set off for the inn. They had little to say. William was regretting his decision, and Richard felt guilty. They hadn't discussed what they'd do if they did meet the attacker and, though neither would admit it, they were now hoping the day would pass without event.

They soon reached the Newcastle Arms. William had never been there before. It was midday, the tide was out and the rooms were full. Pipe smoke hung in thick swathes around the tables, and the walls, where you could see them, were yellow with grime. William was already getting a headache from the stuffy atmosphere and peered warily at the company. The men were strangers and looked ready for a brawl. Those at the nearest table were drinking from large tankards. Others, by the smell wafting across, were supping rum and brandy. Many appeared half-drunk. William was all for going back home, but Richard pushed him forward between the tables where there was an empty settle by the fireplace.

Eyeing them up and down on the opposite settle was an old soldier. With no introduction, he began to relate how he'd lost his leg.

Now William knew why the settle was unoccupied, yet there was nowhere else to sit. He pretended to listen to the veteran and ordered pints of a strong imported ale. Hoping it would give him courage, he drank it far too quickly and ordered more. Before long, he grew anxious that he'd be useless in a fight. He was hot. Sweat broke out on his forehead and he felt sick and dizzy in the airless room. A mist like fine pepper danced before his eyes, and the noise of shouting and swearing came and receded in waves. He swallowed hard, thought he might faint, and gripped his tankard. He concentrated on getting it to his lips without spilling the drink and looking foolish.

Suddenly, Richard nudged him with his elbow and whispered. 'There's the man over there. Don't look now—he's standing by the door. He's about to turn this way.'

William gulped down the last of his ale and wiped his mouth on his coat sleeve. He glanced up to see a mariner striding towards them with a defiant and angry expression.

The man stopped in front of them and spat at their feet. He grinned before shouting.

'Filthy buggers! 'Ow dare tha come back 'ere an' ply tha mucky trade?'

Richard went pale before he blushed. He'd never been embarrassed in public before.

The mariner was determined to engage the whole company. He raised his voice further and turned to the crowded tables. 'We don't want mollies in 'ere, do we?'

The customers went quiet as they peered through the smoke to see what was happening. Eager for entertainment, they banged their tankards on the tables and yelled.

'Out, out, out!'

Above the racket, the mariner shouted at Richard. 'Get up tha slut. If tha's so fond o' back doors, there's one over there—it takes thee out—out of 'ere where tha doesn't belong.' He swaggered forwards, leering, confident of his victory.

As Richard stood up to leave the inn in shame, William leapt up and threw a wide, swinging punch. He caught the mariner off guard, and the man fell backwards against a table. Ignoring the alarm on Richard's face, William followed up his attack. He grabbed the man by the neck and tried to throttle him. No one interfered. William left off the strangling and shook the man so that his head flopped like a rag doll. Realising at last that the man was not fighting back, William let go and gave him a parting punch in the stomach.

'Let that be a lesson. Think next time before you accuse someone in full company.'

As the mariner sank to the floor and vomited over the sawdust, William and Richard stepped round him and headed for the door. When no one followed them outside, William turned to Richard and grinned.

'That's sorted *him* out. You'll have no more trouble.'

Richard was not so sure. 'They know me by sight now. They might report us to the constable.'

'Stop fretting. You forget—they don't know who we are, or where we're from. We're fine.'

As they went to collect their horses, Michael Watson was recovering in the inn. A group of men crowded round him, offering sympathy. One of them was Zak, a friend of John Beale, the man William had punched years ago.

'I don't forget a face,' he spat. 'That man's William Jordan from Reighton.'

A couple of weeks later, an official delivered a familiar letter to William. It was a request for him to appear at the next Beverley quarter sessions and answer 'such matters of misdemeanour as will be objected against him by Michael Watson of Hull in these parts, Mariner, touching ye assaulting and beating ye said Michael Watson.'

Chapter 38

1725-6

William didn't want to explain to his wife or the rest of his family why he'd received the summons for fighting in Bridlington. Instead, he let them think he'd lapsed into his old, drunken and violent ways.

Mary persuaded him to have a word with Matthew. 'You two were close once, and he has influence. Ask him to plead your case. You've nothing to lose, and he is your brother-in-law.'

When William did speak eventually to Matthew Smith, it turned out that he knew this Michael Watson.

'I can't tell you any more,' Matthew confided, 'but I will say this.' He grinned and gave William a subtle wink. 'Watson could get to know you're a customs officer, and then he might hear perhaps that you have information against him... maybe that you know about the next runs of brandy... then he may just think again.'

'You mean he's one of a smuggling gang?' William was beginning to wonder if the mariner was even in Matthew's pay. 'He's not one of your lot, is he?'

'I didn't say that, though I think I can silence him. Leave it to me and don't lose any sleep over it.'

Since Matthew was so confident of success, William left the matter in his hands.

In the middle of September, Sir Richard Osbaldeston, at his seat in Hunmanby, received a letter from Hull from Michael Watson.

'Sir, I being this day obliged to go for London fears I shall not be back time enough to answer sessions At Beverley so I humbly devise your worship to either put it off if you can or make void warrant of the complaint your Worships granted against William Jordan Customs house officer of Reighton for assaulting wounding and bruising of me.'

When Mary heard that William no longer had to appear in court, she was relieved and yet suspicious. Her brother must be far more involved with those in high places than he ever admitted. As to her feelings about William, his reprieve did nothing to lessen her shame. He was a churchwarden and shouldn't be drinking and brawling. He was presenting a very poor example. She was quite aware that others thought him lucky to get away with it.

In church, Mary was embarrassed as the vicar kept glancing at her pew. When she heard him read from the fifth chapter of Matthew, she had no doubt but that he was trying to humble William and curb his violent ways.

'Ye have heard that it hath been said, Thou shalt love thy neighbour, and hate thine enemy. But I say unto you, Love your enemies, bless them that curse you, and pray for them which despitefully use you and persecute you.'

The congregation cried a loud 'amen' to that as Robert Storey, among others, twisted round to stare at William.

The villagers' high moral stance didn't last. Before long, they had far more to think about than some obscure fight in Bridlington. It was already past the usual harvest time and the crops were still not ready.

In November, the women tried to reap the wheat. It wasn't the right colour and it didn't taste as it should, yet they had no choice. Their hands, numb with cold, could hardly grip the sickles, and no amount of goose grease could soothe their chapped fingers. In the end, their efforts were futile; the crop was so poor that the hogs were turned loose to feed among the sheaves.

The winter was severe, the frost continuing into the new year. Young William took the dog to bed with him again; her soft head nestling against his neck brought comfort as well as warmth. One morning though, he complained bitterly when his bare bottom stuck to the icy chamber pot; he dared not move for a while for fear of losing his skin. He got no sympathy from his father.

'You worry over your arse... I'm more concerned for our livestock. Our animals have little to eat except the gorse that's died off in the cold.'

'More gorse for our fires then,' young William replied, and immediately received a clout round the ear.

His mother intervened. 'We shouldn't complain. We should be thankful. We have plenty of fatty bacon and salted beef to eat.' She didn't add that they were short on potatoes and cabbages. By the end of February, even those supplies had run out.

One afternoon, William was cutting down reeds for thatch repairs. He paused in his work to see the sunset transforming the sky. The clouds seemed to be ablaze. It should have been a glorious sight, but his belly was empty and he hadn't slept well for days. The sunset was like a smack in the face, a cruel joke from an unfeeling God. He cursed the cold and trudged home through the frozen grass, his feet crunching with every step. Above him, to compound his misery, the snow still lay in a thick pelt over the darkening hill.

By spring, William's family, like others in the Reighton area, had resorted to eating squirrel or crow stew. Thanks to young William's skill with the sling, they managed to survive and even avoid the prevalent fevers.

The bad winter had not suited the vicar. Living in Filey, John Sumpton had difficult journeys around his parish. By March, he was bedridden with exhaustion and a severe chill, and the wet, thundery weather prolonged his illness. After missing many services throughout the parish, he decided that his brother Robert should take over for a while. No one knew how long this arrangement would last; John Sumpton was very weak after recurring bouts of fever.

William didn't care; he was not a churchwarden this year and didn't want to get too involved in church matters. When the vicar didn't live in the village and share its problems, the church was nothing but cold stone and plaster. William soon found that Robert Sumpton spent no longer in Reighton than his brother had, carrying out the bare minimum of duties. At least, like his brother, he kept the sermons short, a blessing on a cold, wet Sunday. As William sat in his pew, he thought of his own brother Richard who'd been very quiet all winter. He hoped the miserable weather had dampened any craving for men in Bridlington.

In May, news reached Reighton that three men had been hanged in London for sodomy. Thomas heard it first from the blacksmith. Neither man had a definite idea of Richard's inclinations, only vague suspicions. Thomas couldn't wait to tell William.

He found him leaning over the gate to Matthew Smith's pasture, idly watching the cattle. The bullocks were giddy on their first day out on the new grass, charging about and kicking up lumps of turf.

William turned and gave a wistful smile. 'I wish *I* felt that lively.'

'At least you're better off than them hanged in London… them sodomites.'

When William shrugged and offered no opinion, Thomas carried on regardless. He rubbed his hands together in prurient censure.

'Did you know there's a woman in London who runs a place for the likes of them? Mother Clap they call her. Good name, eh? She got a two-year prison sentence. Wish I'd seen her in the pillory. I'd have thrown something—hit her where she'd least expect it. Fancy eh, a milkman, an upholsterer and a wool-comber! Ordinary men with ordinary jobs.'

William remained silent and let Thomas ramble on.

'I believe it was in the London Journal. Apparently, they've discovered houses that run clubs for such things—and that's not counting their meetings in the open at night. Glad I don't live in London. They say it's a vice from Italy. That's probably it. What do you think?'

'I think it's probably exaggerated. Some folk like to stir up trouble.'

Thomas strolled away, disappointed; there was no pleasure in telling William the news these days. As young William was more companionable, he decided to take the boy, just turned fourteen, under his wing. Young William would be a man soon, and he could teach him many things.

Despite the stormy, unpredictable weather, Thomas took young William to Bempton. Food was still in short supply and, if the boy became adept at getting birds' eggs from the cliff, he could feed his family. Thomas knew two of the climmers and persuaded them to let the boy have a go.

'He doesn't weigh much,' Thomas argued as they walked from the village to the cliffs, 'and it's best to learn young.'

The men tied a rope around William and slung a bag over his shoulder for the eggs. He walked to the edge. The sheer height and the vertical drop to the dark sea below took his breath away. He couldn't hear the waves sucking and lapping at the rocks for the screaming of the gulls and, instead of enjoying the fresh sea air, he was repulsed by the shocking stink of bird muck. Suddenly, he ducked as a huge white bird glided past him at eye level. Others flew by with equally wide wingspans and wicked beaks, mocking him with their speed and agility.

'Get on then,' urged Thomas. 'You're on a strong rope. Over you go.'

Young William didn't want to embarrass his uncle. He bit his lip and resigned himself to the ordeal, yet his eyes were wide with fear as he was lowered over the cliff. The stench overwhelmed him and clung to the back of his throat. Gannets dive-bombed and shat on him. When he gagged, he saw his uncle lean over the edge and laugh.

'Don't be put off!' Thomas shouted down. 'Ignore them and fill the bag.'

Uncle Thomas was making fun of him. Angered by that thought, William was now determined to get the job done. He wiped the slime from his face with one sleeve and fought off the birds with his other arm. There was just one way out of his predicament—fill the bag with eggs. Then they'd haul him up to safety.

He gritted his teeth and kept his mouth shut tight. Even so, he could almost taste the bird muck on his face. He channelled his anger and concentrated on the narrow rocky ledges beside him. Whenever he saw a large egg, he leant forward and made a grab. As soon as he'd emptied an area, the men holding the rope lowered him further to reach more nests. At last the bag was full, and he gave two sharp tugs on the rope. Slowly, the men hauled him back to the top. He was covered in bird shit and he stank.

'Well done, lad,' said Thomas, ignoring the boy's scowls and trying not to laugh. 'You'll be allowed to take a few eggs home.'

William sulked as they walked back and couldn't rid his nose of the rancid smell. His uncle did not show enough appreciation of his efforts and the few eggs he carried were not worth the ordeal.

Thomas did not walk his nephew all the way home. At Uphall, he left him with a piece of advice.

'Best show your mother the eggs before she gets a proper look at you. That should help. Off you go.'

Young William trudged down the hill and waited a moment in the garden at the back before knocking on the kitchen window. When his mother peered out, he held up a couple of eggs.

She smiled and opened the door for him. Her smile vanished. 'Oh, my God!' she cried as she put a hand over her mouth and then her nose.

'I have more eggs.'

'That uncle of yours! He'll be the death of you! Oh, get out of your clothes quick. They'll take some scrubbing. And poor you... your hands are covered! Get over there—use that tub to get the worst off.'

There was one good outcome to the day. Apart from his mother being most grateful for the eggs and not minding too much about washing his clothes, his father said he deserved a reward.

'I'm proud of you, lad. I think you've earned the chance to go to Flamborough Fair. Since you've a good aim with your sling, your uncle Thomas might let you shoot.'

Chapter 39

Young William heard from Uncle Thomas that there'd be a shooting contest at the Whit Fair at Flamborough. Visitors were encouraged to shoot as many seabirds as they could. It sounded thoroughly bloody and exciting, so he pestered his uncle to teach him how to shoot.

With the family's permission, Thomas took young William up on the hill for training. He found the boy impatient to learn, which proved a problem. Thomas did not want to damage the precious musket let alone injure himself or William in the process. Since the boy would insist on bringing his dog, he tied Stina to a bush, well out of the way.

First, he named and explained the various parts of the gun, and showed how the gun worked. He loaded it and fired it and then the real work began of teaching William to do it himself, safely.

'Balance the musket on the ground—that's right, muzzle to the sky. Now, put in the measure of powder. Careful, don't spill it, and make sure the ball is well-greased before you fit it in the barrel.'

'It won't go in,' William complained.

'Of course it will, it's supposed to fit tight. That's the whole point. It's a rifled flintlock, as I explained. It's a proper fowling piece of your grandfather's, far more accurate than just any old musket. Go on, ram it home with the ramrod.'

William forced down the lead ball as far as it would go.

'You know what'll happen if you don't push it in all the way to the breech?'

William shook his head.

'If you leave an air gap between the powder and the ball?'

William was getting annoyed. He shook his head again and rolled his eyes.

'Well, my lad, it can make the barrel explode!'

William was shocked. This was worrying information. Apart from the obvious harm to himself, he didn't want the blame for ruining the family gun.

'So,' asked Thomas, 'are you sure the ball is right in?'

William forced the ramrod down again and pushed. He was satisfied.

'Now, don't *ever* forget to take the ramrod out. It's dangerous enough firing a ball let alone a metal rod.'

William put a small amount of fine gunpowder into the flash pan and closed the lid. Now loaded and primed, he turned the cock to full, took aim at a tree stump a hundred yards away and pulled the trigger. There was a flash of sparks at both ends of the gun and a simultaneous loud crack. He hadn't a clue where the ball had gone, probably nowhere near the target. He wasn't comfortable with the gun. It was too heavy. He wanted to throw it on the ground, but his uncle was watching. Instead, he laid it down gently and then kicked a clump of grass in frustration.

'It's no good, I can't do it.'

'Don't give up. You'll improve with practice. You'll get used to this gun in time.'

William sat down on the grass while his uncle explained the finer points of gun maintenance. He learnt that the gun barrel should be cleaned after each shot or else the black powder would foul it and make it harder to reload; the flint must be shiny and well napped or it wouldn't give a good spark; the powder and the flash pan must be kept dry.

'And most important,' repeated Uncle Thomas for the third time, 'always run an oiled rag up the barrel. Use the ramrod to do it—put out any burning embers left in there. A clean barrel is everything. Remember, if there's any embers left in when you reload, they can ignite the powder charge and the gun will fire before you're ready.'

When William looked even more disconsolate after all his instructions, Thomas began to feel sorry for him.

'Alright, another way of avoiding such accidents is just to wait longer between shots. That'll give any leftover embers time to burn out.' He gave William a friendly thump in the chest. 'You're not in an army, you know. You don't have to fire off four shots a minute. And no one is going to shoot back at you—it's only seabirds you'll be aiming at.'

Young William practised loading and caring for the gun almost every evening with Uncle Thomas, and each day he strengthened his arm muscles by holding heavy cobblestones at arm's length. By Whit Tuesday, he was confident.

On the day of the Fair, he got up at dawn and walked to Uphall with his father. He insisted on taking the dog since she went everywhere with him and had grown accustomed to the noise of firing. Thomas joined them and they rode south on horseback.

They reached Flamborough by mid-morning. The place was packed with people who'd come for the stalls as well as the shooting. They found Richard there, in his best clothes, eyeing up the display of stockings and cravats. To young William's relief, his father and Thomas were not a bit interested in buying anything and wanted to move on to the cliffs. Only Richard lingered behind, saying he'd join them later.

When they reached the cliff top, scores of people were there already, and many more were arriving in carriages from Bridlington. There was a carnival atmosphere with tables set out full of bread and cheese for sale, and you could buy port, ale and beer by the pint.

'I don't know why they call it a shooting contest,' Thomas remarked. 'There aren't any winners. You just load your weapon and shoot at leisure.' He pointed towards the sea. 'Look down there in the cove. Those cobles will gather up the dead birds. I've heard that, if you skin and cook a gannet like a piece of beef, the meat's reckoned almost as good.'

He warned the boy to stand well clear of other shooters when he was loading. 'Sparks from their weapons can set fire to your own powder. And see those men over there?' He pointed to a group gathering by the cliff edge. 'I bet they'll be firing lead shot instead of balls, so we'd best keep a safe distance. Here, I'll put Stina on a shorter leash. I promise to keep a tight hold of her.'

Once the shooting started, the noise was tremendous. Despite the racket, the dog sat on her haunches with pricked ears, calm yet alert, her eyes fixed on her young master the whole time.

Young William concentrated and took his time loading the gun. He took aim at a gannet wheeling past at eye level, and fired. He missed, but cleaned the barrel as he'd been taught, and reloaded carefully.

His father was impressed and congratulated Thomas on doing a good job. He watched his son many times as he shot, cleaned and reloaded.

After a while, Thomas got bored and went to get a drink, leaving William to oversee his son and keep hold of the dog.

Without Thomas by his side, young William risked taking a short cut. Until then he'd cleaned the barrel after every shot. It was time wasted that could be spent in shooting. His father wouldn't notice if he didn't do it every single time.

He fired three shots without cleaning the barrel. Nothing untoward happened. For the fourth shot, he loaded the barrel with powder and a ball as usual. Before he could prime the pan, an ember left in the barrel ignited the charge. Instantly, the gun fired. He dropped it in alarm and looked around. He could have hit anyone. Then he saw his father's face as white as his shirt.

'You damn fool! You could have hit me!'

It was then that both of them realised the horror of what had happened. Stina lay flat and motionless, blood spreading from beneath her onto the grass.

Stunned by what he'd done, young William stood still as if nailed to the ground. He watched his father kneel down, move the dog with the utmost care and inspect the wound.

'I'm sorry, son. She's been hit in the stomach. There's nothing we can do.'

Young William couldn't believe it. His legs were shaking as he joined his father. Kneeling by the dog's side, he stroked her head. When she began to whimper, he broke down in tears.

'Can't we do something?'

'Not with a stomach wound.'

'Please!'

At that moment, Thomas returned with Richard. They found William and his son on their knees leaning over the dog.

William turned his head and put a finger to his lips. He stood up and spoke quietly to them out of his son's hearing.

'It's bad. It was an accident so don't blame him—he's upset enough already.'

The boy was now cradling Stina's head and weeping. They could hear him praying to God.

'We'd best put her out of her misery,' William announced. 'I'll do it. I'll shoot her.'

'No,' countered Thomas, 'I'll do it, though not with a musket ball. There's enough mess already.'

'He'll probably hate me for it, but I'm his father. It's best if I do it.'

'No. I've taught him how to shoot. It's my fault.'

Young William was still on his knees, stroking the dog and begging God to let her live.

His father leant over and tried to pull him away. 'Listen, Will, Stina is hurt too badly. We can't help her.'

'No!' the boy screamed, and lashed out with his fists. 'We can help her, get her home.'

'But you can see—she's in pain. She's panting for breath. All we can do is stop her suffering.'

Young William saw Thomas holding the gun. He made a grab for his legs and pleaded for Stina's life. The way his father and uncles avoided his eye, he knew there was no option.

'Let me say goodbye then,' he pleaded. Tears spilled down his cheeks as he brushed his face against Stina's head. She had recovered from the initial shock and was now trembling and trying to get up. He held her still and stroked her back to soothe her. His throat was so tight he couldn't speak, couldn't say all the things she'd meant to him. In despair, he kissed her head for the last time.

'I'm sorry,' he choked.

He saw that Stina kept her eyes on him as he rose to his feet. Then, without warning, his father spun him around and held him tight to his chest so that he couldn't see. His father's arms covered his ears as Thomas brought the butt of the gun down hard and cracked Stina's skull.

Chapter 40

Gunshots continued to reverberate around the cliffs as William let go of his son. He stood by and watched him kneel again by the dog. He remembered the Christmas when he'd brought her as a puppy for his daughter—a beautiful little thing, but now the white chest and the one white leg were red with blood. Taking Thomas and Richard aside, he discussed what to do next.

'We'll have to take her back with us.'

'Then we'll need to wrap her up well.' Thomas, always practical, was thinking of the blood.

Richard sighed as he looked on. 'I wish we'd never come. I'll go back to the stalls and fetch some sacks. We'd all better just go home.'

While they waited for Richard, young William continued to sit by Stina, occasionally fondling her ears. The blood was still oozing from her stomach, though more slowly. He stared unseeing towards the edge of Flamborough cliffs where men were continuing their shooting, oblivious to the accident behind them.

As soon as Richard returned, he helped Thomas wrap a sack around Stina's middle. Then they lifted Stina into another sack. The day was over for all of them.

They walked without speaking to collect their horses, Thomas offering to carry Stina. Richard waved goodbye as William helped his son up on the horse and mounted behind him. Thomas passed them the dog.

Young William held on to Stina as she lay over the horse's neck, and so they began the long journey home. He tried to stay calm and behave as a man, yet every time he thought of what he'd done, he sobbed. He couldn't remember a time without Stina. Whenever he'd been upset, he'd taken Stina on his own for long walks on the beach or on the cliffs and hills—when his sister had died, when old Ben had died, when his father was violent. She was always there when he was just plain bored, there with him for his best and worst times. And she'd been such a good dog, often his only friend. When she chased that duck he'd been so proud, and she'd been so patient while he learnt to use the sling… and then the gun. Always his thoughts came back to the gun, and the horror, and then he couldn't stop the tears.

When they reached Uphall, there was no one about in the yard. William dismounted and lifted down Stina's stiffening body.

'Come on, Will, get down and tie the horse up over there. Dickon'll see to things. We have to go home and explain to the family.'

Young William trudged behind his father and hung back further as they approached the house.

'Be brave, lad. I'll put Stina in the back garden, and then we'll go in together. Come on.'

'I'd rather stay with her for a bit. I'll come in later.'

'Alright, I understand.' William placed Stina under the apple tree and then braced himself as he walked into the house.

The boys were helping their mother, seated round the table getting the white flesh from the claws of a couple of large crabs. They were absorbed and happy in their shared task.

Mary raised her head, wondering why William was back early. The look on his face made her drop her fork.

'No,' he said quickly, 'the lad's fine. It's Stina. I'm afraid she's been shot. It was an accident. There was nothing we could do.'

The boys stopped what they were doing, and Mary put a hand over her mouth. They all knew how much the dog meant to young William. Suddenly, John began to cry and that set off Richard and Matthew.

William sat down heavily at the end of the table. He put his head in his hands and covered his ears. There was only so much weeping he could stand. When he lifted his head, he admonished his sons.

'Whatever you do, don't blame your brother. He's taken it badly enough. We'll bury her tomorrow morning, in the garden if you like.' He surveyed his sons in turn. 'It's no good crying. There's nothing you can do for the dog. You've got to help Will now. I'll fetch him in if you're ready—and woe betide any of you stare at him or ask questions. Understood?' He glared at them until they nodded.

Mary busied herself by the fire, remembering her daughter holding onto the dog's ear before she died. She concentrated on stirring the fish soup, every so often drying her eyes with her apron.

Young William shuffled in quietly through the back door and sat near his father at the table. Black smears streaked his face where tears had mingled with powder shot.

His brothers kept blinking as they tried not to stare.

'We'll have an early supper,' said their father, 'then get to bed all of you.' When they didn't complain, he added, 'In the morning, straight after breakfast, we'll bury Stina.'

Mary dished up the soup, and they finished the plate of crabmeat in silence.

When the boys had been settled for the night, and their mother had left them, John slipped out of his bed and climbed in next to William. He wrapped his arms round him and gave him a kiss.

'Get off!' grumbled William. 'What are you doing, you soft lump o' lard?' When he felt John squeeze him harder, he couldn't decide whether to kick him out of bed or leave him be. On the one hand, it was comforting, but it also made him cry again. He pressed his face into the pillow to stifle the tears, and allowed John to stay.

In the morning, after another silent meal, the boys followed their parents into the garden. Their father had been up since dawn and had already dug a hole by the hedge, not far from the apple tree. He picked Stina up, still in the sack but with her head free, and carried her gently in his arms. Before he put her in the grave, he asked if they wanted to say anything.

The boys shook their heads.

Mary wanted to speak, yet couldn't trust her voice. Already, her throat was tight and she couldn't swallow.

John stepped forward to stroke the dog. Her head was damp and cold with dew, and there was a streak of dark, dried blood on one side.

'I'm sorry, Stina,' he whispered. 'I'll see you in heaven. Be a good dog.' He kissed the soft wet fur on her head and went back to hold his mother's hand.

Young William glanced sideways at his father, not daring to face him eye to eye.

His father noticed. 'Are you sure you don't want to say something?'

Young William shook his head. When he stared at the sack holding her body, he couldn't begin to say what he felt. He'd promised he'd never hurt her. Tears streamed down his face as his father put her into the hole and began to spade over the earth.

After replacing the grass sods, his father said a prayer.

'Lord, look down upon this family with mercy and forgive us our sins. Stina did no wrong—she was better than any of us.' He remembered how he'd lied to his daughter when she was dying, how he'd told her that Stina would go to heaven. 'If ever an animal should be admitted to heaven, it's Stina. Lord, hear our prayer. Amen.'

Afterwards, they went to do their usual daily chores, all except young William who took a walk by himself. He took his favourite route along Oxtrope Lane and then on to the cliffs, his view blurred by tears. Every so often, he paused to take a deep breath and then release a long trembling sigh. He carried on walking northwards, picking up the odd stone to fling as far as he could in any direction. When he reached the second gap in the cliffs, he stopped and sat down to think.

The sea was calm and deep blue, glittering in the morning sunshine. On the horizon, it looked as if waves were breaking, though it was really a line of fluffy white cloud. He wondered if Stina had a soul. Would she be in heaven now? His father's prayer over her grave was confusing. As far as he knew, animals never went to heaven, only good Christians could go there. Dogs couldn't believe in God, so they'd be left out. Did that mean they went to Hell? Or, were they just left neither here nor there? He wished his brother Francis was at home—he'd have known the answer. If George Gurwood had still been the vicar, he could have asked him.

Suddenly, he realised he was not alone. Right behind him was his brother John.

The boy had been following for some time. He'd kept out of sight until he'd seen William talking to himself and waving his arms like a madman. Then, concerned for his brother, he'd rushed out of hiding.

He was not welcome.

'What do *you* want?' William grumbled.

'Nothing. Are you alright?'

'Yes, why?'

'You were waving your arms about—like this.' He did a very good impression.

'Go on home, John. You can't help me. You can't tell me if dogs go to heaven, can you? What does a simpleton like you know?'

John frowned, thinking of Prince the piglet. He'd assumed that all creatures went to heaven. Eager to have this confirmed, he said, 'You should ask the vicar.'

'We haven't got one. Well, I suppose we have his brother instead, but I hardly know him. No, there's no point trying to talk to *him*. He's off back to Filey before the pew's even warmed up.' Then he had an idea.

'Hey, I know—I can walk to Rudston and see Francis. George Gurwood's there. Between them, I'm bound to get an answer.'

'Can I come?'

'No. I'm going to set off now. If I'm not back before suppertime, it means I'll be sleeping there. Tell mother not to worry.'

John walked back with him as far as the village and then waved goodbye as his brother headed south-west.

Part Three

Choices

Chapter 41

As young William strode out of Reighton, he was relieved to be doing something at last to ease his guilt. Stina had been his sister's dog, never his. He should have taken more care of Stina for her sake. How he wished he'd never gone to Flamborough. He could so easily have stayed at home. Stuffing his hands deep in his pockets, he kicked at the turf.

He walked briskly and followed the line of the Argam Dike. He found the wind and the sun in his face the whole way helped to lift his spirits. When he neared Rudston, he left the dike and followed a well-trodden path between fields to join the road. After half a mile of easier walking, he reached the church, high on a mound and overlooking the houses; it was much bigger and more impressive than Reighton's. Though he'd heard about it, he was in awe of the huge upright stone in the churchyard. No one really knew why it was there or who put it there. Suddenly, he had second thoughts about meeting the Gurwoods again. Maybe they wouldn't recognise him. After all, he'd been just eight years old when the Gurwoods left.

Instead of seeking out the vicarage straightaway, he entered the churchyard and strolled up to the standing stone. It towered above him, cold and grey, the height of about five men he reckoned. He walked round it, running his palms across the pitted and ridged surface.

Surely it was there for a reason. He leant his forehead against it and prayed for Stina.

When he'd finished, he touched the stone once more in farewell, then turned his back on it to seek the vicarage. He guessed it was the house standing almost opposite the church's main entrance—a new and large chalk-built place, with its own barn and stable.

He stood outside the gate, chewing his lip. His desperate need for an answer about Stina drove him up the path. When he knocked on the door, a young woman answered. He assumed she was a servant.

'I've come to see the vicar.'

'I'm sorry, 'e's not in. 'E's away fo' day i' Burton Flemin' an' won't be back till late.'

'Do you happen to know then where Francis Jordan works? He's a hired lad from Reighton.'

The woman frowned and looked puzzled. She even blushed. She seemed about to question him, but then thought better of it and gave him directions to the farm.

As he left the vicarage, he grew anxious about meeting Francis. They'd always argued and fought, had never got on. Why should Francis help him now? He dragged himself along the road and, just as he was thinking to give up and go home, he saw his brother emerge from the field ahead.

Francis recognised his brother at once by the lopsided gait. He waved, and then afraid that William was bringing bad news, he quickened his step. As soon as that worry was allayed, he heard about Stina, though not exactly how she'd died.

'The reason I've come,' explained William, 'is that I wanted to ask George Gurwood about dogs going to heaven. Do *you* think they do?'

Francis raised his eyebrows and scratched his head. It was a strange question; his brother lived to torment

310

anything that breathed. They walked on in silence towards the farm while he considered a suitable answer. He knew what Robert Storey would have said, that to get to heaven you must be saved by your faith and by God's grace. Beasts couldn't know Jesus. They had no conscience, couldn't choose between good and evil. Robert would say that salvation was only for people.

'I don't know, William. Whosoever believeth in Jesus shall not perish but have everlasting life. Perhaps if *you* have enough faith, and it must be a strong faith, then that will count for something.'

William had hoped for a better answer. His brother, as usual, was a disappointment. He didn't want to go home without seeing the vicar, and so asked if he could stay the night.

'Perhaps I can sleep at your place, then I can speak with the vicar tomorrow.'

Francis shrugged. He didn't care what his brother did. He showed him the way to the barn and promised he'd bring bread and cheese later.

At dawn the next day, William awoke hungry with no prospect of a breakfast. Impatient to see the vicar, he washed himself in the yard, dipping his head in a bucket of cold water. He used his fingers to comb his hair and remove any bits of straw. Then he smoothed down his breeches and decided he was clean enough.

When the vicarage door opened, he was relieved to see George Gurwood standing there.

The vicar peered at him for a moment. 'Why, it's William, isn't it? William Jordan? Well, fancy seeing you here and so early in the day. You've grown! Come on, take off your hat, and scrape your boots. Follow me into the parlour.' The vicar led the way and then stopped. 'I hope you're not here to bring bad news.'

'No, no,' William stammered. 'I've come because I've something important to ask.'

At this point, they both heard his empty stomach rumble.

'You need food first. I don't suppose you've had breakfast. Let me see what I can get you.'

William smiled. He really was very hungry. When the vicar left him to give instructions to the kitchen, he gazed at the shelves of books. Surely, anyone with so much learning must be able to answer his question. When the vicar returned, William squeezed and twisted his hat between his hands, and then went straight to the point.

'I want to know if dogs can go to heaven.' He swallowed. 'You see, Stina died the day before yesterday.' Suddenly, he heard himself blurting out the truth. 'She didn't die of old age or anything... I killed her.' His voice quivered. 'It was an accident, but I shot her.'

George Gurwood put an arm round his shoulder. 'There now, don't be so hard on yourself. As you say, it was an accident. Now I see why you need to know about heaven. Here, sit down and let's think.'

When both were seated, the vicar rubbed his newly shaven chin. 'Hmmm, it's not that simple.' He thought for a while and then leant forward with his hands on his knees.

'Listen, William, think of all living things in three groups. There are plants—they can feed and grow and reproduce themselves. Then there are animals, and that includes us. We can do these things, yet we can also move and feel things, we have ideas and have a memory. But then, you see, what separates us from the rest of the animals is that we can use our reason, and we have a conscience.'

William frowned. He didn't want a long, difficult sermon on the subject.

'Stina never did anything wrong. She was better than other dogs, better even than me.'

The vicar smiled. 'You may be right. In many ways, we are the same—as I guess you already know. In fact, I bet I could see as many likenesses between a dog and a man as between any two men. I'm sure your dog proved to be a good and loyal friend.'

'Do you think then, if even a bad man might one day go to heaven, then a *really* good dog could get there?'

The vicar leant back in his chair. 'I'm not saying that exactly.' He paused to think for a moment and then stood up. As he began to walk round the room, he tried to explain.

'All things created by God, whether they're people or plants or dogs—they each have a purpose, a role to play that God has planned for them. When they carry out that role—say when your dog was obedient and trustworthy—well then, they glorify their creator. It says in the Psalms, "Beasts, and all cattle; creeping things, and flying fowl—let them praise the name of the Lord." You see?' He stopped walking and stood in front of William with his arms folded. He smiled, pleased with himself.

William continued to frown. He was not satisfied with the explanation.

The vicar sat down again. 'The trouble is, William, the Bible doesn't tell us for sure. I know one thing though, and this is written in Psalm 84, "the Lord will give grace and glory: no good thing will he withhold from them that walk uprightly. Blessed is the man that trusteth in thee." So, William, you must lead a good life and have faith that both you and Stina will meet in heaven. For who hath known the mind of the Lord?'

At that moment, the servant came in to say the breakfast was ready.

William left Rudston with a full belly, and yet didn't know what to make of it all. On the way home, he pondered his life so far, how he'd been careless, thoughtless and maybe even cruel at times. Even if Stina did go to heaven, there was every chance *he* might not get there. In a panic, he wondered if it was already too late to change his ways.

Chapter 42

On his way back to Reighton, young William spoke aloud as he pondered his future, as if he still had his dog as a listener.

'What does God expect from me? I could be nicer to John, be more patient. I could work harder, do as I'm told. Oh, God... ' It was not going to be easy. Tears flowed as he realised how lonely he was without Stina. To cheer himself up, he imagined her running ahead, sniffing for rabbits and then bounding back. For a short while, he was happy with the dream, and then the reality of her death struck him once more. 'Oh, God,' he cried through his tears, 'what can I do?'

That evening, at supper, young William's parents didn't question him. They knew from John what ailed him, and observed without comment. He didn't grab the food as usual, but let his brothers take their share first. Then he chewed each mouthful of the thick, cold ham as if deep in thought. His brothers looked on in silence while his parents put it down to his age, him being neither man nor boy and as likely to blow cold as hot.

At bedtime, young William tucked his younger brothers into bed and even kissed John goodnight.

In church that Sunday, he prayed for forgiveness. As he walked away with his parents, Matthew Smith's eldest daughter suddenly left her family and, pretty as a spring flower, ran towards him.

'I'm sorry about Stina.'

He stared at Ann, dumbfounded. His mother mimed a 'thank you' at him.

'Thank you,' he mumbled. Then she was off, running back to her family.

His father whispered in his ear. 'Don't go getting any ideas about that one. She might be your age, but Matthew will have better suitors in mind.'

Young William blinked. He hadn't thought of such things. He was only fourteen.

Throughout the summer, he remained obedient to his parents and toiled hard in the fields. Often, he accompanied John and worked alongside Dickon. He no longer sought the company of Uncle Thomas, gave up using his sling, and never asked again to borrow the gun. At night, alone in bed, images would flood his mind, tormenting him and keeping him awake; he couldn't rid himself of the sight of Stina lying in her own blood.

Thomas was uncomfortable with the change in his nephew and tried different ways to engage his attention. He coaxed him to wrestle or gamble on some sport or have a ride to Bridlington. All attempts failed. It was quite by chance that he learnt from John that young William hoped to see Stina in heaven.

Thomas thought it ridiculous. If dogs were in heaven, then why not horses or cats and any other dumb beast? There was no way he was going to believe that dogs, like people, could be punished or rewarded after death depending on how they'd lived on earth. The idea was as far-fetched as the news he'd heard from London that a wild boy had been baptised so that he could go to heaven.

At the end of the day, Thomas strolled to the blacksmith, keen to know more details about King

George's obsession with Peter the wild boy. He knew the feral child had been found alone and naked in the woods near Hanover. The boy had lived on berries and acorns, and the fingers on one of his hands were said to be webbed like a duck.

When Thomas entered the forge, he saw his brother William there with Dickon and the hired lads. The blacksmith was holding forth, and his avid audience was sitting on upturned buckets and anything else available.

Phineas rolled his sleeves up higher as he spoke. The subject was the wild boy.

'Aye,' he reported, 'our King still keeps 'im at court. Apparently 'e 'ates wearin' clothes an' won't sleep in a bed—'e just curls up o' floor in a corner.'

'It's all a waste o' time,' Dickon chuntered. 'Lad's been wild over long.'

'Thoo may be right,' agreed Phineas. ''E 'as lessons ev'ry day i' speakin' an' learnin' manners, though I've 'eard 'e doesn't get any better.'

There was silence in the forge as they considered the enormity of trying to teach such a child.

Phineas continued. 'An' 'e'll still only eat greens, an' 'e still throws 'is food about. All 'e can do is repeat a word or two an' make a bow. If I 'ear any more, I'll let thee know.'

As everyone left the forge, Thomas nudged his brother.

'What do *you* think?' he asked as they stepped outside into the road. 'If that wild boy can be baptised and go to heaven, then any other wild animal can. And that's plain daft. I've seen a parrot talking in Bridlington market. It merely repeats what it's been taught. Does that mean, if you baptise it, it'll go to heaven? It walks on two feet, just like the wild boy, so what's the difference?'

William stopped and shrugged. Though eager to get home for supper, he let his brother rant on about the boy.

'I don't believe for a moment that he has a soul like us—do you? To me he's still just a wild animal. I mean he can't think or speak. He knows nothing, doesn't know good from bad.' Thomas sighed and gazed in the direction of the church. 'I mean, just because he *looks* like a person... No, I think he's just a dumb animal—a body without a soul.'

William was surprised by his brother's outburst. 'You're being a bit harsh. It's true the poor boy does *seem* like an idiot, but he *is* still a boy. I think if he could learn to speak and then think, then he must have a soul. He's more than a parrot or a trained dog. He could probably learn in time to be able to choose between good and evil.'

He turned as if to go home, and then added as an afterthought, 'I have to say though, I agree with you about dumb animals not going to heaven.' Immediately, he bit his lip. 'For God's sake don't tell any of my sons I said this. They think Stina might be in heaven. We're all enjoying the change in William. Whatever you do, don't spoil it.'

Thomas sniffed and then spat on the ground. Reluctantly, he agreed to keep the peace. 'Alright, if you want, I'll say nothing.'

As they set off in different directions, Thomas stopped and sent a parting shot. 'So long as your lad doesn't start listening to Robert Storey—you won't want another saint in the family.'

William was not sure if he could trust Thomas to keep his mouth shut, but like everyone else in Reighton, he had far greater worries. The harvest that summer, as predicted, was meagre again. Struggling on from year to year was becoming the norm. As the harvest ended, the yeomen and tenant farmers grumbled. They found fault with each other and blamed their poor crops on bad work habits. William's father was no exception, and complained as he inspected the sheaves in the barn.

'Them fields are not bein' looked after properly. I' my day, we all 'elped to scour ditches. Aye, an' we kept our fences i' good repair.' William had heard this many times before, yet his father hadn't finished. 'Why, there's some 'ere who take bits o' brushwood an' whins from our own fences an' use 'em i' theirs.'

William had to agree. There were lots around the village that could be improved. He guessed the Smiths were of the same opinion. When he left Uphall and went home for supper, his wife greeted him with an interesting bit of gossip.

'I hear that my brother has been dining with the Lord of the Manor and his steward.'

'How do you know?'

'Ah, well, one of his maidservants let it slip.'

William suspected Matthew might be arranging a sale of land or a lease. 'Do you know what he's up to?'

'No, so why don't you ask him here and find out? I never see him except at church.'

William glanced around the kitchen, as tidy as it could ever be with four boys in the house. 'No, I'll catch a word with him early tomorrow. He's bound to be organising things in his yard.'

The next morning, William was at the Smiths' place and spotted Matthew striding ahead to speak with his foreman. He waited until he was free.

'What's this I hear about you and Thomas Cockerill? What's going on?'

'I was going to tell you, but you'll find out soon enough when the Manor Court meets. You'll be pleased to know I've been thinking of ways to improve things here. We've put up with bad practice for far too long. The steward agrees; John Grimston's had talks with Thomas Cockerill and, between us, we've come up with a set of rules.'

William could scarcely believe that Matthew would do such a thing behind his back. The rules had better be worthwhile or Matthew would be most unpopular.

'What kind of rules are you thinking of?'

'Oh, the usual thing—making sure people don't put more livestock in the pasture than they're allowed, making sure no one leaves their cattle in the upfield when crops are growing. I could go on. The steward has quite a list written up—twenty items or more—and there'll be fines for defaulting.'

William was impressed though he didn't show it. His father would welcome the news, and so no doubt would the other landowners, including Robert Storey and John Gurwood. All the same, they wouldn't want to be left out of any talks.

'Can't we decide our own rules—I mean, before they're presented to us? We could meet in the church or at the forge?'

'There's nothing to stop you, but I think it best if you wait and see what is proposed. The steward has eyes everywhere. He knows what bad practices go on.'

'How long have we got? When exactly is the next court?'

'Monday, 14th October. It'll be announced in church this Sunday, and a notice nailed to the door.'

While the landowners mulled over everything from the selling of whins out of town to the geese spoiling the pond, life in Reighton carried on as normal. John Gurwood's wife was heavy with their fourth child and expected the birth in late autumn, and the shepherd was about to prepare the sheep for winter and put the ram with the ewes.

Jack the shepherd had not forgotten his promise to John; when it was time to salve the sheep, the boy could join in and help. Just before the middle of October, there was a spell of dry weather, the perfect time for the salving. He knocked on William and Mary's back door.

'I've come fo' John,' he told Mary. 'It's greasin' time.'

John heard and leapt from the breakfast table. He ran into the shepherd's waist and hugged him.

Jack smiled. 'Thoo's ready then, eh?'

As John gave a huge grin and nodded, his brother William sidled up.

'Can I help as well?'

The rest of the family stopped eating. Young William never offered to help the shepherd.

'Can I?' he repeated.

'Why, aye, if thoo wants. There's plenty o' work.'

'Don't get in Jack's way though,' Mary warned. 'Listen, and do as you're told.'

'We will,' young William agreed. 'And I'll see John is alright.'

His father mumbled under his breath, 'It's not John we're bothered about.'

The boys donned their jackets, pulled on their boots and set out. John skipped alongside the shepherd. Young William bent down to stroke the sheepdog, but she wasn't used to the attention like Stina and shot out of reach. He shrugged, and they carried on until they reached the moor where Jack had the year's lambs in a pen. Four strangers awaited them, rough-looking men in dirty smocks standing beside two broad benches.

John grew shy immediately and hid behind his brother.

'It's only men from 'Unmanby,' Jack explained. 'They're greasers. They're 'ere to 'elp.' He pointed out two tubs to the men. 'Salve is all ready, an' thoo'll see I've added rancid butter. It'll spread easier, an' these two lads 'ere can 'elp thee.' He turned to the boys. 'Stand over 'ere an' watch first.'

He went into the pen, grabbed the nearest lamb and, despite it being almost as large as a full-grown sheep, he dragged it outside. One of the men helped to haul it to a bench where his mate now sat astride. They flung the lamb onto its back and held tight.

John and William paid attention as the man on the bench parted the fleece on the belly. He then dipped his finger into the tub of salve and smeared it on the lamb's skin. Then, about two inches away, he made another parting and did the same. When he'd finished the front, he started on the sides.

Young William sighed. The greasing wasn't a quick job and there was still the lamb's back to do. He stood before Jack with his hands on his hips. 'What are *we* supposed to do then? You said we could help.'

Jack ignored William and spoke to John. 'Thoo can grease lamb's face… an' thoo, William, can grease its tail an' rump.'

Young William scowled. It didn't seem fair, but he kept quiet. Perhaps if he made a good job of it, they could swap over and take turns. He stuck his finger into the salve.

'Ugh, what else is in this stuff?'

'Tar an' tallow.'

William grimaced and then copied how the man had parted the wool to reach the skin. He daubed the mixture on as best he could.

John did the same to the lamb's face. With his tongue sticking out in concentration, he carefully avoided the eyes and mouth.

It took ages to salve one lamb. The four men, Jack and the boys worked non-stop until late morning when three women arrived with food and drink. William recognised one of them as a maid from Uphall. He and John wiped their fingers on the grass and stood by to be served. Once they had a pot of beer each and a hunk of cheese, they sat on one of the benches with Jack. The greasers sat on the other bench.

The women stood together, waiting for the men to finish. Apart from the lambs' bleating, it was quiet. It was only when the first beer had been drunk and half the cheese eaten that conversation began.

One of the greasers watched William leave his bench and return his empty pot. 'Ey up, lad, what's wrong wi' tha leg? Or 'as tha foot been trodden on?'

William frowned. Usually, no one mentioned the way he walked.

'Nay,' Jack answered for him, ''e was born that way.'

'One leg longer than t'other then?'

'Aye, summat like that.'

William sat down again and glowered. The sheepdog was laid near his foot, so he reached down to stroke her black head. This time she didn't move away.

'Aye,' Jack muttered, 'she's a good dog is Meg.'

The maid from Uphall smiled. 'Thoo knows what they say—it's best to 'ave a lame shep'erd an' a lazy dog.'

'Aye, it's true,' Jack snorted. 'It's patience works best. Sheep don't want rushin'.'

John remained silent. He knew the greasers were now looking at him.

'Odd place this is,' one remarked. 'Yon lad never says owt.'

William lifted his head from the dog to defend his brother. 'John's quiet because he thinks a lot. He's alright.'

'Tell me then, John, why are we gettin' greasy an' mucky all day, eh?'

John glanced at Jack as if to ask permission to speak.

'Go on, lad, tell 'em.'

'It's to stop the lambs getting scab.'

'Oooh! 'E knows then. What else?'

'The salve helps keep the rain out.'

Jack intervened. 'An' if we rub fleeces wi' tar an' grease, it'll soften 'em, won't it, John? Make 'em fetch a better price.'

John nodded with a wide smile. 'And when Jack greases our sheep in winter, it keeps them warm.'

The men shut up. They finished their drinks, nodded in gratitude to the women and went back to work.

At the end of the day, Jack thanked the boys. 'Thoo's been a great 'elp. We'll soon be done now, so thoo needn't come i' mornin'.'

William was glad. He didn't like the way the men mocked them, but John shifted about on his feet, reluctant to move.

'Come on, John, it's time to go. Jack'll let you help some other time.'

'Aye, I will. First week i' November thoo can watch me raddle our ram.'

Chapter 43

Matthew Smith attended the meetings at the forge, and paid personal visits as well to the major yeomen. His standing with the Lord of the Manor was at stake, and he wanted everyone's full consent to the list of rules.

On the appointed day, the front of the church was filled with the usual jury of landowners. William sat between his father and Matthew, while John Gurwood and Robert Storey sat behind them. Everyone waited for the arrival of Thomas Cockerill and the steward, John Grimston.

It was late morning, and the low sun streaked through the south windows, cleaned especially for the day. The pews at the front had been dusted and, as William judged by the smell of turpentine and beeswax, they'd been polished too.

Hesslewood, the churchwarden, having brought out the vestry table and set it out with paper, pen and ink, kept glancing towards the door.

When the Lord and his steward entered and marched to the front, a faint whiff of coriander followed in their wake. William winked at Matthew; he knew that Thomas Cockerill chewed the stuff to sweeten his breath. They and the other yeomen rose and waited while the two men sat at the table. No one sat down again until the jurors' names had been called in order of the amount of land owned. On this

325

occasion, the jury was complete; there were no fines for non-attendance.

John Grimston took a long parchment from his bag and placed it on the table. He stood and cleared his throat before making his announcement.

'I call this court baron open this day, the 14th of October, 1726. I have here a comprehensive list of pains. Each one is for the better regulating of Reighton and its common field. You will hear each one in turn, and the payment for each default.' He inclined his head to Thomas Cockerill. 'Shall I begin, my Lord?'

On a nod from his right, he read out the first one.

'The byelawmen shall, on or before 25th May, drive the moor and other pasture, and give account to the chief freeholder. The penalty for default is five shillings.' He waited while the jury members nodded in full agreement, and then read the next.

'No oxen or cows to be tethered in the upfield between May Day and until all the corn be in. For every default, three shillings and four pence.'

Again, everyone consented though it amounted to a day's wages for a skilled worker. William and his father smiled. So far, the list was commonsense. The next two items pleased Francis Jordan even more; there were orders to repair gates and stiles, and detailed instructions on scouring the gutters in the lower pastures, even specifying the width and depth required and when the work should be done.

'About time,' he murmured. He listened rapt as the steward read items concerning whins and brushwood, and many concerning livestock.

All went well until the steward read out Number 17. It was to regulate the collecting of seaweed from the beach. Anything found on the beach was by rights the property of the Lord of the Manor, and yet everyone took seaweed whenever they could. Now, there'd be a fine. John Grimston could not progress further due to the shuffling of boots and the obvious indignation.

Francis Jordan was the first to stand and speak up. 'Nay, we can't 'ave that. We've allus managed before wi' no trouble. Them that 'as means an' labour to gather seaweed should be able to take what they want. There's plenty i' winter, an' it's good fo' soil.' As he sat down again, he chuntered to William. 'I thought these rules were to 'elp us.'

The other yeomen agreed and began to grumble about the number of restrictions mounting up.

The steward looked to Thomas Cockerill for advice.

The Lord of the Manor waved a weary hand. 'Move on. We can come back to that later.'

The yeomen settled down and listened to the next six regulations on the list; they were so various that Francis Jordan grew restless and complained once more.

'See 'ere tha lordship,' he said as he rose from his seat, 'we've sat an' listened well, but there's a lot to take in. I know I'm gettin' on i' years, but I've a clear 'ead. Why don't we try an' abide by these rules till next October? Then we'll meet again an' sign up proper, like.'

There were murmurs of approval from the pews.

The steward sat down to confer with his master while the others discussed things among themselves.

At first, Thomas Cockerill was in no mood to compromise, and then thought a year's wait might be of benefit. 'Mr Grimston, next year we'll be able to add even more to this list. I'm sure you have other ideas for improvements up your sleeve.'

'But what, my Lord, about pain number seventeen? What about the seaweed? It does improve the land.'

Thomas Cockerill was getting impatient and yet knew his steward was being reasonable. 'Oh, very well... let's show some leniency. Cross it out. Do it now, in front of them. It's a minor point in the greater scheme, and then we've finished for the day.'

The steward explained what he was doing and put heavy crosses through the offending sentences.

Thomas Cockerill had to raise his voice above the general hubbub. 'There you see—the fine for seaweed collection has been removed.'

The steward stood and held up an arm for silence. 'Thank you for your valuable time and your patience. We'll take up the matter of these pains next October when the Manor Court meets again. I trust you'll do your utmost to comply with the regulations. I'll leave a copy in the church.'

Thomas Cockerill stood and made his way to the door.

The steward followed and spoke to the churchwarden as he passed. 'Make sure you display the copy in a prominent position for all to see.'

Chapter 44

As November approached, the hired lads at Uphall began to talk in earnest about their futures. There was the ploughing still to finish and the green peas and winter wheat to sow, yet this didn't stop the lads congregating in corners to argue for and against the local farms. Dickon overheard them as they carried out the end-of-year tasks. Bullock Rob wanted to stay, and Dickon could guess why. He'd seen that particular lad make a habit of working with Richard Jordan whenever Richard came to help. Dickon hadn't actually caught them together, but he had a suspicion that they were more than workmates. It was something he never dared mention to his master or to William.

Richard heard from his father the names of the lads that were to leave Uphall at the next hirings. The announcement was made just to him and his brothers. While William and Thomas nodded in approval, Richard was shocked to find Bullock Rob on the list. His first thought was to plead Rob's case, though that might arouse suspicion. He didn't like the hired hand that much, but his presence and the promise of intimacy was exciting. Knowing the lad's short temper, he feared repercussions when the list was made public.

When Bullock Rob heard he was on the list to leave, his eyes narrowed. He was a powerfully built young man in his late teens and was used to getting his own way. He'd spent the past year getting close to Richard and lickspittling up to the family, and had expected to stay at Uphall for years. Now that he was to be dismissed, he could think only of revenge.

He bided his time, waiting for the opportunity to speak with Richard alone. Late one afternoon, at twilight, he followed Richard into the barn.

Richard spun round on hearing footsteps behind him. When he saw who it was, he held his arms wide in welcome.

Rob stepped closer and then shoved Richard away in disgust. 'Thoo's lied to me,' he snarled. 'Thoo's led me on, let me think I could stay on 'ere, work me way up.'

'Don't be like that, it's not *my* fault.'

'Well, listen to this. I'm goin' to tell thy father all about 'ow I was led astray, an' what thoo did to me.'

Richard went pale.

'Or thoo can get tha father to keep me on. Or not. Make up tha mind.'

Richard needed time to think. He shrugged, unable to commit himself. 'I'll see what I can do.'

Rob slouched out of the barn, turning to sneer as he left. 'An' then there's thy mother... she won't be 'appy.'

Richard felt dazed, and sat down on a pile of sacks to think. He was horrified to be threatened in such a way. Only William knew about him and Bullock Rob, so perhaps William could help. With this faint hope, he put off the rest of his jobs for the day and sought out his eldest brother.

William shook his head on hearing Richard's dilemma. 'You've got yourself in a real pickle this time.' He carried on mending the gate of the pigsty while he thought what to do. Straightening up, he looked Richard in the eye.

'Tell me honestly, do you want Rob to stay?'

'Not after the way he's threatened me. But what can I do?'

'Oh God, Richard, the things I do for you.' He kicked the gate into position and then sighed. 'Leave it to me. I'll fix him.'

'Thank you. I'll make it up to you.'

'Don't worry. You're family and that's what matters. Let Rob believe you're working on Father, trying to change his mind. I might need a few days before I can catch the lad on his own—well away from prying eyes.'

In early November, John spent as much time as possible with Jack the shepherd. His brother William often joined him, more to be with the sheepdog than the sheep. When it was time to mark the ram with the raddle mixture, they both hung around Jack's hut to watch.

The shepherd had dug a hole in the ground a foot deep not far from his door, a hole just wide enough to stand a pot over it and not fall in. He had John and William fill the hole with dry kindling and gorse. Then he put a great dollop of pigs' fat into a pot, half a bottle of linseed oil and, finally, a small tub of red dye. He lit the fire and, when it was blazing, he sat the pot over it.

'Is it to help the ram's fleece?' John asked.

His brother sighed. He thought everyone knew why the ram had its chest marked with red. He scratched his head. Surely, at twelve years old, John knew about tupping.

'Listen, John,' he began to explain, 'when the ram mounts a ewe—you know, to make lambs, it leaves some of that red stuff on her back. It rubs off his chest. That way, Jack can tell which ewes have been ridden.'

'Aye,' said Jack, 'it's ridin' season, an' ram over there i' yon pen is keepin' 'is eyes on us.'

The boys faced the sheep in question. It was huge. Although it didn't have horns, neither boy relished having anything to do with it. They turned back to Jack who was stirring the pot with a wooden paddle. A distinctive rich, fatty smell filled the air.

'As a rule,' he said, 'I add oatmeal to thicken it a bit, then I can trowel it on. Today though, we'll 'ave to brush it on.'

When the raddle mixture was ready, he took the pot off the fire to cool. All three sat to wait on the bench by the hut, John swinging his legs, and William stroking Meg. After a while, Jack broke the silence.

'I' November, if frost clings to sheep's wool of a mornin', that's a good sign. But if it melts, then sheep is over warm. It's a sign it's ill. Then I check fo' foot rot.'

William stared at Jack. He'd never known the shepherd say so much. Maybe Jack had spent too much time alone with the sheep.

'Thoo lads might 'elp me wi' yon lamb over there.' He gestured with his head towards a lamb kept separate in a small pen. 'It's blind. Go an' 'ave a look—go on.'

They approached the pen and leant over the hurdle to see. The lamb had a scum over its eyes.

'Can you cure it?' William asked.

'Watch.' Jack entered the pen, held the lamb between his legs and lifted up its head. Then, with his other hand, he took out his knife and cut the corner of an eye. The lamb flinched, yet Jack was so deft that he managed to do the same to the other eye too. He let the lamb go free, a little blood seeping from each eye.

William was fascinated.

John had tears in his eyes. 'Do you have to do that?'

'That's where thoo can 'elp. There's another cure thoo can try. I picked ground ivy leaves this mornin'. Thoo'll find 'em, John, in a bag just inside me door. Go an' fetch 'em, there's a good lad.'

John handed Jack the bag.

The shepherd took out a few leaves and put them in his mouth. He chewed for a moment and then, with his mouth full of juice, he approached the lamb again. He spat into its eyes.

'There,' he announced, 'thoo lads can come an' do this three times a day. It'll save me a job.'

John put a couple of leaves in his mouth and chewed. He gagged straightaway.

'I'll have a go,' William offered. Showing off, he grabbed a handful and stuffed the leaves in one cheek. He concentrated on the lamb as he chewed, finding the leaves quite minty and pleasant at first. Soon though, the taste turned bitter. He ignored the rising temptation to retch as his mouth filled with saliva. Suddenly, he rushed into the pen and spurted the whole mouthful into the lamb's face.

Jack laughed. 'Well, that's one way to do it. Thoo can carry on—'ave that job for a few days.'

John gazed at his brother in admiration although William was still trying to spit out the taste.

Jack left the pen. 'Come on lads, raddle stuff'll be cool enough now. We'll take it into ram's pen an' thoo can 'elp me. John can paint it on.'

William gulped. He wasn't strong like a man.

Jack saw the worried expression on his face and grinned. 'Ram may look fierce but 'e's fine so long as 'e's on 'is own, not with 'is ewes. Once 'e's out o' moor wi' flock... then beware.' He took the feeding bucket and entered the pen.

When the ram followed Jack, William and John ventured in with the pot of raddle. They closed the hurdle behind them.

As soon as the ram began to eat, Jack used the ram's own weight to flip it over onto its back.

'Now, 'old tight, William! 'Elp 'old 'im still! John—get goin' wi' that brush. Daub plenty o' raddle on 'is chest.'

John dipped the brush deep into the pot and then, with wide eyes and a trembling hand, he edged towards the ram and jabbed at it with his brush.

'Again, John,' cried the shepherd, struggling to hold the ram. 'Keep paintin' it on.'

When he saw that John had used up most of the raddle mix, Jack signalled that he'd done enough. 'Get out now, John. I'm goin' to let 'im go.'

William let go of the ram first and shot out of the pen close behind John. They watched as Jack released the ram. Instead of attacking him or butting the walls of the pen, it went straight back to the bucket to feed.

'Well done, lads. Tomorrow it's 'is lucky day. I'll put 'im out o' moor to do 'is job.'

William kept his eyes on the lads at Uphall as they went about their work. At last, just before the hiring fair, he managed to corner Bullock Rob at the back of the cowshed. Armed with a pitchfork, he advanced on him and rammed the fork into the wall either side of his neck.

Rob gasped in horror, unable to speak.

'Next time, I won't miss your filthy throat.' William leant in closer to Rob's face. 'You stop threatening my brother or this is the last place you'll ever work. You're going to leave Uphall and never come back. And if I ever hear you've been spreading rumours about Richard, then I'll seek you out—aye, wherever you are, I'll find you. Understand?'

The cold prongs of the fork pressed against Rob's neck. He nodded as best he could.

When William wrenched the fork from the wall, he noticed the lad had wet himself. He grinned. 'I trust you'll cause no more bother.'

He left him and went to find Richard in the yard. His brother was standing by the trough, clearing out dead leaves. William made it clear that he wasn't happy being implicated in Richard's problems.

'I know,' Richard admitted. 'It's not fair on you.'

They stood together in silence for a while, gazing into the trough.

Richard poked out more dead leaves that were floating there. 'I can't go on like this,' he said. 'I can't keep hoping to find a new and willing lad each November—one I can trust.'

'No, you can't,' William echoed. 'You're a married man. Try harder. Promise me you'll stop working for the chandler. Stay at home with your wife in Carnaby, and work on your father-in-law's farm instead.'

'Maybe.'

William's well-meant comments set Richard's thoughts on a different path. Nearly all the men he'd enjoyed in Bridlington had been older, often married. Yes, he might stay and farm in Carnaby, but what he needed was a steady, older man.

Chapter 45

The day before the Hunmanby hirings, young William went into the cowshed next to the house and took out the shilling he'd hidden there. He showed his father the money.

'I wouldn't have this if Stina hadn't won it for me. She retrieved a duck at Flamborough, and Uncle Thomas gave me this from his winnings.'

'Fancy that then. And what are you going to do with it?'

'I want you to take it tomorrow and buy a dog collar.'

'But—'

'I know, I haven't a dog, but the shepherd has, and Meg is a good dog. I'd like her to have a new collar. Choose a nice leather one.'

William returned from the hirings the next day with a fine red leather collar, and he had another surprise.

'There's someone outside who wants to come in and stay for the week.'

Mary and the boys glanced at each other. No one could think who he meant.

'Is it Stinky Skate?' John asked.

Young William chuckled at that idea. 'Don't be daft. Stinky? Mother wouldn't have *him* in here.' He cast a worried glance. 'You wouldn't, would you?'

'No.'

'Who is it, Father? Tell us.'

'I'll fetch him in.'

They waited, all eyes on the door. They heard boots in the passage, and then suddenly they realised.

'My goodness,' cried Mary, 'it's Francis!'

Her eldest son stepped forward and kissed her on the cheek. 'Father says I can spend my week's holiday here.'

The two youngest shuffled backwards. Their older brother was taller now, and not as they remembered.

Young William's heart sank. He'd have to give up his bed and share with John. It was annoying to see his parents looking so pleased to have Francis back home. His mother was now promising to cook his brother's favourite dinners. Such a fuss they were making, helping him take off his boots and asking endless stupid questions. He thought of the prodigal son in the Bible and knew exactly how the brother had felt. It wasn't fair.

Francis was told to get comfy by the fire. His mother would warm a mug of beer for him. 'And, when you're settled, you can tell us all about Rudston.'

The others were told to sit at the table and listen.

Francis didn't wait for his drink. He turned to his mother, eager to pass on news of the Gurwoods. 'Did you know Priscilla got married this year? It was in April. I was invited to the breakfast.'

'Yes, I remember hearing something. Was it to anyone we know?'

'Cornelius Read. He's from Kilham. I think his family might be from near Scarborough.'

'I wonder if he's any relation to Robert Read who married her sister Jane. Anyway, tell us what she looked like. What did she wear? Were her sisters bridesmaids?'

To satisfy his mother's curiosity, Francis did his best to describe the wedding.

Young William clenched his fists beneath the table and gazed at the empty space by the hearth where Stina used to lie. If he'd had Stina he could have escaped, taken her for a long walk. He didn't know how he'd bear a whole week of this fuss and nonsense. There'd be no peace in bed either with John wriggling all night.

After supper, Francis and his father left the table first. They sat together by the fire while Mother tidied up.

The other boys, no longer so shy of their elder brother, crowded as close to the fire as they could. They watched their father light up his pipe.

Young William asked if he could have a go.

Immediately, Francis complained. 'You're too young!'

'Let him be,' their father said. 'You don't live here now, and your brother can have a pipe if he wants.'

Francis let out a deep breath. 'I think I'll go to bed early. I'm tired after the walk here in the head wind.' He stood up, stretched and yawned. 'Goodnight, Mother. In the morning I'll visit Uncle Robert and Aunt Elizabeth.'

His father flinched.

His mother put down the knitting she'd only just picked up, and said goodnight with a worried frown.

The next day, Francis rose before anyone else, washed outside in cold water and, despite the heavy mist, took a walk down Oxtrope Lane. He strolled to the cliff top and turned southwards, then headed inland towards the church. There was still a thick mist hovering over the lower village, but on the higher ground the sun was beginning to break through. He hadn't told his parents the real reason for his week in Reighton. He'd tell them once he'd discussed it with Robert Storey.

Elizabeth was so surprised and pleased to see him on the doorstep that she wrapped her arms round him and held him tight.

'Leave Francis alone,' Robert cried from the passage. 'He's not a child anymore. Let him come in and sit down.'

Elizabeth bade Francis sit at the kitchen table. She handed him a bowl, and the three of them began to spoon in the thin, milky porridge.

Robert put his spoon down first. 'So, Francis, what brings you to Reighton? Is there not enough work in Rudston?'

'No, it's not that. As it's hiring week, I've been given a holiday.' He swallowed and licked his lips. 'I also wanted to talk to you... It's about my future.'

Robert could see the youth was troubled. 'Go on then, spit it out.'

'There's a young woman there. She works as the maid at the vicarage. I've got to know her through the Gurwoods. They often invite me to dinner.'

'And?'

'She's everything I could wish for. She's learnt to read while she's been there, and she likes to study the Bible. She doesn't drink, and she doesn't approve of others getting drunk.'

'And?'

'I was wondering... I'd like to make her my wife.'

'Francis, you're only nineteen. How old is...? You haven't even told me her name.'

'Lizzie—I mean Elizabeth. Elizabeth Cooke. She's two years older. I'm sure she feels the same.'

'Do you know her family?'

'They're related to my grandmother. She was born in Bempton though her parents live in Bridlington now.'

'Where would you live?'

'I don't know. I've been saving up. I'd like to come back and live here.'

Elizabeth leant forward and grasped Francis's hand. 'Oh, Francis... I don't want to put you off, but you are very young.'

'I won't change my mind.'

Robert agreed with his wife. 'There's no need to hurry these things. I courted Elizabeth for years.'

'Well,' interrupted Elizabeth, 'you needn't wait *that* long.'

Robert frowned. 'At least wait one more year. It'll give you time to be better acquainted.' He winked at Francis. 'Women take some getting used to.' With that, he left the table. 'Let's leave Elizabeth to clear away and do her chores. We can talk further, at our ease, in the parlour.'

It was cold in the other room. No fire had been lit. Robert knelt down to pray and signalled Francis to join him.

'Oh, Lord, we ask humbly for guidance. Your obedient servant here is about to embark on a perilous voyage of the spirit. Watch over him and his daily actions, and bring him safely to harbour. Amen.'

They rose together and took a seat each by the window. Francis stared outside. The wind was getting up again. Tree branches were thrashing, and leaves were swirling round the garden. Occasionally, a twig hit the glass. He knew he was about to be lectured, but this was exactly why he'd come. Only Robert could give the kind of advice he sought.

Robert thought for a moment before he began. 'Tell me,' he asked, 'does George Gurwood know of your intentions towards his maid?'

'I think so. He gives me a certain smile when she enters the room.'

'Be careful. Our old vicar is not like us. Don't let him tempt you to spend time alone with her. You haven't been alone, have you?'

'No! No, we haven't.'

'Very good. Keep it that way. You must remember that Satan has many ways to beguile us through women. Be on your guard at all times. Imagine you're a seafarer trying to reach port, and there are dangerous rocks in the way. Tell me, is this Elizabeth Cooke a comely woman?'

Francis reddened.

'Is that what first attracted you? Be honest.'

'She was kind to me, and always put me at ease when I called at the vicarage. And, yes, I find her... comely. But I'll never take advantage of her generous nature.'

'Listen, Francis, true chastity does not consist of simply keeping your body from uncleanliness. No, it is in withholding your *mind* from lust too. And women are well-armed with their tongues, their newfangled fashions, their breasts and ankles.'

'Lizzie's sober in her appearance. She's quiet and obedient. She's hardworking too.'

'So, you trust she'll make a useful wife and helpmate?'

'Yes and, like I said, she reads the Bible.'

'When choosing a wife, value virtue above learning. And remember, women are the weaker vessel, both morally and spiritually. You must not be led on by her.'

'I'll take care. Maybe I should do as you say and wait another year.'

'Good. And, if you can, find out what her mother is like. The apple doesn't fall far from the tree. Like mother like daughter.'

Francis thought that could wait. He'd prefer to have a year getting to know Elizabeth better before meeting her parents.

'Thank you for your help.' He stood up to go.

Robert showed him to the door. 'I'm glad you thought to come here first. Just remember, beware of bodily fascination. Seek instead her inner qualities.'

As they went past the kitchen, Francis put his head round the door. 'I'm going now. Thank you for breakfast. It's been so good to see you again.'

Robert returned to the parlour while Elizabeth escorted Francis to the door. On the threshold, she held him by the arm.

'Take what he says with a pinch of salt. Know your own heart, Francis. Follow it and be happy.'

Chapter 46

1726-27

While Francis was with Robert Storey, young William took John to see the shepherd. He looked forward to handing Jack the new dog collar. They walked through the mist hovering low in the lane and emerged from it onto the north moor where the sheep glistened in the early sunshine. Well before they reached the shepherd's hut, the sheepdog scampered forward to greet them. Both boys bent down to stroke her, but she stood still for only a moment before running back.

They found the shepherd in his smoke-filled hut warming milk over a meagre fire. The hut had no chimney, just a hole in the roof, and young William reckoned the smoke was even worse than at old Ben's cottage. When he began to cough, the shepherd ushered them outside.

'Wait out there. I'll be out i' leap of a lop.'

Glad to be in the fresh air again, William spoke through the open door.

'I have a surprise—a present for Meg.'

Jack came out cradling a mug of hot milk. 'What's this you say? We've never 'ad any presents.'

William showed him the bright red collar and passed it over. 'I hope it fits.'

'My, my.' Jack put down his mug and ran his fingers over the tooled leather. 'Meg's never 'ad such a fine collar. Come 'ere, Meg, an' let's try it on.'

'She's a good dog,' John announced with one of his widest smiles.

'Yes,' William added. 'A good dog deserves a reward.'

'Aye,' Jack said as he removed the old greasy collar and fastened on the new one. 'I'm sorry about Stina.'

William shuffled his feet. 'That's alright. Come on, John, we'll be off now. We have sticks to gather.'

As they turned to go, John noticed Meg sniffing at her old collar on the grass. He reached into his pocket and pulled out a lump of cold bacon. It had bits of fluff on it, but he held it out to her and she took it from his hand gently before swallowing it whole.

'John, come on!'

'Are we going home?'

'No. Francis might be back and I don't want to see him. You know he didn't even notice Stina wasn't there anymore. We'll stay out all morning and gather sticks.'

The family's meals were improved by Francis's visit because Mary kept giving him some treat or other. Due to pig-killing time, there was plenty of fresh pork, and that autumn there was an abundance of apples to make sauce. She never tired of seeing her eldest son at the table, but could tell that her husband's enthusiasm was waning.

William vented his misgivings when Francis was out of the house. 'That lad finds fault with everything.' Then he imitated his son. 'We don't do it like that in Rudston. In Rudston, we do this. In Rudston, we do that.' He sighed. 'I've just about had enough. As far as I'm concerned, he's outstayed his welcome.'

Mary could understand his annoyance though it cast a shadow over the remaining days.

Francis had not mentioned Elizabeth Cooke to his parents yet. As he was missing her, he decided to cut his visit short. At breakfast on the fifth day, he plucked up courage.

'I'm sorry, but I'll be leaving sooner than expected.'

Only his mother looked upset.

'You see, there's someone in Rudston who I'm thinking of courting in earnest. I'm missing her already.'

Young William choked on his bacon. Both parents stopped chewing and put down their spoons.

'I've spoken to Robert Storey—'

'What?' his father spluttered. 'You've seen *him* about it?'

Young William smirked. It was good to see Francis in trouble though his mother had tears in her eyes.

'Oh, Francis,' she cried, 'why didn't you tell us? You've been here for days.'

'If he thinks he'll get good advice from Robert Storey then I'm a Dutchman.'

'Who is she?'

Francis explained, and was relieved when his parents' main concern was his age. They calmed down on hearing he wanted to save up and would wait a year.

Young William was keen to know when he'd get his bed back. 'Are you leaving today?'

Francis nodded. 'Thank you, Mother, for all you've done. I'll miss your apple pies.'

She didn't answer. She'd used up flour that should have been saved for harder times. Now the family would face smaller rations.

They finished their breakfast in silence.

Francis didn't waste time. As soon as he'd eaten, he grabbed his coat and kissed his mother on the cheek. After a brief goodbye to his father and brothers, he was gone.

Mary announced that she was going out to fetch water. She needed fresh air and women's company. 'And you boys—go and gather more sticks for the fire. I'll be cross if we run out.'

William left the house and strolled to Uphall, shaking his head at the thought of his son courting. He remembered the trouble over Milcah. Now at least he could get on with his work without hearing 'In Rudston we…'

At the end of November, Mary heard that John Gurwood's wife was in labour and that John had gone to fetch a midwife from Hunmanby. She called on her sister Elizabeth, and they joined Martha Wrench at the house. It was still early in the day, dark and dismal. Together, they made Dorothy comfortable and kept the three children occupied.

When the midwife arrived, the women left the parlour and waited in the kitchen until needed. After an hour, they were still waiting, huddled round the table. Hardly a sound came from the other room.

Suddenly, the midwife opened the door. 'It's done. She 'as a lass an' all's well. Come on in an' clear up.'

Mary stared at Elizabeth. The midwife sounded very confident. It must have been the easiest birth in the whole village.

Once the mother was washed and the baby cleaned and swaddled, the helpers gathered in the kitchen for a celebratory drink of warm spiced ale. The midwife, who until now had hardly said a word, began to talk of strange births she'd heard about.

'Wait,' interrupted Mary. 'Little pitchers have big ears. Children, go and find your father and tell him the good news.'

As the outer door closed and the women were left alone, the midwife resumed her alarming tales.

'I 'eard one woman was frightened by rabbits while she was wi' child. Aye, an' afterwards she gave birth to fifteen of 'em—rabbits I mean.'

Mary shook her head. 'I don't believe it.'

'Well, it's been reported, an' surgeon to royal family believes it.'

When the midwife continued to relate stories of babies born with a monkey's or a dog's head and monstrous limbs, Mary nudged Elizabeth.

'We should go now. We've work to do… meat to salt. Martha can stay and help if she wants.'

That night, as soon as everyone had settled to sleep, Mary whispered in bed to William her news of the 'rabbit woman'.

'What nonsense!' he grunted. 'It's not true. Why, I heard she was charged with being a cheat, an imposter. And there's others have tried worse things.'

'What? What could be worse?'

'There was one woman who had animal parts thrust inside her—cats' and rabbits' legs, even bits of an eel's backbone.'

Mary felt sick. She turned away from him and curled up to keep warm. The last thing she wanted after such revelations was another pregnancy.

William's mind was soon on other matters. The harvest had been poor and there was less wheat to sell at the market. Although families didn't need much for their own consumption as they had barley and oats to live on, so much wheat had to be kept back for seed. Based on experience, the Jordans would begin their usual calculations as to how much grain to keep back for release onto the market in spring and summer.

The next morning, William argued with his father that, the longer you held onto grain, the higher price you could charge.

'Aye, but I don't like it an' it's a risky business, allus 'as been.'

Thomas agreed with his father. 'I don't like it either. Haven't we always prided ourselves on being able to feed others? The market at Bridlington depends on people like us.'

William didn't reply. They did have a responsibility, yet times were hard.

Thomas put into words what William was thinking.

'I suppose we've done it before. Instead of taking bushels of grain to the market, we can just take samples. Others do it. We can use them to find out the going prices, and then we'll keep our main stocks to sell to the corn jobbers. When they call round we can negotiate a good price.'

William shrugged and turned to his father for an answer.

'Alright, that's what we'll do, but it's a sorry day an' I'm ashamed. Still, we must look after our own.'

In the spring, small amounts of threshed grain were measured into sacks at Uphall, and William and Thomas took turns to take them to Bridlington. They continued the practice despite their vicar denouncing it from the pulpit. John Sumpton, recently recovered from his long ailment, was in no mood to prevaricate.

'To keep the fruits of the earth to yourselves is an abomination in the eyes of the Lord. Those who hoard corn work against the common good. They grow fat while others starve. They are the enemies of both God and man.'

The yeomen sitting in their pews knew he meant well, trying to appeal to their better natures. But what did the vicar know? He wasn't from round here and, besides, he lived in Filey. They turned a deaf ear.

William noticed that Matthew Smith kept his head down. Only recently, there'd been rumours of him arranging to export grain. Matthew was operating in a different sphere, dealing with Holland and France. Such transactions could make or mar his fortune.

Chapter 47

1727

During the winter and early spring in Rudston, Cecilia Gurwood, daughter of the vicar, had been intent on matchmaking. At the age of thirty-three, she'd given up on her own chances and now spent her energies on others. She had her eye on Francis Jordan and the maid. On Sundays she watched Francis accompany Elizabeth Cooke to church. The couple sat together at the back, but did not let their bodies touch. The two were as chaste as ever, and she guessed they'd probably be thinking only of the service. The courtship was slow and boring; it needed livening up. She thought April was the perfect time for action.

First, Cecilia invented excuses to leave the couple alone in the parlour. When this ploy brought no obvious results, she grew frustrated; she thought her sister Mary might have better ideas.

'It's spring,' Cecilia complained as the two strolled round the vicarage garden. 'If they don't feel like courting now, when everything is bursting into leaf, then when? I don't know.'

Mary stopped in thought and cocked her head. 'Hmm. They're a difficult pair. I know they want to be together, but I don't think either has made a move. Have they even held hands yet, let alone kissed?'

'So, what can we do to help them?' Cecilia rubbed her hands in anticipation. 'Let's think. They don't drink ale or brandy—won't touch anything stronger than small beer. If only they'd have something to warm them up...'

They took another turn of the garden.

'I know,' said Cecilia, 'we'll wait until May Day. Everyone's outside having a good time then, and I have an idea.'

Francis Jordan was not looking forward to the May Day festivities. Like Robert Storey, he disproved of the lack of self-discipline, and decided to keep his distance. He assumed the vicarage maid was of the same opinion. On the previous Sunday, she'd announced that she wouldn't be staying out all night on May Day Eve, and she certainly wouldn't be dancing round the maypole. Neither had bargained on the enterprising Gurwoods.

On the afternoon before May Day, Cecilia picked a bunch of cowslips and tied them with a pink ribbon. She asked her sister to stand by in the parlour and make sure no one caught her as she copied out a verse to go with the flowers. She did her best to write in Francis's heavy-handed and stilted script.

> *Cowslips is for counsel,*
> *For secrets us between,*
> *That none but you and I alone*
> *Should know the thing we mean!*
> *And if you will wisely do*
> *As I think to be the best,*
> *Then you have surely won the field*
> *And set my heart at rest.*

They waited for the ink to dry. Satisfied, Cecilia folded it and tied it to the posy.

'Right, then. Wish me luck.' She strode out of the parlour to seek the maid.

Francis, aware of his role as a suitor, also picked cowslips for his love. He chose them because they reminded him of her. They had the most delicate of perfumes and did not flaunt their scent like other flowers. He liked the freshness of the leaves and the bright, sunshiny petals and, though her eyes and hair were deep brown, her face glowed in just the same way. He walked to the vicarage in the early evening and presented them to Elizabeth at the back door.

'Oh!' she gasped in surprise.

'They're as pretty as you.'

She wondered why he'd given her two posies; having read the verse that accompanied the first, she could only think he was inflamed with passion. Her heart leapt. Blushing from the neck upwards, she murmured a thank you, leant forwards and kissed him on the cheek.

He gulped and took a step backwards in shock.

At that moment, Cecilia poked her head through the door. 'Francis! I'm glad I've seen you. We're all walking out tonight to celebrate May. You must join us. Meet us here first and we'll have oatcakes and a drink.'

It was an unusually warm evening for the time of year. George Gurwood, always in favour of the younger generation making the most of their youth, gave his maid the night off. While he and his wife settled down to a quiet time in the parlour, Cecilia coaxed a nervous Elizabeth into the garden.

'Come on, Lizzie, sit there on that seat while I fetch the drinks. *You* don't have to do *any*thing. I'll be *your* maid for tonight.' As she walked back to the house, she turned her head to add, 'Francis should be here soon. Keep him company. I won't be long.'

Elizabeth perched on the edge of the garden seat, uncomfortable with the reversal of roles and tense at the thought of Francis's arrival. Unable to sit still, she tapped her feet on the grass and smoothed out her skirt. Bees were still humming around the hives and the air was heavy with the scent of bluebells. She lifted up part of her skirt, making sure a little of each stockinged ankle was showing.

In the kitchen, Cecilia poured out just half a jug of small beer, and then topped it up with strong ale. Out of the corner of her eye, she saw Mary waving the bottle of brandy.

Cecilia blinked. 'Oooh, shall we? Oh, why not. Not too much, though, or Father will notice.'

Almost a quarter of a pint went into the jug and Mary gave it a stir.

While the sisters prepared the food and drink, Francis arrived. He gave a formal bow to Elizabeth and sat on the same seat, leaving a wide gap between them.

'It's a beautiful evenin',' she murmured.

'Yes. It should be a fine day tomorrow, though I won't be dancing with the rest.'

She bit her lip in disappointment. 'Nay, me neither.'

'I intend to keep a clear head at all times.'

She sighed. When would he show the ardour of the poem?

He stood to attention the moment he saw the sisters heading towards them with loaded trays.

Mary handed round the oatcakes while Cecilia passed the pewter mugs.

'You may find the drink has an unusual taste. I wanted to make it special so I've added a few herbs and spices.' She watched the maid take a sip. 'It's alright, I sieved them out. It's good isn't it?'

Elizabeth nodded and took a proper mouthful. 'It's warmin'. I can feel it goin' down. Even me stomach feels warm now.'

Francis drank and agreed the beer benefitted from the herbs.

'So,' said Cecilia, 'I'll propose the first toast and then we can take turns.' She sat next to her sister on the other garden seat. 'Here's to a sunny day tomorrow.'

They raised their mugs and echoed the toast.

'Your turn, Mary.'

'To love.'

Elizabeth blushed as she drank and tried to catch Francis's eye.

'Your turn, Lizzie.'

'I don't know…'

'Oh, come on, there must be something you wish for.'

'Alright, to our 'earts' desires.'

'Perfect,' said Cecilia. 'Drink up. I'll fetch the jug, and refill our mugs.'

Mary kept a conversation going about the winter wheat and the number of calves at each farm.

'Aye,' Elizabeth replied, 'I'll be busy makin' butter an' cheese.' Suddenly she giggled and nudged Francis. 'I'll be a busy Lizzie!'

Equally affected by the fortified beer, he gave her a broad grin. She looked so becoming in her print gown; her cheeks were flushed and her eyes glistened.

Mary thought to leave them a while. 'I'll just go and help Cecilia.'

Alone, the young couple were quiet for a moment. Elizabeth was more relaxed with Francis than she'd ever been. She leant back and stretched out her legs.

'It's such a warm night, Francis.'

'It is. And I'm glad I'm here with you.'

She edged closer to him until she could feel his thigh. He didn't move away.

The sisters observed from the kitchen window. Cecilia nodded her head, pleased with the progress so far.

'One more jug should do it,' she announced. 'Go on, Mary, add more brandy this time. They won't notice.'

The sisters came back with the jug, and the mugs were filled to the brim. Cecilia and Mary were accustomed to the strong drink and proposed further toasts at a fast rate.

In order to be polite, Elizabeth kept pace.

'To a good crop of barley.'

'An' a good crop of oats.'

'Here's to the wheat.'

'An' don't forget chickens. 'Ere's to plenty of eggs.'

'You give a toast, Francis.'

'To the prettiest maid in Yorkshire.'

Elizabeth smiled and rested her head on his shoulder. 'I want to say another toast.' Her voice was a little slurred. ''Ere's to finest lad i' Rudston, most 'andsome an' most eligible.' She struggled with the last word, unable to end it to her satisfaction. She gave up and burped. 'Sorry, silly me.'

Francis grinned again. He could feel the heat emanate from her body, the pressure of her thigh against his. Taking one of her hands, he lifted it gently to his lips and kissed it.

Cecilia winked at Mary and encouraged the couple to have one more drink. When they were snuggling even closer and giggling at everything, she decided the time was right. She stood up and took the tray.

'Mary and I will clear away. Remember, Lizzie, you have the evening to yourself. As it's growing cooler now and it'll be getting dark before long, why don't you two go and sit in the barn?'

She saw Francis and Lizzie exchange glances, their eyes sparkling.

'You can borrow a lantern. I'll bring one. It's not often you two have any time alone.'

Chapter 48

Cecilia brought the lantern and set it down beside the garden seat. 'Don't worry about the time, Lizzie. Just come in and go to bed whenever you like. You're not needed until morning.' She left the couple with a glint in her eye.

Francis picked up the lantern and took Elizabeth by the hand. Together, they strolled towards the barn. It was dark inside, lit only by the dull yellow glow from the horn lantern. He searched around for somewhere to sit. The barn was almost empty since most of the sheaves had been threshed. He couldn't let Lizzie sit on the cold, dusty floor and so led her to one end where there was a pile of straw left for thatching repairs.

Elizabeth, giddy from the drink, sat down with a thump.

Francis put the lantern safely on the bare floor, and sat beside her. The low light cast huge shadows.

'Ooh, it's scary,' she cried, and clung to his arm.

'There's nothing to fear.'

She held on tighter; the walls were spinning round now, and she was queasy. 'Oh dear, I think I'll have to lie down.'

Having closed her eyes and lain flat, she recovered from the nausea. Then she was overcome by the most wonderful contentment. It felt so right to be lying on her back next to Francis. She took a deep breath, inhaling the smell of the straw. It reminded her of harvest time. She had an image of her body as a ripe plum... waiting. In an instant, she'd grasped his shirt and pulled him down onto the straw.

He lay on his side, resting on one elbow so he could look at her face. 'You are so beautiful.'

She clutched his shirt again and drew him closer. The kiss was as dizzying as the headiness brought on by the drink.

Both lost themselves in the moment, forgetting all they'd been taught about self-discipline and chaste courtship. Their lips were full, soft and yielding. Once begun, they couldn't stop.

She eased her legs apart so that he collapsed on top of her, their lips still together. When she felt him harden, the sudden pleasure surprised her. The more pressure between her legs, the more she wanted him closer, even inside.

'Francis,' she whispered, 'do you love me?'

'Oh, God, yes.'

'Enough to marry me?'

'Yes, yes.'

The words of Aunt Elizabeth echoed in his head. 'Follow your heart.' Beneath him, Lizzie's young breasts pressed into his chest. He could hardly breathe. When the ache in his groin became almost unbearable, he realised she was trying to pull up her skirt. He shifted to one side to give her the freedom to continue. Once she'd revealed all, there was no turning back. He ripped down his breeches and entered her. Half-drunk, in the dimly lit barn on May Day Eve, it seemed the most natural thing in the world.

Afterwards, awed by what they'd done, they lay in the same position, reluctant to move. Elizabeth, still warmed by the drink and Francis's body, couldn't have been more at ease.

Francis, though, was sobering up. He coughed, pulled away and lay on his back to pull up his breeches. What would Robert Storey say? May Day was no excuse.

He then rolled onto his side. Though he didn't regret what had happened, he must not repeat it. Surely, they'd both be embarrassed tomorrow. Their friendship was based on their moral values, and this evening was an aberration. He smoothed her skirt back down and rose to his feet.

'We'd better go now. You'll be needed early in the morning.'

He walked her back to the vicarage and handed her the lantern on the doorstep.

'I can see my way by the moon. Goodnight, Lizzie.' There were no more kisses.

Elizabeth undressed and got into bed. As soon as she reached over to blow out the candle, the room spun round. She knew she was going to be sick, and only just managed to slip out of bed and pull the chamber pot out in time.

Later, still on her knees by the pot, she groaned and leant her face against the cool bed cover. The enchantment of the evening had faded to a confused memory. She climbed back into bed, blew out the candle and lay on her back. The next thing she knew, Cecilia was shaking her awake.

'Come on, get up and dressed. It's a perfect morning, and we're ready to go out.'

Elizabeth rubbed her eyes. Though dawn, it was still quite dark in the bedchamber. Her mouth tasted foul— enough to make her feel sick again.

'Oh, do come on, Lizzie. A wash in the cool dew is exactly what you need.'

By the time Elizabeth ventured into the garden, the villagers had already hung a branch of hawthorn by the door. She heard them singing their way to the foot of the village, calling on everyone in turn and leaving some greenery. It was beyond her to see how they could be so lively after a whole evening outside.

Cecilia and Mary were waiting for her at the bottom of the garden where the grass was longest. Elizabeth hitched up her gown and stepped over to join them. Together, they scooped up the dew and rubbed it over their cheeks and foreheads. Though this ceremony was performed every May, Elizabeth doubted that it helped their complexions. She sighed and resigned herself to getting the fire going and making breakfast.

As she entered the kitchen, she was glad she'd filled the buckets yesterday with fresh water. The last thing she wanted was to face the women at the spring. She had visions of the previous evening and felt sure everyone would know, simply by looking at her, that she was no longer a virgin. Had Francis really promised to marry her? Surely, she could trust him to keep his word. Today she'd find out.

Francis awoke with a thick head. The room was empty, the other lads having chosen to stay up all night. When the church bells began to ring, he held the pillow to his ears. He couldn't ignore Elizabeth today or pretend that last night hadn't happened. No, he'd have to face the May Day games despite his aversion to such frivolity.

He got up and helped himself to what was left in the kitchen of a cold breakfast. Everyone was out, no doubt decorating the maypole ready for the procession and dancing. He didn't even know who'd been chosen to be the May Queen or her escort, Jack-in-the-Green, and he didn't care. Robert Storey had always warned him of the heathenish goings-on, old customs that just encouraged vanity. Well, he'd fallen far short of his standards last night and no mistake. Perhaps it was for the best though. He knew she wanted to marry him and had probably forgiven him already. He could meet her parents and carry on the courtship in a proper manner.

Elizabeth searched for Francis. As expected, he wasn't in the noisy procession from the forge to the field near the church. Neither was he watching the dancing round the maypole. Finally, she caught sight of him hovering at the back of a group of lads. One of them was holding a piglet under his arm and swaggered to the middle of the field for the contest.

'Who wants to go first?' he yelled.

Jack-in-the-Green, decorated in ivy leaves, was hustled forwards. There was a loud cheer from the crowd as his crown of primroses and ribbons wobbled to one side. He took hold of the piglet and began to sing. He didn't even reach the end of the first verse before the piglet squealed.

The crowd laughed and jeered until another lad tried to win the pig. As the new contestant attempted to get through the song before the pig squealed, Elizabeth waved to get Francis's attention. When he didn't notice, she edged her way through the crowd until she was beside him.

'Why, Elizabeth, I didn't think you'd be joining in today.'

'Nay, an' thoo neither.'

He blushed and avoided her eye, choosing instead to gaze vacantly at the church. He hated the festivities and here he was in the thick of them, having to listen to a bawdy song. Robert Storey was right to tell him to shun such rowdy and colourful displays. It was sickening to see the way the girls danced, kicking up their feet to show their calves. But then he remembered the sight of Elizabeth's thighs last night, and blushed again as he recalled the rest.

He stared at the ground. 'I suppose,' he muttered, 'we must both come to terms with last night.'

'Francis, is thoo sorry fo' what we did?'

At that moment, the piglet shrieked. They watched as it was passed to yet another contestant, and the same song began again.

Francis turned to her. 'It's my fault. I should apologise. As you're the weaker sex, I should have acted better, taken control.'

He noticed her dark brown eyes fill with tears. 'Don't cry. I'm sorry, truly I am. Can you forgive me?'

'Oh, Francis, it's not that... Alright, if it 'elps, maybe we was just caught up in excitement o' May. If thoo really wishes, we can be'ave as seemly as before.'

He smiled. 'Thank you. And I will marry you—though not this year. I need to save more money. Last night won't change anything, I promise.'

Chapter 49

William and Thomas Jordan went to Bridlington with corn on alternate weeks. On a glorious day in early May, it happened to be William's turn. As soon as he'd concluded his business, he strolled down the high street towards the green, thinking to sit outside the Bull and Sun for a pie and a quart of ale. He'd get some more tobacco and enjoy a pipe. Just as he crossed the road, he stopped. His mouth fell open as he stared at the young woman walking towards him. She ignored him completely. He spun round to watch her go up the street, his heart thudding like a boy in love. She was the image of his lost daughter, how he'd imagined she'd be had she lived. He gave up the idea of a quiet smoke and followed her.

The way she bounced along and tossed her head, it was as if young Mary had come back to life. When she loitered by a shop window, he could see the chestnut hair poking out from her hat, just like Mary's. He couldn't take his eyes from her. Even the way she put down her basket and bent to pick it up... it was too much to bear. He pretended to be interested in the shops, and then followed her to the end of the street where she turned suddenly and headed up an alley.

He paused for a moment. It was madness to go further. He'd been upset years ago at his brother Samuel's wedding when one of the bride's sisters reminded him of young Mary. It wasn't good to dwell on the past, yet he didn't want to lose sight of this Bridlington girl. He followed and noted the house she entered. With his heart still racing, he went back to the main street and paced up and down the market stalls, reluctant to leave. He was in two minds whether to go back and knock on her door. He could invent a feeble excuse; maybe she'd dropped something. He could easily buy a kerchief for the purpose.

As he stood looking around for this 'something', he realised he was getting over-excited. He needed to control this urge to see her, to be near her. He must be calm, and think, not act the fool. Taking a deep breath, he strode away to collect his horse. He'd have plenty of time to consider things on the journey home.

William's parents were surprised when he kept offering to do the market chore. They knew there must be an ulterior motive; William was furtive, even feverish at times with wide glittering eyes. One morning, as soon as William and the hired lads had left the kitchen, his mother stood behind Thomas, still at the table finishing his porridge. She nudged him.

'Thoo must know what ails 'im. Is it some woman 'e's taken a fancy to?'

Thomas was taken aback by the accusation, and almost choked. 'How should *I* know?' he spluttered.

His father carried on lighting his pipe by the fire, in no mood to join in.

'Well,' she pestered, 'someone must know what 'e's up to. Maybe it's to do wi' smugglin'.'

'Yes, that's more like,' Thomas agreed, pushing away his now empty bowl. 'There are more customs men employed in Bridlington now. Maybe it's the Flamborough lot William's dealing with; they'll be looking for other landing places further north.'

'Thoo could ask 'im an' find out.'

'If he wants to tell me, he will.'

'Well, thoo could follow 'im. Find out where 'e goes an' who 'e meets.'

'I can't do that! You can't expect brothers to spy on each other.' He certainly wouldn't want someone following *him* on his pursuits beyond Reighton. 'Think about it, Mother, we'd be turned against each other. There'd be no end to the distrust.'

'Aye,' said his father, taking the pipe from his mouth, 'that's last thing we need. Jordans stick together.'

'Well,' his mother chuntered on, 'I bet some woman's at bottom of it.'

'Hush, Dorothy. If it *is* a woman, then it's nowt to do with us. Keep tha peace an' let 'im an' Mary sort it out.'

William's wife was worried. Her husband was often preoccupied. There he sat at breakfast with a vacant expression, pushing porridge into his mouth. She could have fed him anything and he wouldn't have noticed. God alone knew what was in his mind. Whenever she tried to speak to him and find out why he was so distant, he made an excuse to leave the house. If they were in bed, he pretended to be asleep. Yet, on those mornings when he was going to Bridlington, he was a different man. Then he was eager and happy to be setting off; he'd grab his younger sons in mock wrestling holds and ruffle their hair. Though he was kind, Mary knew he'd be in a foul mood when he returned, and so it would continue until the next trip.

Each time William went to Bridlington, he searched for the girl. He reckoned she was about eighteen or nineteen, just the age young Mary would have been. She wasn't young Mary, he knew that, but at the sight of her, his stomach dropped. The mere thought of her made him feel so alive that his only desire was to see her as much as possible. If a market day went by without a sighting, he was distraught. Until he could go back to Bridlington, he'd be on tenterhooks, unable to sleep or concentrate on ploughing the fallow. When he did chance to see her, this fuelled his need even more. As each market day approached, he grew nervous and excited as he visualised himself following her at leisure and watching her every move.

When he didn't see her for two weeks in a row, he panicked, thinking she must be ill. On the third week, he feared she might have died. He trudged in misery through all the passageways off the high street before riding home in a daze.

The Bridlington girl had not died, but both she and her mother had seen William leaning against the wall opposite their door.

'Aye, aye,' said Ruth one week later as she peered from behind the curtain, ''e's there again. I've seen 'im a lot. 'E's allus 'angin' round market an' 'e's often followed me.'

Her mother yanked her back. 'Get away fro' that window! Thoo should 'ave told me. Thoo mustn't encourage 'im.'

''E's odd, aye, though 'e's never 'urt me.'

Her mother glanced out of the window. 'If 'e follows thee back 'ere again, I'll be waitin'.'

The next week, Ruth went home, followed as usual by William. As she opened the door, her mother dashed out wielding a heavy pan.

'Get away, damn thy eyes! If thoo doesn't shift, I'll bray thee.'

William backed off.

'An' I'll call fo' constable if I sees thee 'ere again.' As William turned and slunk away, she yelled, 'That's right! Stop botherin' us.'

Though William didn't want any more trouble with constables, he was horror-struck at the prospect of not seeing the girl again. He didn't know how he'd cope without her.

For two long weeks, William let his brother Thomas go to the market instead. This didn't prevent the image of the girl haunting him day and night. Sometimes, he cried silently in bed, and the only time he felt any relief was when he planned to spy on her without being seen.

In the middle of June, he offered to go to the market once more. As the day approached, he grew tense. When Mary dropped a knife on the table, he leapt as if shot.

Mary wondered what on earth was the matter with him. Maybe a smuggling venture had gone wrong, or maybe the Jordan family had got into debt. Maybe William owed money. Whatever it was, she'd be the last to find out.

It was still misty when William set off for Bridlington. A thrush was singing from the top of his apple tree and the sheep and lambs were bleating in the distance. As he climbed southwards onto the high road and emerged from the mist, he could hear larks singing above the fields. It was a perfect June morning and, full of hope, he rode faster than usual, keen to get to the market early.

Once he'd arrived, he was determined to strike a quick deal. He arranged a sale to a local miller and then ambled from stall to stall, always keeping his eyes on the lower street where the girl might suddenly appear. At first, he felt in control, but the longer he wandered about and waited, the more anxious he became. In despair and beginning to panic, he strode up and down the high street, always slowing as he passed the entrance to her alley. He fought off the impulse to go to her house, and went into the Black Lion instead.

As soon as he stepped down into the dark room filled with smoke and noise, he regretted the idea. What he needed was peace and quiet, yet he stayed and bought a brandy. He stood and drank it in one gulp, and then had another while he thought what to do. Growing more desperate, he drank a third brandy. Only then did he have the courage to satisfy his urgent longing.

He pushed through the men crowding the doorway and marched straight to the girl's alley, that beautiful place where she'd brushed against the brick walls, where her feet had touched the cobbles. He leant drunkenly against the wall opposite her doorway and gazed at the upper storey window. She might be there, ill in bed, or she might be in the kitchen. Perhaps she was helping her mother prepare dinner. If he could just watch her and not be seen. That's all he wanted—to look at her. It wasn't much to ask. He prayed for her to appear at the window or, better still, leave the house and go out shopping. How he loved to see her. Like young Mary, she was as fresh as hawthorn blossom, as lithe as a young lamb on new grass.

All at once, her door opened.

It wasn't the girl who came out; it was her father and brothers. They pounced on William before he could move, and dragged him into the house.

'Is this 'im? Is it?' they demanded of the girl.

She nodded and smirked, excited by the attention.

'Go on then, Ruth, go an' fetch constable. We'll 'old onto 'im till thoo gets back.'

They shoved William roughly into a chair and, since the brandy had made him sluggish and weary, he had no stomach to fight. It hurt to see the girl smile so horribly at his expense, and either the brandy or the kitchen reeking of stale fish made him feel sick.

When the girl returned with the constable, William gave his details meekly and apologised for causing any trouble. 'It's God's truth,' he mumbled, 'I never meant any harm.'

'That's fo' justices to decide,' announced the constable. 'Thoo'll be gettin' a summons. Now be off wi' thee, it's a long ride back to Reighton. Thoo'll 'ave plenty o' time to sober up an' think o' thy be'aviour.'

As William slouched back up the high street, he passed the new brick house of Allan Lamont, collector of customs. The magnificent house set him thinking. It's alright for some, he thought. There's me working in the fields every day, struggling to make a living and where has it got me? As a customs officer I've been led into bribery and corruption and nothing but trouble. And when I find something to bring light back into my life, a little something to hang onto, to give hope and pleasure, then it's taken away. What do I live for?

By the time his horse had carried him back to Reighton, he'd decided to resign his post with the customs. It would be one less bother in his pathetic life.

Chapter 50

The first thing William did on his return from Bridlington was knock on Matthew Smith's door. As soon as the maidservant opened it, he walked past her and announced loudly, 'I'm resigning!'

Matthew heard from the kitchen and came out into the passage. 'What's the matter? Come in the kitchen, William, let's talk this over.'

'No, I won't come in. I won't disturb your family. I've made up my mind.'

'Are you sure about this? You'll have to ride to Scarborough and see to it in person.'

'Never been more certain. It'll be one less bother in my wretched life.'

Matthew leant against the passage wall and sighed. Apart from wondering what had changed for William, he was trying to think who could replace him. Suddenly, he had an idea.

'There's a man I know in Hunmanby!'

'What?'

'Your replacement. I know a man in Hunmanby who'll do. Risden's his name.'

'Not old Risden! Why, he's far too old for the job.'

'Exactly.' Matthew winked. 'The perfect choice. And I'll tell you what—I'll take him to Scarborough myself and explain about you—save you the ride. Just give me your journals and anything else you need to hand in.'

William shrugged. It seemed too easy. As he thanked Matthew and left to go home, he thought of Risden. He hoped the poor old man would stay at home on winter evenings and keep warm and out of trouble.

Though relieved to have given up the customs job, William remained despondent throughout June. While he waited for his summons to arrive, he kept away from Bridlington, toiled long days in the fields and attended festivities with little pleasure.

Mary let him be. She thought he might be missing his role as a customs officer, thought he'd lost his self-respect. Even the news of King George's death evoked a negative response.

'It's just another George we're getting,' he complained. 'He's only interested in Germany and his military campaigns. I, for one, won't be celebrating the new king.'

When the summons letter arrived in July, Mary was shocked and embarrassed to find that the complaint came from a woman. William was to appear at the next quarter sessions at Beverley 'to answer to such matters as shall be objected against him by Ruth Lumbert of Bridlington, singlewoman'. Until that time, he was enjoined to keep the peace 'towards his majesty and all his liege people and especially towards ye said Ruth Lumbert'. It was signed by Richard Osbaldeston.

'Oh, William, what have you done?'

'It's not what you think.'

'How do you know what I think? And what will the village think? Oh, William, how could you!'

'Just listen to me and I'll explain. This Ruth Lumbert is *so* like young Mary. It's as simple as that. I only wanted to see her. I did nothing more, I swear.'

Mary didn't believe him, and neither did anyone else. They'd all noted his eagerness to go to the market, seen his wild eyes. William's brother Thomas had his own ideas and confided them to Dickon one morning by the stable.

'Mother was right. There's one thing makes a man like that.' He leered and thrust his hips forward in a bawdy gesture.

Dickon pursed his lips as he considered the matter. He forked another load of soiled straw into the barrow before replying.

'Aye, maybe thoo's right. 'E's been gaddin' about all spring, but I like neither egg nor shell of it. There's allus more to summat than meets eye.'

'Oh, come on, Dickon, you have to admit...'

'Nay, I'll admit nowt, an' I don't listen to gossip. We'd best get on. There's work to do.'

Thomas left Dickon to finish cleaning out the stable. It was too menial for him, and there were far better jobs in the warm, dry weather. He glanced at the sky devoid of any clouds. Yes, it was a fine day, but the fields needed rain. Last year it had rained too much early on, and this year it hadn't rained enough. The chalk in the soil should have held plenty of moisture, yet the wheat and barley crops were puny. At this rate, most of the grain would have to be kept as seed, and oats would be their staple diet once more. He was getting fed up with farming.

In Rudston, the maid at the vicarage missed her third monthly bleeding in a row. Though her body looked the same, there was no longer any doubt in her mind. She waited another week before daring to speak of it. As she carried a pile of sheets upstairs, she found one of the vicar's daughters alone in the chamber. Cecilia was brushing her hair.

'Remember May Day?' Elizabeth asked, placing the fresh linen in a chest. 'And the night before it... you know, when Francis came?'

'Yes, indeed—a beautiful evening.'

'Well...' Elizabeth closed the chest, turned to Cecilia and cleared her throat. 'There's summat I need to tell thee.'

Cecilia put down her brush. 'What is it Lizzie? Come on, girl, spit it out.'

'Me an' Francis... we...' She blushed and looked to the window in desperation.

'We what?'

She blurted it out. 'I think I'm wi' child.'

Cecilia put a hand over her mouth. 'Oh, my! Oh, Lizzie! Are you sure? I know of ways to find out.'

Elizabeth nodded. 'I'm sure.'

'I have heard that if you touch the blood left on someone else's soiled monthly cloths, then you'll miscarry. Do you want that?'

Elizabeth hung her head. 'No... I don't think so.'

'Then you'd better tell Francis.' She picked up her brush and then giggled. 'Francis! Fancy that! You did well there, Lizzie.'

Elizabeth bit her lip, trying not to cry. 'I won't tell 'im yet. I'll wait until after 'arvest time. Then we'll 'ave more time to sort things out.'

Despite the meagre crops, August and September were hectic months. William thought of Ruth Lumbert every day and, though he now realised he'd been a fool and the girl was not worth the trouble, he dreaded the visit to the Beverley sessions.

On October 1st, with the harvest not quite finished, he set off to face the JPs once more. He chose an early start, determined not to stay overnight. It was an unusually dark morning and everything felt damp after a night of rain. The smoke from the houses did not rise but drifted down the thatch and, judging by the low clouds, he guessed there'd be more rain to come, rain that was too late for the crops. Now he'd have a miserable journey along bad roads with their ruts full of water.

By the time he reached Driffield, a heavy shower had chilled him to the bone. He stopped briefly at an inn to give the horse a rest and allow himself time to steam his hat and coat dry by the fire. Then, with a brandy and a hot mutton pie to warm his insides, he took the road to Beverley, now busy with wagons and carts. He avoided conversation with other travellers, eager to arrive at the sessions in time. He had no idea if Ruth Lumbert would appear in person. He hoped not. It was humiliating enough to face the charges without having to see her disdain.

He arrived in Beverley, stiff and cold, and with no appetite for the place. It cost him more to leave his horse at a small stable near the sessions, but it meant a quick escape from town later. On entering the large, imposing building, he found the main room packed. The sight of wigs, the bustle and the stacks of official papers intimidated him as before. He took a seat at the end of one of the benches. Though he'd not been there for eight years, there were the same bleak walls streaked with damp, mould now growing near the windows. As far as he could make out, there was no Ruth Lumbert.

The JPs entered and the sessions were opened. William noted the absence of old Richard Osbaldeston, which could be either a good or a bad sign; the eldest son attended as a JP instead, and was the image of his father.

William's name was called; he duly answered and awaited his turn. He listened while a number of men and women were fined for giving short measures at the market, then a man heard he'd face a whipping for stealing corn from a granary. William had no sympathy for the fellow; he didn't appear to be starving and would sell it on rather than feed his family. His own 'misdemeanour' seemed paltry in comparison. It would not be easy, though, to explain why a forty-six-year-old man kept following a young woman.

William's turn came after a group of men were fined for drunken brawls and blasphemy. By now it was late morning, and the backbenches were shrouded in steam rising from damp overcoats. He could tell that everyone was ready for dinner. His own stomach was grumbling and William Osbaldeston had yawned more than once.

The clerk read out William's charge. 'Over a period of time from spring until June, William Jordan of Reighton did harass and behave in a threatening manner towards Ruth Lumbert, singlewoman of Bridlington. He also fought with her two brothers and her father.'

William could hardly believe it. When asked, he didn't want to plead guilty or not guilty.

'I may have caused upset to the woman. It's true I'm guilty of following her and waiting near her house. But I never fought with her family—ever. That's a lie.'

The constable stood up and gave an accurate account of his finding William held down in a chair in the Lumbert home. None of the family had come to give evidence.

'William Jordan had been drinking. He stank of brandy and was wild.'

William Osbaldeston JP intervened. 'In the absence of witnesses, I'm at a loss to understand what happened before the constable arrived.' His fellow JPs nodded in agreement. 'So, Jordan, you have our ear, but be brief. What did you do and what is your excuse, if any?'

There were titters of laughter throughout the room.

William sighed. No one would believe him.

'She reminded me of my daughter...who I lost when she was just a girl.' He paused to swallow. 'She was only seven. The vicar and his daughters loved her, taught her to read and write. She could recite whole psalms, and she was so lively and bonny. I only followed the young woman so I could look at her. I thought it did no harm.'

No one was laughing anymore. While folk around the room murmured their views, William Osbaldeston whispered to the Chief Justice next to him and then gave the verdict.

'In view of the lack of evidence, I ask you—do you regret your actions?'

'I do.'

'And do you promise to keep the peace from now on, and especially leave Ruth Lumbert alone?'

'Yes.'

William Osbaldeston stifled another yawn. 'William Jordan—a five shilling fine. Now, let's adjourn for dinner.'

While a relieved William was waiting to pay his fine, he caught a glimpse of the magistrates in their private dining room. The table was loaded with food and bottles of wine. He didn't envy them; they were fat and red-faced. All that sitting down indoors and overeating, they'd never make old bones.

Outside, in the fresher air, he smelled roast chestnuts. An old woman was selling the simple fare by a brazier. He bought a bag and put it inside his coat to warm himself, and then chose a beef and onion pasty to eat in the Wednesday market. After washing it down with a pint of ale, he was ready to collect his horse. He was keen to return home and thought most of the journey could be managed before sunset. There'd been a full moon the night before without any clouds; he should see the rest of his way home by moonlight.

Satisfied that the day had not gone too badly, he rode out of Beverley through the North Bar and over the ditch. He'd had his fill of the crowds, and ignored the grand houses and gardens on his way to Molescroft.

Once he was on the quieter country roads, he appreciated the stillness of the autumn landscape. As the recent rain had refreshed the air, and the sky was still clear, he decided to take the longer road home via Burton Fleming.

He inhaled deeply, at ease with himself for the first time in months. Thank God he was no longer a customs man. He was free to be a better farmer, a better father and husband. To make up for the payment of his fine and the loss in wages from the customs, perhaps he could find work as a carrier. He could work in the winter months when farm work was slack, but avoid going to Bridlington market; it would be best to avoid any chance of bumping into Ruth Lumbert.

The girl's face still haunted him. If he could trust himself to stay away from her, then one day he might even be free of the constant ache, the craving for his lost daughter.

He held his horse on a loose rein and found comfort in its steady rhythmical walk. As the horse could be trusted to find a sure footing, perhaps he should trust God in the same way. He should let go, leave his life in God's hands; certainly, he wasn't faring too well in his own. A time to heal and a time to break down, the Bible said; a time to weep and a time to laugh, a time to mourn and a time to dance. There was the answer—let go and trust things to arrive in their own time.

He was riding slowly over the high point on the wolds above Hunmanby as the sun set behind him. Filey Bay stretched out in the distance before him with the large full moon rising above the sea. All was calm with a hint of frost in the air. With a long sigh of relief, he whispered into the cool breeze, 'Thy will be done.'

Chapter 51

On Saturday 11th October, bonfires were lit to celebrate the King's coronation. In Rudston, Elizabeth Cooke took the opportunity to break her news to Francis. She could hardly have left it any later as there were limits to what her apron could hide. The couple stood to the rear of the crowd as the brushwood caught fire and flames leapt into the black sky. She stood on tiptoe and whispered into his ear.

'What?!' he gasped in horror.

'Thoo 'eard me.'

He didn't answer. Instead, he stared at the flames as if he was being condemned to burn in hell.

She shook his arm. 'Francis? Francis!'

He didn't respond, his body rigid as wood. Then, as she was about to run from the scene in tears, she felt him shudder and go limp.

He turned to face her. 'It's my fault.' After a quick glance at the bonfire, he sighed. 'There's no use now in me trying to save money for next year. We'll have to be wed—and soon.'

'November's allus a good time...'

He removed his hat and rubbed his hands roughly through his hair. 'Damn!'

'What's the matter? Don't you want to marry me?'

'Of course I do. I'm just thinking what Uncle Robert will say. I've let him down, let myself down, let everyone down. And by November you'll be showing, won't you? Everyone will see.'

They stood in silence while the other young villagers whooped round the fire. They had never joined in such madness, but what did it matter now whether they had or not?

'Francis, if thoo'd prefer, we could marry i' Bridlin'ton. Me family's there so it's only proper. Come wi' me an' meet me parents an' vicar. We can sort things out.'

'I'm going to have to face George Gurwood first. He's going to lose his maidservant.'

'Speak to 'im i' mornin'. 'E's a generous man. 'E'll understand.'

Francis banged his hat against his leg and cursed again. 'I haven't even thought where we can live.'

They gazed at the bonfire in silence, watching it collapse and burn less fiercely. As the last flames died down, Francis took hold of her hand and escorted her back to the vicarage. He said goodnight on the doorstep and then, as he was about to leave, he bent his head to give her a gentle, lingering kiss on the cheek.

'You know, in truth, I can't wait to be married. My aunt Elizabeth did tell me to follow my heart.'

That night, Francis couldn't sleep. By the time the other hired lads returned to their beds, drunk and stinking of bonfire smoke, he'd finished praying for guidance and had reached a state of acceptance. Tomorrow, he'd see the vicar.

As it was a Sunday, the vicar had services to give at different churches, so Francis had to wait until the evening.

'I've betrayed your trust,' were his first words on being shown into the parlour.

The vicar raised a hand to shush him. 'Don't stand there dithering. Sit down, lad. I know what's wrong with Lizzie. My wife's had enough children for me not to notice.'

'But I always meant to wed in chastity.'

'Don't we all? I mean, your own mo... No, it doesn't matter. There's many a marriage started this way. What matters is how you finish.' He reached for the brandy, noting he'd soon need to open another bottle. 'My wife must be using it in her cooking,' he murmured as he poured out a couple of glasses. 'Come on, just this once, Francis. We'll drink to your future. It's about time you two were wed.'

As they sat by the fire, George Gurwood hinted that there might be a cottage to rent, if not in Rudston, then maybe in Reighton.

'Would you like to stay here? There's that little cottage at the north end, you know, by the forge.'

'I think I'd be better off going back to Reighton. There's plenty of work at Uphall, and I noticed last year how my grandfather's slowed down.'

'Perhaps you're right. If you like, I'll have a word with your vicar now he's well again. I did hear there's that glebe cottage at the bottom coming vacant soon. It might be in need of repair, but Robert Storey would probably supervise. I'm sure though, that if you worked on it yourself and tended the land properly, then you'd be able to afford the rent.'

Francis had turned pale.

George leant over and rested an arm on his shoulder. 'Ah, yes... I suppose you'll have to tell Robert. But he can't change what's happened, can he? He'll just have to accept things as they are.'

Francis finished work early the following Friday and walked towards Reighton. As he reached the high ground above the village, he paused to admire the sunset. The fiery orange ball was about to dip out of sight yet still lit up the fields, making them glow. Reluctant to enter the main street, and preferring to remain outdoors, he walked further north onto the moor. A mist was forming on the lower ground, the sheep ghostly in the still air. As the light faded, so did the colours, leaving the autumn landscape a washed out ginger and grey, difficult to define, just like his future. He frowned, turned back to the village, and headed for his family home on St Helen's Lane.

At the end of the lane, he came face to face with his father also on his way home. He hurried forwards to greet him before being asked questions.

'Father, I'm glad I've seen you. I have some news.'

'I hope it's better than the meeting we had at the forge. Next Tuesday it's Manor Court day and we're all still splitting hairs over the new rules and fines. You'd be interested to hear them.'

Francis shrugged. 'Yes, maybe, in good time...' He strolled alongside his father. 'What I wanted to tell you was—' He hung his head and blushed. 'I'm getting married... next month.' It was such relief to say it to his father and not the whole family. To his surprise, his father laughed and crashed an arm round his shoulders.

'Well, lad, I never thought you had it in you! Am I right in thinking it's a rushed job?' When Francis nodded, his father suddenly stopped walking. 'It *is your* child?'

'Of course! Elizabeth's not like that.'

'Neither are you, or so I thought. Well, well...' He shook his head in disbelief and then gave Francis a hearty slap on the back. When they set off walking again, he found it hard to stifle a smirk.

The moment they entered the house, young William looked aghast. 'Oh, no! Do I have to lose my bed again?' He received a clip round the ear from his father.

'It's just for one night. Francis'll go back in the morning.'

Francis watched young William rub his ear. No doubt, the boy was puzzled as to why his brother was there at all. His mother was equally concerned, judging by the way she stepped back from the fire with a worried frown. He cleared his throat.

'Mother, I'm getting married.' He noticed his father give a wink and point a thumb at his belly. 'And, yes, I may be coming back to live in Reighton.'

Before she could congratulate him and ask questions, young William spoke up.

'There's no room *here*!' he blurted out, and received another clip.

Francis glowered. 'I'm not going to live here, you dolt, not with a wife and...'

'Leave Francis alone,' his mother ordered. 'Let me dish out supper. Move up, lad, and make a space for your brother.'

While his brothers were occupied with eating their boiled fish and potatoes, Francis whispered to his mother. 'Would you mind telling Uncle Robert for me? I dread meeting him.'

'I'm sure he'll be disappointed, but what can he do? Listen, though, your aunt will be pleased for you. Cheer up, it's not the end of the world.' She went to fetch a jar of pickled cabbage. 'There you are, your favourite. I do wish I'd met your future bride though. You'll have to ask her father's permission... do it properly.'

'I will. We're going to Bridlington on Sunday.'

After supper, when the boys were sent to bed, Francis stayed up with his parents. His father warmed a pan of ale, added sugar and spice, and asked Francis if he wanted a pipe or a pinch of snuff. His mother settled down by the fire and picked up her knitting.

'You used to like knitting, Francis. You were good at it. Oh, I do hope you'll come back to live in Reighton. I can help with the baby. I'll have more time now that your youngest brother's old enough to work in the fields.'

His father poured out the ale and winked at Francis. 'Your mother's a step ahead. Let's get you married first and settled in somewhere.'

Francis did not refuse the drink. It warmed his stomach and, if it weren't for the thought of Robert Storey, he'd have enjoyed it all the more.

Chapter 52

Ever since the coronation bonfire, young William had been moping around the house and garden. His father put it down to his age and ignored him. Eventually though, fed up with his son's long face at the table, he asked him outright.

'For God's sake, what's up with you? You take forever to do your chores, and you play around with your food. Are you sickening or something?'

Young William scowled and put down his spoon. He mumbled with his head down. 'We've never been taught to read and write.'

There was silence as the family tried to take it in.

'What's that got to do with anything?' his father cried. 'You've never shown the slightest interest before.'

'Well, I want to learn now—before it's too late.'

'Too late for what?'

Young William blushed.

John, in all innocence, spoke up. 'Uncle Matthew's children can read and write—even Ann. She—' He stopped as his brother kicked him under the table.

'Shut up, John.'

'Ah,' said his father. 'It's to do with Ann Smith, is it? Don't waste your time there, son. She's not for you.'

No more was spoken about it that evening, and his father soon forgot the conversation; the imminent meeting of the Manor Court and the finalising of the regulations occupied his thoughts.

The following Tuesday, William and the other landowners crunched through the frozen leaves to attend the Manor Court once more. They knocked their boots against the churchyard wall and entered the church to find Thomas Cockerill and his steward John Grimston already there, waiting. William, as before, sat between his father and Matthew Smith. As far as he knew, most were content with the way the rules were being followed in the village and were ready to accept them formally with their signatures. There was just one worry; last week, Matthew had hinted that more rules might be added.

When everyone was seated, names were read out and, again, there were no absentees. The steward began.

'Before I read out the full list of pains, there are a few additions.' He read out a new instruction for both freeholders and tenants to dig up whins by the roots on their pastureland; they were to clear thirty yards every year until they reached the foot of the hill. Worse still, the work had to begin next month, and the thirty yards had to be completed by Lady Day next March. Otherwise, there was a fine of four shillings.

William nudged his father. 'This is a tough one.'

'Aye', his father mumbled. 'It's not a bad idea though. It'll let more grass grow.'

They heard a rule forbidding anyone to glean corn with rakes at harvest time when the land wasn't theirs. Such a rule was welcome, but the final one puzzled them. Already there were items regarding the number of livestock allowed per land owned, and the need to report such numbers to the byelawman each year. Now, there was another specific rule about the sheep. At any time the byelawman could now demand to know exactly how many sheep each man owned. There was a fine of two shillings and six pence, more than a day's wages.

William whispered to Matthew. 'Is this to do with smuggling fleeces?'

Matthew smiled with a knowing wink. 'Could be. It all depends on how keen the byelawman is. We needn't fret too much.' He put a finger to his lips and said no more.

The others talked among themselves for a while before reaching full agreement. Now they just had to listen while the steward held out the long roll and read out the full list of pains, all twenty-six of them, before asking for signatures.

Matthew Smith, as the chief freeholder, signed his name first in an elegant, fluent hand. Richard Maltby followed and then William with his father, both signing more awkwardly as they pressed too hard on the parchment.

Six of the landowners signed with various marks, including Robert Storey who signed with a flowing capital R. On returning to his seat, he gave William a black look.

William shrugged; it wasn't his fault Francis had to get married.

Afterwards, the men strolled to their various homes, wondering how many of the new duties would be carried out let alone overseen. As William's father was about to cross the road to Uphall, he chuntered to his son.

'We don't want to be only ones scourin' ditches an' stubbin' up whins. That byelawman 'ad better do 'is job properly.'

'I bet Dickon'll be pleased, though, when you tell him there's a ten shilling fine for putting scabby horses in our pastures.'

'Oh, aye, 'e'll be 'appy wi' that. But I don't see as lasses'll be able to keep ducks an' geese out o' pond. They didn't keep 'em out last year.'

William watched his father shuffle away, not picking up his feet; he looked as though he might fall flat on his face at any moment.

Robert Storey stood in the churchyard, biding his time. As soon as old Francis Jordan was out of earshot, he approached William.

'Three score years and ten... that's our allotted span. Your father can't be far off.'

'Oh, he's fine. He has a few years yet.'

'And I hear Francis's wedding is to take place during the hiring holiday next month.'

'That's right.'

'Will you be attending?'

'No,' he hated to admit. 'It's in Bridlington.' He'd been avoiding the place all year because of Ruth Lumbert, and Mary had agreed with sadness that they wouldn't go.

'You're doing the right thing. It's best if no one attends. It's nothing to celebrate—marrying in sin. My wife will argue differently, but what do women understand?'

William bit his tongue and started to walk away.

Robert held him back. 'Elizabeth's persuaded me to help them get that glebe cottage to rent. I've already seen the vicar about it.'

'Thank you, Robert.' He made another effort to escape.

'Listen, William, I'll help your son get on the correct path again. There's time to turn him back to godliness and chastity. I'll make it my purpose in life.'

Disheartened and full of foreboding, William left Robert and trudged down the hill. There was too much going on, too many changes. His brother Richard wasn't settled; he'd been seen lately at Hunmanby market more than was necessary. No one knew why he went so often or if he met someone there. It was another worry, and his brother had better be discreet so close to home.

When William reached the foot of the hill, he groaned. In less than a month they'd have to start digging out the gorse. Thirty yards to clear by next March was an added labour. On the other hand, his eldest son would soon be there to help. As for young William, he was fifteen now and should be working full hours as a man. He paused in the lane, lost in thought. The lad had not been the same since he'd lost Stina, and was often found in the garden sitting by the dog's grave.

William scratched his forehead and walked on. As soon as he'd entered the house and had taken off his coat, Mary began to question him about the pains. He sat at the table before answering.

'Oh, they're much the same as before. I wish, though, that I'd been able to talk about them right at the start. It's fine for your brother—he's well in with the Cockerills and that John Grimston.'

Mary lifted the pot of stew from the fire and carried it to the table. 'Talking of my brother, I did hear that *all* his daughters are learning to read and write, not just his sons. They have a tutor from Hunmanby comes over twice a week. It must cost them... I heard he used to teach at the Osbaldestons' place.'

Young William raised his head immediately. 'So, can *I* learn then?'

His father soon put paid to any grand ideas. 'We can't afford a tutor, and there's no one at the vicarage to teach you.'

'I'm wondering what's best for the future,' Mary said as she began to dish out the stew. 'Don't you think it *would* be a good idea if William *did* learn? Our youngest boys could learn too.'

Young William's face lit up. He glanced at his father who was scratching his head but also smiling.

'Alright, son, I suppose I could teach you myself—maybe start this winter.'

'Father,' the boy cried in excitement, 'I think there's a sand tray you used with my sister. It'll do for writing practice.'

Mary shook her head as she slopped food into his bowl. 'I think, son, whatever your hopes are, you're heading for disappointment.'

Young William was undeterred. Already he could imagine himself sitting next to Ann Smith, sharing a book. He was soon dreaming of what he could say to her in a letter.

His father sighed as he noticed the faraway look in his son's eyes. The boy was growing up so fast. He thought of his own future when there would be changes at Uphall. His parents were getting old now and, when they passed away, he expected to inherit everything. His parents, though, were always reticent on the subject, and William knew his brothers would hope to get a share.

He watched his sons tuck into their food, and remained deep in thought. Though he was anxious for young William's aspirations, there was the imminent concern for Francis's return to Reighton. As he began to spoon in his dinner, he wondered how Francis and his new wife, poor soul, would deal with the inevitable clash with Robert Storey.

Appendix

The Jordan Family Members

The sons of Francis and Dorothy Jordan of Uphall:-

William* (see below)
Francis (living at Argam)
Thomas
Samuel
Richard

The sons of **William*** and Mary Jordan, living on St Helen's Lane:-

Francis
Young William
John
Richard
Matthew

Coming soon
(The last in the series)
Book Five

1727 to 1734

Change brings conflict for the Jordan family as one generation succeeds another. Who will inherit Uphall? And who will help the newlyweds, Francis and Lizzie, as they grapple with the puritanical teachings of Robert Storey?

Young William sets his sights on Ann Smith, knowing her father has better suitors in mind. He ignores all warnings at his peril.

The story takes place within the farming seasons and the Christmas, Shrovetide and harvest festivals. Young women learn to make soap and plait rush mats, boys learn how to tend oxen and set rabbit traps. William and Mary's vulnerable son John adopts an orphan lamb and soon settles into the peaceful occupation of shepherding. Will he be the one, against all expectations, to hold the family together?

About the Author

Joy Gelsthorpe writes under her maiden name, Stonehouse. Her father came from Filey, and then moved to Hornsea before the Second World War and married Gladys Jordan, a descendant of the Jordans of Reighton. Her interest in family history led to the series of novels set in the East Riding.

She writes and researches local archives in the winter, often spending days at The British Library at Boston Spa and The Treasure House in Beverley. During the summer she visits local museums. Favourite places are The Yorkshire Museum of Farming at Murton, near York, and The Ryedale Folk Museum at Hutton-le-Hole.

Joy lives on the east coast and finds inspiration by walking in the area, especially along the cliffs and beaches. Memorable times include a walk above Speeton as dawn was breaking, and a visit to Reighton church for a carol service on a frosty, starlit evening.

For more information and details of other books by local authors:-

www.hornseawriters.com